S Ledbetter treet

A Novel of Second Chances

Susan P. Baker

Refugio Press

LEDBETTER STREET
- A Novel of Second Chances
Copyright © Susan P. Baker.

ISBN: 978-0-9962021-8-3

This is a work of fiction. Names, places, characters and incidents are either the product of the author's imagination or are used fictitiously, and any resemblance to any actual persons, living or dead, organizations, events or locales is entirely coincidental.

Front cover design by Alexander Von Ness
Interior formatting by Laurie Barboza

Produced in the United States of America.

For information and/or permission to use excerpts, contact:

Refugio Press
P.O. Box 3937 Galveston, TX 77552.

Books by Susan P. Baker

Novels:

My First Murder
No. 1 in the Mavis Davis murder mystery series

The Sweet Scent of Murder
Mavis Davis No. 2, Mavis's search for a missing teenager turns into a murder investigation in Houston's Ritzy River Oaks.

Death of a Prince
Mother & daughter criminal defense lawyers defend the alleged murderer of a millionaire plaintiff's attorney

Ledbetter Street
A mother fights the system for guardianship of her autistic son.

Suggestion of Death
A father who can't pay his child support investigates the mysterious deaths of other deadbeat dads.

UNAWARE
Attorney Dena Armstrong is about to break out from under the two controlling men in her life, unaware that a stranger has other plans for her.

Nonfiction:

Heart of Divorce
Divorce advice especially for those who are considering representing themselves.

Murdered Judges of the 20th Century
True stories of judges killed in America.

www.susanpbaker.com

Dedication

For my brother, David, the bravest man I knew.

Contents

Acknowledgements

I owe many thanks to the following folks:

Lorin Oberweger for her wonderful first edit. Juli Bahlinger, for sharing her cancer experience. Patricia Arnold, Cheri Brinkman, and Kate Holmes, for information about resale shop operations. Dennis Hill, for help with questions regarding the Texas Department of Family and Protective Services. Judge Kathy Stone for verifying the workings of a Probate Court in Houston, TX.

To Sandra Gardner and Saralyn J. Richard for editorial assistance.

Thanks also to Vicki Rust and Catherine Roberts, my critique group in Fredericksburg, Texas during early drafts. The Galveston Novel and Short Story Writers Group for their thoughtful critiques on later drafts.

Thanks to my readers, early, middle, and late: Bonnie Baker Palmer, Charlotte Greineisen, Kathryn Lanan, Susan Johnston, Gabriella P, Kathy Sanford, Suzanne Turner, and Jenny Wolfe.

And the Writers Retreat Workshop family, specifically Lorin Oberweger, Jason Sitzes, and Roman White.

Chapter 1

MARIAN REID FELT LIKE SHE'D been blind-sided. After no-shows at the 10-year reunion, the 20-year reunion, the 25, the 30, the 35, why had Bryan Mosley sent her a friend request on Facebook the day before the 40th? Had he found out about their son?

She moved the cursor to *Confirm* and jerked her hand back as though her finger had been blistered. Something told her no good could come of it, but she couldn't bring herself to hit the *Not Now* button. She stared at the screen, her stomach churning. Her imagination ran as wild as the fish in the nearby Gulf of Mexico.

What if she confirmed and didn't hear back from him? What if he decided he'd made a mistake asking to friend her? She'd be almost as destroyed as she'd been in high school when she returned from her grandmother's to find him going steady with that bitch, Sheila. Well—not that devastated after 40 years, but still . . .

At the end of the day, her last two customers huddled at the front door, not wanting to go out into the slackened rain. Marian had offered umbrellas, but they wouldn't budge. She stood at the glass door with them, her little black-and-white poodle-mix dog, Anna, in her arms.

She wanted to close up and be alone to contemplate her options, but the plump little woman and her elderly mother were firmly planted in place. They'd said they had nowhere to go but home.

The trolley lurched by, spraying the curb. Speeding cars splattered the sidewalk. People dashed about. The old homeless woman who slept in the alley trudged past, oblivious to the weather.

Over her customers' heads, Marian could see Eva in Coffee & More across the street, bustling from behind the counter with a coffee pot in each hand, pouring refills for customers. Marian wanted to call her or wade across the street and show her the email, get her advice. Should she *Confirm* the man who'd been the love of her life?

She scratched between Anna's ears. She couldn't throw the ladies out. Reid's Ritzy Rags catered to such customers—those on fixed incomes who weren't able to buy new clothing but wanted something to spice up their wardrobes.

Putting Anna on the floor, Marian leaned toward the daughter. "How about I get your car for you and pull it up to the curb?"

"Oh, would you?" The woman's face brightened. She squeezed Marian's forearm and sought approval from her mother, who broke into a wispy smile. "That would be so kind."

Finally, success.

"Could we keep the umbrellas?" the old lady asked.

"Yes, of course. I buy bulk umbrellas for such occasions. You never know when there might be a shower in Galveston."

She found a clip to hold back her long hair. Donning a raincoat, she stuck her feet into a pair of rubber boots. After locking up her purse and the cash register, she pointed behind the counter and

2

addressed her dog: "Go to your bed." Anna gave her a look and scampered away, disappearing from sight.

"It's the maroon van two blocks down on The Strand," the younger woman said, handing Marian the keys.

When Marian opened the front door, a small metal bell hanging over the entrance chimed. She popped open a golf umbrella. "You ladies have a seat on the husbands' sofa. Help yourselves to coffee and cookies or boxed wine. I'll be right back."

Letting the door swing closed, she sloshed through the warm water that was about to lap over the curb, past the shell of the five-and-dime that had been closed for a generation, and waded across Ledbetter Street. She waved at Luther, a young artist who stood smoking a cigarette under an awning. She hurried by the barbecue on the opposite corner, the acrid aroma of something grilling causing her belly to rumble. She slogged across the alley behind Coffee & More, past the front entrances of a closed gallery and a defunct jewelry shop and, just beyond the side entrance of a credit union, finally found the decrepit, maroon minivan on the corner.

She drove to the shop and helped her customers to their van.

"Y'all come back soon when the weather's better," she said, as she closed the passenger door on the older woman. She waved as the pair drove away, relieved that she could return to pondering whether she should pay heed to the warnings in her head.

Back in the store, grateful no new customers had arrived, she locked up and pulled down the flowered window shade. Scurrying to the computer, her muscles taut as the stays in a corset, she re-read the friend request.

What was the worst thing that could happen if she replied?

He'd opened up so many possibilities . . . . If she confirmed, then what? Did he just want to see what she was up to? Did he want to see her? Was he still married to Sheila?

Or was he just contacting her because most people coming to the reunion were logging onto Facebook to find out who was going to be there?

The rain had slowed to intermittent sprinkles. The setting sun dimmed the sky. The historic building facades across the street looked like sleepy faces. Marian glanced between the mannequins in her front windows into Eva's place.

Eva stood behind the counter, her spiked hair like yellowed grass. She was chatting with a customer, looking up at him, her hands doing most of the talking.

Marian called her on her cell phone. Eva's customer moved away. She snapped her cell from her waistband and eyeballed it before looking through her own glass door toward Marian's shop.

"What's up?"

"You won't believe who wants to friend me on Facebook."

"Quick, I'm busy."

"Bryan Mosley! Bigger'n Dallas. What am I going to do?"

"Was it him in the picture?" Eva started picking up cups and trash from her tables, her cell tucked between her neck and shoulder.

"No photo, just that silhouette thingy of a man. What should I do?"

"A search."

"Just a minute." Marian put her phone on speaker and laid it on the counter. She typed Bryan's name into the search block. "One recently dead English actor born in 1931, several black guys, a football player, and a man who looks like he works construction, but not my Bryan Mosley."

"Hah! *Your* Bryan Mosley? Well, how do you feel about his contacting you? You're scared to death, right?"

Leaning on the counter, Marian stared across the street. Her

4

heart wanted what her heart wanted. "You think I shouldn't contact him?"

Eva walked to her front window and put her forehead to the glass. "The only way to find out what he wants is to confirm."

Blood rushed in Marian's ears. "It's killing me."

"Suppose he just wants to see if you're going to the reunion?"

"But he didn't send his registration fee."

"What else could it be after all this time? Maybe he wants to see you and is thinking of showing up and registering at the door."

"Surely not." But people had done that at the other reunions.

"It's what you've been dreaming of—"

Marian exhaled and fisted her shaking hands. "Okay, back to the question, should I or shouldn't I?" Her common sense told her to click Not Now, but the palpable, yet pleasing, discomfort in her heart, the taste of anticipation on her tongue, froze her hand in midair.

"I'm not making that decision for you, girlfriend," Eva said.

"I'm hitting confirm. Be over after I finish dinner."

Moments later, her breath shallow and difficult, she tapped the *Confirm* box. Staring at the screen, chewing her lower lip, she waited to see what would happen.

Nothing.

Slamming the lid on her laptop, she said to Anna, who sat nearby, "I'm too old to behave like this."

She'd give it time. She straightened the clothing on the rounds and checked to make certain the sizes were in order.

Back to the computer.

Nothing.

She rehung the clothing left in the dressing rooms. Re-checked the computer.

Nothing.

Paired up the shoes. Wiped the fingerprints from the glass case that held jewelry. Tallied her sales for the day. Re-checked the computer.

Nothing.

Pulled the excess cash and made up a deposit. Mopped the puddle of water just inside the door. Packed away the chocolate chip cookies after eating one. Dumped out the coffee and tea. Refrigerated the boxed wine. Swept the shop. Sanitized the doorframe and handle. Snuffed out the orange-and-mango candle. And every few minutes her eyes, if not her body, ventured back to the computer. Nothing. Nothing. Nothing. What was she, fifteen?

Before she took Anna upstairs to the condo for dinner, Marian raised the computer cover one last time and typed in her password.

Nada. Nilch. Nothing.

She shut down the Facebook window and opened it again to see if that made any difference.

Nope.

She drew a deep breath and pulled her shoulders back. Just as well he didn't respond right away. She needed time to think about her biggest concern—how their getting back in touch with each other might affect Robert.

Chapter 2

THOUGH ONLY A FEW DAYS had passed since Eva's helper had quit, the toll of being the only person running the coffee shop had etched itself on her face. Instead of the hyper-energetic, forty-something jogger Marian knew and loved, Eva moved like an old woman who'd scrubbed too many floors. Her apron was covered with stains, her khaki shirt needed pressing, and her feet, normally clad in wildly colored socks, were bare in high-top tennies.

"Good grief, you look exhausted," Marian said when she arrived after dinner, the scent of coffee greeting her at the door. "I can help for a couple of hours." She began picking up discarded cups and napkins, tossing trash, straightening chairs, and cleaning spills.

"I put an ad in the paper, but you wouldn't believe who—or should I say *what*—responded." Eva wiped the counter and started another pot of coffee brewing.

"I hate to imagine." Last time Marian ran her own ad the people who showed up were not the type she'd ever invite to dinner.

The rain had stopped. Outside sat a young couple reading novels and sipping from steaming cups. The inside stood empty for the moment. "You never saw such a bad lot. Didn't their mothers ever tell them to wash before going on an interview?" Eva asked.

"You poor thing. Bad enough trying to run this place with only one helper. You've got to find a way to cut corners so you can afford two part-time students. You could force a dress code on them. Have you thought of dropping the grocery line and just doing coffee, pastries, and sandwiches?"

"I'm ignoring that last bit, and what I'm looking for is part-time high-schoolers who won't give away the store to their friends."

"That goes without saying." Marian pulled the trash bag out of the can and tied it off, replacing it with a clean one. "Glad my hours are so short, though I need someone, too."

"Wish my grandmother had left *me* an inheritance." Eva shoved a chair under a table.

Marian picked up the garbage bag and traipsed out to the dumpster behind the shop. She had to dodge a little river of water that rushed toward the deep drain hole not far from the back door. The alley had been repaved many times, but the drain cover hadn't been reset level with the pavement. She threw the garbage into the dumpster and glanced up. Clear skies, clouds headed East, cool breezes from the Gulf. If she didn't have to help Eva, it would be a good night to sit out on the balcony with a book and a glass of wine, though she probably wouldn't be able to concentrate.

Back inside, a line of customers had arrived. She stepped up to the counter. "Next person, may I help you?"

The shop closed at nine, except on poetry reading nights. Marian didn't mind helping out when she could, but she didn't have the energy to do it every night. And Eva sorely needed time off. You'd think in a bad economy there'd be decent folk who would appreciate a part-time job with benefits. At least they had each other to keep watch as much as they could through their plate glass windows.

When the place cleared out again, Eva asked, "Get a reply?"

"No, at least not by the time I came over here."

"Bring your cell?"

"No, I forgot."

"He's probably working. He'll email you later; you'll see."

"God, I hope so. I mean I hope he has a job. Don't want anything to do with him if he's a bum. That might not be an option anyway. He could just be contacting everyone he remembers who he might want to see at the reunion—if that's what this is about."

"You're right. At least you know he remembers you." Eva turned the oven on.

"I should hope so. We went together for two years. What're you doing? I thought you only baked in the morning."

"Supper, girlfriend. I'm starving."

"Tell you what," Marian said, switching the oven back off, "you go upstairs and have a decent dinner, and I'll mind the store."

"You're a doll. I won't be long." She patted Marian's arm.

"Take your time. Rushing will only give you indigestion."

"Yes, Mother." Eva hustled up the stairs.

Marian leaned on the counter and stared out into the night. A car splashed by with a hiss of spray, but the mass of water had gone down, so the little couple still reading at one of the tables outside weren't soaked. She'd like to have a relationship like that, where she and her lover sat together reading in comfortable silence.

She tried to remember when she'd had that pleasure. Never, really. Her ex-husband hadn't been much of a reader. The daily paper and car magazines were the extent of his personal reading.

He'd always said he had to read too much at work. He'd chide her when he caught her hunched over a novel. What had she seen in him in the first place? She shook her head, having trouble remembering. She'd been young, in her early twenties. And wanted to get away from her mother. Well, enough of that.

Another customer came in, Sam, a medical student and one of her rarely-seen tenants.

"You helping out, Marian?" He stroked his lower lip and looked down at the few remaining pastries in the bakery case.

"Yep, what can I get you?"

"Just a tall cup of coffee."

"Sure you don't want that apple Danish?" She chewed the inside of her mouth, thinking she might like it, herself.

"Nah, just the coffee, thanks."

She filled his order and took his money. "See you."

When he left, she got out the broom and brushed the area behind the counter. Many bits of paper and a lot of what could be salt or sugar layered the floor and the cushy mat that stretched from one end behind the counter to the other. When she finished, she went after the aisles in the grocery area. Had Eva or her helper dusted the shelves or glanced at the floors in the last month or two?

She was in the middle of the coffee shop, bent down, scooping dirt into a dustpan, when a car drove up and stopped on the Ritzy Rags side of the street—just stopped—right on the trolley tracks. A man inside sat facing her shop. Marian rose, wondering what he was about. He didn't get out. He didn't cut his engine. He just sat there looking in the direction of her shop, his back to her.

A few moments later, she could hear the trolley in the next block. The trolley drivers—two retired men who switched off their shifts—didn't much like it when cars parked on the trolley tracks. Marian walked to the door and peered out as the trolley rolled slowly toward them. The man in the car didn't move. Maybe he didn't hear; his windows were rolled up and his motor running. The trolley continued en route. The couple reading at the tables turned and watched. When the trolley drew close to the car, it blasted its whistle one, two, three times.

The man lurched in his seat. His car lurched in the street. He glanced behind him, forward, and around toward Coffee & More. His eyes made contact with Marian's before he sped away. Though forty years had passed since she'd seen him, she could swear he was Bryan Mosley.

Chapter 3

MARIAN WASN'T OUT OF HER nightclothes when she checked her computer the next morning, chastising herself for feeling the way she did, wanting to hear from Bryan, wanting to see him. She'd slept badly. Waking in the middle of the night. Wondering if she should check for a message. Worrying about what it all meant.

A message was waiting for her like it was the most normal thing in the world. "Hi, Marian. I hope you remember me, Bryan Mosley? Are you going to the reunion tonight? I'd like to see you."

Was he trying to be funny? Did he have a weird sense of humor? Without taking the time to mull it over, she wrote back, "Yes, see you there," and went to the phone to schedule a mani, pedi, and hair appointment now that she had someone she wanted to look her best for.

Hours later, she wondered if the Facebook contact had been a big joke. The reunion was three hours old, three long hours that Marian had spent staffing the registration table. Now, sitting alone and feeling like a fool, the blare of the Beatles burst forth when the ballroom door opened. The reunion organizer, Sarah, a woman Marian had known since fifth grade, slipped out and headed her way, followed by the smell of fried shrimp.

Sarah pulled up a chair next to Marian and whispered, "He hasn't come. I've been so nervous all night, but he never showed up."

Who did she mean? Who had Sarah dated in high school that she wanted to see so badly? No one else was in the foyer, so Marian focused her attention on Sarah.

"I've come to every reunion hoping to see Royce, but he never shows up." Sarah held her hands in her lap, kneading her fingers. "I just want to see if he still feels the same way about me as I do about him. I know he's married, but I just need to know."

Sarah could have been reading from Marian's script.

"We loved each other very much, but his mother broke us up. She couldn't allow her precious son to marry me."

"What did you do that was so bad?"

Sarah shrugged. "Humph. I'm a Jew."

"And I'm Catholic, so . . ."

"So the big cheese doctor's wife didn't want her son marrying a Jew." Sarah shrugged. "I guess he's not coming again. It's just as well. I'd probably pee in my pants. See you later." She headed back inside.

Marian had almost spit out her own story and would have if Sarah hadn't cut her off. She punched Eva's number into her cell. "Hey, kiddo, it's nine o'clock, and Bryan's a no-show. Guess I'll pack up and go home."

"That's strange. I wonder what all that Facebook crap was about. Well, you still had fun, right?"

"Sure. Sitting out here at the registration desk, relying on old friends to bring me food and drink."

"Still, it was good to see them, right?"

"Yeah, I guess. The food was good. The wine chilled. I got lots of smacks on the cheek from guys I never dated."

"Better than a kick in the seat of the pants."

"So do I have your permission to go home now?"

Eva snorted. "Yes, my dear. You can pack up and say goodbye forever to the reunion committee. If you want to come over here when you get home, you can help me finish a bottle of white."

"I might just do that after I get out of these clothes. *Adios*." Marian put her cell away and began gathering the reunion materials into a box.

"Marian—" Bryan's unmistakable deep voice.

She couldn't breathe. At fifty-eight she should have aged out of the adolescent thrill thing, but butterflies circled in her stomach. She kept her eyes on the registration list, afraid to look up.

"Marian. That's you, right?"

Chills swept up from her toes. Bryan sounded neither older nor huskier than on high school graduation night. His voice was strikingly similar to their son's, though Robert's usually came out in a monotone. A very loud monotone.

She raised her eyes. Bryan's face, shopworn and thinner. Yellow hair gone white but as thick and curly as their son's. Azure eyes the same as Robert's, though Robert wore glasses. Here stood the man who had fathered the child she'd been forced to give up. The man who'd married another woman.

Bryan wore a pressed sport shirt and Bermuda shorts on his lean, tall body. His open-toed Huaraches brought a smile to her face. He'd waged many high school battles to get to wear them to class years ago.

"Marian Vernon."

"Reid," she said. "My married name is Reid." Her eyes tried to pull away from his face; his eyes held them captive. She wanted to stand, but her legs would have collapsed. She wanted to run into his arms. Good grief, could she think any more like the heroine in a romance novel?

She glanced behind him. Had he brought Sheila?

"Marian, you look just as lovely as the last time I saw you."

Heat extended to the tips of her ears. She weighed fifteen pounds more than in high school. Gray intertwined with her black, thinner hair. Crows' feet accented her eyes. But Bryan couldn't have given her a sweeter compliment. *Lovely.* "Thanks. You look good yourself."

Still no Sheila.

He grinned the same grin he'd worn when they'd surfed together. But it was all long ago—their sophomore and junior years. By the time they were seniors, her life had taken an abrupt turn, and Sheila had become the recipient of those smiling eyes, that toothy grin.

"One?"

"One what?" he asked.

"One late registration?" She returned his smile.

The ballroom door opened, and the refrain from "Hey Jude" drifted out. They'd danced to that song, long and slow, the dance and the song seeming to go on forever.

She continued, "Sorry, but you have to pay the full fee, no early discount. Seventy-five for one if you're doing the whole weekend." She waited for his answer, pleased to have a moment to gaze upon his face. Robert was practically his spitting image, except for the hair and Robert's pale skin. Not that she had known Bryan at forty, Robert's age now, but only seventeen years separated father and son. "No photo name badge either. You had to early register so we could make one." The back of her neck tingled; her feet throbbed with heat, her sandals tight as gloves. Her sundress felt damp. Aged out of all that nonsense? Not hardly.

"Will you take a check?" Bryan fished in his back pocket for a wallet.

"Sure." Marian made out the receipt, holding her hands stiff to hide the trembling. The last day she'd seen him, he sauntered across the stage for his diploma. After the ceremony, he hugged another woman, Sheila, who became his wife.

Marian fumbled with the receipt book, trying to tear off his copy, eyes blurred in memory. When she held up the receipt, Bryan stared at the Ladies' Room door across the foyer.

"I'm paying for two, I think."

"Oh."

A moment later, Sheila came out, and a chill ran through Marian. She busied herself with writing a second receipt and hoped neither of them would be able to read the disappointment in her eyes.

"Am I getting yours?" Bryan asked Sheila.

"I'll pay you back later." Sheila held out her hand. "Hey, Marian. You look great. How're you doing?" A cloud of flowery scent swirled around her.

"Hi yourself." She shook Sheila's tiny, damp hand and wondered what kind of weird monetary arrangement they had. "I'm doing just great, thanks for asking."

It took only a few moments for Marian to size up the woman Bryan had abandoned her for all those years ago. Sheila looked like she could don her old cheerleader's outfit and blend right in with girls a third their age. Her jet-black hair, probably dyed, still fell in a shoulder-length pageboy. Her face didn't sag. She didn't wear glasses, bore no wrinkles on her upper lip, and showed little sign she was near the age of fifty, much less sixty. Of course, Sheila could have had work done. Marian knew that was a mean thought, but she just couldn't help it.

Bryan handed the check to Marian, his hand brushing hers.

Had that been intentional? Their eyes met, but she couldn't read anything in his. The check displayed his name and an island address. When had he moved home?

"Y'all can go on in." She handed him the two receipts. "Wine, beer, and soft drinks are free. So is the seafood buffet." Marian feigned a smile. "Cash bar for mixed drinks. Have fun."

As they walked away, Sheila looked as good from the back as she did from the front. Her backside was still small and perky when every other fifty-something woman's rear end had fallen flat.

The door closed behind them, cutting off a Jan and Dean song in mid-melody. Marian heaved a huge sigh. So much for hoping Bryan was divorced. What had that Facebook business been about?

She sipped a glass of warm Chardonnay, a sour taste coating her tongue. She'd go home, tail between her legs like a wild animal to the safety of its lair. It had been a mistake to get her hopes up, to think the Facebook message meant anything more than he just wanted to see her—the same as anyone else in their class.

Marian flexed her shoulders as she stood and crossed the hall to the ladies room, the bank envelope with cash and checks safely tucked into her purse. When she pushed open the door, Sheila's sweet flowery scent assaulted her. Harsh white light illuminated the wall of mirrors and her reflection.

Bryan and Sheila might still be together, but just the same, she was glad she'd gotten her nails and hair done. The fuchsia and green sundress flattered her, showed her cleavage. She looked good even though she would never be competition for Sheila, who would always be smaller and daintier.

Now she was in a hurry to leave. The idea of Bryan and Sheila dancing, laughing, having a good time while she watched from the sidelines was just too much. She didn't want to see them holding hands and draping their arms about one another.

She called Eva again. "Hey girl, I'm still here and guess what? Bryan showed up."

"Great! How'd it go?"

"Sheila was with him."

"Oh, I'm so sorry. Where are you calling from?"

"The bathroom. I had to get away for a moment. I'm not quite through packing up."

"Well, when you're done, come over. I'll still be nursing this bottle of wine, and you can tell me all about it."

"Okay, but if you don't hear from me, you'll know I threw myself off the seawall."

"Come on. It's not that bad. You still have me."

"Thanks, friend. See you in a bit." She hung up, took a deep breath, and flung open the door. Bryan stood at the registration table, a glass of white wine in each hand. When their eyes made contact, his face brightened. She smiled through clenched teeth as she clutched her purse and crossed the carpeted gulf separating them.

Bryan held a glass toward her. "Buy you a drink, Mrs. Reid?"

Marian accepted the glass, but before she could ask about Sheila, Bryan said, "Let's toast. To reunions. May they hold that which we desire."

Her eyes fixed on his face, adrenalin rushing in her limbs, she took a sip and again started to ask about Sheila, when he said, "How about a dance?"

"Sheila won't mind?"

"No more than Mr. Reid, I expect."

"There isn't a Mr. Reid anymore."

He cocked his head. "Oh, I'm so sorry."

"I mean, I'm not married anymore. I—I'm divorced."

He grinned and raised his eyebrows. "Sheila and I aren't married anymore, either."

Don't blow it, she thought. Holding up her shoulder bag, she said, "I have to bring the receipts."

Bryan took it and slung the strap over his shoulder. "Well, come on, woman, before the song ends." He led her into the ballroom where The Beach Boys crooned, "California Dreamin'." They set their glasses down on the nearest table, and he pulled her against him, wrapping his long arms around her. Memories of their surfing the waves together whirled in her head.

She buried her face in his chest as he steered her across the dance floor. The starch in his shirt and the earthy scent of perspiration barely masked by aftershave smelled the same as in high school. Her head still fit nicely into the curve of his shoulder. The words he murmured into her hair and the warmth of his hand on her back made her want more of him.

When she started to speak, Bryan said, "Shh. Later." She allowed herself a few moments of reminiscences and what ifs before giving in to the pleasure of being in his arms.

After the song ended, Marian pried loose and stepped back, trying for a deep breath. "W-When did you get divorced?"

Bryan tugged at the bottom of his shirt. He toyed with a few strands of her hair, tucking them behind her ear. Taking her elbow, he guided her to the edge of the dance floor. Some of their classmates stared, but she didn't care. She just smiled and focused on him.

"When did you divorce Mr. Reid?"

"He's been out of my life for years."

Bryan laughed, his eyes flashing. "Same here. Sheila and I are just good friends."

She could drown in his eyes if she weren't careful. "You moved home?"

"I'm back in Galveston. You live here, I know. Anyone else in your life?"

Marian shook her head, though she wondered if it was wise to be so honest.

Another slow song began. When Bryan touched her, she floated back into his arms. He brushed her hair behind her ear again and ran his fingers along the back of her neck. "I've found you again, Marian, and I'm never letting you go."

Marian closed her eyes. She didn't want to see the ballroom, its tall columns wrapped with purple and gold crepe paper, or the white-linen covered tables. She wanted to dance in Bryan's arms as though she could erase the years between now and the last time he'd held her. When the song ended, they stood staring at each other.

"Let's retrieve our wine," he said, his voice husky, and led her to where they'd left their glasses.

"Hey, Bryan," a man said. "How's it going?"

"It's going." They shook hands.

Another Beach Boys' song came on, a fast one. Bryan handed Marian her shoulder bag. "Want to get out of here?"

"What about Sheila?" She didn't give a hoot about Sheila but thought she should ask.

"I just picked her up at the airport, that's all. She's staying with friends." He took her hand.

"Just a minute." She skirted her classmates until she found Sarah. Pushing the moneybag at her, Marian said, "Mine showed up. I'm out of here." She patted Sarah's arm and headed back to Bryan.

They ran hand-in-hand through the warm, salty air across five traffic lanes to his car, parked on the beach side of the seawall. A mild breeze blew strands of hair across her eyes.

Before he opened the passenger door, Bryan pulled her into his arms. "I've got so much to say to you. Where can we talk?"

Marian wanted to do more than talk. She hadn't been with a man in years, but there were other considerations. She knew her own heart. Now was her chance to get things straight, to have them turn out as they should have been. That's what she wanted, but what did he want? She had to find out, and so she withdrew and reached for the car door. "IHOP is open twenty-four-seven. Want to get coffee?"

He nodded and tried to kiss her. She turned her head so the kiss ended up on her cheek but cupped his face in her hands and smiled so he could see she didn't mind. His breath smelled like wine.

"Let's go, okay?" she asked. He opened the door for her and, as he jogged to the other side to let himself in, all she could think was that he wanted her. Her. The girl who had gone away to give up their baby and found him with someone new when she returned. Striving to appear composed, Marian gripped her purse in her lap.

"That was you last night in front of my shop, wasn't it?" Marian glanced sideways.

"After you answered my Facebook query—after you friended me—I looked you up. I hope you don't mind."

"I knew it was you. Not when you first stopped, but when the trolley blasted and you glanced into my friend's coffee shop as you drove away. I was inside, helping her out."

"That was you? All I saw was a woman."

After they settled in a booth and ordered drinks, Bryan went to the restroom, and Marian texted Eva. "OMG Im w/B. Dont wait up."

Within a few minutes, other classmates arrived and grabbed booths and tables near them. Voices rose to an almost deafening level.

She and Bryan settled into the camaraderie of old friends, catching up on their lives, talking until the early hours of the morning. Marian chose not to tell him about Robert. If they saw more of each other there would be plenty of time to give him the full story. If not, it wouldn't matter. Around dawn, they ordered breakfast. When Marian could barely hold her eyes open, Bryan drove her back to her car. They promised to meet at the pool party that afternoon. It didn't matter that Marian hadn't planned to go, that she had no one to cover for her, no one to keep the shop open. None of that mattered now. Bryan had risen to the top of her list of priorities.

Chapter 4

AFTER A DAY AT THE Galvez Hotel pool, after an evening of formal dinner and dancing, Marian found herself alone with Bryan. This time they were in her condo where she'd invited him for a last drink.

She poured them amaretto on the rocks and wandered to the windows, to her favorite place, where she frequently watched the world go by without being observed. Late as it was, Eva's light burned from an upstairs window.

They'd had no contact other than a text from Marian to Eva, before she'd gone out that evening, asking Eva to take care of Anna for one more night. Marian left her cell phone in her apartment, not wanting the time with Bryan to be disturbed.

A few people were on the street, though it was after-hours for almost every place on the island except the dives, the bars a few blocks east of her place, nearer the wharves. The stragglers undoubtedly were cleanup crews for area restaurants.

"What was it you liked about me in the first place, Marian?"

Startled out of her reverie, she flinched. "Let's see. Your politics?"

"My politics? Why you—" He pulled her toward him and brushed her lips with his. "You don't even know what my politics are. Or is that is? Politics is?"

More than anything she wanted to drag him to her bed, but there was a question he had to answer before she could give herself up to what she hoped would be the sexual experience she'd dreamed of. She pushed him away. "I hope you haven't changed since high school. We had similar opinions back then."

"That was a long time ago." He pulled her back and wrapped his arms around her.

"Yes, a very long time ago." She rested her head against his shoulder. During the months she'd lived with Nana, the last months of her pregnancy, she'd dreamed of dancing with Bryan. During the past two days, they'd danced almost nonstop.

He nuzzled her temple. "What are you thinking?"

She gazed up at him. "About the last time we danced together."

"This evening?"

"The last time we danced together when we were in high school." She laid her head back down. "Remember?"

"The Junior-Senior Prom. We were juniors. You wore that long blue dress with the empire waist that made you look pregnant."

Her breath caught. That was the perfect opening to tell him about Robert, but she just couldn't do it. She didn't want anything to threaten their relationship. Robert needed a man in his life, but whether Bryan needed Robert was one of the questions she had for him. "You thought I looked pregnant? You never told me that."

"All the girls looked pregnant in those dresses," he murmured as he stroked her arm.

"I can't believe you remember what they were called." She

pulled away from him, wanting to put distance between herself and that subject.

"Isn't that right? Empire? All the girls wore them. The guys liked them because they could see cleavage. Not a big deal today, since it's everywhere you look, but—"

"The things we remember." She moved to the next window. A curtain stirred upstairs in Eva's condo across the way.

"Yeah, I definitely remember you in that blue dress, babe. You were one hot chick. Just like now." He followed her. "We can make up for lost time. I've got plans for us."

"I'm glad we've had this time together." Her voice sounded unnaturally loud in her ears.

"You're making it sound like it's over." He enfolded her in his arms. "I'm going to show you the world the way it should be seen."

He spun her around and kissed her neck, her ear, her temple.

Before she could stop herself, she said, "I just want to ask you one thing."

"Anything, babydoll." He planted little kisses around her mouth.

She was determined to get the unsettled business between them out in the open. Fear made it hard to breathe, but she forced herself to ask the question anyway. "The summer before our senior year, why didn't you wait for me to come back?"

He held her at arm's length, solemn-faced, mouth opened. He entwined her hair in his fingers. After a few moments he whispered, "I made a mistake, a stupid mistake."

Her insides quivered. She sat on the sofa and clasped her hands between her legs, to warm them and stop the shaking. He followed her.

"I didn't think you'd ever come back."

"You didn't even wait three months." Her voice sounded accusing, but she wasn't going to back down.

He sat beside her and took one of her hands in his. "Can you ever forgive me for making the biggest mistake of my life?"

She wanted to trust him, to be confident he'd be there for her in the future. "I want to, Bryan," she whispered. "I've just never understood."

He kissed her forehead. "Give me a chance to explain."

"That's what I'm waiting for. This sounds harsh, but why? Why didn't you wait for me?"

"You mean now? Explain now? I thought—"

She shook her head. "I have to know."

He swallowed from his drink, and his eyes studied hers. "You disappeared without saying anything."

Her mind went back to the day she'd left town. The morning after school recessed for the summer, in the early days of June, her mother had shaken her awake while it was still dark.

"Get up and get dressed," she said. "We've got to go."

Wiping the sleep from her eyes, Marian spotted her bulging suitcase standing in the doorway. "What's going on?"

"There's no time to waste, young lady. Get your clothes on right now. I'll explain on the way. We need to leave immediately." Her mother jerked the bedclothes down and stood over her as Marian dressed. As soon as Marian tied her tennis shoes, her mother took her by the arm and escorted her out the door.

Now, Marian shook her head. "My mother didn't give me a chance. She said we had to leave right away."

Bryan's fists were clenched. "When no one answered the phone, I didn't know what to think. Your mom didn't pick up the phone for several days."

Marian glanced away. "She took me to my grandmother's in Fort Worth."

"Finally one day your mom answered and said you were gone. I asked her if you'd be back after summer vacation, but she said I just needed to forget you. She hung up on me."

The fights with her mother came rushing back at her as clear as if they'd just occurred. Her mother said Marian could either give the baby up for adoption or go live in the streets. When Marian finally agreed to give up the baby, her mother had swept her out of town.

When they were miles from Galveston, her mother told her the truth.

"I'm taking you to Nana's house until your bastard is born."

Marian cried all the way to Fort Worth. When they arrived, her mother grabbed her suitcase and marched her inside. She instructed Marian's grandmother: "She's not to use the phone, and you're to keep her inside and away from the windows. The less known about this, the better for all of us."

"Claire," Nana said, with a shake of her head, "it's not the end of the world. It's a baby. A beautiful gift from God, for heaven's sake."

"You agreed to take her in under my terms. If you can't do that, I'll make other arrangements." Her mother had stood over her grandmother with a bone-crushing look in her eye.

"I've been thinking about it, Claire. If Marian wants to keep the child, as she has said she does, why not let her live here with me? There's plenty of room, and I'd love to have her."

Marian's mama swelled up like a blowfish. "Don't even try it, Mother. Don't even try to interfere."

Marian fled to the guest room. She crawled under the covers and pulled them over her head. When she came out, her mother was gone.

Now, she said, "I'm so sorry, Bry."

"One day I went to your house and waited on the porch until your mom came home. She spotted me when she pulled into the driveway. She began backing up, but I ran to the car and grabbed the door handle. After she dragged me several feet, she finally stopped."

"Oh, God, I didn't know."

"She said she would never tell me where you were, that you were never coming back. That I might as well forget you and find somebody else." His lips turned white as they stretched over his teeth.

"She said she'd found your nasty, dirty panties and confronted you about what we'd been doing—" His face creased in anguish, Bryan put his hand over hers. "You don't need to hear this."

Marian squeezed his hand. "I have to know *everything* she said."

"The only thing that counts is that we're together now. Let's put this behind us and plan our future." His eyebrows drew together, and his eyes looked sad. "You do want to be with me, don't you?"

She nodded. "But I need to know." She clenched her jaw. "Tell me everything you remember."

"I'll tell you the parts I'll never forget." He fixed his eyes on hers. "She said . . . no daughter of hers was going to be known as the town whore."

Marian could still feel the too-small girdles her mother had made her wear. And her stomach growling even after eating one of the sparse meals her mother allowed her. "That's nothing new." She gritted her teeth. "What else?"

"She said you didn't want to see me anymore, that you thought what we'd done had been a sin. I didn't believe her and asked if she'd send you a letter. She said she would, and I gave it to her. You never wrote me back."

"I never received your letter. She said you never called or came by, that you didn't care, you were just using me for sex." She wiped her eyes. "At the end of the summer when I returned, you were with Sheila."

They reached for each other at the same time. His cheek felt scratchy and warm. As she clung to him, she forgot Robert, the adult Robert, for a moment and thought about what her life would have been like if her mother hadn't been so controlling. Then she focused on Bryan.

And Bryan focused on her.

She led him into the bedroom where they yanked each other's clothes off. They fell onto the bed.

"Wait," she said, pulling away. "What about a condom?"

"I haven't been with anyone since Sheila and I split up." He reached for her.

"My husband was the last person for me." Marian had an overwhelming desire to giggle, so she did. "I can't get pregnant anymore either."

Afterward, Marian pulled the duvet over them. Astonished at the weekend's events, with his hot breath against her temple, she fell asleep.

Chapter 5

AFTER THE REUNION GOODBYE BRUNCH, she and Bryan made a date for a night during the week, and Marian drove to Houston to see Robert where he lived with Dorothy, the woman who had been his foster mother and was now his legal guardian.

Though it had only been a week since she'd been to Dorothy's small home, something seemed different. The house looked like a neglected child. The grass needed mowing, and clumps of weeds made a patchwork of the yard. When she'd called, Dorothy hadn't said anything about either of them being ill or otherwise *indisposed* as Marian's mama would say. Her mama. She forced that thought from her mind.

Finding the screen door latched, she pounded on the wooden frame. She stood on the veranda and breathed the soggy, polluted Houston air. Perspiration oozed from her scalp, dampening her dark, gray-streaked hair. Her cotton blouse and capris clung to her body.

Shifting the package she held and her purse to the other arm, she exhaled a deep breath. What could be taking so long?

She hated the limited time she was allowed with Robert but couldn't blame Dorothy, a real sweetheart. A judge had issued the order a lifetime ago.

Finally, Dorothy, sans glasses, eyes seeming out of focus, unlatched the screen. Her curly gray locks sprouted like a garden. "Sorry, honey. I was lying down. Thought Robert would let you in."

Marian reached up to kiss the taller woman on the cheek as she stepped past her into the air-conditioning. When they hugged, Dorothy's bony shoulder blades stuck out like a knife. Her blouse smelled of Ivory soap and body odor. Holding Dorothy at arm's length, Marian asked, "Are you okay?"

"Tired, that's all." Dorothy shifted her eyes, and led Marian to the den. The television blared. "Robert, Marian's here."

As soon as she and Robert returned from their outing, Marian was going to get to the bottom of the situation if it took all night. Dorothy might not want to ask for assistance, but if she needed something, Marian wanted to help. It was the least she could do after all Dorothy had done for them.

Marian stood in the doorway and watched her son for a few moments. He sat cross-legged on the floor and stared at the TV, like a child. "Hey, Robert."

"Be in the kitchen if you need me," Dorothy said.

Marian walked over to him and crouched down. He was as pale as a slice of onion. If she'd been allowed to raise him, she would have made sure he spent time outside every day, every season of the year. They would have taken long walks on the beach, shed their shoes, waded in the shallows, and wiggled their toes in the sand. But the judge said it would never be.

Robert sat with his back against the threadbare sofa. She got

31

between him and the TV and looked into eyes the same color as the clear, hot sky outside. Taking his cool hand, she squeezed it and said, "I said, *Hey, Robert.* When someone greets you, you're supposed to greet them back."

"Hi, Marian." His voice just missed being loud enough to bounce off the walls. His breath smelled of salt and grease from the potato chips that half-filled a glass bowl next to him. "This is my favorite show." He shifted to see around her. "My favorite show." His face was unshaven. The face of a man. The behavior of a boy.

"Yes," Marian said. "We'll talk when it's over." She resisted the urge to pull him to her, knowing he didn't like touching. Instead, she stroked his head, his auburn curls shorn for the summer, something Dorothy had done for as long as Marian could remember.

"Okay, Marian." He nodded, his eyes anywhere but on hers. "This is my favorite show. Okay."

Something pinched in her lower back as she got up off the floor. She found a cushiony spot on the sofa and settled down with the Houston paper.

Staring at the back of Robert's head, she realized she'd never thought to ask if he minded going around practically bald until the end of the summer when his hair began growing back. If she'd been allowed to raise him, she would at least have asked him how he felt about it. At his age, he could have an opinion.

"What are you watching, Robert?"

"Animal Planet," he said in a monotone. "My best show. Animal Planet."

"But what show?" she asked the back of his head.

"Every show, Marian. Every show on Animal Planet."

"Every show on Animal Planet is your favorite show?"

He didn't respond.

"Robert. I didn't hear you."

"Yes, Marian. My best show."

"You need to speak in complete sentences. How have you been?"

"I want to watch the three o'clock TV show. Three o'clock." He pointed at the clock that hung above the set. "It is my best TV show."

"Your favorite, you mean." Marian tapped her lips and waited for the pang in her chest to subside. Just because she wanted her visits to take priority, didn't mean he felt the same. He liked things to fit into boxes and schedules. She liked to expose him to new things, knowing from experience that once she got him out of the house, he'd be okay and even enjoy himself—at least as much as he could.

"Everything seems to be your best show, Robert." She reached forward and caressed his sleeve, trying to get his attention. "I thought we could visit for a few minutes."

Robert called to Dorothy in a loud monotone, "Mother." He unfolded himself and left the room.

Marian felt a twinge when he called Dorothy *Mother*. Putting the newspaper aside, she waited. He soon returned, all six feet of him towering in the doorway.

Wiping her hands on a dishtowel, Dorothy stood behind him, her eyebrows drawn together. Dorothy actually looked more like his mother, being just as tall, while Marian was shorter than the average woman.

Marian cocked her head. "We have different ideas about how to spend our time." She didn't have to add *as usual*. They both knew that already.

Dorothy chuckled. "I completely understand." Turning to Robert, she squeezed his hand like Marian did. "Marian came to see you. You need to visit with her. We can record your show on the DVR, and you can watch it later." Nodding at him until he nodded back, she left again.

33

"Robert, I brought you something." Marian held out the package. Robert looked at the present and back at the TV. He picked up the remote and punched buttons before turning back to Marian.

She pulled on his sleeve until he sat next to her. She touched his chin, bringing his face to hers so she could look him in the eyes. Robert stiffened but didn't pull away. "Look at me, Robert. This is a gift for you. A book about trains. Hot off the press. You'll like it. I promise."

Robert made brief eye contact, took the package, and tore off the paper. "A book about trains." He stroked the cover, which bore a big, full-color photograph of a locomotive. "I like it. I promise."

"Why don't we look at the book together?"

"I like the book about trains," Robert said, standing up.

"Sit down, Robert." She patted the sofa cushion next to her.

Robert sat beside her and opened the book. "A lot of pictures."

"Yes, lots of pictures of trains. And this book has information about train museums. Would you like to go to the train museum?" Her voice sounded almost as loud as his. She lowered it. She didn't want to be one of those folks who talk louder to people who don't understand.

"Lots of pictures." He turned the colored pages one at a time, patting the photographs.

As they sat together, his arm touched hers, his masculine scent filled her nostrils, and joy flowed through her. She hoped she meant as much to him. A bit later, Dorothy leaned her head through the doorway. "Robert, show Marian the changes you made to your room."

"Come to my room, Marian." Robert stuck the book under his arm and rose from the sofa, departing with a few quick strides. Marian scrambled up and hurried after him.

Though small, his bedroom had a view of the backyard. With

---

the café curtains pushed aside, she could see the vegetables he put in every spring. Often when she visited, he would be staring out the window. She wondered what went through his mind. She'd also come upon him in the backyard, squatting and staring at the plants as though he could see them grow. Maybe he could.

Robert had rearranged his living space. A smell of new paint floated in the air.

"I made new bookshelves, Marian. See. New bookshelves." Robert pointed to a six-foot wooden bookcase.

"It's wonderful, Robert. Did you build everything? It's wonderful." She sounded more and more like him lately when she spoke to him. "I see you've sorted your books." He'd arranged his books by color, like a rainbow, all the red covers together, then the orange, the yellow and so on. In each section, he grouped the title color so that red with white words came after red with black lettering. She knew it made sense to him, and no one else mattered in his room.

The H O Scale model train she'd given him when he was a teenager ran along the upper part of the wall on a track mounted on a shelf above the doorway, window, and bookcase. To make space for the bookcase, he'd moved his single bed to the other side of the room and put his chest of drawers at its foot. His desk stood under the window. A braided rug lay in front of the shelves. "Robert saved money for new bookcases and shelf for train," he said.

"Good job, Robert, but you know it's *I saved money for new bookshelves*. It's truly very nice."

"I can sort books better. Have room for train."

Marian rested her cheek against his forearm. He wore a T-shirt and shorts, and his arm was cool from the air-conditioning. "Your room gets nicer every time I see it. You have quite a knack for fixing it up."

Robert looked at her, deadpan, but let her touch him for a moment before pulling away.

Back in the den, he again opened the book Marian brought him. What thoughts bounced around that mind? Did he want to put the book away and turn on the television again? Did he look at the book only because she expected him to do what she wanted?

Marian wished she could see inside his brain. She knew he recognized her, though he couldn't know she was his biological mother. The judge had ordered her never to tell, not to confuse him with the facts. He'd never known anyone as his mother except Dorothy. The people who'd testified said he wouldn't handle the information well. Though Marian thought it horribly unfair, her lawyer had advised her to be grateful for the right to visit and not make waves.

Did Robert ever wonder who she was?

Marian studied him, the shape of his ear, his jawline. His dark, thick, unruly eyebrows and long, straight eyelashes were just like Bryan's. A small nick on his neck appeared to be healing. When he turned the last page a few minutes later, he pointed to the clock. "Okay. Time for TV now." His voice was singsong.

"Would you mind skipping that program, too? I thought we could go to the train museum."

"Skip? Skip?" Robert fled the room. "Mother."

In a few moments, Dorothy and Robert returned, Robert standing behind Dorothy like a child hiding in his mother's skirts. "Now what's wrong?" The dishtowel lay draped over her shoulder.

Marian rose from the couch and stepped closer. "Didn't you tell him about the museum? You said you'd tell him before I got here." She tried to keep from sounding irritated. "Remember they're having an event today for special people?"

Dorothy blanched. "I completely forgot, honey. Did we talk about that at your last visit?"

"We did. The museum event is this afternoon, and then I want to take him to the cafeteria. You said it would be okay."

"It's no problem." Dorothy turned to Robert. "Go change your clothes. Marian's going to take you to the train museum and to eat at the cafeteria. You know how much you like the cafeteria. Go change into tennis shoes and long pants." Her eyes met Marian's. "You don't mind if he wears his T-shirt, do you?"

"No, that's fine." He wore the same T-shirt almost every time she visited. Or at least one that looked like all the others. Black T-shirts, ranging from new and dark to faded gray, crowded his closet. In that way, she supposed he was like other obsessive people.

"Mother, my show." He stared over Marian's shoulder.

"I'll record it, too. Now go change your clothes, Robert." Dorothy waved him away. "Put on long pants and tennis shoes. Go now."

Marian watched their interplay. Dorothy stood firm and stared into Robert's face. Robert made brief eye contact and, shoulders drooping, walked toward his bedroom.

"I feel terrible taking him away from the TV." Marian frowned. "Don't you think he'll like the museum once we get there?"

"Of course he will." Dorothy sighed. "He has too much screen time as it is."

Marian followed her to the kitchen. "Guess what I did last Friday." She leaned against the counter.

"No idea." Dorothy seemed to be searching for something. She went from the counter, to the stove, and back to the counter near the refrigerator.

"Went to my class reunion. What are you looking for?"

"The dishtowel. I had it a few minutes ago."

Marian pulled it from Dorothy's shoulder. "Here it is."

"Thanks." She strung it through the refrigerator door handle.

"Is something wrong?" Marian took Dorothy's elbow. "Something on your mind?"

"Just tired. Your class reunion? How many years has it been?"

Marian shook her head. "Dorothy, you know how many years— forty. Robert will be forty-one this August, remember?"

"What am I thinking? Of course." She swiped her hand through her hair. "Of course."

"I wasn't going to go, but Eva talked me into it. Swore I'd regret it for the rest of my life if I didn't. So I signed up to volunteer. And then—"

"Eva?"

"She lives across the street from me, Dorothy. You know who Eva is." Marian stared up into Dorothy's face. She'd get to the bottom of this if she had to drag it out of her. "What's going on?"

"Nothing, dear. I'm glad you're taking Robert on an outing. I could use time to myself." Her eyes gave nothing away.

"Something's not right. Didn't you have a check-up last month? Did the doctor say you're okay?" Marian continued to look her in the eye. "Is there something you're not telling me?"

Dorothy sighed again. "I—"

Robert appeared in the doorway. He wore black and white high-top tennis shoes, no socks, jeans, and his black T-shirt under the Houston Astros jacket Marian had given him years earlier.

"Chicken leg." He looked at Marian and said, "I will have a chicken leg."

"See, it's not that hard. Thank you for making the effort." She patted Dorothy's arm as if to say they would have to talk another time. "You can have all the chicken you want, Robert. But first, we're going to see the trains. Then we eat. You're going to be awfully hot in that jacket. Don't you want to leave it here?"

She knew he'd say no. If anything, autistic people were set in their ways—if you could call it that. She knew it, but still tried to treat him like anyone else most of the time. He wasn't stupid, just autistic, though lately Dorothy had let him lapse into bad habits, like not speaking in complete sentences. He was capable of many things. He'd graduated from high school, with special circumstances.

"We will ride in car, Marian. And go to the museum." He held up the book.

"Bring the book if you want. Let's say goodbye to your mother." Marian winced inside.

Dorothy leaned against the kitchen counter. "You two go on now."

"Go take a nice long nap, and don't worry about us." Marian hugged her friend. "I'll bring him back safely, I promise."

"Of course you will."

Robert stood by the door, arms dangling.

"Go on." Marian stood behind him, waiting for him to open the door.

"Goodbye, Mother." Robert pulled open the door and walked through the doorway, leaving Marian standing there.

"We need to work on your manners," Marian called after him.

🌿 🌿 🌿

When they arrived back at Dorothy's, Marian opened the door. "Goodnight, Robert." She stood on her tiptoes to kiss him on the cheek.

"Goodbye, Marian," Robert said. "Hello, Mother," he said to Dorothy who stood just inside the door. He clapped her on the back, patting her several times.

"Go get ready for bed," Dorothy said. "I'll be there in a minute." To Marian, she said, "Come inside for a cup of decaf tea."

Marian accepted and sat at the dinette table. "Sometimes I have an urge to say, *Thanks, Mom.*"

"Lately I feel old enough to be your mother, honey." Dorothy hugged herself and rubbed her arms as though she were cold.

"You're not old." Marian passed her fingers over the embroidery on the napkin. "Why don't you sit down?"

"Let me see to Robert, make sure he gets to bed. I'll be right back."

Marian stirred sweetener and milk into her tea and took a sip. Lukewarm. She got up and pulled the teabag out of Dorothy's cup. When she opened the cupboard under the sink to drop the bag into the trash, the teakettle rested on top of the garbage. Though shiny and clean on the top, the sides were charred and blackened. The bottom had a hole the size of a quarter burned through. Marian dropped it back into the trashcan as if she'd burned her fingers and slammed the cupboard door.

Her mind raced back to her visits through the winter and early spring, searching her memories for hints, signs, confirmation of the suspicion that now lay in her stomach like thick dough. She'd been so caught up in herself and her life that she failed to notice all was not right with her friend. She shivered, goose bumps covering her body.

Marian microwaved her tea, wanting to busy herself. The machine's hum made her aware of just how fast life went by while people weren't looking.

One minute. One minute to heat up her tea.

One minute everything was wonderful. She had a lovely boyfriend. One minute later she was pregnant and her life changed forever.

One minute she'd been married and pregnant. One minute later, the child died and her husband left her.

One minute her nana, the woman she most adored, was fine. The next, she died of a heart attack.

In only a minute, life could be turned upside down. The illness of a friend, a mentor, a mother. The bell dinged, and Dorothy returned to the kitchen.

Marian resisted the urge to run to her, wrap her arms around her, and never let her go, as though she could protect her from what was to come. She sipped her tea, allowing Dorothy to break the news in her own way.

She owed Dorothy so much. She'd welcomed Marian into her home, let her share their lives, and twice spoken up for Marian in court.

"Anything exciting been happening?" Marian asked, hoping her words would be an easy lead-in.

"They have a new manager at the grocery store." She sat down across from Marian and gripped her cup as if she were trying to warm her hands. "Robert may lose his job."

"Why?" For once Marian didn't want to talk about Robert, but she'd be patient and let Dorothy tell her when she was ready.

"The new one's impatient. From what the kids at the store say, the new man doesn't like to explain to Robert what he wants him to do." She grimaced. "You know how literal Robert is. He doesn't understand someone barking orders and expecting him to understand without an explanation. The man won't leave him alone and let him do what he's always done."

"He'll find another job with an understanding person. He always does."

Dorothy reached out to Marian. "That's the least of our problems. I did go to the doctor to have my annual physical."

"You're fine, right?" Marian held her breath.

"Marian, I've suspected it for a while but thought it was just old age. Things kept getting worse." Her eyes clouded over. "You must brace yourself, my dear. I have Alzheimer's."

Chapter 6

IN THE WEE HOURS OF the next morning, Marian walked to the picture window at the front of her condo. The street below, still lit by antique lamps, and the dark upstairs windows across from her, gave off ambiance. Her favorite part of the morning was watching the day begin on Ledbetter Street. Giving the window a tug until it opened, she leaned out, inhaling the humid, salty air.

Something about Galveston—the water, the air—she didn't know what, energized her, gave her strength. A seagull squawked as it flew behind a brown pelican. Patchy dark clouds drifted overhead.

Ledbetter Street, though two lanes wide, felt narrower. The buildings opposite hers might just as well be only a few feet away. When the curtains and blinds stood open in the daytime, anyone could see deep into the interior of both the first and second floors.

The street glistened from an overnight rain, light reflecting off the trolley tracks that ran down one side. Neon signs backlit The Pit and Coffee & More, though the windows above the shops remained dark. Early light cast shadows on the historical buildings, their facades looking like long, drooping, pastel faces.

Movement on the street caught Marian's eye. A man wearing a dark T-shirt and dark pants, a jacket slung over his shoulder, ambled past. A woman with raggedy-cut hair, and a baby in a sling across her chest, followed a couple of strides behind, her long skirt dragging the ground. The woman jogged every few steps, struggling to keep up.

A light appeared in a second-story window at the end of the block, above the Taqueria. Did the owners see her light and wonder about her as she did them? Too great a distance was between their two places so she couldn't see much more than light leaking through the blinds.

Something had changed at the small shop catty-corner from her own, the one where the drug people had been busted, next to Eva's shop. Brown paper covered the downstairs windows from the inside. No one had said anything about the building having been sold.

Marian had slept little the night before, tossing and turning, hearing Dorothy's words in her ears. She needed to talk with Eva, but her lights were still out.

The night before, when Dorothy had said *Alzheimer's*, images filled Marian's head. The first time she'd seen her in court, a much younger Dorothy, tall and lean. The way Dorothy had clutched herself in protective body language when she testified—describing Robert's attachment to her—his head-banging when he was a toddler, his constant demands for books, books, books, her efforts to reach him.

The Dorothy who had welcomed Marian into her home—against the social worker's wishes—secure in her role as Robert's mother, casting them together as frequently as Marian could visit, taking the lead in developing a relationship between the biological mother and son.

The angry Dorothy at the second court hearing, who was facing attachment issues at the thought that Marian might steal Robert away.

The forgiving Dorothy who had again welcomed Marian and had become as much a mother to Marian as to Robert in the last twenty years.

Dorothy's face faded into a shadow as the memory of deep loss burrowed out of Marian's heart, where it had lain dormant since her father's disappearance. Marian yearned to go back to earlier in the day on Sunday, before learning that her life was not going to follow the trajectory she'd day-dreamed about.

When her vision had cleared, Marian leapt across the gap between them and cried, "It can't be! You seem fine."

"That's a lie, and we both know it," Dorothy whispered, winding her arms around Marian.

Marian stroked Dorothy's hair. "Tell me there's a mistake. Tell me you're going for another opinion." She knelt on the floor before Dorothy. "Are they positive?"

Dorothy cupped Marian's face in her hands. "They can only be 100 percent positive by doing a brain biopsy after I'm dead, but, yes, they're as certain as can be. And that includes the specialist I've seen."

"What can I do? How can I help? Is there medicine you can take? Will your daughter come stay with you?"

Dorothy's grip on Marian's arm was like a vise, the look in her eyes distorted.

"Dorothy, quit looking at me like that. They'll be able to do something, right? I mean, these days they know more about it, don't they?"

Dorothy caressed Marian's cheek again. "There's medicine that might help, but you need to prepare yourself, dear girl."

"No. There has to be something they can do. Get another opinion."

"I told you, we've done that, honey." Dorothy exhaled a huge breath. "Veronica's been here on and off and dragged me to doctors all around Houston."

Marian pulled up a chair and sat knee-to-knee with Dorothy, grasping her hands. "I could've helped. Why didn't you call me?"

Dorothy shook her head. "There was nothing for you to do."

Dorothy—kind, gentle-spirited Dorothy, loving Dorothy— didn't deserve to end her days that way. Marian hated to think of the suffering Dorothy would experience.

She searched Dorothy's face for—what? She didn't know. For many years, Dorothy had been the only family she'd known.

She wept hard, choking sobs. Each time she thought she had herself under control, the idea of life without Dorothy struck her again. When she got a grip on herself, she dried her face and peeked at Dorothy. She wanted to be strong for her, as strong as Dorothy was, herself.

"Honey, I understand how upset you are." Dorothy pushed back Marian's hair. "I don't want to lose you, either."

Marian knew she shouldn't be thinking about how empty her own life would be without Dorothy instead of how terrible Dorothy's life would be as her health deteriorated. Dorothy met her eyes with an understanding smile.

"I waited as long as I could to tell you. The doctor says it's progressing rapidly. I'm already having memory lapses." She glanced toward the cabinet where the kettle lay in the trash.

Marian dropped back into the chair. She didn't think she could stand hearing any more.

"We need to talk about Robert, sweetheart."

What would happen to Robert? He'd be devastated. "Will he go to live with Veronica? I'd hate it if he went that far away. I don't know if I could bear it if I didn't get to see him at least once a month."

"Veronica can't take him. She has a husband and my grandchildren to take care of."

A prickly sensation nibbled at the back of Marian's neck. She blew her nose again. "What do you think the court will want? We know he won't do well if he has to go to strangers."

Dorothy's eyes bored through hers. "Marian . . . you're his real mother."

Marian shook her head. "What are you saying?"

"You should take him. He should go live with you in Galveston."

"You—they—would the judge give him to me now? After all these years?" Marian pushed back her chair and stood again. "When I fought for him, they said I could never have him. Never. Are you saying they'd give him to me, finally, when he's a middle-aged man?"

"That was Children's Protective Services." Dorothy spoke as though to a child.

"But when I applied for guardianship when he turned eighteen, the probate court refused me. Why would the judge change his mind now?" A knot formed in her middle and grew with each word. She began to pace.

"Robert was so attached to me. You know how he behaved when Victor abandoned us and filed for divorce." Dorothy clutched the edge of the table.

"So, now . . ." Marian turned her back and covered her mouth with her hands. Thoughts flashed through her mind. Testimony in past court hearings. The looks people had given her. Why would they let her have him now? She'd wanted him her whole life and been told no. No. No. Never.

"So now that I'm—I've got Alzheimer's, and you've been visiting him all these years, things'll be different. The court will see it differently." Dorothy turned Marian to face her. "Marian, the results of another court hearing, another trial, won't be the same. You might not even need to have a trial."

Marian crossed her arms and continued pacing. "You don't know that." She didn't know why they were even having the conversation. She couldn't go to court a third time. Be told no a third time. She couldn't take it. Get her hopes up again and be let down again. It would kill her as much as Alzheimer's would kill Dorothy.

"I phoned the court investigator. Made a case for you to take him."

"I don't know what to say. I have a business to run. I have tenants to worry about. I—" She had people in her life who didn't know her secret. Most of her friends. Everyone on Ledbetter Street except Eva. And now, Bryan was back. *"Bryan,"* she whispered. "Dorothy, Bryan is Robert's father. He doesn't know."

"And Robert is your son," Dorothy said, her voice bringing Marian back to reality. "At least consider the idea." Dorothy loomed over Marian.

"Don't get angry." Marian's heart pulsed in her temple. Her vision blurred. She hadn't had a real migraine since the last time she'd seen her mama. "I'm just shocked. It never occurred to me. Never. Not since the last time we went to court, and the judge ruled in your favor." She shook her head. "I mean I always dreamed of it, but the judge said never, and I took him at his word. My whole life has been built around knowing I'd never have custody."

"Will you at least consider the idea? Robert would do so well with you now. He knows you."

"I don't know how to take care of an autistic person." Marian flailed her arms as though she could wave everything away. "I read everything I could get my hands on, but all I've ever done is visited, brought him a few gifts, taken him out alone occasionally. You know how little caretaking I've ever had to do, Dorothy. How little the court even allowed me to do."

"You've always been good with him, Marian. He needs you. He'll be way better off with you than in a home somewhere. God knows how he would be affected at his age if he were sent to strangers in a strange place." She lifted Marian's face up to hers. "You know you want him."

Marian stared past Dorothy. Did she still want him? Of course she did. But she had to think.

"Let me give you the court investigator's number," pleaded Dorothy. "Put your feelings aside and think of what would be in Robert's best interest."

Marian took two steps backward and held up her hands as if to ward off Dorothy. "It's no life for him, in a women's pre-owned clothing store. What would I do with him all day? Where would he sleep?" Marian needed time to think about everything, talk it over with someone.

Dorothy sank into a chair. "He's not a dog. You'll find things for him to do. You have plenty of room to make space for him in your condo." She pulled a card from her pocket and held it out. "Call Yvette and talk it over. Could you at least do that?"

Marian pocketed the card. She knew she'd do it. She loved him. She'd never wanted to give him up. This was it, her best chance. Her only chance. Her last chance to get her son back. No way could she risk his health and welfare by letting Adult Protective Services send him away. She had to protect him. She'd driven herself back to Galveston in the dark of night, having difficulty navigating through blurred eyes.

Now, on Monday morning, Eva's condo lights came on, but

the drapes didn't move. A ball of paper blew down the street. The couple with the baby had disappeared. As far as she could see east to west, no one else had risen before dawn. The mist from the harbor had begun to burn off, leaving a purple sky. The kettle screamed from the stove. A giddy feeling enveloped Marian as she pulled her head back inside.

When Eva's morning rush was over, Marian would head across Ledbetter Street. After all, what were best friends for if not a sounding board when a person was in need?

Chapter 7

EVA BEST OVERSLEPT. SHE NEEDED to get downstairs and get the coffee shop open pronto. Her fingers brushed the grape-sized lump in her breast. From the pea shape she'd first found, the mass had grown until she couldn't put off action any longer. If the cancer that had taken her mother and her aunt thought it had come for her, it had another think coming. She'd beat it. She'd run it out of town and off the island. Time to begin the fight. Put up her dukes. Show it how serious she could be. And she would do that, as soon as the doc called her about the biopsy results on Monday.

Eva wanted—no, she *needed*—to talk to Marian. She hadn't told her what was going on because she didn't want to spoil Marian's excitement about the reunion. She'd thought she might as well wait until the results came in. After receiving Marian's text messages, she knew she'd made the right decision. She couldn't wait to hear how things had gone with Bryan. She'd texted her back on Saturday morning, "OMG is rt! Come over or call and tell all asap." But

Marian hadn't and now that Monday morning had dawned, Eva didn't think she could wait to talk to her much longer.

Her mind went back to her cancer. Taking a couple of deep breaths to calm herself, she focused on getting ready for the day instead. She'd never let her customers see her upset. Some of them were annoying enough without letting them into her personal life.

Eva shuddered and hooked her bra. She would have to make a decision soon. She scrubbed her face. After drying off, she moisturized, brushed a bit of powder across her cheeks, and ran pink lip balm around her mouth. She wanted to look and act normally though it struck her as hilarious that she thought of moisturizing so she wouldn't be so wrinkled when she grew old. She might not get to be old.

Okay, *that* was the wrong attitude. What she needed was one swift kick in the rear end to adjust her thinking. And who'd be good for that? Marian. But enough of that. If she didn't see her earlier, she'd see her at the Taqueria. Mondays were their regular dinner date. Right now, though, she had to get to work. After baking in the early hours, she had run back upstairs for a nap and slept through the alarm. She stroked mousse into her hair so it would stand up in a spike. After zipping her red shorts, she buttoned a sleeveless red plaid blouse, tied her feet into a pair of red high-tops, and hurried downstairs to open Coffee & More.

Stale coffee and yeast fumes hung in the air. Mazie Phillips peered through the window, her hand cupped above her eyes, and tapped her keys on the glass. None of the rest of the early regulars had waited.

Eva propped open the door to let fresh air inside. Mazie followed her to the counter. "What's up, Eva? Why you opening so late?"

"I'll have your cappuccino in a minute," Eva said, stepping behind the counter and flipping on the cappuccino machine. She forced a smile as she set up the coffee maker and filled the water pot for hot tea.

Mazie pressed her nose to the bakery cabinet glass and gazed at the muffins and breads, a ten-dollar bill in her hand. "A lot of people went down to Harry's, Eva. I saw them. But you know I would never do that, not me. I don't like Harry. He's a smartass. You keep opening late, though Eva, you're going to lose business."

Eva cringed. Harry again. She rued the day he bought the gallery in the next block. Always up to something. Always complaining. Always causing trouble. He didn't like the trashcan applique. The streetlights were too dim. The palm trees each building owner had sprung for were too expensive; he couldn't afford to put one up. Eva's face flushed, and she fanned herself with her hand. She could slow down. Mazie wasn't going anywhere. Mazie didn't like Harry.

Eva flushed and blotted the back of her neck with a paper towel. "I'm not competing with Harry." She couldn't be having a hot flash. Wasn't forty-five too young to go through menopause? No way she could be going through the change. No way. No way in hell. "It's no big deal. So he sells a little coffee—"

"He sells tea now, Eva." Mazie smirked. "Packaged tea as well as brewed. Not as much variety as you could buy at a wholesaler's like Maceo's, but still, if you need tea bags or want packages of loose tea, you can get them at Harry's."

Eva grunted and wished she had earplugs so she didn't have to hear one more blessed thing about Harry. Staring at the cappuccino maker, she willed the machine to hurry. In just a few more minutes, Mazie could take her muffin and cappuccino and head on down the road.

Eva smiled again when what she wanted to do was scream. "Harry's main thing is his art gallery. He's just trying to make his customers comfortable while they decide what they want to buy.

You want a muffin or a slice of carrot cake?" Standing behind the bakery case, her shoulders even with the top of it, Eva stared, glassy-eyed, at Mazie.

Mazie pressed her palms on the glass as though to do pushups. "What about that gelato machine? Is he going to let them walk all over the gallery with melting gelato in their hands? No, Eva, I think he's trying to compete with you."

"Muffin or carrot cake," Eva repeated, wondering whether Mazie ever thought about who had to clean those finger and nose prints off the front of the glass.

"If that's a plain bran muffin, I'll have a muffin. I could use a good cleaning out."

Eva flinched. Too much information. She had to remain calm, bide her time until the old blowhard made her purchase and departed.

"I'm just warning you, Eva, that's all. Just giving you time to prepare if Harry keeps infringing on your territory."

Eva wrapped the muffin and handed the bag to Mazie. She mixed the cappuccino and handed that to her as well, though she wished she could dump it on the woman's head. Instead, she smiled through gritted teeth as she took the money and rang up the sale. "I just can't worry about it."

Why couldn't Harry stick to art and let her do coffee and tea? The Starbucks a few blocks away was bad enough. Why did Harry have to make her life even harder? She handed Mazie the change and came out from behind the counter.

"Well, girl," Mazie said in a confidential tone, "maybe you ought to worry. He has a line of extra-large cups and saucers with big artsy prints on them, gift-type items. Next he'll be selling tobacco products and newspapers."

"Maybe I'll just start selling art," Eva said, escorting her to the door. "I appreciate the warning, Mazie. I can't do any more than what I'm doing. You have a good day, you hear?" Eva hustled her out onto the sidewalk, resisting the urge to push her in front of the oncoming trolley, and dragged the bundles of Galveston County Daily News and Houston Chronicles inside.

When she stood, Eva found her breath coming fast. God, maybe she should start working out with free weights. Running wasn't a strength builder in spite of the miles she put in several nights a week. She hated getting older and feeling worn out. She didn't want anyone to accuse her of being weak. If they did, she wanted to know she could pummel them. Grinning, Eva imagined punching Harry in the nose. That would be worth lifting weights for. She flexed her biceps and bounced up and down like a boxer.

Sipping a latte, she cut the strings on the papers and set them out. Though it tasted rich and sweet, it landed in her stomach like wet cement. As soon as she was ready for the day, she'd run back upstairs and cook an egg. No fattening muffins for her.

When she took the dust rag to the shelves on the other side of the store, she saw that the shelf with the fried fruit pies needed restocking again. No way. People didn't buy them that fast. A quick glance told her the thief hadn't taken anything else. Eva could understand a fondness for fried pies. As a kid, she had loved them herself. The ooey, gooey lemon or cherry oozing through a hole in the crust. Yum. But someone was stealing her stock, and she'd be damned if she'd let that go. She wiped the bare spot where the pies had been and moved on to the next shelf, vowing to keep a better watch.

Another of her regulars entered.

"Hey, Willie," she said. "Black coffee?"

"Hey, Eva. And a pack of Marlboros." He picked up a newspaper.

"I like what you did to your hair, but if it gets much shorter, you're going to look like a guy."

If she had cancer and lost her breasts, her girls, she'd really look like a guy. "Thanks. I think there was a compliment buried in there somewhere."

Willie winced. "Sorry. I just meant—well, that maroon color suits you, that's all."

"Red. It's red, Willie, and thanks anyway." Climbing a three-step ladder, Eva retrieved the Marlboros from the rack above the counter and handed them to him. When she gave him his coffee and took his money, she smiled and said, "Have a great day." Watching him leave, she wondered whether the next person would be politically incorrect enough to call her a dyke. If that happened, she'd really throw a punch, not just think about it. Couldn't a woman dress the way she wanted without everyone voicing an opinion?

After popping more loaves of bread into the oven, Eva grabbed the broom and went out to the sidewalk. She needed to clean around the entrance, wipe the tables, fill the sugar and creamer containers, and make sandwiches.

Another customer drove up while Eva swept. She followed the woman inside.

"Do you have apricot tea?" The woman lifted her sunglasses and peered at Eva as if she were a bug under a rock. "I only drink apricot tea."

Before Eva could answer, a young boy hurried inside and headed down the aisle to the back of the store. The shoplifter? She tried to keep an eye on him in the large magnified mirror hanging in the corner. "Sorry, no apricot," she told the woman. "Have you ever tasted Chai? Spicy, exotic, rich, and musky. You'll love it, I promise."

"No, not interested." The woman tapped her French-manicured

fingers on Eva's counter. "If you don't have apricot, do you know if Harry does?"

The boy moved to the far end of the aisle where Eva couldn't see him. "Tell you what, why don't you go ahead and try Harry's? I promise I'll have apricot the next time you come in." She wanted to tell the woman what she could do with it, too, but once again forced a smile instead.

Eva escorted the woman to the door. If she had someone helping out, she could run errands when she needed to, like going to a wholesaler's for a variety of packaged tea. Having Marian watch the front of the shop just wasn't enough. To run across the street and serve a customer, Marian had to abandon her own place since she rarely had help either. Hell, if she could find someone to work part time, Eva could do many things. Like sleep closer to eight hours. Like have surgery if necessary and recover like a normal sick person. Like not kill herself doing everything. With all the unemployed people, why did she have such a hard time finding help?

She hurried to the back. She didn't recognize the boy, but that didn't mean he wasn't a legitimate customer. "What do you need, kiddo?"

Bags of chips lay on the floor. The boy had piled some back on the shelves but not in neat rows the way Eva liked them. "Sorry." He looked sheepish. "Supposed to buy chips for the kids at the K.C. pool. Almost knocked your whole rack over."

Eva picked up one of the bags. "How many do you want?"

"Six. Three Cheetos. Three potato chips."

After the boy left, Eva glanced at Marian's place across the street. Early that morning, Marian had stared out the window as though lost in a time warp. They hadn't seen each other much lately. Being springtime in a tourist town, business had improved for both of them. Marian could close occasionally, but Eva had to be open seven days a week. After she paid the doctor bills, maybe she'd get her head examined. She must have been nuts to open a coffee shop.

Marian hadn't returned to the window. Eva missed spending time together, Marian giving her advice. If she had a mother, she would have called her for advice. Her mother would have helped out in the shop when Eva needed her.

But she didn't have a mother. She had a best friend. And she wanted to ask that best friend to sit with her in the recovery room when she had her breasts removed. Oh, she knew she should be thinking positively. Not assume the worst. Stay in the present moment. Wait until the doc called. But Eva had become more of a glass half empty person lately. All she could think of was asking Marian to take care of her like the time Eva had swine flu. Of course, cancer was worse, much worse, but whom better than Marian to help her through the healing process?

Another customer arrived, a fifty-something, lanky man in a blue sports shirt and knee-length shorts. "I'm your new neighbor from next door, Troy Sumner."

Eva shook his hand. "Eva Best." She peered around him at Reid's Ritzy Rags. Though she didn't open on Mondays except by appointment, maybe Marian would come downstairs like she sometimes did, to sort stock, then Eva could run over and talk to her.

"Eva Best, you got any chocolate-coated biscotti?"

Eva pointed to a jar on the counter under the cigarette rack. "How many pieces, sir?"

"Not 'sir.' Troy."

"Okay, Troy. Sorry."

"Just one piece. And a regular coffee, black with sugar."

She poured his coffee. "You can do the sugar thing yourself." She pointed to a shelf where she kept the fixings. "Make yourself at home." She watched him for a moment. "I saw the brown wrapping on your windows. What did you say your business is going to be?"

Troy paid and put the cellophane-wrapped biscotti in his shirt pocket. He flashed a grin as he picked up two packets of sugar and slipped them into his shorts pocket. "Didn't say."

As he headed next door, Eva wondered what he was up to. That's all they needed on Ledbetter Street, some guy who thought he was cute. Just wait until she told Marian about that.

Chapter 8

JANE PULLED THE SCARF TIGHTER around her head and scrunched under the layers of coats and bits of blankets to keep the morning dampness at bay. She must be dreaming. The streetlight at the end of the alley had faded out, but the sun hadn't fully dawned. Voices at this hour? What the hell?

Everyone knew this was her alley, her place behind the dumpster. She wanted to sleep another half hour. Could they just leave her alone for a few more minutes? Could they shut up and leave her be? God. Times like this she really missed living in her own place and sleeping undisturbed in her own bed.

"Goddamn bitch. Get up." A man's voice, rough, a heavy smoker's voice.

He couldn't be talking to her. She rolled over. Breathing through the scarf filtered the rotting smell. She wrapped the scarf tighter and ducked down, pulling her covers closer to her chin. The inside of her mouth tasted like a dustbin. Wiggling her foot back and forth, Jane touched the bottom rail of her grocery cart, relieved her stuff hadn't been stolen in the night. She'd always hoped she would wake up if someone tried to rip her off but knew she might not. She hunkered down, still hoping for a few more minutes of sleep.

"Look at me when I'm talking to you." The man's voice again.

Jane peeked out of one eye. On the other side of her dumpster stood two sets of feet. Opening the other eye, Jane pushed her hair and scarf aside and focused on her surroundings as much as she could without her glasses. The ragged hem of a dark skirt dragged the ground. A woman's dirty clogs moved under the skirt, stumbling over the broken asphalt. Near a small suitcase on wheels, black, pointed-toe cowboy boots sprouted below frayed jeans.

"You say one more word, Chloe—"

"But—"

A loud smack made Jane cringe, and something banged against the dumpster, a deep, echoing metallic sound rattling in the alley. Glass shattered near Jane's feet. A baby wailed. The woman fell to the ground on her back, her head bouncing. The baby, hanging in a sling of thick blue plaid across the woman's chest, fell with her, protected by the woman's arms. Jane's head pounded as though it were she who'd hit her head. She longed for the sun to do an about face and go down so she wouldn't witness the scene, what she could see of it from her position behind and under the dumpster.

Shrugging out of the sling, the woman pulled the fabric tight around the bundled baby and crawled down the alley, away from the boots and Jane's dumpster, pushing the baby ahead of her, staying low as though to avoid an ambush. Jane curled up, small as possible. She didn't want to watch, but her eyes betrayed her while her stomach revolted at the woman's pain.

"Come back here, bitch."

The man ran at the woman and kicked her. She went down face first, the baby's howls muffled beneath her body.

Jane turned over on her stomach and could see between the garbage bags on the ground. The early morning light revealed the woman's face, young, pale, and scared, yet somehow defiant at the same time. The baby was hidden behind her back like a surprise.

"Stop, Darryl. Please. I'm sorry." She held her palm out like a shield. Easing upward, she shifted her body to protect the baby, out of sight but still screaming.

The man didn't stop.

Jane felt each blow in her own stomach. Was it sympathy for the girl, or had she eaten something she shouldn't? She pulled the pile of coverings down. Why did they choose her home for this invasion?

"You stop that!" Jane said, scrambling out of the pile of rags. She grabbed the neck of a broken beer bottle with one hand and a clump of broken asphalt with the other. "I said, stop!" Jane pitched the asphalt rock and hit the man in the side of the head.

"What the fuck?" The man turned as though in slow motion and faced her.

The whole event reminded Jane of a movie. Not that she'd seen a movie in a long time. She pointed the broken end of the bottle toward him.

"Don't come any closer." Jane waved the bottle in the direction of his face. "You want to beat her, find someplace else. This is *my* alley." She wished she had someplace else to go, a place to get away from people like him.

The man took two steps toward Jane. His face was as mean as a house in the slums.

"I been out here a long time, Mister. You might wallop me a good one, but I'll cut you so bad you won't forget it." Her stomach felt like raw nerves, but she wasn't backing down. She couldn't. Not living on the street. When a person started something, they'd better finish it, or word would get out they were soft.

He stopped, as though weighing her words. The woman gathered up the baby and got to her feet.

"Go on now," Jane said, pointing the bottle toward the end of the alley. "Get out of here."

He turned to the woman. "Get your shit and come on, Chloe. And stop that kid from crying." With one finger, the man hooked his black leather jacket over his shoulder. He brushed his blond hair out of his eyes and stepped toward the street, calm as could be, as though Jane wasn't even there.

Jane had seen his type before. As soon as she turned her back, he'd be all over her like a bad case of the shingles.

"I can't, Darryl." Chloe coughed. In a raspy voice, she said, "Give me a minute. Please."

Chloe had striking green eyes, dark hair, and creamy skin. Not Mexican. At least not like any Mexican Jane had ever seen. Not with green eyes. Maybe part, but too fair. Chloe took several deep breaths as she rewrapped the baby and fixed the sling about her chest. The baby looked like a tiny papoose, dark hair like his mother's but with a yellow face. He could be a few days or weeks old, nothing more.

The woman brushed at her clothing. Bits of rock, trash, and broken beer bottle fell to the ground. She wobbled toward the suitcase on wheels, as if she didn't trust her legs to work right. Taking the handle, she glanced at Jane, nodded and shrugged, and lurched toward the man.

As they turned the corner, the woman asked where they were going to live.

The man answered, "Not on Ledbetter Street. Fags, artists, and old furniture . . . " The volume of his voice fell as they moved out of Jane's earshot.

Jane had to pee. As soon as she couldn't hear them talking any more, she dropped the beer bottle into the dumpster and stilled her shaking hands, glad the man hadn't called her bluff. She piled her things in the basket and headed in the opposite direction, stopping to squat in a crevice in front of a garage door. Using a found napkin from her basket to dry herself, Jane tried to be careful her pants didn't get wet.

A few moments later, she rolled her cart out of the alley and onto Twenty-Second Street. As she turned the corner, the Reid's Ritzy Rags woman came out her back door with a bag of garbage. Jane hurried out of sight. The woman's garage door had been the one she used the restroom in front of. She hadn't meant to do it, but fear always made her have to pee.

Heading in the direction of the wharves, Jane aimed to look in the dumpster behind the coffee shop. Sometimes the Coffee & More woman threw out day-old sandwiches. After that, she'd go to Our Daily Bread to see if they'd give her something for breakfast. Maybe the line wouldn't be so long.

Across the street, she spied young Luther stumbling toward the Strand, his easel, canvas, and paint box under his arm. He looked like a walking skeleton.

She wondered what her friend painted now. When she'd talked to him a year earlier, before she'd lost her apartment, he'd set up his canvas near Pier 20 where fishing boats docked. Luther painted with the prettiest hue of blue she'd ever seen, matching his eyes. She'd asked him once why he painted fishing boats when everyone painted fishing boats. He looked at her for a long minute and said, "I have to paint what people want to buy. I can't do art."

Jane pushed her basket into the alley behind the coffee shop. She had to find food. Maybe later she'd walk to the wharf to see what Luther painted. She liked him. He'd been kind to her, and something about him reminded her of her son. A look. His dimples. Something.

The coffee shop dumpster wasn't anywhere near full, so Jane pushed her basket up against the drab rusty metal and climbed on top of her bags to boost herself over the side. She swatted at the flies and, after a whiff of the putrid odor, breathed through her mouth. Since the tobacco store on the far side of the coffee shop had closed, there was a lot less trash. Their closing had its goods and its bads. Less stuff to trade, but she hadn't liked the people anyway. They'd yelled at her and told her to get lost. At least while that building was empty she could look for food more easily. Maybe the next people wouldn't be so mean.

Years of being married to Howard had made her methodical. He'd liked everything just so, the son of a bitch. In her next life, she hoped she'd have a happy family. A child who would live to adulthood. A man she loved who would love her back.

She arranged the plastic bags in rows. She tore open the sides, fishing around with her fingers. When she found a whole half a chicken sandwich on wheat, she gobbled it up. A quarter sandwich of ham on rye, she saved for later, wrapping it in the cleanest napkin of the lot. Someone had folded the back half of a slice of cheesecake, the part with the crust, in clear plastic. She licked her lips. She liked cheesecake, didn't matter what flavor. She wanted to eat the pieces of cookies she found next but didn't want to spoil her breakfast any more than she already had, so she placed them in a small white paper bag she'd emptied, along with the other bits.

After finishing, Jane tossed her find over the side of the dumpster into her basket. Getting into the dumpster was easy. Climbing out, though, she had to pile bags on top of bags until the mountain of trash was tall enough for her to reach the dumpster's lip. Being careful not to catch her overalls or tear her hands on the rusty edge, she hiked her leg back over the top. Pulling herself up and easing back down into her basket was hard, but months of practice had improved her agility. After resting a moment, she reached solid ground without a spill and decided, in spite of the rude awakening she'd had, the day was off to a good start.

When she turned to head out of the alley, though, she came face to face with the coffee lady carrying a bag of trash.

The coffee shop lady stood only a mite taller than Jane and had eyes the color of the Gulf of Mexico after a storm. Jane hunkered down and waited for the screams. They didn't come.

"'Scuse me, ma'am," Jane said, hunching over her basket and hurrying to the end of the alley. As she turned the corner, she glanced back at the woman who had barely moved. Jane grinned and waved as she hurried away.

Chapter 9

BEFORE SHE GOT A CHANCE to go to Eva's, Marian's doorbell rang. The only people who came by on Mondays were friends who knew she didn't mind being disturbed when the store was closed. She expected to see one of the girls from the barbecue next door to Eva's or one of the Moraleses from the Taqueria with a last-minute need to buy something for their new hire.

When she opened the door, there stood her mama in all her finery. She pushed past Marian. "Close the door. You want to pay to air-condition the whole world?"

What had she done to deserve a visit from her mama, the last person she expected or wanted to see?

Claire's perfume followed her inside, bringing back memories Marian usually managed to keep hidden. She would struggle for days—sometimes a week—to put them out of her mind.

How had her mama known? No one could've told her about the Robert thing. For heaven's sake, the woman lived almost three hundred miles away. So how could she know Marian stood on the verge of making a huge decision that would affect the rest of her life? Or she should say: *another. Another* huge decision.

She stared at her mama, not wanting to be the first to speak, crossing her arms about her chest, trying to breathe deeply but silently, in a way her mama wouldn't notice and ask what all those deep breaths were about. She was almost afraid to speak. Now that she knew what her mama had said to Bryan to drive him away, she could've grabbed the hag by the hair, opened the door, and tossed her into the street.

Claire looked as though she'd recently stepped out of a hair salon, which she probably had, her blue-blonde hair—backcombed helmet hair—frozen in place and in the past. Her clothes, an advertisement for Neiman's. They should've paid her for all those years as a walking billboard. Her mid-heel pumps were two-toned, no white for Claire, even though Easter had passed. For a woman in her eighties, with the work she'd had done, she could pass for someone in her sixties. Maybe even as Marian's sister, though, thank the Lord, Marian resembled her father. She would've hated looking in the mirror and been reminded of who, or should she say what, had given birth to her.

"Aren't you going to invite me up?" Claire's two-tone matching handbag hung on the crook of her left arm. Thick gold bracelets dangled at her wrist. Her right hand rested on the stair rail, a small indication she might be growing a bit infirm, might need steadying now and then.

"I didn't invite you *in*." Marian didn't want to think about her own attire: pre-owned shorts and tank top, flip-flops, barely combed graying brown hair, and no makeup.

"It would be the polite thing to do."

"To what do I owe the honor?"

"I was just passing through." Claire started up the stairs, moving with the same grace she'd displayed her whole life. An *almost*-Miss America when she was young. An *almost*-Mrs. Houston later.

Marian rolled her eyes for her own benefit, reverting to childish feelings for the time it took to climb the stairs. What had she done to deserve this visit?

Anna's unwelcoming bark, a yip, almost a cry, as if she knew about Marian's mama, greeted Claire as they reached the landing. Marian didn't attempt to settle the dog down.

Claire stood, not moving, glancing from Marian to the dog. "What is it?"

"A dog. You're supposed to put your hand down for her to smell, so she gets to know you. But you wouldn't know that since we never had a dog. Or, as I recall, anything more than a stuffed animal."

"I can't believe you, Marian. Getting a dog." She leaned down and opened her palm. "Are you sure she won't bite?"

"She hasn't yet." *If only*, Marian thought. But knowing her mama, she'd sue Marian, hoping her homeowners' insurance would pay the max.

"I am not amused."

"Turn your hand over." When her mama didn't respond, Marian did a two-fingered twist of her mama's wrist so her hand hung palm down.

Anna sniffed Claire's hand, growled low in her throat, and backed down the hall in the direction of the bedroom. Marian had an overwhelming desire to do the same. Instead, she said, "You might as well come in and sit down."

"What's wrong with that animal?"

"Anna doesn't like strangers." Anna knew a toxic person when she smelled one. Too bad people didn't have that ability.

Claire shook her head as she laid her purse on the table. She didn't sit. She examined the condo, slowly pivoting as though wanting to be sure she didn't miss anything. When she'd made the complete circle, she said, "So this is where you live."

"May I offer you something? Iced tea?" Marian gripped the back of a chair so she wouldn't lapse into any of the behaviors she'd engaged in when she'd been small and lived under her mama's critical eye. Just keeping her hands occupied would help conceal the feelings she'd hidden since the last time she'd seen her. The feelings she'd never vent at her mama because all the experts said not to—it wouldn't do any good. They would say to try to mend the relationship and, if that didn't work, taper off, like kicking a drug or a bad habit—kind of like when she'd quit biting her nails. Well, she'd tried both. Neither worked. So she stayed away. She'd avoided her mother for ten years.

"What is that you're wearing?" Claire asked.

"Chanel Number Five."

"Marian, really. You know I meant your clothes."

"Do you want something to drink or not? It's hot outside, and I thought you might be thirsty." If she made it through this meeting with her mama, it might be considered one of God's major miracles. "I promise you the tea's not instant. I made a couple of fresh pitchers this morning, one decaf. I have lemons and limes and sweetener or sugar. I washed the glasses myself in my dishwasher with soap and hot water. No discernible germs. Would . . . you . . . like . . . something?"

"Marian . . . really." Claire pulled out a chair, sat down, and then with a change of attitude, she smiled and said. "That would be nice."

Marian busied herself with pouring their tea. Her neck felt like a chunk of ice sat on it. She returned to the table, setting out yellow linen napkins, two small crystal bowls, one with sliced lemons and limes, the other, sweetener, and two iced tea spoons from her silver set. After retrieving the glasses, she sat across from her mama—out of touching distance—and waited for what she could only think of as the inevitable.

Her mama mixed her tea, took a sip, and set the glass aside. "So this place is how you spent your inheritance from your grandmother."

"You've known that for years." Marian pressed her lips together and kept her eyes on her mama. What did her mama see when she gave the place the once-over? Other people loved it, loved her view of the street, loved the open concept, loved her furniture, loved the art on the walls. Certainly not every place was to everyone's liking, but she knew she had done well with her condo. She loved it there, inside the condo and outside on Ledbetter Street. She was certain, though, that after her mama passed judgment and departed, she'd question her choices. Why had she come?

"Now that I see it, I better understand. Though I'm not sure it's worth what you paid."

"You don't know what I paid, Mother."

"Well, I can just imagine. Do you have any of your inheritance left?"

"You don't even know what Nana left me." Marian cocked her head as she had an aha moment. "Unless . . ."

"It's a matter of public record." Claire stirred her tea more.

"You went to the courthouse and pulled the court records?" Red flashed like lightning in front of her eyes. "I suppose you got a copy of the inventory and appraisement?"

"She was my mother, Marian. I had a right to know, since she left me out of her will, other than acknowledging my existence."

Marian shook her head. No way would she repeat anything Nana had said to her. "You didn't need the money."

"That's beside the point. I was the natural heir of my parents, just like—"

"Just like I'm your natural heir? Is that what you were going to say?"

"Well, regardless, I had a right to know. I feel I have a right to know how you've spent it. At least you didn't blow it on a fancy car or a trip around the world."

"There's enough left. I still might." Was that why she'd come? If money was all the visit was about, Marian could live with that. But fear that her mama might know about Robert or Bryan—she didn't know which would be worse—gnawed at her.

"You're so amusing, Marian. So you have enough money to get by? To pay the expenses of your upkeep?"

"Yes, Mommie Dearest. The will was probated many years ago. Why, all of a sudden, are you concerned?" It must gall her that Nana skipped her and set Marian up to be self-supporting. But it pleased Marian no end.

"I can take it then, that you won't show up on my doorstep and ask for a handout?" Claire sipped her tea and watched Marian over the rim of the glass.

"I've never shown up on your doorstep with my hand out, and I never will."

"Figure of speech, Marian, dear, figure of speech. I'd hate to add up all the money I've spent on you over the years. I'm sure it would break my heart."

If you had one. Marian studied her mama for any clue as to what she knew. If her mama didn't tell her now, it would be because she wanted to keep Marian in suspense. Even if she accepted no responsibility, Claire knew the reasons Marian had needed money when she was younger.

"So what have you been doing with yourself?" Claire strolled toward the front windows. Almost everyone eventually gravitated to the windows to look out at the street. Maybe it was the different perspective the view from above gave of their little Ledbetter Street world.

Marian followed her. "Oh, nothing special. Had a trip to the Hill country last month to—"

Claire did an about face. "No time during that trip for your dear old mama?"

Marian could have bitten off her tongue. "Only a short trip—to pick up clothing from an estate in Kerrville to replace what we lost in the fire. A woman died leaving every room in her house full to the gills. I got the clothes, really good stuff."

"You had a fire?" Claire's eyes flared. "When were you going to tell me about that?"

Marian brushed her hair back. The twelfth of never. "Oh, it was only a small fire—smoke damage, really, and water damage from the fire hoses."

"Fire hoses? It was big enough for the fire department to be called? Marian, really, these old buildings—I imagine they're like tinderboxes. Very unsafe. Did you think of that before you purchased this place?"

"You see why I never tell you anything? You get carried away." As if that was the real reason. Her mama would eventually figure out how to use any information she had against her.

"I don't think worrying about you living in a hundred-year-old building that could burn down at any minute is getting carried away."

"Hundred-and-thirty." Marian feigned a smile.

"That's not amusing, Marian. This is a dangerous neighborhood. Didn't you think of that? What a bad location for you to choose to open a business, but then your judgment—"

"If you came here to insult me, Mama, it's time you left. Thanks for stopping by." Marian headed toward the stairwell.

"Don't be so melodramatic. I'm just saying that you need to be careful about living here. Do you have fire alarms? What about a sprinkler system? And, most importantly, fire insurance?"

"Oh, that would be most important to you. The insurance proceeds. As if you're *my* natural heir." Her big mouth. God, Marian didn't want to get into that. Next her mama would ask her whom she was leaving her estate to, and Marian couldn't very well tell her she'd set up a trust for Robert.

"Oh, now stop. I didn't mean it that way. You always did exaggerate everything."

"Look, we're not doing each other any good. You don't want to hear me out about what happened. You just want to pass judgment, make me feel bad about myself and my choices. This is not a productive conversation. You should go." Marian stood at the head of the stairs. Since the door was down below, she couldn't open it and usher her out. But any idiot could read Marian's body language.

Claire sat back down at the table. "Don't get so excited. Come and sit down. I'll give you a chance to explain everything. I don't like it when you get like this." She sipped her tea with an air of nonchalance. "Come on. I apologize."

She didn't like it when Marian stood up to her. And she thought an apology made up for everything, or, as Marian's therapist had said, she used it as a manipulative tool.

Marian sat back down and crossed her arms. "The fire was next door."

"There was no fire in this building?"

"This building has brick walls about a foot thick. Except for the roof, this building is unlikely to sustain any fire damage unless the fire starts inside." Why was she explaining?

"But the roof could've caught fire, and the fire could have come down inside the apartments upstairs and come down to burn your condo and gone downstairs and burned your inventory—"

"Stop it." That red flare again. "Could've, should've, would've. It didn't. That's all. Any more than any other building or your house for that matter. For heaven's sake."

"I don't see why you couldn't have opened your business in a mall somewhere. They're so much safer." She squeezed another lemon wedge into her glass and held it out to Marian. "Seconds, please. You do make a mean pitcher of tea."

She might give her seconds on tea, but no way would she ask her to stay for lunch. She needed to talk to Eva, tell her about Bryan and Robert. Get her advice. Ask for help.

"Was there no time to stop by and see me when you went to Kerrville?"

"What, are you sick or something?"

"Well, it's easier for you to come see me in Georgetown than for me to come down here to Galveston to see you. After all, I am twenty years older than you. And anyway, you were in the neighborhood."

"I hate to tell you this, but Georgetown was two hours out of my way. My helper, Paula, had given notice. I didn't want to leave her alone too long with keys to the place. I rented a truck and away I went. And my class, uh well—other things were going on." Did she have to spell it out? She had a life, and her mama not only wasn't in it but would never be in it. Even if the woman accepted responsibility for what she'd done to her, Marian would never make her part of her life.

"Ten years, Marian. It's been ten years since I've seen you. Since Nana's funeral."

Marian entwined a lock of hair behind her ear. "I've been really busy. Besides, Mother, I'm not trying to be unkind, really I'm not. We've been over all this before—we've never been what you would call close." And never would be. If she saw her mama any more frequently, she might very well have to go back into therapy and never come out.

"But I'm getting older, dear. I could die at any moment."

"We all could die at any moment. A guy almost got run down by the trolley right here on Ledbetter Street last week. He didn't look a day over twenty-nine."

"You can make jokes, but I think we should be closer. I want to have more of a relationship with you. Be a part of your life." Claire reached out, but her hand didn't extend to the far end of the table where Marian sat, and Marian didn't bridge the chasm.

What had she done to deserve this? So maybe her mama didn't know about Robert or Bryan. Not that she should know. Not that she could know. Except she'd always seemed all-knowing. Maybe the visit was to mend fences. To try to get Marian to go see her once in a while or invite her down to stay with her. Relieved, Marian smiled again. But she still didn't trust her. Would never trust her. She'd make noises of agreement and get rid of her. The therapist said to taper off, try to work things out—which Marian had done for many years—and then wean herself from the toxic person. Which Marian had also done. Being agreeable during the conversation and ushering her mama out the door was the solution. And hopefully, it would be another ten years before she saw her again.

Maintaining her feigned smile, Marian said, "Tell you what, when you get home, why don't you look at your calendar and write me with good dates to visit next year. I'll compare it to mine and see what I can do, okay? Now I don't want to be rude, Mother, but Mondays are the days I catch up. I've got a lot of work to do and errands to run."

"You don't understand. But how could you? The reason I was asking you about money, and whether you'd be needing any, is that

I'm about to make an investment which will, I think, not only make my budget tighter but will give us a chance to be a lot closer."

Marian stared long and hard, afraid to ask what she meant. Fear clutched at her. Her mama couldn't be serious. She couldn't really think they'd ever be close. Not after all the things she'd put Marian through.

"We'll be able to spend a lot more time together soon. I'm buying a house on East Beach. I'll be living here on the island a great deal of the time."

Chapter 10

MARIAN ENTERED MIGUEL'S TAQUERIA AND inhaled the pungent aroma of cumin. She skirted a group of Red Hat Ladies, bantering like a flock of chickens as they stood in line at the cash register, and headed to a yellow-and-orange covered table for two in the corner by the window looking out on Ledbetter Street.

New piñatas hung from the ceiling and red, yellow, and orange tablecloths draped the tables. Lupe, who always dressed in embroidered Mexican blouses and matching multi-colored ruffled skirts when she was in the restaurant—part of her marketing plan to be a real Mexican restaurant, she'd said, rang up the Red Hat Ladies while monitoring the wait staff's activities. She called to Marian, *"Hola, Amiga!"* and flashed a set of white teeth. Peppering her conversations with Spanish was part of her game plan, too.

Marian waved and slid into the chair facing the window. Ledbetter Street drew a heap of characters, strangers and acquaintances alike, and she enjoyed people-watching. Just then the homeless woman who slept behind the dumpster in the alley behind the shop rolled her basket across the street toward the Taqueria.

The woman had appeared out of nowhere about a year earlier. One morning, when Marian put out her garbage, a pile of rags lay bundled under the dumpster next to the building. She thought it was a dead body. She ran inside and dialed 911. An ambulance roared into the alley. Several EMTs jumped out and ran toward what turned out to be a sleepy old woman scared half to death by all the commotion.

That night, to make up for the phone call, Marian had left clean clothes and a pair of shoes on her stoop. When they disappeared, she hoped the woman was the one who took them. Later, when the weather turned cooler, she had put out a jacket and socks and a thick blanket.

Now, seeing the homeless woman, she was struck by the contrast between her and Marian's mother. Luckily her mama ended up wealthy and not living in the streets. She wouldn't have lasted long. The homeless woman looked much tougher. The women could have been the same age; though Marian would lay odds the homeless woman was the nicer of the two.

Marian fought to put the scene with her mama out of her mind, which wasn't totally impossible, since there was a blank where the memory of her reaction should have been. She only remembered asking her to leave. Claire, red-faced, picked up her things, and Marian flushed like a woman having a hot flash. As her mama complained about the way Marian talked to her, Marian followed her down the stairs and bolted the door after her mama flounced outside. Could Marian have told her off and not remembered? Maybe she did need to go back into therapy.

"Hey, girlfriend, what're you staring at?" Eva stood at her elbow.

"I didn't see you come in." She grinned and reached for a hug. Some things were constant. Some people. Eva was one of those.

"Yeah, you were definitely in another dimension." Eva slung her purse over the back of the chair across from Marian. "I've been trying to talk to you all weekend. Where've you been?"

"I'm sorry. It's been crazy. Let's order first. You won't believe everything that's happened in the last three days." Marian motioned to a waitress.

"I've got news, too." Eva slapped the menu down on the table. "I don't know why I'm looking. I always get the same thing."

"Creatures of habit, both of us. Hey, I'm looking for help in the shop. Saturday was Paula's last day. Know anybody?"

"If I did, I wouldn't tell you. We both need someone. I'm so tired of doing everything myself." Eva bit into a chip. "Um, nice and toasty. I'm getting a glass of wine. Where is that waitress?"

Marian dipped a chip into the green salsa and munched on it. She didn't know which to tell Eva first. Her mama was the freshest on her mind, but then there was Dorothy and Robert and Bryan.

A young, dark-haired waitress arrived. She wore the customary red shirt embossed with the restaurant logo, but instead of black slacks, she was dressed in a long skirt that dragged the floor.

Something about the girl tickled Marian's memory. She recognized her from somewhere. If she gave it a few minutes, she'd remember.

Lupe appeared at their table. "We got a new waitress. Chloe, these are *mis amigas*." Lupe's dark eyes sparkled. She swept the air with her hands as she spoke. "They usually come in on Mondays and stay for a long time." She laughed and said to Marian and Eva, "Not that I'm complaining. But Chloe, save this table for them on Monday nights."

"Yes, Mrs. Morales."

The girl barely made eye contact, but in the moment she did, startling green orbs peered back at Marian. She wondered whether Chloe wore colored contacts.

"And you probably saw the table needs to be set up with chips and iced tea just before my girlfriends arrive. So if you aren't busy, you can help with that. *Entiendes?*"

"Yes, ma'am. May I take your order, ladies?" Chloe stood with her pad and pen and stared at the floor.

Lupe patted the girl's arm and headed for the kitchen.

"Number three," Eva said. "Extra cheese and onions for the taco and more salsa when you get a chance. Oh, and a glass of the house Merlot."

"Yes, ma'am," Chloe said. She turned Marian's way, still looking down. "And you, ma'am?"

"I know you, don't I?"

Chloe's eyes swept the room as though looking for the nearest exit.

"Marian thinks she knows everyone. Ignore her." Eva dipped another chip into the salsa.

"Your order, ma'am?" Chloe asked in something like a stage whisper.

"Be quiet, Eva. Let me think." Marian stared at Chloe. "You have a baby?"

Chloe blanched. "He's with his father when I'm at work. May I take your order?" she asked again, her eyes darting to the cash register where Lupe now stood.

"I saw you walking down the street early this morning. It was pretty dark, but it was you, wasn't it?" Marian glanced down at the girl's skirt.

"Would you just order, Marian?" Eva said.

"Yes, ma'am," Chloe said. "We moved into the apartments above Ron's Grocery."

"So you work during the day, and your husband works at night?"

"Marian," Eva whispered, "you can't ask people their personal business when you don't know them. Order, will you?"

Marian gave Eva a look. Couldn't she see how pitiful the girl was? Obviously Chloe needed their help. "Chicken nachos. Chloe, I own the clothing shop down the street—Reid's Ritzy Rags. If you ever need anything, you come to me, okay?"

"Thank you, ma'am. I have enough clothes right now."

"No. I mean, *anything.*"

"I'll be right back with more chips and salsa." Chloe took the menus and retreated to the kitchen.

"Miss Social Worker," Eva said. "I love you for it, but I came to spend time with you, not Lupe's employees."

Lupe returned tableside. "You finally make your order?"

"I'm worried about that girl," Marian said.

"You don't even know her," Eva said.

"No, but I'm going to keep an eye out for her on the street."

"I'm trying to look after her," Lupe said. "She came in yesterday looking for a job. Her *esposo* is a strange one. At least, I think he's her husband. Has mean eyes."

"I saw them walking down the street way early this morning. She followed at least two steps behind, if you know what I mean."

Eva looked askance, shook out her napkin, and spread it on her lap.

"*Momento*, Eva." Lupe put her hand on Eva's arm. "You should see how much she eats. They get to eat one meal as part of their pay."

"A lot?" Marian asked.

"Like a truck driver," Lupe said. "I already don't know if she's going to work out. It's not the food, but her husband came in and wanted her to take the baby. She's at work her first day, what is he thinking?" She shrugged. "Enjoy your meal," she said and whirled away like a flamenco dancer, her red, white, and green gathered skirt sweeping around her.

Marian smiled at Eva. "Okay, I'm sorry. That girl just looks so pitiful. So who goes first?"

Eva frowned and shook her head. "You can. My news is pretty bad."

Eva's grim expression told Marian it must be serious. "I hope it's not as bad as mine." How much worse could Eva's news be than her own, at least as far as Dorothy's Alzheimer's? She pressed her napkin to her lips and laid it back on her lap. "You go ahead, mine can wait."

"No, that's okay. You've been so tied up all weekend—I've got to hear what's going on with you. Not even to call me—it's got to be bad."

"I apologize. It's good and bad." She sipped water. "Okay, if you're sure, here goes. You got my text that Bryan and I got together Friday night. Saturday he spent the night and stayed until I had to throw him out yesterday so I could go to Houston to see Robert. Then last night when we got back from the train museum, Dorothy told me she has Alzheimer's and wants me to take Robert to live with me. God, can you believe it, Eva? My poor friend—"

Eva made a consoling sound and stopped eating chips.

"Then to top that off, this morning my mama showed up and informed me she's buying a place down here so we can be closer. I can't stand it." Marian didn't know whether to scream or cry.

Eva choked on her water, coughing, sputtering, and spilling it on her lap. "Jesus Christ. Your mother?" She wiped at the water.

"Don't say that. You know I hate it when you say that."

Eva shrugged. "Are you going to bring Robert to live with you?"

"If the court will give him to me this time, and Dorothy thinks they will." She toyed with her fork. "He knows me, so the transition should be much better than if he went to strangers. Autistic people don't do well with change."

"Poor Dorothy." Eva finished mopping up the water and put the wadded up napkin on the empty table next to them. She glanced over her left shoulder and then her right. "The whole world will know about Robert. Don't you care?"

"It doesn't matter who knows now. Besides, I never wanted to keep him a secret. It was my mother. I never should have let her make me give him up." She gritted her teeth at the memory.

Eva cocked her head. "You were just a kid."

"Well, she can't control me now. She can't make me do anything now."

"And Bryan." Eva tapped her lips. "I had wondered if he'd show up at the reunion."

"God, it was so great. At least I had two days with him before all this other stuff came up."

"So you told him about Robert?"

Marian shook her head. "No way. Not yet."

"Jesus Christ," Eva said again. "How can you keep holding out on him?"

"I wish you'd stop saying that." Marian dipped another chip into the salsa and bit down on it. After a few moments of crunching, she swallowed, and a bitter laugh came out. "I think I'm getting hysterical."

"You sure it's not that hot green salsa? Where's my glass of wine?" Eva craned her neck toward the kitchen. "What did your mother say?"

"Greatgodalmighty, you think I told her anything? I'm only afraid somehow she already knows. The all-knowing, all-seeing mother." Marian sat back as Chloe approached with the wine and another bowl of salsa. Pointing at the wet napkin, Marian said, "Another napkin for my friend, please." After the girl had gone, she said, "I feel like I can't breathe. Tomorrow the social worker comes. I'll find out what hoops she wants me to jump through to get Robert."

"And *then* you'll tell Bryan and your mother?" Eva gulped her wine.

"I don't know. Don't tell anyone. At least, not yet, okay?"

"I won't. How long does Dorothy have before she has to give him up? Does Robert know what's going on? Does he want to come to Galveston?"

"I don't know. And no, Robert doesn't know a thing. It's best not to let on, at least not yet. As for a change in where he lives, I don't know if I told you how bad he got when his foster father left. Anyway, he's my son. I want to take care of him, but I'm feeling overwhelmed."

"So, not wanting to sound like a lawyer, I hate to ask you, do you think you can handle a forty-year-old autistic man?"

"He'll be forty-one this summer."

"You know what I mean. Have you thought of the consequences of his coming to live with you? Or will he live in one of your apartments?"

"He can't be left alone that much. He'll have to live with me. I'm going to hire a carpenter to make my bedroom into two rooms. It's big enough, and that way I'll be able to supervise him but we'll both have privacy."

"Well, good luck is all I can say. Whatever I can do, you know that. At least when I'm not dealing with my own problems."

Their eyes met. "That means a lot to me, Eva. Thanks. I'm scared, but somehow I've convinced myself everything's going to be all right." She pulled her shoulders down from around her ears. "It has to be. Now tell me what's going on with you, besides needing help in the shop."

Chloe brought their dinner then, platters of steamy beans, veggies, and meats. The singed smell of chicken and onions made Marian's mouth water. When Chloe left, Marian slapped a flour tortilla into one hand and began piling guacamole, *pico de gallo*, chicken, onions, and peppers into it until it was too large to roll up. She treated it like an open-faced sandwich and bit in. When she raised her eyes, Eva had eaten half of her first taco but watched Marian.

"What?" Marian paused.

"They'll bring you more tortillas, you know."

"Yeah, but they're flour—very fattening." Poised to take another bite, she asked, "So you going to tell me what's going on? What could be worse than a mother-figure who is dying, a secret child who has to be brought into the open, and a mother who'll do anything to make her daughter miserable?" Maybe Eva wouldn't feel as bad about her own problem now that she'd heard Marian's. She shifted the tortilla to the other hand and reached for her glass of water.

"Cancer," Eva said. "I get to have a radical mastectomy."

Chapter 11

MARIAN BURST INTO TEARS.
"If you're going to do that, I can't talk to you about it," Eva said.

Marian covered her face with her napkin. Not Eva, too. Disease sure didn't discriminate. If it did, surely it would have bypassed both Eva and Dorothy and gone for all the mean, evil people in the world. Like her mama.

"Are you going to quit, or am I going to leave?"

Marian wanted to stop crying. Wanted to be supportive. The tears just wouldn't cooperate. "I can't help it," she mumbled through the napkin. "First Dorothy and now you."

"I'm giving you one minute to stop. I thought you'd want the details."

Marian blotted her face and took several breaths. "Okay, I'm listening." She'd try to hold it together while Eva explained. It was just too much.

"Take that napkin away from your face and act normal. I'm trying to be strong, and I need your help."

Marian pulled the napkin into her lap and through blurred eyes, tried to focus on her friend.

"That's better." Eva launched into a description of the lump and how she'd ignored it until she couldn't any longer. She talked about the trips to the doctor, the hospital, the exams—the mammogram and the follow-up tests. When she stopped talking, she asked Marian to stay with her before and after the surgery, in recovery, until she was taken to her room.

Another sob slipped out of Marian. "I'm so sorry, honey. Why didn't you tell me before?"

"I don't know." She shook her head. "I don't know. I've gotta go." She pushed back in her chair.

"I'll come with you. You shouldn't be alone right now."

"No—I do—want to be alone. I'll see you tomorrow." She left her half-eaten meal, empty wine glass, and money to pay for her dinner on the table and rushed out.

Marian watched her go. Eva was probably barely holding herself together, too. When she described the cancer history in her family, and her own discovery, her hands were shaking. If it had been Marian, she'd have wept all over the table, like she had anyway.

Marian held the napkin to her face again. How would she get through the next weeks and months? She clenched her teeth. She'd have to be strong, help Eva fight. She couldn't imagine life without her. Eva just had to beat it. She wiped her eyes. She needed to pull herself together.

And then she thought of Dorothy and the tears welled up again. It just wasn't fair.

She glanced around the restaurant. Lupe stood on the other

side, speaking with a customer at a large round table. Marian tried to think of other things. Happier things.

Carrying a tray, Chloe passed by the table on the way to the kitchen. Maybe Marian could at least help the younger woman. Get her into the shop, and get her good work clothes.

After slipping money for the bill and a tip under her plate, she went to the kitchen door. When Chloe came out, Marian coaxed her to the side where they could have a private conversation. She could see what a tiny thing Chloe was. For once, Marian was taller than someone other than Eva.

"Did I do something wrong?"

"No, honey, Eva and I left money for our bill and your tip on the table."

"Thank you, ma'am." She chewed on her lower lip.

"And listen, I'm not trying to butt into your business, but I noticed you aren't wearing slacks like the rest of the staff."

Chloe glanced down at her dirty skirt. "As soon as I get my first paycheck—"

Marian pointed in the direction of her shop. "My shop's just down the street, Reid's Ritzy Rags. I just got in a couple of loads of clothes and bet I can find you something. No charge."

"I pay for what I need," Chloe said, the muscles in her neck taut.

"Really, it's okay. We girls have to stick together."

"I appreciate it, ma'am, but I can pay." She relaxed, a hint of a smile gracing her mouth. "Maybe with some of my tips."

"Okay, sweetie. I'm just trying to help. You come on down when you get a few minutes. Bring your baby. I'd love to see it."

Chloe stared at Marian. "Him, and I don't know. I'll see if I can." She backed into the kitchen.

Marian said goodbye to Lupe and went outside. Something was going on with Chloe. She'd give her a couple of days and, if she didn't come into the store, maybe Marian would go over to her apartment and see the setup for herself. Ron's reputation as a landlord wasn't all that good.

Crossing the street, Marian kept pace for a few moments with the homeless woman who pushed a grocery basket full of newspapers, plastic bags, and smelly unrecognizable stuff. Marian walked with a sprint in her step, whereas the withered woman pushed the basket as if it were loaded with a ton of granite rocks.

The more she thought about it, the more she thought she knew the old woman from someplace besides behind the dumpster. The layers of clothing and the baseball cap seemed to work as camouflage. She just couldn't place her. The woman muttered something unintelligible at her feet, never looking up.

Marian knew how fortunate she was that Nana had left everything to her. The money had made all the difference in her life. She didn't know where she would have been without it.

As she approached her shop, a man came out of the once-empty building across the street, the one wearing brown paper in its windows. Tall and thin like a runner, he wore Dockers and a Polo-style shirt. In spite of knowing how her makeup must look, smeared eyes and all, she crossed back over. "Hey."

"Hey. You one of my neighbors?" He gave her a cockeyed grin.

"If you're the new owner or tenant of this building I am. What are you doing in there anyway?"

He chuckled. "You people sure are a nosy bunch, aren't you?"

"People on this street are like family. Now that you're here, you'll be part of our family whether you like it or not." She forced a laugh. "Might as well like it."

He arched an eyebrow. "Oh, so that's the way it is. Well, the new guy doesn't reveal everything about himself until he feels safe, wouldn't you agree?"

"So you're a psychologist? Awfully expensive real estate for a store-front practice."

"And you're what, an investigative reporter?"

"Touché." Marian glanced at his tanned face. Attractive. Quick sense of humor. She liked him already. "Okay, so when're you taking that paper off the glass?" She walked close and tried to see in through the edges.

He crossed his arms and leaned against the front door. "You don't give up."

"Just curious about what you're hiding. You're not dealing drugs like the last tenants, I hope."

"Say, how are the girls at the barbecue down the street? Any more action? I heard there was a fight, and you broke it up."

"At The Pit? So you already know who I am. You've been getting around." She held out her hand. "Marian Reid."

"Troy Sumner." They shook. His hand was warm and dry, a little rough. "So you did break it up. What are you, the street boss?"

"More like the street Godmother. It was just a family squabble between two old—uh—partners."

He raised his eyebrows. "I understand. They do make good barbecue."

"You've been in there?"

"And met the former partner."

"So you know what's going on. You gotta problem with gays?"

"No, ma'am. No way. Not this lad. You?"

"Okay." She pointed at him. "I have to go, but I'm going to figure out what you're doing. I have my eye on you."

He smiled. *"Et tu."*

He was something else. What, she didn't know yet, but she'd figure it out. She sidestepped like a crab to the other side of Ledbetter Street, avoiding a passing car, and unlocked the door, keeping her eyes on him to show him what she meant. He saluted and went inside his place. She grinned, in spite of everything, and went inside her own. She needed to get to work straightening up the place before the social worker came in the morning. Her mama's visit had put her behind schedule. When she had time, she'd sit down at the computer and make out another schedule to post on the bulletin board behind her desk in place of the old one. She liked everything to run smoothly as possible. And on that spreadsheet, she'd plug in a few minutes for a good, no-holds-barred cry.

Chapter 12

THE NEXT MORNING, MINUTES AFTER she'd stashed Anna across the street in Eva's apartment, Marian greeted Yvette Denby, the court investigator. Considerably younger than Marian, the woman wore yellow spike-heeled sandals with no hosiery under a yellow skirt suit and white tank top. She had a French manicure, and her hair looked professionally coiffed.

Marian had met her at Dorothy's. Yvette had always dressed down, nothing fancier than a blouse and slacks. Was her formal appearance now supposed to telegraph a message? Marian glanced at her own slacks, cotton blouse, and sandals and hoped they didn't send the wrong message back.

"Come in out of the humidity and make yourself at home," Marian said, hoping her anxiety didn't show.

"It's quite a climb." Yvette followed Marian up the stairs, shoes clicking on the steel plates attached to the front of each step.

"You get used to it." When they reached the top of the second flight, she pulled out a chair for Yvette. "Why don't you sit here at the table, and I'll get us drinks. Coffee or tea? I have iced tea in the fridge."

"That would be nice. It's already so muggy out." Breathing hard, Yvette set her briefcase on the oak table, her dark eyes sweeping the wide expanse of the living room, dining room, and kitchen. Her cropped black hair barely moved.

"Sit down. I'll be right with you." Marian's hands trembled as she filled a glass with ice and poured the tea. Gathering the iced tea things, she set them in the center of the table.

"So, this is where you reside, Ms. Reid?" Yvette pulled out a pen and a wad of papers and placed her satchel on the floor next to her chair.

"Yes, this is it." She wet her lips. "I leased at first and later bought. Downstairs is Reid's Ritzy Rags, my vintage and pre-owned ladies' clothing business."

"Sort of like a flea market or a thrift shop?" Yvette mixed her tea. "Do you have a straw?"

Marian winced at Yvette's comment and got up to retrieve a straw. "I sell only quality, pre-owned clothing, so no, not like a thrift shop or flea market. But I can understand your confusion." She wanted to cooperate and reminded herself that Yvette wasn't responsible for what had happened in court in the past.

"Whatever," Yvette said, stacking papers.

Marian bit her tongue. Was APS really interested in her having Robert? Or were they merely interviewing her, so they could say they'd done a home study, and she hadn't been approved? But wait, hadn't Dorothy said it should be a piece of cake?

Marian's name and address were pre-printed on the paperwork. Robert's name appeared at the top in tiny letters with a case number, his date of birth, and his social security number. Yvette frowned when she caught Marian reading upside down.

"I'll need you to complete these forms." Yvette handed her several pages. "We have basic information already so you don't need to do that today, but as quickly as you can, send it back to me. Some of it is just updating what we already have. I'll get other info from you in a few minutes."

Marian glanced at what she'd been handed and set it aside.

"Okay, Ms. Reid, you understand that Dorothy Young's Alzheimer's has moved into a stage that can't be helped with medication, so she can't take care of Robby?"

"Yes. No. It's all so confusing. I didn't even know she had Alzheimer's until recently. But she told me she can't manage him much longer, and Robert—we call him Robert—can't stay with her. Dorothy wants him to come live with me."

"Not so fast." Yvette daintily sucked on the straw. "Let's go ahead and get this other data now; then you can show me around your apartment and shop."

"Condo—condominium. What do you need to know?" She felt like she was on trial. She tucked her cold hands under her legs so Yvette couldn't see them shake. What strings would the court attach if they let her have Robert? Would they nose around her business, day in and day out?

"How much money do you make each year? Do you have a copy of your last two years' tax returns that I can attach with your statement of income?"

"I can get those from my office downstairs before you leave. My income is sort of confusing. I have money invested from an inheritance. The rest I used to buy this building. Besides my store, I have three apartments upstairs I rent out." Was she talking too much? She couldn't stop her hands from shaking.

"So you have liability if they're unrented?" Yvette gazed steadily at Marian.

"Liability? I have insurance and taxes to pay, but I own the building. I don't have a mortgage. Of course, I'd like to have every unit rented, but there's no problem if one is vacant for a few months. As I said, I have funds set aside, and I do well with my clothing store."

"Okay." Yvette made notes on a legal pad. "You understand you have to hire a lawyer to do the formal paperwork, file the petition, etcetera. The guardianship will have to be changed over to you."

"I don't really understand the guardianship thing now that he's so old. Why would I need to be guardian? I'm his mother. I'm not an attorney or anything, but wouldn't I get my son back as his mom if Dorothy gives up guardianship?"

"Okay, let's start from the beginning. Robby—"

"Robert."

Yvette gave Marian a look. "Robert's autistic, unable to live on his own even though he's moderate-functioning. He requires a guardian. When he became an adult, the juvenile court dismissed the permanent managing conservatorship." She tapped her pen on the paperwork.

"Yes, I know about that." Marian ignored Yvette's patronizing tone.

"Dorothy Young petitioned the probate court for guardianship of the person and the estate. The court file indicates you applied, too. You need to do so again since circumstances are changing. If I approve you, there will only be the formalities to take care of in court.

Marian straightened in her chair, determined to make the woman understand that she was more than capable of taking care of her son. "I just didn't realize I'd have to go to court again if the home study was approved. So no matter how old he gets, he'll always need a guardian, and the court will be involved?"

95

"That's correct. If there's no guardian of his estate, he could receive his government stipend and spend it any way he liked. That wouldn't be so bad, but often these people are taken advantage of. You would not only manage his money, but as guardian of the person, you would have the capacity to consent to marriage, medical treatment, and court action in his behalf."

"Marriage . . . "

When Yvette smiled, she had a sweet face. Marian wondered whether the stress of the job overwhelmed the woman.

"I'm not saying Robert should marry, Ms. Reid, but there are predatory women out there who would marry Robert to get his money." She pushed back in her chair. "I know the monthly check's not large, but still . . ."

Marian could see that happening. He was so docile. "I understand. If I get physical custody of Robert, I would have to manage his entire life like I would a child's."

"Exactly." Yvette's eyes met hers, pen poised in mid air. "Would that pose a problem?"

"No." Marian massaged the back of her neck. "I guess Dorothy's been managing his money?"

"Yes. The money is there for his care—food, clothing, and other needs. Dorothy Young has an order from the court that says how much money she can take out of his account each month. The attorney you hire will help you file the guardianship papers to achieve the same results, assuming you're approved."

Were Yvette's last words a threat? Marian couldn't tell.

"Of course, you have to go to court in Houston. You might want to hire an attorney there—someone who knows the ins and outs of the Harris County probate courts."

Marian's mind began to race again. Having Robert would impact so many things. No freedom to go out when she wanted.

He could be left alone for short periods, but otherwise she'd have to have someone to stay with him. And what about Bryan? Would she have to give up their private time? Their sex life? She hoped not. Wait—what was she thinking all that for? No matter what, having her son would be worth it.

Yvette interrupted her musing. "Mrs. Young has been a good mother. But, Ms. Reid, except for simple tasks, Robert requires twenty-four hour supervision."

"I've been giving this a lot of thought. I'll have to adjust." Marian stared into Yvette's unfathomable chestnut eyes. Was the woman judging her? Did she think ill of her for not winning guardianship when Robert was eighteen?

"Do you have anyone who can help you? Your mother, perhaps?"

So that was why her mama had been there. "My mother? What do you know about my mother?"

Yvette looked away. "Just what I read in the file. I've set up a meeting with her, as I will all your references."

"Oh no you didn't." Her breath caught.

"Is there a problem? I don't understand."

"M—my mother is not involved in this. She's an old lady, and we're not close. She's never been a part of Robert's life. It's important you know that."

"I understand."

"No, you don't. You absolutely cannot involve her. This is between me and Adult Protective Services."

"If I'm to do a complete home study, I have to speak to everyone involved. You do want me to do the home study, don't you? I know you've fought in court for him twice. I can see you want him." She tapped her lips with her pen. "You do want him?"

"Absolutely. But my mother is *not involved*. She's not part of my life. *Or* his. Nothing she says will have any bearing on our situation. She hasn't been in my life for ten years."

"I'll consider that, certainly. But she *is* your mother."

Why did this caseworker decide to involve her mother when none of the others had?

"You want me to go on with the study?"

That sounded like a threat. "Of course I want you to do the study, but I'll need time to get ready for Robert to move in." Marian hoped Yvette couldn't see her fear and confusion. She couldn't tell the woman what her mama was really like. No one would believe it. She would have to hire a lawyer immediately.

Yvette arched an eyebrow and made more notes. "All right. There's not much time though. Veronica will be able to stay with her mother for a while, but she'll have to go home to her own family soon. Caregivers will have to be hired to assist Dorothy."

All Marian could do was stare.

"Do you think you understand the legalities? What your duties and responsibilities under the Texas Probate Code will be? You said you want to take your son, but you need time. Correct? To get your place ready, etcetera."

"Yes. I don't really understand what Robert's capabilities are. But I've done my homework on autism and understand it better than most people."

"That's all very well, but there's still a lot to learn about Robby personally. Nothing like living with a person . . . "

Was she deliberately goading Marian by calling him Robby? "I know Robert has different needs than he did as a boy. But I've been visiting him regularly. He knows me. He responds to me. We'll be able to work it out."

"I hope so. Robby is very attached to Mrs. Young. The specialists believe Robby's health will seriously deteriorate when she uh—can't take care of him anymore."

"Just how bad could he get?"

"Were you visiting him when Mrs. Young was divorced? When Mr. Young abandoned her and Veronica?"

"That was twenty-five or thirty years ago."

"His file says Robert crawled under his bed when Mr. Young left and wouldn't come out. For several days, he wouldn't eat. He wouldn't sleep. He wouldn't speak."

"I was there, and it was a difficult time. He was a child then. He's an adult now."

"He was a teenager with a child's mentality. Now he's an adult. He's childlike about some things, and others—well, it's unclear exactly what he'll do when the time comes."

"He's doing so well right now," Marian said. "I'm sure it won't be a problem."

"The case notes say Dorothy and Veronica worked with him every day after Mr. Young's departure. Dorothy crawled under the bed and held him. She spoke to him, coddled him, finally persuading him to come out. The healing took a long time." She stabbed her pen in Marian's direction. "He became physically ill because he wouldn't eat even after he came out from under the bed. With a lot of work, he eventually recovered."

Marian remembered what really happened. Dorothy called her to come and help. So Marian drove to Houston with a gift for Robert, a toy locomotive—a windup. She took turns with Dorothy, crawling under the bed, winding up the locomotive for him, watching it chug out from under the bed into the middle of the room. Eventually Robert followed it out. He was ill, seriously ill, and confused about his foster father's disappearance. Thinking about it now, Marian was not surprised Children's Protective Services made no mention of her part in the situation. CPS had always minimized her participation in his life.

She refocused on Yvette. "What are you saying?" She was getting mixed signals.

"Robert knows you. He's going to have trouble adjusting no matter where he goes. I think he's likely to have less trouble going with someone he's known for a long time than with strangers. But there's always the possibility that strangers would do a better job, especially if you're not up to the task."

"But *I am—I am* up to the task. I'm his mom. I can take care of him better than anyone."

"Let's proceed on that assumption for the time being." She made more notes. "May I see your premises, please?"

Confused and more than a little disconcerted, Marian headed toward the bedroom. She turned on the lights and took the caseworker all the way back to the alley window.

"This apartment is really quite large," Yvette said.

"Twenty-four hundred square feet. I have four walk-in closets, but two are full of my grandmother's things. I need to finish going through it all."

"I only see one bedroom, Ms. Reid. Where would Robert sleep?"

"I'll have a carpenter remodel this room into two bedrooms."

Marian led the way to the bathroom, explaining there was another one downstairs in the back of the shop. Giddy at the thought of Robert actually living with her, she showed Yvette the huge tub, the shower, double sinks, and the closet that held the washer and dryer.

"And you've seen the rest of the place." Marian walked to the front window and looked out. The new guy, Troy, came out of Coffee & More and went next door. The trolley rolled by.

Yvette glanced out the window, and then they traipsed down the back stairs to the garage. "Let's scoot by the car and into the store through this back door," Marian said. She showed her the small kitchenette and restroom. "I usually lunch back here. I built that partial wall for privacy and to conceal the storage area."

She showed her the dressing rooms and the office. "Let me find my tax returns while we're here." Marian squatted in front of the file cabinet. She pulled two files and made copies of her tax returns while Yvette walked to the front.

"This is my clothing store," Marian said, rounding the wall to hand over the copies.

"You have no employees to help out?"

"Paula quit recently, but I'm looking for someone else."

"Explain to me, Ms. Reid, what a typical day is like for you." Yvette climbed onto one of two tall stools that stood behind the cash register on the counter. "You don't mind, do you?"

Marian forced a smile, offended that this woman thought she could come into her place of business and make herself at home in a private space as though she were the owner.

"I get up, eat breakfast, shower, not necessarily in that order, clean up the kitchen, dress, and come downstairs where I work all day except for lunch break. Sometimes I spend more of the day sorting and tagging clothing than I do dealing with customers, except when cruise ships are in port. Also, people come in not only to buy clothes, but to sell them. I may take a few days off and travel a little just to get away, but not often. Sometimes short trips to conferences for people in this business."

"And after you close your shop?"

"Walk on the seawall. It's the only exercise I get. Or down to one of the restaurants on the wharves. Grocery shopping. Errands. I'm open most days, closed on Sunday mornings and when I go to Houston to visit Robert unless I have someone who can work for me. I have a sign that says Mondays by appointment, which I put out when I have a lot of stuff to do." Marian showed her the sign. "That's it. See my friends a bit. Sometimes I'm across the street at Eva's Coffee & More. We do things together: movies, plays, the Opera House, dinner." She leaned against the front door.

"Which place is Eva's?"

"Directly across the street. She's my best friend. Are you going to interview her?"

Yvette eased down from the stool, walked to one of the racks and pushed the hangers back. For a few minutes, except for the squeak of the hangers on the circle as Yvette looked at several garments, silence fell. Marian glanced across the street. Eva stuck her head out and put her hand to her ear. Marian gave her a thumbs-up.

"You have pretty things."

"Thanks. I'm selective. I buy from estates as well as individuals. I purchase things outright, but I've been thinking of taking on consignment."

"Well, Ms. Reid, I think I have an idea of the life you lead. I'm not sure where Robert would fit in."

Chills spurted through her body. "What? Why?"

"You may want him, but what's here for a forty-year-old autistic man?"

"He's my son. I can make a place for him in my life."

"But is that what would be best for him? Robert has led a very sheltered life with Dorothy. You don't have room in your life for an autistic man, son or no son. It's time he was around people of his own kind."

"I don't believe that! I love him. I want him with me. Even you said he would do better with someone he knows than with strangers."

"Well, I'm afraid my report will reflect my feelings on the matter, although I do empathize with you."

Marian's head pounded. "But he wouldn't be just in the shop. He would go places and do things with me." How could she explain she wanted to be the kind of mother to Robert that she'd never had. A loving, devoted mother who had only his best interest at heart.

"If you want him, you're going to have to hire an attorney, and let the court decide," Yvette said, heading up the stairs. "I simply can't recommend you. And," she added, "I can tell you this. The judge will never approve your home until you have a bedroom for Robert."

Marian's face felt hot. Her hands shook. "I don't understand. Dorothy said—"

Yvette snapped her head around, "Dorothy has nothing to do with this."

"You're not even giving me a chance," she said to Yvette's back.

When Yvette didn't reply, Marian stood by as she packed her briefcase. She walked her down the stairs to the front of the building. When she opened the door, the hot, humid air rushed in, full of the smell of garlic and onions cooking across Ledbetter Street at The Pit.

Yvette held out her hand as though to shake Marian's, but Marian couldn't touch her. She met the woman's eyes and nothing more.

"I suppose it's a difference in philosophy. I'm doing what I think best for Robert," Yvette said and walked out onto the sidewalk.

"You can't be," Marian muttered. "What are you going to say for yourself when Robert reacts badly to the move—if he becomes ill? *I'm sorry? I made a mistake?* You *know* he'd be better off with me."

"No, Ms. Reid, I don't." She pivoted and marched away.

Marian pushed the door closed and locked it, wishing she could lock out the nightmare Yvette brought with her. Hard to believe Yvette would risk Robert's health. Marian couldn't and wouldn't let that happen.

Chapter 13

❝ MAY I HELP YOU?" THE young woman at a desk in the County Clerk's office asked Marian.

Marian didn't want to broadcast her business so she hesitated, wondering whether she should try to get information elsewhere. But no, she was there. She'd worn a dress and heels and fixed her hair in anticipation of speaking with a judge or other court official, and she'd follow through. "Would you mind coming to the counter?"

The clerk bounded out of her chair. "Sure. No problem."

Marian leaned forward and said, in a very low tone so the man behind her couldn't hear, "I was wondering whether I could talk to a judge." She held her trembling, fisted hands down at her sides.

The clerk peered over granny glasses and leaned in toward Marian. "Um, what are you trying to do? What do you need a judge for? Like, are you wanting to get married?"

"Nothing like that. It's just—I have to file a case in Houston—in the Harris County courts. I thought if I could talk to the same kind of judge here that my case would be in front of in Houston, I could find the right kind of lawyer to represent me. I want somebody who knows what they're doing."

"Un-huh, yes, ma'am. Well, I can't speak for the judges, but I don't think any of them would make a referral to a particular attorney."

"Well, how does someone find the right kind of lawyer? The ones I had before didn't do me much good. Should I Google the subject matter?"

"Well, there's an attorney referral service through the State Bar of Texas if you go online."

"So I can't see a judge?" She didn't like the idea of finding a lawyer on the Internet, with no personal recommendations.

"That's not for me to say. You'd have to call for an appointment. The probate judge's office is one floor up, but you can't get to the actual office without a security clearance. Can I help you with anything else?"

"Excuse me," said the tall, bald, young man behind her. "I couldn't help overhearing. Maybe I could be of assistance."

Marian glanced at the clerk.

"This is Parker Benavides. I can vouch for him." She winked. "He practices law down here. Maybe he knows someone."

The man stepped up beside Marian. "Thanks, Andy." To Marian, he said, "Would you like to come with me to the break area and talk about it?"

Did he hang around courthouses looking for business? That's all she needed, some ambulance chaser. But he looked decent enough. He wore a khaki-colored suit, the shirt collar unbuttoned. The tongue of a tie hung from the breast pocket.

"I'm trying to find a lawyer in Houston."

"Yes, I heard. Why don't we sit down and have a cup of coffee?"

"I guess it's okay."

"Don't worry, you're safe with me."

"Did I say that aloud?" She bit her lip.

"Yes, ma'am," he said, smiling again. "It's okay."

She followed him to a large area with tables and vending machines. "What would you like?" He put money in a machine, pushed the buttons, and waited while it spit coffee into a paper cup.

"I-I'll get mine." She bought a diet soda and sat at a table with him.

"Parker Benavides," he said and held out his hand. He looked about the same age as Robert.

"Marian Reid." She shook his hand and opened her drink, taking a sip. She needed to get back to the shop. Every minute closed was money lost, but she needed a lawyer worse than she needed money. She hoped he knew someone who could help her. A feeling of being overwhelmed followed her everywhere, like a man one step behind her with a huge burlap bag. She wished somebody would take her away from all her problems.

"Mrs. Reid, why do you need a lawyer?" He relaxed in the hard plastic chair, leaning back.

She launched into a description of her situation. "I wanted to talk to the judge who hears cases involving guardianship of adults. I thought he could tell me of a lawyer I could hire to represent me in Houston." In spite of her hesitation, she relaxed in response to the crevices in each cheek when he smiled.

"The clerk was correct when she told you that judges aren't supposed to refer people to attorneys. Exactly what kind of case is it? Maybe I can point you in the right direction."

"A disabled adult who has been in the care of the state for his whole life, kind of."

"Kind of?"

"From foster care to guardianship. He's forty. The guardian is unable to continue caring for him."

"What's your interest in this, Marian? Okay if I call you Marian?"

She nodded. "Otherwise I'll have to call you Mr. Benavides, and it seems kind of ridiculous since I'm old enough to be your mother." She studied him. His clean-shaven head shined above thick black eyebrows and hazel eyes.

"I don't know about that." He flashed his dimples again.

"I am, and no need to apologize." She took another swallow of her drink. She might as well confess her connection. Her gaze met his. Embarrassment burned her skin. "The guardianship is for my son," she whispered.

"I see," he whispered back.

"It's a long story."

He glanced at his watch. "I have a few minutes to kill before my next hearing."

"You're a lawyer, right?"

"Yes, ma'am."

"So do you know any in Houston? Could you give me the name of one who could help me, either in Houston or who would go to Houston?"

He stared at her over his coffee cup.

Marian bent forward. "Do you do that type of work?"

He leaned across the table and whispered, "Is there a reason we're whispering? Is this a state secret?"

"You could say that. It's been a deep, dark family secret for forty—almost forty-one years." Three people on the island knew about Robert now. Four, if she counted her mother. The load she'd carried for all those years seemed lighter with each new person she told.

His face wrinkled up. "Like something you only read about in the funny papers."

She shrugged. Her chest felt like a balloon slowly inflated inside her. She glanced at the clock on the wall. How many customers had turned away from the door of her shop? She didn't ordinarily worry about money, but times were changing.

"One of the attorneys in my firm is board certified in probate law," he said. "He handles guardianship cases."

"Could you give me his name? He wouldn't be afraid of the judges in Houston?"

"Could you tell me a bit more about the situation? What's the nature of your son's disability? Are you asking to be the guardian? Does he want you to become his guardian?"

"He knows me, but he doesn't know I'm his biological mother. He thinks Dorothy is his mother. She's had him since the adoptive parents dumped him back on the adoption agency when he was an infant, and the adoption agency dumped him on the foster care system." She rubbed her hands together.

"You gave him up for adoption."

"My mother forced me. Back then girls didn't keep their illegitimate children like they do now."

"Hmmm. That could go against you."

"It already did. I've been to court twice to get him and lost each time. The first lawyer is dead. The second one I didn't care for."

"Why'd you lose?"

"The caseworker said Robert was too attached to Dorothy to separate them. He'd have an attachment disorder. They knew he had a kind of mental disability, but thought he was retarded at the time of the first hearing; he was so little."

"And later?"

"Same thing only by then they'd found out he's autistic."

"Wow. There's a lot of that going around."

"If there was then, no one really knew it. Dorothy was wonderful about taking Robert around the state, trying to get him help."

"So you were involved then?"

"The first time, Dorothy told me I could come see him. She told the judge at the second hearing, when he turned eighteen, that she'd been letting me see him. The judge made an order, not that we needed it. Dorothy's—" A cry erupted from her throat. Marian covered her mouth. "Like a mother to me."

"I see." He squashed the paper coffee cup and tossed it in the trash. "So what's up with her now? Is there a reason you want to go for guardianship again?"

"Alzheimer's." Marian pressed her lips together.

"Sweet Jesus. Poor lady."

"She's so good. Before she even told me, she already talked to the court investigator about me getting Robert."

"So what's the problem?" Parker asked.

"The court investigator thinks Robert should go to a home—be with others like himself."

He shook his head and leaned back in his chair again with a sigh. "That's rough. Judges often follow the investigator's recommendation."

Not what she wanted to hear. "You think I can't get him?"

"Oh, you definitely have a case, since you've had a relationship with him. It's just harder when the investigator is against you."

Marian rested her face in her hands. Maybe she should give up. But no. She wanted her boy more than anything. It was her last chance to be the mother to him she always had wanted to be. He would do well with her. She knew that. She glanced up. "You're not saying I can't get him?"

He shook his head again. "Not at all. It'll be a fight. An uphill battle. How bad do you want him?"

"More than I can say. Do you think your associate or whoever would take my case?"

"That associate is me, if you want me." He ducked his head and raised his eyebrows at her.

Marian laughed. "So you like to play your cards close to your chest. I don't know what to think about that."

"I am a lawyer, after all."

She tilted her head and closed one eye. "Aren't you awfully young to be certified in something?"

"Don't let this baby mug of mine fool you. I'm a lot older than I look. In fact, I'm a bit older than your son."

He was easy to talk with, like a big old boy. Had a good sense of humor, kind of a teasing manner. Her intuition told her to hire him. He had good energy. "Okay. You're hired. Do I sign a contract?"

"Tell you what, Marian." He looked at his watch. "I need to get to court. Let me give you a card. You call my office for an appointment. Today."

"Today?"

"There's no time to waste if the investigator already made up her mind. I have an idea how I'd approach your case. I need more background. We have a lot of work to do, but I'm in a rush. Have to be in court in five minutes."

"How much is this going to cost me? Are you expensive?"

He stood. "Very expensive. We'll discuss fees when you come in." He grabbed her hand and shook it. "You'll find I'm worth it, though. We're going to get you your son."

"I believe you."

He picked up his briefcase and walked away. For the first time in several days, the man with the burlap bag was falling behind.

Chapter 14

A FEW DAYS LATER, WHILE DRESSING mannequins in one of her display windows, Marian sensed movement on the street. Glancing up, she spotted Yvette Denby walking away from Coffee & More. Decked out in a little turquoise cotton suit and heels, Yvette carried her briefcase with one hand and, in the other, held a clipboard.

No one on the street dressed like that, especially in the summer. Everyone wore shorts, T-shirts or halter tops, and sandals or tennis shoes.

Marian leapt from the front window and ran outside. She hurried over Ledbetter Street and caught Yvette before she could cross at the corner and go in the opposite direction. "Hey, Yvette, what's up?" Marian squinted in the late morning sun.

Yvette frowned. "Speaking with your references like I told you I would." She stood with her clipboard clasped to her chest as though concealing something.

Anger shot through Marian. Just doing her job, *with fervor.* "So you already know you're recommending against me, and you're still speaking with my references?" That didn't pass the smell test. "So what have you found so far?"

Yvette pushed Ray-Ban sunglasses up on her head and arched an eyebrow. "I haven't changed my recommendation, if that's what you're hoping, Ms. Reid. I just don't think a women's clothing shop is any place for someone like Robby."

"Robert." Marian sank her hands into her shorts pockets and hoped Yvette hadn't noticed she wore a beer T-shirt. Who knew what the woman would use against her. "Let's give him dignity, and call him by his proper name."

Yvette's look told Marian she'd struck a chord. "Robert, then. You know he'll be better off with his own kind."

"No," Marian said, trying not to clench her teeth. "I don't. He's not from another planet. He's a human being who will do well anywhere he's loved. Wouldn't you like to come inside, out of the heat, and talk about this more?"

Yvette shook her head. "I'm not going to argue with you, Ms. Reid. I don't think there's anything else to talk about. We'll let the court decide." She turned away.

Marian sidestepped ahead of her. "I've got other plans for him as well, Yvette. He won't just be living above a dress shop. Galveston has a lot to offer people. Community college. The arts. Music. Theater. And The University of Texas Medical Branch has excellent doctors."

"I need to get going. You're not going to change my mind." She pulled her sunglasses back down on her nose and picked up her pace.

"Yvette, aren't you concerned about how he'll react to being moved in with strangers?" She kept pace with her. "He'll be better off with me. I just want you to give me a chance. I can be a good mother to him."

"If the judge wants to give you guardianship, that's fine. I'll make my recommendation, but the judge makes the final decision. Now back off, Ms. Reid."

"Just so you know," Marian called to Yvette's retreating back, "I've hired a lawyer. I'm not giving up. I want my son."

Yvette shook her head and kept walking. What had Marian ever done to be treated like that?

"Oh, by the way, have you been to Dorothy's lately?" Yvette asked, turning back toward Marian.

"I've called every day. I've been busy." She'd been making room for Robert in her life, not to mention Bryan. If she didn't spend her time in the shop, which she did a lot since Paula had quit, she spent it clearing out closets and moving furniture. She'd interviewed carpenters and found one who had the same vision she did for the remodel, to turn her bedroom into two smaller ones. The man would start work in a few days. And she and Bryan spent what little time there was left over, together.

Yvette tilted her head slightly to one side. "Too busy to find the time, I take it."

"What's that supposed to mean?" Perspiration ran down the back of Marian's neck. The temperature hovered in the low nineties, too hot to stand out on a street corner and have any kind of conversation. Marian was reaching her boiling point.

"If you love your son so much, you'd get down there more often and see what's going on for yourself."

Goosebumps rose on Marian's arms. She didn't like the idea that Yvette knew something she didn't. She'd run up to Houston when she closed for the day.

"The Alzheimer's is progressing rapidly," Yvette said as she took a few steps backward. "So now you know." She turned and strode away. "Oh, I forgot to tell you," she said as she pivoted again. "I met with your mother." She turned again and hurried away.

Heat swept over Marian. In spite of what she'd told the woman, Yvette had persisted in contacting her mother. There was more to that story, a lot more. She ran after Yvette and grabbed her arm. "What did she say? What did my mother tell you? I haven't seen her in ten years, except for when she dropped in on me unexpectedly a few days ago." They were so close Marian could smell Yvette's perfume, too sweet for her taste.

"Just some background."

"What on earth could my mother have told you that has any bearing on Robert? She has nothing to do with this. She knows nothing about Robert's situation."

"She does now. I must say she was quite surprised when I told her what you're trying to do."

A murderous rage built inside Marian. "You've crossed the line, Yvette, bringing my mother into it. Just where do you get off—"

"I needed more background information, Ms. Reid. Let's just say she was able to fill me in on the big picture, and leave it at that."

"What's that supposed to mean?" Marian put a hand to her abdomen when her stomach gurgled. No telling what her mama had told Yvette, and what Yvette had told her mama. If Yvette had found out about Bryan, had she told Claire about him as well? Marian stood rooted to the pavement, thoughts spinning like a pinwheel, and watched Yvette's departure, her walk not unlike a child's skipping.

Marian fled into Coffee & More and found Eva behind the counter. "Give me a strong cup of coffee," she said. "The strongest you've got."

"You don't like coffee."

"I'd rather have a belt of bourbon, but I better not. Just give me a coffee—cappuccino, better yet, espresso—something to give me a jolt."

Eva wiped her hands on the dishtowel that hung around her waist and charged over to the counter where her machines stood.

Marian sank into one of the chairs at the nearest table and put her head in her hands. "What did that woman ask you, Eva?"

Eva brought her a small cup. Marian slurped it then swallowed a huge mouthful. "Hot! It's dark and black. Uck."

"Uh huh. Strong. That's what you wanted. Come over here." She led her to the back door and spoke in a low tone. "That woman's got it in for you, girlfriend."

Several customers sitting at other inside tables glanced at them.

"I know. What I don't know is why she hates me so much."

"I don't think she's the type that likes to be crossed." Her face scrunched up. "And speaking of crossing, she questioned me as though I were a witness in court. Is she an attorney? She sure acts like she's one. That woman's a bitch."

"Yes, she is." Marian swallowed the remainder of her drink. "I feel revived, but don't ever let me do that again. That's bad-tasting stuff." She shook her head. "I don't think she'd be working at APS if she had gone to law school. They don't get paid squat. What'd she ask you?"

"Did you talk to me about Robert? Was I going to be a witness? Did I think you could care for a grown man with a disability? And about your habits."

"Like drinking?" Marian couldn't imagine what was on Yvette's mind. Why was she plotting against her?

"Yeah. Girl, I don't know what she's up to. I told her how long we've been friends, and how I've never seen you drink more than a glass or two of wine."

"Did she seem to think that was okay?" Marian's stomach rumbled, rebelling at the coffee.

"Who knows? She wanted to know if you smoked cigarettes."

"She would have smelled smoke when she was in my house if I did. Idiot woman."

"I'm just telling you what she asked." She swiped at her short hair. "And drugs. Do you use drugs?"

"What? For heaven's sake. You told her no, didn't you?"

"Just told her what I've seen you take for aches and pains."

"Stuff everyone over fifty takes, but she wouldn't know about that, being practically a little girl herself."

Eva laughed. "That's what I said. She sure is nosy."

"Did she ask about men?"

"She knew you had a boyfriend, and asked if I knew his name. Maybe she saw Bryan coming and going."

"I wonder if she's been following me or watching my place, like on TV. What did you tell her?"

"If she wanted to know, she should ask you. God, she practically gave me the third degree." Her eyes focused on something behind Marian. "A woman just went into your shop."

Marian edged toward the front door. Whispering, she said, "She talked to my mother. I'm fifty-something, and she talked to my mother."

"How'd she find her?" They walked out onto the sidewalk.

"I don't know. How did she find out anything? So now I have to face my mother, bad enough she came over the other day, and if Yvette knows about Bryan and told my mother—"

"Well, you knew it wasn't going to be easy, girlfriend."

Marian glanced at the sky as though an answer to her prayers might be there. "I'm going to have to tell Bryan about Robert before he finds out from someone else."

"What are you going to say?"

"Only that I have a son."

"Not—"

"Only that I have a son. You didn't tell her, did you?"

"No way."

"Thanks, Eva. You're the best." Marian started to leave and remembered Eva'd had a hospital appointment. "By the way, what happened at UTMB?"

Eva let out a deep breath. "They scheduled my surgery."

Marian gripped Eva's arm. "Oh, honey. When is it?"

"I'll text it to you so you can put it on your calendar, but it's soon. You're going to be there, right?"

"Absolutely," Marian said. "Nothing would stop me. Send me the date today so I can plug it in."

Eva hugged Marian's neck. "I'm so scared."

"Oh, sweetie, I know you are, but everything's going to be okay." She wrapped her arms around her friend. "I'm sure you'll be fine. Millions of women survive breast cancer every year. You'll be fine," she repeated as she jogged across to her shop. And hoped what she said was true.

Chapter 15

JANE SAT ON A PILE of rubbish and watched the new guy carry what looked like paintings and light fixtures into the back of his shop. Shielded between two dumpsters, she spread the cleaner napkins across her lap. She munched on bits of barbecue and pickles she'd found, washing the food down with warm beer from almost empty cans the barbecue girls had thrown out. Their garbage had become a lot sloppier lately and smelled nastier, what with the rancid mayonnaise from the potato salad and coleslaw. Used to she'd only find things like rib and chicken bones, used napkins, and empty cans and bottles. The new barbecue girl wasn't as careful as that old one, that tall one who'd been so mad one day. The new girl probably didn't know about the roaches yet or the rats. Jane hoped she'd be slow to learn.

Though her head swam in perspiration under her hat and semi-circles of fluid ran from under her breasts, Jane happily waved the flies away as her stomach quit growling. The beer made her sleepy. The new man whistled as he moved in and out of his store. Chirping like a bird, he wheeled in crates from a truck. His whistling reminded her of her dead husband.

When Howard was young, he used to whistle. In his twenties, his eyes had sparkled when he came home each day from his teaching job. He'd dance her around the kitchen. During the spring and summer when he'd work outside in his vegetable patch, or in the garage, he'd whistle all day long. The off-key notes would have been maddening if she hadn't loved him so much. She smiled at the memory of what life had been like when she'd been a young wife, her whole world a new adventure.

Now, a shadow appeared. The new guy loomed over her like a large, dark bird. Jane squinted up at him and hoped he wouldn't start yelling. She didn't like yelling. If he'd just give her a minute, she'd finish her lunch and be on her way. She watched and waited, but he seemed to expect her to say something. His face didn't look mad, what she could see with the sun above him, but he stood with his hands on his hips, like a boss would stand. After a few moments, he walked away. Still, Jane thought she'd best go. No telling who, or what, he might bring back with him. What she couldn't swallow quickly, she stuffed into a bag. After wiping her hands and wadding up the napkins, Jane maneuvered to her feet. She brushed off her bottom, straightened her floppy straw hat, and pushed her basket toward the West side of the alley.

"Hey, wait a minute," a male voice called from behind her.

Jane pushed harder, faster.

Something touched her shoulder. The new guy towered over her. Jane flinched and hovered over her basket, her arms held protectively over her head.

"Here," he said, handing her a plastic grocery bag. He patted her shoulder a couple of times and walked back to his store. Jane stared after him. What the hell?

Inside the bag were a ham sandwich, a pickle spear, coffee in a Styrofoam cup with a lid on it, a can of orange juice, napkins, and one of those wet napkin things in a small square package. Jane snickered. Food. Fresh food. She drank the hot coffee and hid everything else in her basket under the raggedy blankets she used for bedding. Glancing back at the door to the new man's shop, Jane hoped to catch a glimpse of him, to thank him. When he didn't come out after a few minutes, she forged onward toward the street and the seawall. She would tell him another time. Right now she had a mind to go swimming.

Chapter 16

WHEN MARIAN ENTERED HER SHOP, she found Chloe looking at the racks, her drawstring bag over one shoulder. The baby hung in a sling across her chest, barely visible. When she approached, Chloe started for the door.

Marian followed. "It's okay, I'm open."

"I don't know," Chloe said, holding the door wide.

"Don't know what?" Marian took her by the arm and pulled her inside. "Let's not run up my air-conditioning bill." The baby cooed like a dove.

"Whether I should be here. Darryl went out, and I didn't ask him before he left."

"Darryl your husband?" Without waiting for an answer, Marian said, "Doesn't matter. He couldn't be opposed to your buying something to wear—pre-owned even." All she'd ever seen the girl in was that long, dirty skirt.

Chloe bit her lower lip and glanced outside. She caressed the baby's head and looked in the other direction. "Well, maybe . . . if I hurry."

Marian led her to a rack. "I have many small things—lots of things in your size. What exactly were you thinking of? Pants for work? Skirts? Dresses?"

Chloe affected a smile. "Things for my job, I guess."

"You're still at the restaurant?" Marian reached for the baby. "I'll hold him. That is, if you don't mind. Been years since I held a baby." Remembering what Lupe had said about Chloe's husband, Marian wondered whether Chloe had any retail sales training. Maybe she could put her to work in her store. She could keep the baby with her. Put up a crib in the back. Darryl couldn't cause her problems over him that way.

"All right." Chloe lifted him out and put her cheek to his for no more than a breath before handing him to Marian.

He wore a long nightgown and socks even though the temperature was ninety plus degrees outside, but what did Marian know about dressing babies these days? The store could get really cool if you stayed inside long enough. The baby seemed rather light, but Marian didn't ask any questions. She put her nose to his neck and sniffed. "Babies always smell so yummy." He wiggled in her arms, and a hint of a smile tugged at his rosebud lips, which he pressed firmly together as though determined nothing would enter his mouth. Her daughter, Greta, had done that. Once she had her fill, a crowbar couldn't pry her lips apart.

"You pick out some things. There are curtained areas in the back where you can change," Marian said. "I'm just going to pull up a chair. Oh," she said when the baby opened his eyes and seemed to focus on her. "He has the darkest eyes I've ever seen for a baby so young. Beautiful."

Chloe smiled, revealing a missing tooth on one side. The poor girl probably didn't have money for dental care. While Chloe picked through the pile, Marian cuddled the baby. "What's his name? He's a boy, right?"

"Leonard. Supposed to be after Darryl's father. But I call him Leo, after Leonardo DiCaprio, the actor." She covered her mouth, muffling a snigger, and a light gleamed in her eyes.

"Nice to meet you, Leo," Marian said as she gazed into the baby's face. Had Greta lived, she could have had a baby by now. Marian could have been a grandmother.

"I found three pairs of pants that might fit," Chloe said. "How much are they?"

"Oh, don't you worry about that," Marian said. The baby clasped her forefinger. He had a strong grip for someone so small.

"I have to. Ms. Reid, right?"

"Yes. I know I'm old enough to be your mother, almost old enough to be your grandmother, but please call me Marian. I'd feel so much better." She smiled at Chloe, thinking Greta might have been close to her age.

"Okay, if you say so, Marian. How much?"

"Have you ever sold retail?"

"Worked in a convenience store once. Really, M-Marian, I need to know how much money I'll have to pay."

"You don't even know if they'll fit yet. Try them on, and then we'll negotiate. Do you like to negotiate? I do. My nana taught me. She'd haggle over anything." Marian rocked the baby in her arms.

"I guess I've never had to negotiate anything," Chloe said. "Except with Darryl."

Marian studied the girl. She didn't want to offer her a job right off, but if they were going to let her go at the restaurant because of Darryl, maybe she could use her.

Chloe stood, eyes flitting around the room.

"Something wrong?"

Chloe stared, deadpan. "No, ma'am, it's just that I should hurry."

"Let's go to the back." Marian walked Chloe behind the separating wall, to one of the two changing rooms. A hook held the curtain off to the side. "Go on in. Leo will be fine. I'll just sit with him in my desk chair here."

Chloe dropped her things and put the pants on a chair.

Marian released the curtain. She hoped Chloe would relax after a few minutes and maybe warm up to her.

The bell out front clanged.

"Be with you in a minute," Marian yelled. She stroked Leo's head. Soft, as only a baby's head could be.

Chloe stepped out from behind the curtain. The black denim slacks fit her like they were custom made, but Marian thought they were a bit short. "Try another pair, honey. See if you can get some that aren't so high water. I'm going out front to see who's there."

"Wait, Marian—why were you asking about retail?"

Marian held up a finger to stop her. "I'll be right back." She carried the baby around the dividing wall. Two women she didn't like the looks of said they wanted to look around. She didn't like the idea of the two women being alone in the front with no one watching them. She'd lost inventory that way when she'd first opened. One had distracted her while the other secreted things away. Marian hurried back around the separating wall to give the baby to Chloe. "Chloe, you're going to have to take Leo—" She flung open the curtain. Chloe gasped and spread her hands over her nakedness. Deep purple and yellow bruises the size of salad plates covered her thighs and buttocks, so dark Marian could see them through Chloe's skimpy white panties.

"What in the name of God?"

"Get out. Get out of here!" Chloe jerked the curtain in front of her body.

Stunned, Marian backed away. Those injuries were no accident.

Leo began to fuss. "I'm sorry," Marian said, alarm running through her body. No wonder Chloe walked around in long-sleeved blouses and long skirts. Marian pulled up Leo's gown to see if he, too, had bruises. She was almost afraid to look, but if that beastly Darryl, whom she had only glimpsed one time in the dawn, had hurt that dear little Leo, she would have to do something. Leo looked fine, unlike his mother. Marian wondered whether there was something she could do for Chloe. She'd considered offering her a job, but the young woman needed more than that, much, much more.

"Give me my baby," Chloe said a few moments later, dressed again.

Marian, still reeling, could only stare. She dared not let her eyes glance downward. Chloe had one pair of pants draped over her arm. Marian handed her the baby.

"How much for this pair?" Chloe's grim face had a determined set. Her eyes wouldn't meet Marian's. She headed toward the front of the store, not waiting for Marian's reply.

"Two dollars," Marian uttered.

Chloe stopped before she got to the counter, stuck her hand under her blouse, fidgeted a moment, and pulled out two folded one-dollar bills.

"I'll put them in a bag."

"No. No bag, Marian. You'll hold Leo for only a moment more." She handed the baby to Marian, folded the pants, and positioned them in the bottom of the baby sling. Leo went in on top of them. "I'll be seeing you." Draping Leo and the sling across her breast, she hoisted her drawstring bag over her shoulder and headed out the front door.

Marian started after her. "You could work here, Chloe. You could even bring Leo. I've been looking for someone to help out." After she said the words, Marian's brain kicked into gear. Did she really want to put herself in the middle of a wife-beating situation? Chloe didn't turn around. Marian stood on the sidewalk and watched the girl's receding back. Just as well. All she needed was Yvette telling the court that a wife-beater lived on her block, and his wife worked in the store where Robert would be spending the better part of his days.

Chapter 17

JANE WAS PUSHING HER BASKET toward the seawall when Rory, a man who resembled Santa Claus and lived in the alley behind the Lutheran Church, waved at her. "Come here, Jane," Rory called. "I need to talk to you."

"No. I ain't going down that holey alley. You come here." Rory never hurt her. The least he ever wanted was to tell her about something he'd heard on the street. The most he ever wanted was to have sex with her, which she'd do if he had five dollars. He was the only man she had sex with and, unfortunately, didn't often have five dollars.

A person never really knew what she would do until times got hard. Jane never thought she'd have sex for money, and here she was wishing Rory had money more often. She kind of liked him, though he could smell like the inside of a dumpster. In another time or place maybe they would've had a decent relationship. No charge. Like normal people.

"Well, hold on," he called. "I'm coming. I really wanna tell you something." He waddled to her as quick as he could.

Jane didn't want to have sex that afternoon. She wanted to go to the beach, but she had to get money when she could. She stopped and waited to see what he wanted. She wasn't walking down his alley for nothing. Too much broken glass and trash.

"What do you want?" Maybe she could still go to the beach after the sex, if he'd just hurry. She'd found a house with a water faucet outside and would need to get washed before the people came home.

"Where are you headed to?" Rory asked as he drew near.

"Going swimming." She didn't tell him about the faucet. She didn't want anyone to know about the faucet, or they'd all be up there drinking out of it and washing their pits. The faucet was hers; finders keepers.

"Sure is hot."

"Galveston's always hot in the summer. You want something, or you just wasting my time?"

"You know that artist boyfriend of yours?"

"He's not my boyfriend," Jane said, straightening. "He's a kid." She liked him to tease her but tried not to smile.

Rory grinned. Most of his teeth were missing, and the ones he did have were as brown as the cardboard box he kept his stuff in. Jane still had her teeth. She brushed them, but her toothbrush was so worn out, the bristles were almost gone. If he gave her five dollars, she might buy a toothbrush. She sure didn't want her teeth to look like his.

"I'm just playing with you," Rory said. "I know something about him you don't know."

"Well, hurry up and tell me. The day's growing as old as us."

"What'll you give me if I tell ya?"

"Nothing. I ain't giving you nothing. I don't care if you don't tell me." She rolled her basket a couple of steps toward the seawall.

"Aw, come on now. I know something you could give me." He chuckled.

"I'm sure not giving you that. You have to pay, like always. Who do you think I am, Mrs. Croesus?"

"Okay. You don't got to get so mad. Somebody beat that boy artist up last night."

She stomped her foot. "No, Luther? Where is he? Did you see it? Was he hurt bad? What'd they do that for? Luther never hurt anybody."

Rory hooked his thumbs in the waistband of his tattered navy pants and strutted in a circle, bow-legged as an old ranch hand. "See, this car pulled up, and the boy artist sat in the front with this older man. They started arguing. I think the man wanted him to— you know—and he wouldn't. The man got out, went around, and pulled the boy out and flung him against the alley wall like an old cat. He hit him a bunch of times and drove away."

"What did Luther do?" Jane glanced back up Twenty-Second Street toward Luther's apartment.

"He laid in the alley all night. This morning I poured water on his face, and he practically crawled upstairs. He didn't look too good."

She weighed the information. If Luther could get up the stairs, he was probably all right. She wanted to go to the beach. She pushed her basket toward the seawall.

"Ain't you gonna do nothing?" Rory bellowed.

"I'm going swimming," she said and aimed for the shady side of the street.

She arrived on Seawall Boulevard in thirty minutes. She left her basket behind the convenience store dumpster. Walking another half block, she crossed at the traffic light. She liked to swim where the Balinese Room used to be. Nobody else much went there. Even though the wave action could be dangerous, it was the most excitement she ever got. Barnacles could slash her feet if she got too close to the old posts under the water, and oftentimes she had to fight the current. Several times, she waded out into the warm green-brown water and let a wave wash her back to the shallows.

A large swell pushed through the deep water and headed her way. She surged forward, toward the sand, and stroked with all her might. The wave caught her and propelled her body. She threw both arms over her head and let the water wash over her. Moments later, she could touch bottom. She sat in the shallows. Should she go back out or should she go to the faucet? Digging into the sand under the water, she rubbed it over her body and her face and ears and neck. Lying down, she let the water rinse her. She would go out one more time.

The water felt wonderful. She was happy. But there were days when she didn't think she could tolerate the life she led much longer. Sometimes she thought the easiest thing would be to swim out to where she couldn't touch bottom, and let the good Lord take her to him. It would be so simple to quit trying, let her old bag of bones sink to the bottom. Who'd care?

When she got chest deep in the water, she began to swim. The breaststroke was her best thing. Her backstroke wasn't bad either. She turned over and swam. "See? I'm swimming," she said to the blue sky. "I'm okay. I'm really okay." Memories of swim meets and medals clustered in her mind. If only her life had been frozen in her teenage years or even college. Before she met Howard or before their son had been lost to the flu.

The current pulled at her, but she was stronger than the current. She turned somersaults in the water, remembering when she'd been in water ballet as a child. "I can still do stunts. I'm good. I'm a good swimmer." Who was she talking to? The warm water soothed her, made her sleepy. Time for her nap.

She put her feet down. No sandy bottom met her toes. The shore looked very far away. Was it really that far, or was her eyesight getting worse? She treaded water for a few minutes, tired from her stunts. Somehow she'd gotten out past the breaker line. No waves came to wash her to the shore. As she tried to decide what to do, Jane hung in the water like a piece of seaweed. Maybe it was time to go to the Lord.

Chapter 18

MARIAN HUNTED DOWN HER MAMA. She knew the type of food her mama liked. She knew some of her mama's friends, too. It only took a few phone calls to locate where Claire was staying and where she was having lunch that day. She found her down on the waterfront inside a Greek restaurant.

"Do you want to tell me just what the hell you've been doing getting into my business with Adult Protective Services?" Glaring, Marian stood over Claire, hands on hips.

"Marian, really. This is hardly the time or place." Claire glanced around the restaurant at the other customers. "Do you remember my friend and now new neighbor, Latrice Lattimer?"

Marian nodded at Latrice. "Hello." She turned back to her mother. "If you don't want me to really embarrass you in public, Mama dear, then you'd better come out on the deck with me." Marian clenched her teeth. Her anger had grown since she'd spoken to Yvette. Now it was boiling over. "Nice to see you, Latrice." She stalked to the door, down the ramp, and onto the deck, which jutted into the harbor.

Standing with crossed arms, Marian didn't have to wait more than thirty seconds for her mama to catch up. She didn't care if it was ninety degrees in the shade, and that the old woman would really feel the heat in her panty hose and summer suit. They were going to have it out right then and there.

"How dare you speak to me like that in public!" Claire shook her finger in Marian's face.

"No! How dare you mess in my personal life again. I thought I was rid of you when you moved to the Hill country, but, no, you've got to show back up down here on the island, waving all your money around, trying to buy back your friends. What happened in Georgetown? They get sick of you and your trouble-making?"

Claire raised her hand as if to slap Marian, but Marian caught it in mid-air. "Not anymore, Mama dear. You will never hit me again." She squeezed her mother's hand as hard as she could and threw it down like it was a piece of trash. "Now you tell me right now what you said to Yvette."

Her mother glared, her breath coming in short takes as though she'd been running hard. "I didn't approach the woman. She came to me. She wanted to know your background, verify what she found in their file, and find out if there was anything she should know that wasn't contained in the files."

"You'd better tell me right now what you told her."

"I may have mentioned your medical history."

"My what?"

"You know, one or two hospitalizations."

Marian could hardly contain herself. "And did you bother to

mention to her what was behind those hospitalizations? Or should I say *who*?"

"Oh, I don't know why we have to get into all this, Marian. You know you have no business getting guardianship of that man."

"*That man* happens to be my son. My son who you made me give away forty years ago. My son who has a disability and needs my help. My son who is losing the person he loves most in the world. If I can do anything to make up for what I did to him, now is my chance."

"Oh please, Marian. Be sensible. He needs to be with his own kind, not some stranger."

"I'll have you know, Claire, I'm no stranger to Robert. I've been visiting him for years."

Claire reared back. "I'm so sure."

"No thanks to you, I'm good at keeping secrets. I've kept Robert a secret for most of our lives, but even better, I've kept it a secret that I've been seeing him for years. Only Nana and my friend Eva knew about him and my visits. So, you see, he won't be coming to live with a stranger, he'll be coming to live with the person who loves him more than anyone on this planet. Me. His mother. And so help me, if you interfere with that, if you do anything to cause me not to be able to get my son back, I—I can't be responsible for what I'll do to you, old woman."

"Now you listen here, Marian Reid. I not only will most certainly do everything in my power to prevent you from getting him, I'll do you one better. I promise you, that if you go forward with this scheme, if you go to court for him, you will regret it."

"You don't frighten me. You don't have power over me any more. I don't need you. I don't need your money. I don't need your help." Marian started to walk back toward the parking lot.

"How badly do you need Bryan? Do you want Bryan?"

Marian ran back and grabbed her mother's forearm. "Just what are you talking about?"

"You go ahead, you go to court for that man, and see if Bryan doesn't suddenly come into information about the son he never knew he had."

Marian had to restrain herself from slapping Claire. She wouldn't lower herself to that level, to treating her mama the same way her mama had treated her. The only thing stopping her from strangling the woman at that moment was the thought that Robert would be sent to a home.

Marian, stiff with rage, walked away, shaking her head. Would Claire stop at nothing? As if threats could control what Marian would do about Robert. How little her mama really knew her. And how much her mama must really dislike her.

She'd risk her relationship with Bryan. She had to. Not that she believed Bryan would listen to anything her mama had to say. Claire had been the one to cause him to give up hope of ever seeing Marian again. No, she didn't think Bryan would have anything to do with Claire. At least, that's what she pinned her hopes on.

Chapter 19

JANE STARED AT THE SKY. The sun felt hot on the parts of her body not under the water. Though blue sky was overhead, gray clouds appeared north of the island. Rain clouds maybe. Not the best thing for a person in her situation. She pondered what she should do. So tired. She could float a bit longer but not as well as she could when she had fat on her body. Should she just let go and let God, as the saying went?

It seemed fitting that she, who had loved the water her whole life, who'd been in synchronized swimming as a kid—water ballet—who swam competitively in high school and college and had gone as far as the Olympic trials, should end her days in the Gulf of Mexico.

Better to swim out farther where the water would be cooler, better to totally exhaust herself, better to give in to one of the elements, than to catch some deadly disease on the streets or get beaten to death in an alley, her basket of goods—of junk—stolen by another desperate person. No one would miss her except maybe Rory, and he'd forget her in a matter of days. Too many people on the streets, too many dying of one thing or another for any of them to mourn very long.

A person should be able to choose how she ended her time. If she exhausted herself and just allowed herself to sink, no one would know until it was too late. Until her body washed to shore. No one would be able to resuscitate her, to keep her alive by artificial means, to throw her back on the streets.

She ran her fingers along the top of the water, making a little splash in a circle. She lay back, bent her knee, raised her leg, felt the muscles protest. Now the left leg. Now a scissor kick. A few back strokes. So tired. Time to turn over and swim, swim as though she wanted to catch that cruise ship she'd dreamed of being a passenger on.

"Swim out too far?"

A voice. Was she having a heat stroke? Or was someone really there? Through the water in her ears, it sounded like Luther. Couldn't be Luther. She turned her head and saw a blurry figure. Where were her glasses when she needed them? "Is someone really there?"

"Beach Patrol. I came out to help you, lady."

Someone laughed, and Jane realized it was her, as though she didn't inhabit her own body. When she scrunched up her eyes and looked closer, a suntanned young man sat astride a surfboard.

"You're really there?" Jane reached for the end of the board.

"Are you okay? How long you been out here? Is the sun getting to you?"

"Think it's time I went in," she said. "Think maybe I got out past where I should be."

"Yes, ma'am," he said, sliding into the water. "If you can climb on, I'll swim us both in."

Struggling against fatigue, with the lifeguard's help she managed to pull herself on top of the surfboard. Closing her eyes, she let him do all the work. Guess it hadn't been time. God had sent someone to rescue her.

After they reached the beach, she convinced the lifeguard she was all right, and he left. She sat on a pink granite boulder until the small crowd, who'd stood watching, faded away. An audience, she didn't need. She wanted to rinse off and dress before the faucet people came home.

Chapter 20

AFTER LEAVING HER CAR IN the parking garage where she rented a space, Eva crossed the street and walked down the alley toward the back of her shop. Miguel, Lupe, and their employees regularly picked up trash and pulled weeds behind the Taqueria on the corner. Miguel and Lupe recycled. They didn't have to recycle cans. If no employees were interested, they'd put the cans out in plastic bags, which would disappear on their own.

A truck stood in the alley near Troy-the-new-guy's open back door. A strong paint smell drifted out. Eva couldn't resist seeing what he was doing inside. She stepped over the threshold and glanced up the enclosed stairwell where she heard Linda Ronstadt singing in the distance.

Troy had remodeled the rear part into an office. Down a short hall were a restroom, a small kitchen, and a table and chairs. A bit farther, past a ten-foot high movable wall that separated the back from the large interior room, Eva found herself in an art gallery.

A new art gallery next to her shop. It would improve her business, especially during Artwalks.

Footsteps fell on the stairwell behind her, leading down into the office. Her exit blocked, Eva didn't try to hide. She entered the main part of the gallery, where it looked like he was ready to hang paintings. Wooden crates leaned against walls and each other. Track lighting hung in rows from the tall ceiling. He'd painted each wall a slightly different shade of white from the next. Pearl, alabaster, and cream or whatever decorators called white these days.

"Seen enough?" Troy Sumner stood behind her with a big smile. Barefoot, he wore tailored shorts and a polo-style shirt. His hair glistened as though he'd just gotten out of the shower. If Eva didn't have other problems, she might be interested, though he was closer to the end of fifty than the beginning.

"Not quite, but I'll wait until you get everything unpacked." She snooped inside the crates, looking to see if he'd uncovered anything. She'd love to see what kind of art he'd be displaying, not that she knew much about art.

"So my secret is out." He followed close behind. "What do you think of the paint job?"

"Not much to it, but now I know what you've been doing in here. Nothing stays secret very long on this street. If you haven't learned that yet, you know it now." Eva snorted. "By the way, you should never leave your alley door unlocked, not even for a moment."

"Yeah, I see what can happen."

"I'm the least of your worries. Galveston is the end of the line for lots of desperate people. They could be in and out with your property in a matter of moments, and you'd never hear them."

"Whoa. Thanks for the warning." He gave her a lopsided grin. "I'll be more careful. I've only seen that old woman. I doubt if she could move that fast."

"She's become a regular in the last few months, but there are lots of others and always new, down-on-their-luck people living in the streets."

He nodded. "I have an alarm system."

"Use it. I can't afford one, but all I have to lose downstairs is food and reading material. I have two double dead-bolt doors between the downstairs and upstairs where I live. I'm very safe at night."

Troy snapped his heels together and saluted. "Thank you, ma'am. I'll pay more attention to security."

Eva laughed and wondered why she felt so giddy. "Hate to sound so harsh. Just be careful, and you'll be all right. By the way, how was lunch?"

Troy's brow wrinkled.

"You bought a bag of food, remember?"

"Oh. Oh, yes. Good sandwich. Thanks."

"You like the bread? I bake it myself."

"Good texture."

"Ham okay? I bake them with sauce my mother used to make."

"Yes. I could go for more." He licked his lips. "Well, if you're finished looking, I have an appointment."

"Sorry. Didn't mean to keep you. Just being nosy." Eva eased back the way she'd come. "Are you going to be open for the next Artwalk?"

"Plan to be. Going to take an ad in the paper since I was too late for that advertising handout."

"Great. Your place will be good for the street, Troy."

"You remembered my name."

"Of course. If we're going to be family, we have to know each other's names." She reached the back door.

"Is there any way I could persuade you to keep quiet for a few more days?"

"If it's important to you. I'm good at keeping secrets, but since I'm bursting with this one, hurry up. You'll come over and have coffee with me sometime?"

"Um, I'm seeing someone."

"And I've got breast cancer," she said. "So I'm not looking for a relationship."

He gaped, and then said, "I'm sorry. Is there anything I can do?"

Eva sized him up. He looked okay that day, but sometimes he wore tight shorts and muscle shirts. Could he be gay? Could be another interesting development for Ledbetter Street. "Just be my friend."

"I'd like that—uh—"

"Eva. Eva Best." She entered the alley. "And be sure to lock the door behind me, even if you're only running back upstairs for a moment."

"Yes, ma'am. Nice to see you again," he said and closed the door, the deadbolt clicking into place.

Seeing Troy's gallery elevated Eva's spirits. Business would pick up, which would mean more money would come in, which would mean she would be better able to pay her hospital bills. Now if only solving her other problems could be as easy.

Chapter 21

AFTER SHE WASHED AND DRESSED, Jane pushed her basket down the seawall until she approached the intersection of Twenty-Second, the street that led all the way down to Luther's. Tourists overflowed the sidewalks. A boy bumped her but didn't say anything. No accident. People were like that sometimes. She kept her head down, pushing, pushing, and turned the corner. Cars raced past her in both directions. Quitting time for workers? Her old watch kept bad time.

Finally, she banged on the door to Luther's apartment building. He lived upstairs over a store. Luther didn't come. No one came. Someone had installed individual doorbells since she'd moved out. Squinting because she was too tired to fish in her basket for her cheaters, she thought she could make out an L under one bell. She pushed the button. No response. She pulled on the handle. The door opened. She took out the food the new man had given her and left her basket next to the antique mall's dumpster. Swimming had worn her out, but the sun was still up. There was no place to sleep until much later. After dark, she could go to her spot in the alley.

"Luther," she said, as she reached the top of the stairs. Banging on his door, she called his name several times. When he didn't answer, she turned the knob. The door opened, so she went inside. "Luther." The air was still. Hot. No air conditioning. The windows were raised. Someone drove down the alley too fast. She hated them speeding down the alley, especially the wrong way, ignoring the ONE WAY signs. People should go by the rules.

The apartment was emptier than last time she'd been there; the walls barer. She crept to the single bedroom. No bed anymore. Luther lay on a blanket on the floor, asleep. Jane set her bag down and shook him. "Luther." His skin was as white as a flour sack except for a huge bruise. His arms thin, his trousers baggy. Luther looked like other friends of Jane's. Street friends. She shook him again.

"What?" he mumbled.

Jane eased herself onto the floor next to him. "Rory said you got beat up."

Luther opened his eyes. "Jane."

"Rory said you got beat up."

"What time is it?"

"Don't know. Quitting time, I think. Or past. Are you okay?"

"It's night?"

"Almost. Are you hurt?"

Luther sat up and held his head. "Ugh. I must have been here all day."

"Rory said he gave you water this morning, and you went upstairs."

Luther looked at her with the prettiest blue eyes she could remember for a long time. Reminded her of her son. One reason she liked Luther so much. She liked blue. Blue eyes. He had that blue color in his paintings. She wondered if he was feeling blue.

"So that's Rory."

"He's my . . . friend, sometimes. Is anything broken?"

Luther moved his limbs. "I don't think so." He stood and reached down for her hand, to give her a lift.

She let him help her up. "I have food. Want some?"

"I ate."

Jane picked up her bag and pulled out the contents. Luther still had an old wooden table, but no chairs. Jane set out the food. "We can share. Got a knife so I can cut the sandwich?"

He stared at her. "I ate, I said."

"Yesterday, I bet. That man. He fed you, I bet. If you don't have a knife, I can pull the sandwich apart. I had a bath. My hands are clean."

Luther shook his head. "You're not my mother."

"I'm hungry." She pulled the sandwich into two ragged pieces. "You can have the big half. I already ate today. Those barbecue girls were good to me."

Luther wolfed down his part.

"Got a glass?" Jane ripped the silver-colored strip off the top of the orange juice can. "I like orange juice."

Luther produced a glass, and Jane shared her juice. They both gulped it down. "I would like water, please, Luther."

Luther came back with water in a glass and handed it to Jane. She considered the pickle. "You can have the pickle spear. I don't like pickles much." She gave it to him, wishing she had more to share. After drinking the water, Jane tore open the wet wipe and washed her face and hands.

Luther stood over her for a moment, staring. "I'm going to take a shower."

"I already had mine. Mind if I take a little nap?"

He shook his head. Jane lay down on the bare floor and went to sleep.

Chapter 22

THE WEEK AFTER HER CONFRONTATION with Yvette and her mama, Marian saw the homeless woman approach Eva's shop. She realized she'd seen the woman outside Coffee & More in the past.

The old woman pressed her nose against Eva's window. A moment later, she pushed open the glass door and stuck in her head. Marian started across the street. The woman approached Eva's sweet stand. Marian ran inside when the woman began stuffing fried fruit pies into her pockets.

"Caught you." Marian grabbed the woman's wrist. "You're the culprit."

The woman jerked and tried to free herself. She cowered like a whipped pup and smelled like sweaty socks.

"I've seen you on the street bunches of times. You know where to go for food."

"Lemme go," the woman said, her voice muffled. Her head hung down on her chest like her neck was broken.

Marian dragged her toward the back of the store. "Stay right there. Don't touch anything." She strode to the bottom of the stairs and called out, while trying to keep an eye on the woman at the same time. "Eva, get down here. Now!"

When she glanced back, the old woman had gone.

"Eva," Marian shouted. "Hurry!" She ran out the front of the shop and spotted the old woman making the corner, past the Taqueria.

Marian took off, but when she got to the corner, the woman had disappeared again. She was fast. And with a basket, too.

Breathing hard, Marian hotfooted it down the block toward the alley behind the strip of shops, resolving to get more exercise soon.

"Marian!" Eva called from behind her.

Marian kept running. "Shoplifter!" When she got to the corner, she spied the woman passing the first dumpster. Marian continued to give chase even with a pain in her side.

"Stop!" Eva yelled. "Too dangerous."

Marian ran down the alley as the woman reached the second dumpster. "Hold it!" She caught up to her and grabbed old woman's baggy shirt.

In what felt like slow motion, the old woman let go of the basket, which cascaded toward the street at the other end of the alley. She turned toward Marian and stepped down onto the manhole cover—the one several inches lower than the alley surface—and fell, her head smacking the ground with a crack. The breath whooshed out of her, and she lay sprawled on her back like a dead insect.

Marian screamed and dropped to her knees as Eva reached them. "Call 911! I think she's dead!"

Eva pushed Marian away. She put two fingers to the side of the woman's throat. After a moment, she said, "She has a weak pulse. Go bang on Troy's door, and see if he'll call an ambulance."

"I didn't do anything. I grabbed at the back of her clothes. She fell."

"I know. I saw everything. Go on, Marian."

Marian, still panting, hurried to the back of Troy's building and hammered on the door. She hoped the old woman didn't die right there in the alley.

Troy opened almost immediately. "What's up?"

"Call 911. There's been an accident." Marian pointed.

Troy stepped outside, took in the scene, and snatched the cell off his waistband, punching numbers.

Marian returned to Eva, crouching down and peering at the woman. With her eyes closed, she looked sweet-faced, if dirty and smelly. "Is she still breathing?"

"Yeah, she's breathing," Eva said. "Get her basket."

Marian darted to the far end of the alley and into the street where the basket had come to a rest in the nearest lane. Plastic bags hung from the handlebar. A blanket covered the bottom, the rest of the things on top. One of the bags smelled like rotten fish.

A siren wailed in the distance. Marian rolled the basket into the alley. Smashed aluminum cans rattled in a large grocery bag. The old woman had stuffed a threadbare quilt down one corner. Another bag held clothes and a pair of huge, worn, black flats.

Food scraps Marian didn't care to try to identify lay on the bottom of the plastic bag that emitted the bad odor. A smaller plastic bag inside the first one really was too gross to contemplate, but Marian picked out the bag and let the contents drop to the ground. A rotten fish, a stiff, sandy black-striped mullet, hit the asphalt like a plank of wood. The only time she'd smelled anything worse was after Hurricane Ike when decayed, putrid fish washed up on the beach. For several weeks everyone except gawkers had avoided the beachfront.

The odor could make the faint-hearted collapse. Marian picked the fish up with the plastic bag and threw it into the nearest dumpster. The larger plastic bag went in as well. No wonder the old woman was stealing fried pies.

A police car rolled into the alley from the East end. A police officer hopped out and rushed to Eva. "Is she dead?"

Marian sifted through the rest of the bags and got rid of every perishable thing. She wanted to trash it all but guessed the basket's contents represented everything the woman owned.

A second officer spoke into a microphone from the front seat of the police unit. Red and blue lights flashed. Troy came back out of his shop. By that time, Miguel had hurried outside as well, a long white cook's apron tied around his middle.

Marian pushed the basket to Eva's back door, out of the way.

"Take my keys, and lock the front of my place and come out the back, okay?" Eva said.

Marian didn't want to leave, but both of them could be ripped off big time. She left and locked both stores and entered the alley from Eva's. More people had gathered. She pulled the basket into the back of Eva's shop.

Troy followed her. "What're you going to do with that?"

"It's the old woman's stuff. Someone will steal it if we don't take care of it."

He looked into the basket. "I don't think so."

"The other homeless people. You can't set anything down in the alley without it disappearing."

He made a disgusted grunt. "So I've heard, but that junk?"

The EMTs came into the alley at the other end from the police. Eva stood next to the old woman while they checked her over.

"I guess I'd better see if they want my statement," Marian said. "I didn't mean to hurt her . . . I didn't hurt her . . . I just chased her for shoplifting." She peered up into Troy's face, hoping for an ally. He had nice eyes, with smile wrinkles.

He patted her shoulder. "I'm sure the cops will understand. Don't worry."

Marian sighed and frowned and headed to the center of the crowd.

"Fried pies. I found them in her pockets," Eva said to the officer. "I'm not pressing charges."

The cop turned to Marian. "So you're the one who got into the altercation with her?"

"There wasn't really an altercation." Marian wished she knew the cops, but she didn't.

"What do you call it, ma'am, when you knock someone down?"

He was about a foot taller than Marian. Sunbeams spiked around his head as he stared down at her. Marian cupped her fingers at her brow. She was in no mood to argue with the police. "I didn't knock her down."

"I'm her attorney," Parker Benavides said, having materialized behind her. "And if this kind lady says she didn't knock the woman down, she didn't knock her down."

Surprised to see Parker there, Marian turned back to the police officer. "I don't need a lawyer. I'll tell you what happened."

"You don't have to," Parker said, his hand on her arm.

"I want to. It's okay." She spent a couple of minutes giving the officer a rundown. "And about the time I caught up to her, she stepped into that depression around the manhole cover and fell."

"Uh-huh," he said and started writing on a new page. "You're Marian Reid, right? You saw her take the pies?"

"Yes. But I never touched her after I caught her. See how deep that depression is? You have to look under the ambulance to see it now. Every time they repave these alleys, the holes around the manhole covers and drains get deeper."

When the EMTs had her stabilized, with oxygen clamped on her face, they lifted her onto a stretcher, put her inside their vehicle, and drove away. The cop walked over to the depression in the alley.

"Do you think she's going to be all right?" Marian asked Eva.

"She was breathing. They think she might have a fractured skull."

"Oh my God. I feel so bad. I shouldn't have chased her."

Parker put his arm around Marian. "Don't say anything else. Let's go inside. We need to talk about your case."

"Forget it," Eva said. "You're not responsible."

When he returned, the officer said, "Okay. Got what I need. What are you going to do with her basket?"

Marian and Eva exchanged glances.

"Save it for her," Marian said. "I got rid of the . . . perishables."

"We'll let her know, and she can come get it when she gets out of the hospital," Eva said.

"If she does," the officer said.

Marian squirmed. "Don't say that."

He shrugged and walked back to his car. The crowd had mostly dispersed. At the other end of the alley, a little old man who Marian thought looked like a dirty Santa, watched them. His foot rested on the bottom rung of his basket. When the police car backed out onto the street, he did a U-turn and plodded away.

Chapter 23

EVA HAD BENT OVER THE old woman in the alley. After she got past her scraggly looks and body odor, as she held the woman's head in her lap and waited for the ambulance, the old woman opened her eyes a bit, peering into Eva's, her lips upturned. Something inside Eva reacted almost violently to that brief engagement. Compelled to find out what it was, she made a trip to the hospital.

"What's your name?" Eva asked, surprised at how small the woman looked against white bed sheets. When she'd seen her on the street, the woman wore layers of clothing, which made her look larger. She'd bathed or been bathed. Her hair was shampooed, the gray strands glistening under the fluorescent lights. She smelled like bath soap. Even her nails were trimmed and cleaned. She could be anybody's sick grandmother.

The woman stared at Eva but didn't reply.

"Your chart says your name is Jane Doe," Eva said. "I asked the nurse when I came in. God, how can you stand the medicine smell in here? Phew."

The woman's watery brown eyes followed as Eva circled at the foot of the bed. She jerked the curtain dividing the space between the old woman's bed and the empty one next to it, the metal balls spinning on the hooks.

"Listen, old woman," Eva said. "I want to help you." She spun on her heel and faced off with her. "Look what I brought you."

Eva pulled a fried fruit pie from each pocket and dangled them in the air. She put the cherry one in the table drawer next to the bed. She peeled a thin strip of waxed paper from the lemon pie, the ripping noise the only sound in the double room except for their breathing. She broke the pie in half, lemon filling oozing.

The old woman held out a bony hand. "Jane," she said in a raspy voice.

Eva handed her the pie. "Have it your own way, Jane." She dragged up a chair next to the bed.

Jane bit into the middle of the pie. The yellow, lemony goo covered her lips like gloss. "Used to eat these at camp when I was a girl."

"I know you love them. Had trouble keeping them in stock."

"Oh," Jane said. She licked the filling as her eyes locked with Eva's. "Knew I knew you."

"It's okay. I didn't come here to yell at you."

They sat silently a moment, looking each other over.

"Did the doctors say what's wrong with you? Do you have a concussion? Marian didn't mean to hurt you."

"The woman from the clothes store?" She shook her head. "Didn't hurt me, except made me run fast. Haven't run that fast in a long time."

"You remember what happened? Marian said you stepped in a hole and fell."

"Yup. Doctors said I had a mild heart attack." She took a large bite. After chewing a moment, Jane said, "Could you pour me some water? Pie's thick in my throat."

Eva poured water into a plastic cup. Jane seemed like a nice old lady. She spoke well. What made her start living in the street? She waited until Jane drained the glass. "Want more?"

"No, I'm fine. They treat me good here. I get lots to eat and drink." She put the remaining bit of pie on the table and wiggled around until she sat more upright. "You could plump the pillows behind my back."

Eva boxed the pillows and positioned them behind Jane. She wondered if someone missed her. Did she have any family?

"Thank you." She smoothed the covers across her chest. "Eva."

Eva sat back down. "You saw my name in what, my garbage?"

"Yup. I've seen lots of things. You should be more careful with your trash. Get one of those shredders."

Eva nodded. "What else should I do?"

"Well, you make pretty good sandwiches."

"I haven't been missing any of those."

"I've had bits that were thrown out. And the new guy gave me one."

Why didn't she try to help Jane the first day she saw her instead of doing what everyone else in the country did, pretend the homeless weren't there?

"What's your prognosis?" Eva got up and opened the blinds, letting light into the room.

"Oh, I'll be all right. They're going to keep me for a few more days for observation. Gave me a talking to. It'll work out."

"Where will you go?"

"Back where I came from," Jane said, her expression defiant.

She'd be back in the street. Eva studied Jane's face and wondered whether the woman had any other options, but from the set to her chin, knew she'd better not ask. At least not yet. "I have your basket."

When Jane smiled, her wrinkles seemed to crack. "Wondered what happened to my stuff. Will you keep it until I can get it?"

"Sure. It's safe in the back of my shop." Eva stood and brushed at the wrinkles in her shorts. "Okay if I come see you again?" Surprised at her feelings, Eva needed to get out of the room before she started blubbering.

Jane nodded. "Sure. You're nice.

"Thanks." Eva edged toward the door.

"Yup. I like everybody on the street except that mean man who lives with the girl with the baby."

Eva stopped, momentarily distracted from her own feelings. "I don't know who you mean."

"That girl who works at the Taqueria. The one who had that baby in a sling across her front."

"Oh." Eva had forgotten all about her.

"He's a wife-beater—a hard, mean man."

"How'd you know that?"

"He knocked her down and kicked her. Woke me up."

Eva found herself back inside the main part of the room. "No wonder she's like a frightened rabbit."

"Did she come back from wherever she's been? She wasn't around for a few days before my—my accident."

"I haven't seen her lately, but you know how of these transients are." Eva realized what she'd said. "I didn't mean you, Jane."

"That's all right. I'm not a transient. I used to have a home, but I ran out of money."

Was Jane giving her an opening? "Is there someone who could help you? Is there someone I could call for you?"

Jane picked up the pie and bit into it again. "You're too late. The hospital social worker already talked to me about it." She folded the waxed paper over the uneaten part.

"So there is someone?"

Jane didn't answer. She licked her fingers and wiped them on a tissue.

"It's okay if you don't want to tell me." Eva shrugged one shoulder. "Just wanted to help. I'd better go. I have a doctor's appointment myself."

"Would you put these bits in the drawer with the other one?"

Eva did what she asked and closed the drawer. "It was nice visiting with you, *Jane*."

"Just lovely," Jane said. She scooted down under the covers. "Goodbye."

After her doctor's appointment, Eva went to the grocery store before going home. As she approached the alley, a full grocery bag in each hand, a siren wailed and an ambulance rumbled past her. God, what now? Spying Troy about to go inside his gallery, she hollered out his name.

"What was that about?" She hoped it had nothing to do with Marian.

Troy pulled off his sunglasses and rubbed the bridge of his nose. "I found a young guy lying between the dumpsters. He looked pretty dead."

"Never a dull moment around Ledbetter Street. Was there blood? Did he break something?" That's all they needed right before Artwalk, bad publicity. "Last year a boy fell off the top of a building. A bunch of them were drinking and partying and climbed out a window and onto the roof."

Troy winced. "I don't think it was anything like that. He's real skinny. When he opened his eyes, they were this weird color blue and the whites were as yellow as his skin, like he had jaundice."

"Sounds like Luther." She set the grocery bags down on his stoop. "Haven't seen him around lately."

"Don't know him. But then, I don't know many people yet, mostly only those on this block."

"He's an artist. A very good artist, but things have been slow lately. His parents used to subsidize him, but his father died, and his mother remarried. Her new husband cut him off."

"Sounds like the step-father's a real sweet guy."

"Not. But if Luther can hang in there long enough, he's due to get a trust fund at thirty-five. Trouble is, that's about ten years from now."

"He'll never live that long. By the way, how's Marian? She was pretty upset the other day."

Eva wondered about his interest. "Got family problems she's trying to work out."

"Everyone's got something—well, good deal. Got to get going. Artwalk's coming up, remember?"

Eva held up her bags. "That's why I'll be baking a lot this week. See you."

He saluted her before closing his door.

Eva walked the short distance to her own alley door. Jane's basket sat just inside where they'd left it. She liked the old lady. Reminded her of her mother. What she could remember of her mother. Maybe she and Marian could figure out a way to help her. Eva was pretty sure Jane had nowhere to go when she got out of the hospital. Maybe they could find her a job and a place to live on Ledbetter Street. She had an idea but needed a few days to mull it over.

Chapter 24

❝ I WISH I'D TOLD BRYAN about Robert years ago when we were kids." Marian sat on a stool as Eva baked. The bread and cookie scents were better than perfume.

"Why didn't you?" Eva wiped her hands on the dishtowel around her waist and reached for a potholder.

"Claire shamed me. Bullied me." She cringed inside at the memories of her mother's words. "She said Bryan wouldn't stick by me. Called me a whore and made me promise not to tell anyone."

"Afraid people would think she wasn't a good mother because you got pregnant?" Eva pulled a tray of cookies out of the oven and reached for the tin of muffin dough.

"Exactly, but said she didn't want me messing up my life by having a baby to raise."

"Guilt—pure guilt she put on you, and you've had to live with it ever since."

"My nana was wonderful, though. Think how different my life would've been if I'd stayed with Nana and raised Robert."

Eva sprinkled colored sugar across what would be huge sugar cookies and set them near the oven to wait their turn. "Make up your mind?"

"I'm going to tell Bryan. Things will start happening fast now. Can I tell you what a great friend you've been?"

A car pulled up, and a man jumped out, hurrying toward them.

"Bryan's coming for me in a little while, picking up Chinese, and we're going to his place for dinner. I'll tell him after."

"After dinner, or after . . ."

"Ha ha," Marian said. "Listen, I want you to know how grateful I am for your support."

"Thanks. Backatcha. You mind waiting on my customers while I grab a quick shower?"

"Sure. I'll stay here until Bryan comes."

"You're a doll," Eva said, and headed for the stairs.

After serving the man who'd run in, Marian perched on a stool behind the counter. It was warm but not unbearable. The blueberry muffins called her name, but she resisted. She had enough problems without adding to her thighs. She phoned Bryan and told him where to find her.

A few customers later, Bryan pulled up outside. Marian checked her makeup in the tiny bathroom mirror and yelled up the stairs. "I'm leaving, and I think the muffins are done."

"Have a good time," Eva called down.

Bryan gave her a peck on the lips when she got into the car. Everything would be all right; he loved her.

He lived on the top floor of a condo on East beach, a short distance from where Claire would live. He'd decorated it as though it were an historical cottage rather than an ultra modern apartment. They ate dinner in an oblong-shaped room furnished with a tiger-oak table and six chairs with silk cushions, and matching pie safe.

He'd set the table with bone china, silver flatware, cloth napkins, and crystal wine glasses. Was he trying to impress her?

He poured them each a glass of plum wine and proposed a toast. "To us. The best is yet to come."

The three bedrooms would be large enough for all of them if Bryan wanted to get married. Robert could have his own room, and Bryan could still have an office at home. He seemed so delighted with her, himself, and their being together that she found it hard to break the spell. She'd waited weeks; the news about Robert could wait a few more minutes. Bryan entertained her with stories of the people he'd worked with and how Tennesseans were different from Texans. Finally, as they cleared the table, she said, "I have something I really need to talk to you about." She carried the serving bowls into the kitchen.

Bryan took the bowls out of her hands and placed them on the counter. He kissed her, her neck, her mouth.

Marian's resolve weakened. She caressed his back and ran her fingers through his thick, curly white hair.

A few moments later, he said, "I wanted to kiss you all evening."

"What stopped you?"

He ran the back of his fingers across her cheek. "Your skin is so smooth."

Part of Marian wanted to push him away, insist they needed to talk, but another part wanted him as much as he wanted her. A few minutes later, she found herself naked in his king-sized, cast-iron bed. Conversation could wait.

They made love slowly at first, enjoying each other's body. He layered kisses on her face and neck. She reciprocated. They worked themselves into a frenzy. She came with a vengeance, and cried out, "I love you, Bryan."

"I love you too, Mar." With a few small pushes and one final fierce one, he let himself go.

As she lay in his arms, she regretted saying those three little words. She'd wanted to save them for a gentle moment. Should she tell him again now? Though he had spoken those three words several times, Marian had saved hers until she was sure. Now was that time for her. "I love you very much, Bryan."

He looked into her eyes and chuckled. "Didn't I just hear that a few minutes ago?"

She giggled. "In the heat of . . . passion. But I want you to know I'm sincere. Saying how I feel isn't easy."

He caressed her cheek with the back of his fingers and curled her hair behind her ear. "I have loved you for so many years . . . and in these past weeks realized just how deep my feelings go."

She toyed with the fine white hairs that grew from his nipples and his chest, trickles of perspiration drying in the air-conditioning. She dozed a bit, and then awoke, startled to find herself still in his arms. Her eyes met his.

"There are so many things I want to show you," he said. "Have you ever been to Paris?"

She shook her head. "Never had the time or money." A rock of dread lay in her stomach.

"I want to take you to Europe. Perhaps next summer, so we'll have plenty of time to plan. I get four weeks vacation. In just a few years I can take early retirement, and we can travel to every place you've ever wanted to go—"

Marian put a finger to his lips. The rock-hard feeling in her stomach had grown so large she knew she had to tell him right then, before he went any further. She searched his face for reassurance, and blurted, "I have a grown son who has Autism Spectrum Disorder.

He's been in the legal custody of the state since he was little, but now he has to come live with me."

Bryan jerked his arms from around her and sat up. "What?"

She pulled the sheet over her breasts and said it again. Bryan stared, his eyes skittering across her face. A seagull's cry outside the window broke the room's utter quiet. The air conditioning blew cool air on her back as she gazed across the breadth of the bed at the man in whom she had placed her faith.

"Did you know this at the class reunion?"

Marian silently implored him to be the understanding person she wanted him to be. "That he'd be coming to live with me? No."

He rubbed the faint white stubble on his chin. His eyes, burning blue, were a stark contrast to his ashen face. "Why didn't you tell me?"

"I'm telling you now. I tried to tell you on several occasions, but the words wouldn't come out."

He sat cross-legged on the bed and pulled a corner of the sheet over his lap. "Let's take this slowly. Explain the whole ball of wax to me."

"It's a little awkward." She reached for her almost empty wine glass on the night table. She rolled the wine on her tongue as she tried to pick her words.

They stared at each other for a few moments.

"Take your time," Bryan said.

She tucked the sheet around her and plumped a pillow behind her back while she tried to gauge how much to tell him.

Bryan sat as far on the other side of the king-sized bed as he could, a view of the Gulf in the window behind him.

"Robert's been in the care of the state since he was a toddler. For years they didn't know he was autistic."

His eyes never wavered from her face. "I don't understand. Why hasn't he always lived with you?"

"My mama—uh—persuaded me to give him up."

"And now she's moving to Galveston. You don't think she'll interfere?"

"Oh, she'll try. But I'm strong enough to engage in hand-to-hand combat with her now."

"So you weren't married when he was born?"

"Right." She felt like she'd been sliced open, her insides exposed.

"Why didn't you get him back—like when you got married?"

"I did try, twice. I hired attorneys, went to court, but the judge said he should stay where he was."

"And now?"

"The lady with whom he's been living has Alzheimer's." She wished she could read his thoughts.

He stroked his chin again.

"I've been visiting Robert for years. Dorothy's a wonderful woman . . . " Her voice broke.

Bryan moved to her side of the bed and took her in his arms. "You poor girl."

The smell of his aftershave made her feel warm inside. "She's like a mother to me." She spoke into his chest. "A good mother."

"So, a double whammy. Lose her and get him at the same time."

"Yes, but getting him would be a good thing. At least I hope so. I have to petition the court again." She wiped her eyes with the edge of the sheet. "Robert doesn't know I'm his mother. He's going to lose the only mother he's ever known." Marian laid her head on Bryan's shoulder again. Everything would be all right. He kissed her bare shoulder, his lips warm.

"I've visited him a lot, on Sundays, though when I was married I didn't go regularly until after Greta died." She pulled back. "In fact, I never told my husband about him. Greta was too little. I'm so ashamed because I've made so many mistakes. I know the investigator is going to use the gaps between visits against me. But I was afraid my husband wouldn't want me and later, that Greta wouldn't understand why Robert couldn't come home. Of course, when she died, that didn't matter any more."

"It's all right, baby." He caressed her hair. "So now, you want him, but the investigator doesn't want you to have him?"

"She's with Adult Protective Services. She thinks he should be in a home or a halfway house or whatever they call it for autistic people."

"And you don't?"

"I'm his mother. He belongs with me. I've wanted him for almost my whole life." What was Bryan was getting at? "Robert doesn't do well with change, so it'll be scary for both of us at first. But I know he'll be okay eventually."

"There's a lot out there about autism."

"Way more than years ago."

"So you want him to come live with you?"

Why did he keep asking her that? "More than I've ever wanted anything in my life. If the judge doesn't give him to me this time, I'll never get another chance."

He pulled her close, resting his chin on her head. "How much longer can he stay with that woman?"

"Not long. Her daughter is helping out now."

"She can't take him?"

"Sure, but Veronica is married and has a couple kids. Besides, she doesn't really want him."

"And you do."

"We've been separated long enough."

"I think I understand, Mar. Of course you want him. I didn't realize how tough your life had been." He patted her arm as if she were a pet.

"I want you to meet him. If he's going to be part of both our lives, you've got to meet him."

Bryan exhaled heavily. The ticking of the wall clock was loud. A line of brown pelicans sailed past the window. She wondered what he thought.

"Bryan—"

"Yes, of course." He kissed her cheek. "When can we do that?"

"Soon." She laid her head on his chest. "I want to ask you something else. Could you get off work and come testify for me?"

He tightened his hold on her. "Sure."

She wanted to reveal her last secret, but something stopped her. "You're the best, Bryan. I love you so much."

He stroked her shoulder and pecked at her neck with little kisses. "You want to stay the night, sweetie? Or should I take you home?"

"Home," she said. "But will you hold me a little longer first?"

"Gladly." He leaned against the headboard, pulling her with him.

Marian let the man she'd loved for so many years coddle her. Though they'd taken the long way around to having a relationship, plainly they were meant to be together.

When he dropped her at home later, Marian checked her voice mail. "Marian, I need you. It's an emergency!" It was Veronica. Dorothy's daughter.

Fear chilling her to the bone, Marian returned the call.

"Mother wandered off last night—"

Marian pounded the table. "Why didn't you call?"

"We looked for her all day. You can't imagine—"

"Did you find her?"

Veronica howled. "In a ditch. They only knew it was her because of her Alzheimer's bracelet. She was there all night."

"Is she going to be okay?"

"Oh, Marian. No. They think she was hit by a car."

Marian collapsed onto the floor. She clutched her chest. She couldn't stand it. For Dorothy. For herself. That poor wonderful woman wandering around in the night. Stumbling in the streets. Looking for home. Confused. Frightened. Run down by a car.

Marian lay on the floor, hugging herself. She listened but couldn't respond. She couldn't lose Dorothy so fast. She'd just made peace with Alzheimer's taking Dorothy away. What would she do without her?

"Marian," Veronica said after some time and blew her nose into the phone.

Marian reached for the tissue box on the coffee table and blew her own nose. "I'm here, V." Sniff. "Are you okay?"

"No," she said with a long, long sigh. "But there's something I have to tell you."

Marian lay down on the rug on her back and stared at the ceiling, afraid to hear whatever it was Veronica was going to say.

"Marian . . . are you still there?" Veronica had stopped crying, yet her voice, husky, held a tentative note.

"What? Is it Robert?"

"Marian, I called Yvette. I—I thought if the guardian dies the county should be informed. I'm so sorry."

"I don't understand. What is it?"

"Oh, Marian, when I told Yvette my mother had died, Yvette came for Robert! She took him away."

Chapter 25

JANE LIKED THE HOSPITAL SOCIAL worker. The woman sat on the foot of her bed with her clipboard and took down Jane's medical history. She'd gotten a little pushy about Jane's family and gave up when Jane wouldn't tell her anything. The name Jane Doe fit her. She certainly wasn't the same Jane she'd been when she'd been married to her husband and borne him a child. Ever since he'd died and left her with nothing, she was a different Jane. Yes, she liked Doe. A female deer out in the wild on her own.

She smoothed the sheet and coverlet across her flat chest and pushed her hair back. Time for her favorite soap. Since coming to the hospital, she'd been able to catch up with what happened since she'd sold her television. Not much. Soaps were like life. Time seemed realer. No, *more real*. That's right.

The door opened and a tall doctor with one eye a bit off-kilter came into the room. "How are you doing today, Mrs. Doe?"

"Miss Doe." Jane folded her hands on her lap. "No missus." He reminded her of her son before—well, before he'd left this world.

"Whatever you say, Miss Doe."

"I don't think I really have a bad heart."

"Oh you don't?"

"No. Did I tell you how much like my son you are?"

"Where is he?"

"Oh, he's no longer with us."

"He's deceased, you mean?"

"Flu. Years ago."

"Was he your only child?"

"I don't know why the Good Lord never gave us another one." She twiddled her thumbs. As soon as he left, she could turn on the TV.

"How are you feeling today?"

"Fine. But I don't want to leave."

He wrote something in her chart. "Two things. I want to monitor you for a few days since I gave you that heart medication. Secondly, you're going to have to leave eventually. Social Services will see what they can do for you, though."

She'd miss looking at him. She might be old, but that didn't mean she couldn't appreciate a good-looking man—especially one who looked like an older version of her son. "You're such a good man."

He put down the chart. "Let me check your heart."

Jane didn't mind someone with his looks sticking that cold stethoscope inside her hospital nightie. She started to say something, but he put a finger to his lips.

"Lean forward so I can listen through your back."

The doctor smelled like soap, some kind of man's soap.

"Everything sounds good. Your heart attack was very mild. The fall gave you a slight concussion and, of course, you're malnourished, but other than that—"

"So, you're really kicking me out, Doc?"

"It won't be long, Miss Doe." He took her hand. "Are you sure there's no one we can call to come get you? If you were my mother, I'd want to know where you were."

Knock. Knock. Eva Best poked her head inside. "Should I come back another time?"

"Come on in," Jane said.

"Are you her daughter, ma'am?" The doctor hooked the chart on the foot of the bed.

"Oh, no. Just . . . a friend."

"Well, I'll leave you two alone." He detoured around Eva and left, closing the door behind him.

"Cute doc," Eva said. "Bet you're getting a kick out of that. Was he checking you out?"

"What are you doing here again?" If people kept coming in, she'd never get to see her soaps.

"Just thought I'd see how you are."

"Want to play rummy?" Jane reached into the drawer next to her bed and came up with a pack of cards.

"Whatever makes you happy."

"Drag up a chair." Jane started dealing the cards. "They're kicking me out soon. You still got my stuff?" She hoped no one had gotten her spot at the dumpster.

Eva arranged her cards. She licked her lips. "Yeah." She glanced at Jane. "But I gotta confess we went through it and got rid of things. Especially that mullet. Reeked so bad."

"Well, thank God for that." She drew a card and threw down another one.

"Where will you go?" Eva laid a queen on the discard pile.

"Why, did somebody take my place?" She had three tens, two

pair, and a bunch of other cards like what Eva had been discarding. She could safely throw down a queen, too.

"That's not answering my question. Do you have someplace beside the street to go, Miss Doe?"

"What's it to you?" Jane drew a third jack and discarded an ace. "If you're not going to let me live in your house, what do you care?"

Eva stabbed the air with the card she drew. "Hey, don't get your panties in a wad, old woman. I just wondered if I could help." She stuck the card in between two others and discarded with a vengeance.

Jane almost laughed at how defensive Eva got. "What are you, a social worker? I can take care of myself." She didn't want Eva to see the idea pleased her. Could Eva really do something? Could she let her?

Eva threw her cards down and stood. "Jesus, I just wanted to help." She headed for the door.

"I'm sorry." Jane reached her hand out. "I didn't mean so sound so harsh."

"I don't know. I had an idea, but it may not work."

"Don't go," Jane said. "Stay, and let's finish this game at least." She liked Eva and the idea of Eva helping her.

Eva stared at her as though mulling things over. "I'd better go."

"I didn't mean to be such an old windbag," Jane said. "Stay?"

Eva stared at her for a moment. "I'd best go for now." She left before Jane could say anything else.

Chapter 26

MARIAN REACHED ACROSS THE CONSOLE and took Bryan's warm hand in her cold one. They were driving to Houston to see Robert. She'd thrown up before Bryan picked her up and fought the urge to do so again. "I'm glad you're finally going to meet Robert."

"I wouldn't miss it. He's part of you, your history. Are you worried about it?" He glanced at her with their son's eyes. He wore a little smile, one she'd grown fond of over the past few weeks. He exuded confidence while she felt discombobulated.

"You've read about autistic people so I don't think you'll be surprised by what you see." A hollowness hovered at the base of her throat. She wasn't as nervous about his meeting Robert as she was about his recognizing him. What would he do if he did?

She had to risk it. For their relationship to go anywhere, he had to know what Robert was like. And when Bryan sat on that witness stand, Marian wanted him to be able to answer honestly that he'd met Robert and would accept him as part of their lives.

"He probably won't talk to me much, right? How will I know if he likes me?" He changed lanes to avoid construction.

"You won't know one way or the other." She couldn't remember Robert ever having expressed a dislike for something, except missing his favorite television shows and some foods. He definitely didn't like squishy mashed potatoes.

Bryan nodded and watched the road. They drove in silence most of the way. Marian stared out the window and tried to hold her hands still. She wondered what Bryan was thinking. He'd gone along with her request with no protest. Although he seemed very quiet, she didn't think it was more than usual.

Was it just a few days earlier she'd gotten that terrible phone call from Veronica? She had immediately called Parker Benavides. Parker had been wonderful, assuring her he'd take care of everything, which he had. The following morning he'd gone down to the Harris County Courthouse, filed the paperwork, and gotten Robert moved back to Dorothy's house under Veronica's supervision.

When she and Bryan pulled up in front of Dorothy's home, Yvette's car sat out front. How she had the nerve to show up after what she'd done, and after the judge called her boss and ordered Robert returned to Veronica, Marian had no idea. The woman had chutzpah. What were her motives? When they rang the doorbell, Yvette came out onto the stoop as though she'd been lying in wait.

"What are you doing here?" Marian asked.

Yvette's smile didn't extend to her eyes. "Robert is on my caseload, Ms. Reid." She stood on the step above them like she was the queen on her throne.

"Mind moving aside and letting us pass? It's hot out here." Marian stepped up and took the door handle, forcing Yvette to step back inside. Bryan squeezed Marian's hand when she pulled him in behind her. Heavy summer drapes covered the windows so the inside was cool from the window units. The smell of something scorched came from the kitchen. Muffled voices came from another room.

Marian switched from her sunglasses to her regular ones. She started to ask how Robert was doing but stopped, realizing Yvette was totally the wrong person to ask.

Yvette stood between Marian and the den. "You're not to say anything to him about your lawsuit."

She had no right to tell her that, but Marian wasn't planning to talk to him about it anyway. "What's he doing?"

"You'll see for yourself. He barely eats. He wanders. He doesn't understand change, Ms. Reid—Marian. He doesn't understand why his foster sister is living here and Dorothy is not."

"Don't you think I know he doesn't understand change? Don't you know that's why we had you bring him back here? We're all worried and concerned about him." She frowned at Yvette.

"Aren't you going to introduce me to your friend?" Yvette turned her attention to Bryan.

Robert entered the room and passed them without indicating he'd seen them as he headed toward the kitchen.

"I'm sure you know this is Bryan. Bryan, Yvette."

Bryan put out his hand. "Nice to meet you."

Yvette looked him over before extending her hand.

Marian gritted her teeth and wished Yvette weren't there.

Robert meandered back the way he'd come. Barefoot and dressed in a wrinkled black T-shirt and Dockers, he looked like he'd just woken up.

"Hi, Robert," Marian said, reaching for his arm. "Is Veronica here someplace?"

"In the den," he said, continuing into the den. "Watching television with Robert."

"Bryan, let's go in there."

Yvette said, "Veronica's very sweet, Ms. Reid. She loves Robert. But Robert is very needy. You know that."

Marian wanted to slug her. "He'd be a lot less needy if you hadn't jerked him out of his home, agitating him. Is V having a problem?"

"Veronica has trouble watching Robert. He's restless. The whole situation is impossible."

"It wouldn't be if you'd just agree to let me take him."

"I can't do that. That's for the judge to decide." She gave Marian what could only be described as a pointed look.

"At least let me have him after the funeral until the trial."

Yvette snorted. "Do you think I'm stupid? Then you can tell her honor how well things are working—whether they are or not."

Marian went into the den. Robert perched on the floor in his usual spot, the television blaring. Marian grabbed the remote and reduced the volume.

Veronica sprang from the far end of the sofa. "I'm so glad you're here." Like her mother, she towered over Marian and bent down to fold her in her arms.

"How's the social work business?"

Veronica's hair was disheveled, her face lined and pale. Her body was too thin, but to Marian, V always looked underfed.

Veronica pushed her long, blond hair over her shoulders and slapped a gold barrette around it. "The ranch takes up so much of my time that another worker and I share a position now. I'm only working half days." Her skin had grown leathery, as though she had spent too much time in the sun.

"It's good they'll work with you like that." The air in the room smelled stale. "They had no problem with you coming down to Houston for a while?"

"I have a good boss." She indicated Robert with her head.

"Veronica, I brought Bryan to meet y'all. Bryan Mosley. The man I'm dating."

Marian went to the doorway and found Yvette and Bryan just outside, engrossed in conversation. What could they possibly have to talk about? "Bryan, want to come in?" She took his hand and hissed, "What'd she want?"

"Tell you later," he whispered.

"Veronica, Robert, I want you to meet Bryan Mosley, my friend from Galveston." Her breath held, Marian watched Bryan, wondering if he'd notice that the shape of the younger man's head, his hands, and even his lean body were a reflection of his own.

Veronica held out her hand. "Very nice to meet you."

"You, too," Bryan said when he shook her hand.

Veronica studied Bryan's face for a moment and glanced at Marian, eyebrows raised.

Marian leaned down to Robert. "Robert, I want you to meet someone."

"TV show, Marian. TV show." He didn't look up.

Marian glanced at her watch. "Okay, ten minutes, and then I want you to talk to me." She stood. "Sit on the couch, Bryan. I'll take the easy chair."

They sat in silence for several minutes, everyone staring at the TV. Yvette stood in the doorway. "Guess I'll be seeing you on Friday, Marian. Goodbye, everybody."

"*Adios.*" Marian didn't know what she meant, but wasn't going to give Yvette the pleasure of knowing that. When Veronica returned from seeing Yvette out, she said to Bryan, "You're not—"

"From the island? He is now, Veronica. He moved away and recently moved back." She tried to communicate with her expression that Veronica shouldn't ask questions, but Veronica didn't seem to be reading her.

"That's not what I was going to ask."

"Sorry. Hey, could we get something to drink?"

"Oh, I didn't mean to be so rude. It's just with everything that's been going on. Coffee?" Veronica started for the door.

"Sure," Bryan said. "I'll take a cup." He sat with his hands in his lap.

"I'll take tea, myself," Marian said. "You want decaf, Bry? Or caffeinated?"

"Caffeinated. Want me to help?"

"No, you just stay put and watch TV with Robert. We'll be right back." Marian followed Veronica. When they got to the kitchen, Marian found a new stainless steel kettle on the stove. She emptied it, refilled it, and put it on the fire.

"Marian," Veronica said, as she set out the cups, "is he who I think he is?"

"Pu—leeze don't say anything, V."

Veronica stared down at her, eyes flaring. "He doesn't know?"

"I don't want him to know, not yet, anyway."

"Any idiot can see Robert is Bryan's spittin' image—except for the hair."

"You've got to promise me you won't mention it," Marian begged. "Promise."

"Okay." Veronica chuckled. "It's not my business anyway." She filled two cups with coffee from the coffee maker. "What does he take?"

"I'll fix it." She doctored Bryan's coffee. "Will you take it in while I brew my tea?"

"Sure. And mums the word." She picked up two cups and left.

Marian pulled the boiling kettle from the fire and poured water over her t-bag with shaking hands.

When Veronica returned, she said, "So y'all have court on Friday?"

"Where'd you get that idea?" She poured some milk into her cup.

"Denby. She really doesn't want you to get Robert. She can be a real bitch, by the way."

"Parker must have forgotten to tell me in all the brouhaha."

"He must. Denby said you're asking for temporary guardianship pending a final hearing. Pretty smart move if you ask me."

"It's all happening so fast now that Dorothy . . ." Her eyes met Veronica's, both of them tearing up.

Veronica fanned her eyes with her hand. "It's for the best, Marian. I can't stay forever. The sooner you take Robert, the better. He's so agitated. He wears me out, constantly pacing, looking for her. He's not sleeping and barely eating. Remember when he was little and my dad left?"

"Oh, he's not that bad, is he?"

"Just about. I'm having such a hard time. I've still got the funeral to tend to and then this house to deal with—"

Robert lumbered into the doorway where he hovered, thinner than just a month ago. His T-shirt and pants hung on him.

Marian took his hand. "Want something to drink?"

"TV show over."

"Okay. I want to introduce you to my friend. He was in the den with you. Will you please shake his hand when I introduce you?"

Robert looked at her, past her, but didn't pull his hand away.

Marian took her cup of tea, and they walked back to the den. She dropped Robert's hand. "Say hello to Bryan, Robert. This is my friend, Bryan. Say hello."

"Hello, Bryan."

Bryan kept his seat but held out his hand to shake Robert's. "Hello, Robert." Bryan gave Marian a look.

Marian wasn't sure what that meant, but merely said, "Shake Bryan's hand, Robert."

Robert put his hand in Bryan's, shook it up and down once, and dropped it. He stepped over beside Dorothy's empty rocking chair and stood there silently.

"Would you like to show Marian's friend your room?" Veronica asked, glancing at the three of them.

Robert walked out of the room.

"Go with him, Bryan," Marian urged. "Follow him. It's just around the corner."

Bryan set his coffee down and left the room also.

Veronica said, "Do you think you could come see Robert every day? He'd get used to seeing you frequently."

Marian ran her fingers through her hair. "I want to, but with the shop . . . I just can't get away. I've lost my help. I had an idea of someone to hire, but . . ." She bit her lip. "I just don't know how reliable the young woman would be. And the carpenter is supposed to come make changes upstairs." Shaking her head, Marian said, "I'll see what I can do about getting back here before Friday, at least."

"I understand." Veronica sipped her coffee and put the cup on the table. "Everything is such a mess."

"Listen, V, what is Yvette's problem?"

"She just doesn't want you to have Robert."

"Well, I know that. I just don't understand why."

"She doesn't confide in me. She knows we—I think you should have him. She just stops by, seems like every five minutes this week, and asks if you've been here."

"She doesn't seem to care that I have a business to run, and that I have to have a room built for Robert." Marian began pacing. "I can't do everything at one time."

"She's not thinking about you at all. I don't think she's thinking about Robert, either. It's like she's got it in for you." Veronica reached for her cup.

"She's been like that since she came to my place. And I bet my mother only made it worse. She popped up from nowhere and found out what's going on and threatened to do all kinds of things."

"What's that about? Why does she care at this point?"

"I've never understood my mama. Can your own mother be pure evil? I don't think she ever wanted me, and she never wanted me to have Robert."

"I'm glad my mom wasn't like that."

Tears ran down both their faces.

"God, I loved your mother."

"Me, too." Grabbing a tissue from a nearby box, Veronica wiped her eyes and sighed. "Anyway, I've been wondering. Who's going to testify for you?"

"Me—and Bryan. I don't know if I can get anyone from the street. They're all so busy, and Artwalk is the day after the hearing."

"What about Eva?"

"Eva's can't come. She doesn't have anyone to help her in her coffee shop."

"So I guess that means she won't be coming on Friday. What about next week? Think she'll find someone by then?"

"Oh, Holy Mother—next week is Eva's mastectomy. If the hearing's on Friday, it wouldn't last until Monday, would it? Are you sure Yvette said this coming Friday?"

"I'm sure. She was angry. I heard her on her cell. She isn't ready for something."

Marian slapped her knee. "Not ready for the hearing. That could be why Parker got it set so soon. To get the jump on them."

"All I know is she spent more time on her cell than talking to me or Robert."

"I've got to call my attorney. Got to find out how long he thinks court will take. I'm supposed to be at the hospital next Monday with Eva. I promised her."

"I don't think you're going to make it," Veronica said. "Yvette was talking about several people testifying."

Marion stood and sat down again. "Eva's my best friend in the whole world. I can't let her down."

"Don't plan on it." She patted Marian's knee. "Maybe something'll come up."

Bryan followed Robert into the den. She glanced at their faces. Both deadpan. Identical. If Bryan caught on, would he say something? Or would he be distracted by Robert's affliction? Marian waited for him to speak, but he sat down and picked up his coffee cup, sipping from it.

She turned to Robert. "Thank you for showing Bryan your room."

"You are welcome, Marian." He touched Dorothy's rocker as he slid down and sat cross-legged on the floor again. Picking up the remote, he began flipping channels.

Chapter 27

AFTER A SUBDUED RETURN TRIP, Marian begged off and said goodnight. Even though it would have been her preference to spend the rest of the evening with Bryan in her bed, she had a lot to do before the hearing on Friday. She walked down to Ron's Grocery, which, though it stood only half a block from her place, might well have been in a different world. Ron sold beer and wine and cigarettes and lottery tickets and kept lewd magazines under the counter. Upstairs he had four apartments that rented by the week, which, she supposed, was better than by the hour. No one Marian knew had ever been upstairs.

Little black blobs of grime covered the sidewalk. Cars often double-parked while someone ran in for beer in a brown paper bag. The dumpster overflowed within feet of the entrance to the alley, the stench hanging in the air.

Marian had made a decision and wanted to act on it before she could change her mind. She pushed through the glass door and found Ron behind the counter.

"Ron," she said, standing beside the line of customers, none of whom she knew or had any desire to know. "How's it going?"

"Miss Reid, what brings you into my humble establishment?" His grin was a leer. His stubble looked dirty. His teeth could have been whiter. His shirt could have been buttoned up over his thin, sleeveless undershirt.

"Which apartment does Chloe live in? I need to talk to her." Marian sidestepped a tattooed woman in a skimpy muscle shirt.

"Three, but she ain't there."

Relieved she would not have to climb a bug-infested staircase, Marian pressed on. "She at work?"

"She in jail." He raised his eyebrows and leered again.

"No, seriously." Marian could understand if Darryl had been arrested but not Chloe.

"Cops arrested her and Darryl and took the kid."

Marian shivered. "Leo? What happened? Was he okay?"

"Screaming bloody murder so I guess so." He handed change to a man and then crooked his finger at Marian and walked down to the end of the counter.

Marian breathed shallowly. Ron's body odor was almost as bad as the smell from the dumpster.

"Look," he said, "you can't tell nobody. I ain't one to rat out nobody, but one of the other kids in my apartments told me Darryl was hurting that kid while the girl was at work. So I called that number out of the phone book."

"Oh, Ron, you did the right thing." If it'd been anyone else, Marian would've reached out to him, but she could only bring herself to nod. "Why didn't they just arrest Darryl?"

"Who can figure out a cop's mind? Not me. Anyhow, I gotta get back. Maybe you can help that girl."

Marian watched him for a minute as he went back to ringing up sales. She had new respect for Ron. He was probably doing the best he could. Everyone had to make a living. From the looks of things, his business greatly surpassed hers.

She skirted his customers on her way out. It was almost nine p.m. Visiting hours at the jail had to be way past. She wanted to see Chloe. See if she could help her, get her out of jail. There was so much to do before the hearing on Friday. Talking to Eva topped the list. Marian headed toward Coffee & More.

She didn't want to leave Eva in a lurch, but surely she'd understand if the court hearing carried over to Monday. Eva would have to find someone else to stay with her. Not that she really needed anyone. The hospital didn't require it. It was just something that Marian had promised, that she thought a friend should do. Who could take her place? Lupe? One of the girls at the barbecue? If Marian told Eva right now, tonight, as she intended, Eva would have several days to ask around.

Marian pulled open the door of Coffee & More. No one was inside. "Eva," she called. No answer. The floor was wet. Water ran somewhere in the back. Marian tiptoed past the counter. Eva stood wringing out the mop over the sink.

"Hey, what are you doing?"

Eva shrugged. "Business has been slow tonight so I thought I'd clean up and close early."

"Need help?" Marian rubbed her lower lip.

"Nah. Just about finished. You take Bryan to see Robert?"

"He saw him all right. And said almost nothing all the way home."

"He out there?"

"Went home. I told him I had lots to do, and he didn't try to persuade me any different." She'd mull that over later, but now she needed to address the problem of who would take her place at the hospital.

Eva leaned the mop against the wall and dried her hands. "Want to get something to eat at the Taqueria?"

"I'm not hungry, but I'll go with you."

"I'm famished. Can't face another of my own sandwiches."

After Eva locked up, they walked down to the corner. Candles burned in red jars at every table. Marian and Eva took their regular one.

"Hey, girls. What's up?" Lupe asked, putting out a basket of chips and salsa.

"Nothing much. Eva's hungry. I'll just have iced tea," Marian said. "I guess Chloe's not here."

"She's in jail," Lupe said. "The Sheriff's Department arrested both of them yesterday." She got a pitcher of iced tea from a nearby stand and returned, pouring them each a glass.

"That's what I heard. But why arrest her is what I don't understand. When she was trying on clothes, I saw bruises he put on her."

"Jane told me she saw him hit and kick Chloe," Eva said, shaking salt over the basket of chips.

"Who's Jane?" Lupe asked.

"That homeless woman I chased down the alley," Marian said. "Eva goes to see her at the hospital."

"Eva," Lupe said, "that's sweet of you."

"I just wanted to make sure she wasn't going to die or sue Marian or me."

"I told you I didn't do anything to her." She stirred her tea.

"That's what she said. She's really nice. She used to have a home." Eva scooped salsa onto a saucer and spooned it onto a chip.

"She's not a dog," Lupe said. "Don't think you can take her in like a pet. I know how you girls are."

"It's not me, this time," Marian said. "It's her." She wasn't ready to mention offering Chloe a job yet. What if it was Chloe who hurt the baby and not Darryl? Or worse yet, both of them? Or Chloe knew Darryl hurt Leo and didn't stop him?

"You need to hire someone in your shop, Eva, so why don't you hire the old woman?" Lupe asked.

"Jane. She says her name is Jane Doe," Eva said.

"You didn't answer me," Lupe said.

"I've thought of that. She needs a job and a place to stay, but I don't have any place for her to stay."

"She can stay at the Salvation Army for five days," Lupe said, "after that she'll have to pay."

"You have that storage room in the back of the shop," Marian said with a teasing note in her voice.

"It's full of my shit," Eva said.

"Donate your shit," Lupe said. "I'd help you clean it out. I think it's nice you want to help that old lady. You have a bathroom downstairs so she'd have a room and a bath, and there's the downstairs kitchen you use for baking."

"Her name is Jane," Eva said. "Quit calling her *that old lady*." She gave Lupe a look. "And I'll think about it. Would you take my order? I'm hungry."

"*Sí*. You're always hungry." She put her hands on her hips. "You want your usual?"

Eva nodded. Lupe flipped her skirt and headed for the kitchen.

Marian pointed at chip at Eva. "See what you started?"

"I don't care. It's a good idea. I like her." Eva busied herself with her napkin, not meeting Marian's eyes.

"What's that about?" Marian asked. "You're not crying?"

"I don't cry," Eva said. "You should have seen her when I took her those fried pies. She was so pitiful. I can't stand the idea of her going back on the street. Our country should be disgusted with itself at how we treat poor people."

"You're right. But you need to be careful before you jump into something you can't handle."

"Look who's talking. Anyway, turns out Jane is pretty feisty. Makes me laugh."

"Uh huh."

"By the way, remember Luther? That little artist with the bluest eyes in the world?"

Marian picked up another chip. Bluest eyes except for Bryan and Robert. "Everyone knows Luther."

"You didn't hear about him? Troy found him in the alley. Turns out he's half-starved and has hepatitis."

"I thought he was a trust baby," Marian said.

"He will be if he lives to thirty-five." Eva gulped her tea.

"Omigod. Is he going to be okay?"

"Maybe I'll go see him when I'm at the hospital seeing Jane."

"I was just thinking about Chloe. We've all got problems, but she really does. If Children's Protective Services got ahold of Leo, she'll never get him back."

"We're talking about Chloe, not you."

"I know. By the way, Eva, I've got to tell you something, and I hope you won't get mad."

"When have I ever gotten mad at you?" Eva stirred the salsa with a chip. "What's the problem?"

"I'm so confused. So much has happened I can't even remember what I've told you."

"What now?"

Marian scratched her head. "Remember I told you I hired this lawyer, Parker Benavides, and he was going to represent me in Houston so I could get Robert?"

"Yeah, sure, he does probate work in Harris County."

"And after Dorothy died, Yvette took Robert. Then Parker got the judge to make her bring him back. I told you about that."

"Right, I'm with you."

"We're having an immediate hearing because APS wants to ship him off—"

"You want to cut to the chase here?" Eva's eyes could have bored a hole through the side of ship.

"When I was at Dorothy's today with Bryan—"

"Yeah? I'm getting confused. How did that go?"

"That woman was there."

"The Denby woman?"

Marian took a swallow of iced tea. "She's really got it in for me. I don't know what's with her, but she talked to Bryan out of my hearing, and I don't know what she said and then she left and—"

"Marian—" Eva made bug eyes at her.

"Okay. Okay. Turns out, court is this coming Friday."

"This Friday?" Eva's eyebrows drew together, making her forehead one huge wrinkle. "Wait. What are you saying?"

"Eva, you know I'd do anything for you. You're my best friend—sometimes I feel we're even closer. You could be the younger sister I never had."

Eva slammed down her glass. "You're going to court this Friday?"

"Wait—what're you doing? Let me explain."

"If you're saying you can't be with me next Monday at the hospital—I think I'm going to be sick."

Marian twisted her napkin. "My attorney . . . Parker . . . says he doesn't know . . . but thinks we can't get through the hearing in one day."

Eva's face turned red. She scooted her chair back and rose. "Goddammit, Marian. You promised."

"He's my son. He's the most important thing—" How could she explain it so Eva would understand?

"And I'm what? Not important?" Eva's face looked like it would explode.

"If it's possible, I'll be there, but until we get into the hearing, we just won't know."

"Oh, be honest. You never wanted to be there with me in the first place." Eva stood over Marian, her fists and teeth clenched.

Marian reached for her friend. "That's not true. You know how I feel about you."

"How could you *do* such a thing?" Eva stamped her foot.

"I didn't schedule it, Eva. Anyway, I have to make a choice. He's my son."

"So you chose Robert over me. I guess I do understand." Eva threw her napkin on the table. "Well, I hope it all works out for you." She stalked out of the restaurant.

Marian watched her go, knowing there was nothing else she could say, nothing that would make Eva feel better. Lupe walked up holding Eva's hot plate with a kitchen towel. "Take it back," Marian said.

Lupe shook her head and left. Marian stayed for a few more minutes, just staring into the street.

When she left the Taqueria, it was almost ten. Troy had begun pulling the brown paper out of his windows. He tapped on the glass, beckoning her inside. She didn't feel like company. Her insides were jittery, and she felt terrible that Eva thought she didn't care. She didn't want to hurt Troy's feelings, but she didn't think she could be civil at that moment. She waved and kept going.

"Hey, Marian." Troy ran to catch up with her. He grabbed her elbow. "What's up with you? I thought you'd like to see my gallery."

He wore a T-shirt, khaki shorts, and flip-flops. Same body-type as Bryan. What was it with thin men around her? Why couldn't he be short and fat?

"I'm not in the mood right now." She started away and burst into tears, covering her face with her hands.

He kept pace with her. "I'll buy you a Dr Pepper."

She stopped and looked up at him through her tears. Why couldn't he be rude and insensitive instead of sweet and cajoling? "What do you want?"

"Nothing." His eyes roved over her face. "Just thought you'd like to see inside since you were trying to peek through the paper the other day. Something's wrong, right?"

She wiped her eyes. "A lot of things."

"Aw, come on, I'm a great listener and besides, there's nothing a cold Dr Pepper can't cure."

She laughed in spite of herself. She might as well go with him since he wouldn't give up. He led her inside, his arm draped over her shoulders as if she were a little child and he, the comforting teacher.

The acrid smell of patchouli floated out when he opened the door. The Beach Boys' "Surfer Girl" played in the background. "Sixties retro," she said.

"Not original, I'm afraid, but—" He held his hands out.

"Still, with so many baby boomers out there, I think you'll attract attention." LP album covers were scattered over one wall. "And you have the range of the decade, from rock and roll to hard rock. Look at that old surfboard. I remember when they used to be that long, what is it, six and a half feet?"

"A little more."

"Who's your featured artist?"

"She's from California. Rain Fennel. You probably haven't heard of her."

"Rain?"

"Well, actually, she's literally a child of the sixties." He'd shoved his hands in the back pockets of his shorts and stood watching her. "Her parents were activists at Berkeley. You might have known them. They graduated from Ball High."

"I don't think I knew any Fennels." Marian smiled halfheartedly, trying to be polite. He was nice, and she didn't want to be rude. "But Rain, hey, that's cool. Know what I mean?"

He laughed. "That's not her real name. Not her last name. Her father's name was John Lloyd. Her mother was a Benavides. Marie Benavides."

Too coincidental. There couldn't be a connection to Parker. No way. "They have any relatives left around here?"

"I think Marie has a brother who works at one of the refineries in Texas City."

Unlikely connection. But it didn't matter.

"Rain's coming in tomorrow night for the weekend. She'll be the one on Saturday night dressed like a hippie. Right out of the pages of Rolling Stone, back then. Wait until you see her." He put his hand on her back and walked with her.

Was he just being gentlemanly or was he hitting on her? Regardless, she liked the warmth of his hand. "I wish I had more energy," she said. "Maybe on Saturday I can get a good look at everything. Do you mind?"

Troy stepped behind the counter and pulled out two Dr Pepper glasses. Behind him was a faux Dr Pepper dispenser that was really a refrigerator. He filled both glasses and handed one to her. "You want to talk about it?"

"Not really." She took the drink. "Why don't we talk about you? You're married? Divorced? I haven't seen any signs of a wife."

"She died in a car wreck. And you?"

"Oh, God, sorry." She hoped he wasn't offended. "My husband

left after our daughter died. On top of Greta dying, my mama drove him nuts, always interfering. Just wish he'd taken me with him. She's still causing me grief." She glanced up to see him watching her. "Don't know how you got me started on that."

"I used to be a therapist. People tell me things."

"Way more than you wanted to know. Sorry." Marian perched halfway on a barstool and ran her finger down the smooth edges of the glass counter. "So, are you excited about your first Artwalk?"

He nodded. "Very."

"I saw your write-up. Pretty good. People like to get free food and wine or punch. You're having food, right?"

"Yep. What did we eat in the sixties?"

"Fritos and canned bean dip."

"Got some of that."

"Dr Peppers and RC Colas."

He held his glass toward her. "Got those as well as Coke and Seven-Up and a few Big Reds."

"All right. We didn't drink a lot of wine."

"Yeah, but I'm not providing rum and Coke or bourbon and Coke for everyone on the island. Just this one time I have all those sodas, but I'm not going to have them all the time."

"Don't blame you. I'm having a hard time remembering what kind of junk food we ate in the sixties besides Fritos and bean dip."

"Chex mix. They still serve that in places."

"Ugh." She put a hand on his arm. "Let me get out of your hair now. Thanks for letting me have a look."

"Marian." His hand rested on hers, his face all eyes and a small pursing of the lips. "Seriously, I'm a good listener. I got it that your mother is a problem, but I suspect there's more to that story."

"A lot more. I've just had to make hard decisions."

"We all do sometimes." He walked her to the front of the gallery and opened the door. "Tell Eva I appreciate her keeping my secret."

Marian nodded. She suspected she wouldn't be telling Eva anything for a while.

Chapter 28

MARIAN WAITED IN THE JAIL'S visitor room, surprised at the appearance of most of the people. They looked just like her, regular folks.

When Chloe picked up the telephone that connected to the one Marian held, she said, "I didn't hurt Leo. I could never do that."

"Where's Leo now?"

"With a foster family. A Child Protective Services worker told me."

"I hope you get him back before he's forty."

Chloe frowned. "I hope I get him back, period."

"Did you know I have a son?" Marian didn't know why she was telling the young woman her personal business.

"I knew you had a daughter."

Who had told her about Greta? Didn't matter. "But I also have a son. He's lived with other people for forty years."

Chloe nodded and stared at Marian as if she knew the story. "What's his name?"

"Robert. Don't you want to know why he hasn't lived with me?" She watched Chloe watching her.

"If you want to tell me, Ms. Reid."

"Marian." She tilted her head at Chloe and looked at her over her glasses. "My mama made me give him up for adoption. And he's autistic. That means his brain developed differently from other people's."

"I know what Autism Spectrum Disorder is."

Surprised, Marian pursed her lips. "Well, good then. I'm trying to get the court to let my son come live with me. The lady who has been caring for him died." She took a deep breath and let it out.

"So after all these years you might get him back? I hope they give my son back."

"I'm trying, anyway." At the expense of a hurt best friend.

"Good luck," Chloe said. "But why are you telling me this?"

"How much is your bail?"

Chloe looked surprised. "Twenty-five thousand."

"Where's your husband?"

"Jail, same as me. But his bail is a hundred thousand. He won't be getting out either. Why are you asking?"

Marian inspected Chloe's face. There was something about her that drew Marian in. Had from the first time they met. "I need your help, Chloe. My hearing starts tomorrow, and I need someone to work for me."

"But I can't make my bond."

"I'll pay the bail bondsman. That is, if you promise not to run off. If you promise to come work for me this afternoon. I'll pay you a fair wage, and you can have clothes at a huge discount."

Chloe stared back and didn't respond. Her brow wrinkled as though thinking required extreme effort.

"And I forgot, but when you get Leo back, you can bring him to work. We'll set up a little area for him in the back. Put a baby bed or a playpen back there."

"Why would you do this for me? For Leo?"

"I need you. You need me. We can help each other." She hoped Chloe wasn't too proud to accept her offer.

"You don't know anything about me."

"Lupe vouched for you. And I like what I've seen. You're a hard worker."

"I don't know. Darryl—"

"Darryl wouldn't like it, I know. But Darryl's in jail and probably doesn't have anyone to make his bail."

"True. But when he gets out . . ."

Marian hoped that would never happen. "We'll deal with him when that happens. Around here they usually don't let child abusers off easily."

Chloe flinched.

"I hate to sound impatient, but if you don't accept my offer, I've got to find someone else." She started to get up, hoping Chloe would stop her.

"Okay," Chloe shouted into the phone. "I'll do it."

"I'll make the arrangements, and as soon as you get out, come to my store."

When she got back to the shop, Marian put together some outfits for court. She made a list of things Chloe needed to know and one for herself because there was so much to remember, she needed reminders.

A few hours later, Chloe, dressed in her black pants and the Miguel's Taqueria shirt, came inside carrying coffee from Coffee & More. "Here I am, Ms. Reid. You're my angel."

"Marian. Stop with the Ms. Reid. Marian."

"Marian. You're still my angel. My benefactor."

"Your employer, and your friend, I hope." They had something in common. The government was involved in both their lives. "Good timing. I'm just getting ready to go to my lawyer's office. Ready to get to work?"

Chloe set her coffee down on the counter. "Yes, ma'am. And I want to tell you again how much I appreciate everything you're doing for me. Especially because when I go to court I'll be able to tell them I have a job where I can keep Leo."

"We're helping each other, Chloe, remember that. I need you as much as you need me."

"I don't know about that, but anyway I sure am grateful."

They sighed at the same time. Then laughed. Marian set about going over the list with Chloe, starting with the most important things. Chloe picked up on most of it right away, to Marian's relief. She could meet with Parker to review her testimony without worrying.

Chapter 29

FRIDAY MORNING, EVA ASKED WINNIE, from the barbecue, to cover for her while she went to the hospital. Jane sat on the side of the bed and faced the window. The yellow pullover and stretchy polyester pants that Eva had dropped off to one of the nurses, hung on her.

"Hello, Jane."

Jane gripped the bed rail and turned toward the door. "Eva."

"I wanted to talk to you. I heard you were getting out this morning. Okay if I come in?" Jane nodded so Eva hurried to the chair next to the windowsill and rubbed her arms to keep warm. "It's cold in here. I should've worn slacks and long sleeves."

"What do you want? I was just getting ready to leave."

"You're in a good mood. Aren't you happy to be getting out of this joint?"

Jane stared at Eva. "Y'all still got my stuff?"

"You keep asking me that. Of course. Where will you go?"

"Why? Did anyone take my space in the alley behind the clothes shop?"

"I don't know," Eva said. "I was just wondering. I mean, Jane, are you still sticking with that name, Jane?"

Jane continued to stare, arms crossed.

"Well, anyway, okay, here's what I want to know. Could you use a job?"

"You and a bunch of do-gooders go out and find me a job?" She shook her head. "I don't need charity."

"A job isn't charity, *Jane*."

"You keep saying my name."

"Isn't it your name? *Jane?*"

Jane laughed. "You just want to give me a hard time. All right. What kind of job? What would I have to do? I don't want to baby-sit. I'm too old to take care of a bunch of loud-mouthed brats. And I'm not very strong. I can't bag groceries at the Super Walmart. I ain't going to be a greeter, either."

"You like to play the mean old bitch, don't you?"

Jane's lower lip quivered. "I'm not your responsibility. You're a nice girl, but you don't have to find me a job. You didn't have to buy me these clothes. What happened wasn't your fault." Her voice broke briefly, but her eyes never wavered.

"Okay, here's my theory. This country is screwed up. People are suffering. If my mother were alive, she'd be pissed that I've wrapped myself up in my little world and let people like you go hungry. So, here's the deal. I want you to let me make up for my dereliction of duty."

"Quite a speech, young woman."

"I'm serious. I've been thinking a lot about it. Are you going to take me up on my offer, or did you like living in the street?"

"I've done pretty bad things since I got out on the street."

"As long as you didn't murder anyone, I don't care." Eva tilted her head to one side. "You didn't, did you? Don't answer that. Anyway, I can be pretty bitchy. Think you can handle that?"

"Sure. I've had to handle way more than that since I went out on the street."

"Okay, we're even."

Eva bounced her feet up and down to keep warm. "The job is at my place. I need someone to help me with the customers and baking and to watch for shoplifters."

"I sure know what to look for there."

Eva ignored that comment. "In exchange, I'll give you a room, a small salary, and at least a meal a day."

Jane hugged herself.

"There's a little room in the back of the shop that I'm storing a lot of junk in. It needs to be cleaned out, but you can stay upstairs with me until we get that done. If that's all right." Eva hoped she wasn't coming on too strong.

Jane's eyes grew wide. "Upstairs in your place?"

Eva thought of the sofa bed, which was really uncomfortable, but was still better than the street. "I have a couch that makes into a bed. It's not great, but I'll give you lots of pillows and comforters to make it more cushy."

"How do you know I won't rob you blind?"

"Will you?"

"No." Jane rubbed her hands together as though washing them.

Eva draped a hand on top of Jane's bony fingers. "There's just one hitch. Next week, I'm having a double mastectomy. I'll need recovery time."

"So I'm out on the street after that?"

Eva shook her head. "No, I'll just need you to work harder until I recover. Think you can do it?"

"Hell, yes. If it means I have a roof over my head. You'll see. I'm a quick study."

"I'm counting on that. A couple of other people on the street will probably help out once they find out what's up."

"So how many days do I have before I'm on my own?"

"Today, tomorrow, and Sunday."

"But you'll be around if I have questions?"

"When I get out of the hospital, I'll be right upstairs."

"I can do it," Jane said. "I know I can."

"Well, okay then."

Jane squeezed Eva's hand. "Thank you, Eva."

"Thank *you*, Jane." Eva ignored the lump in her throat and jumped up. "That's enough mushy shit. Got your stuff? I'm going to find the nurse. We'll get you a wheelchair, and we're outta here."

Chapter 30

MARIAN SAT AT THE TABLE where Parker pointed and put her clutch bag beside her. She wore very little makeup, a white cotton blouse with a Peter Pan collar, a blue, unlined jacket over a plaid skirt, and flats. She didn't trust herself on heels.

When Parker picked her up, he said, "You could be anyone's mother."

While Parker unpacked his briefcase, she checked out the other people in the room. A court reporter sitting in front of the judge's bench. Yvette in a little pink outfit. A bulldog-looking man in a tan suit next to Yvette. And Bryan, who'd gotten his hair cut and wore a gray, pinstriped suit. He sat in the very back row. When she walked by, she leaned down and let him buff her cheek and squeeze her hand. "For luck," he said.

Marian didn't ask Veronica to testify because she had to take care of Robert and finalize plans for Dorothy's funeral on Saturday.

They rose and sat again when the judge, a stately woman

Marian had never seen before, entered the courtroom. Parker hadn't mentioned what had happened to the last judge. He could be dead now. It was thirty some odd years since the last trial. No, that wasn't right. Almost twenty-three years. Of course there'd be a new judge.

Marian held her cold, shaking hands in her lap.

The judge called the case. Parker stood. The bulldog stood. He must be Adult Protective Services' attorney.

"What's this hearing about?" The judge's deep smile lines made Marian hope she was good-natured.

"May I summarize for the court?" Parker still stood, solemn-faced, the fluorescent light above reflecting on his bald head.

"Go ahead, Mr.—"

"Benavides."

The judge didn't know him? Marian thought the judge knew him. What was he planning to say to the judge? Did she need to remind him about everything? She tugged on his arm. When he leaned down, she whispered, "Bryan's in the courtroom."

Parker gently pushed her away. "Thank you, Your Honor. First, I'd like to invoke the rule."

The judge glanced at Bryan. "Sir, in the back of the room." She pointed with her pen. "Are you a witness?"

Bryan stood. "Yes, ma'am."

"Then you'll have to wait outside. That means no talking about the case with anyone other than one of the attorneys, no listening at the door, that sort of thing, or I'll have to hold you in contempt." She smiled. "I know you don't want to see the inside of our jail."

"No, ma'am," Bryan answered and left the courtroom.

Parker said, "If I may proceed—"

The judge inclined her head.

"This is a case wherein a biological mother, who was forced by her own mother almost forty-one years ago to give up her child for adoption, is asking the court to make her guardian of the child—now, obviously Your Honor, an adult."

The judge thumbed through the file as Parker spoke. Didn't she already know the facts? After all, she signed an order making Yvette return Robert to Dorothy's house.

"Not that it matters at this late date, but were your client's parental rights ever terminated?"

"No, Your Honor."

"Who's the guardian at this time?" she asked, eyes piercing.

The bulldog cleared his throat. He'd also remained standing. "The court named the foster mother as guardian at the time the ward reached his majority."

The judge flipped through some pages. "What's her situation now? Is she too old to care for the ward?"

"She's deceased," Parker said, "but before she died, she advised APS she wanted the bio mother to take guardianship."

"Is that true, Ms. Denby?"

Yvette stood. "Yes, Your Honor, but I'm opposed to that."

The judge's eyes cut over to Marian. "The nature of the ward's disability is?"

"He's autistic, Your Honor," Marian said, stumbling to her feet. "She wants to send him to a home where I won't be able to see him."

"Shh. Sit down." Parker pushed her back into her chair.

She sat down, the taste of bile in her throat. Of all things, she wanted to impress upon the judge how calm and cool she was. She hoped she hadn't blown the case already.

"He doesn't function well enough to live alone," Yvette said with a bemused look at Marian. "I believe, and I've had consults to back me up, he'll be better off in a placement with his own kind. I—"

"We'll get to that in your testimony." The judge cut her off with a dark look. "Whoever's going to testify, stand up and raise your right hands."

Stand up. Sit down. Marian wished they'd make up their minds.

The judge swore them in. "Call your first witness, Mr. Benavides."

"Marian Reid," Parker said.

Marian approached the witness stand, her eyes fixed on the judge. A bailiff—a man in a deputy sheriff's uniform complete with gun—held the chair for her.

"Scoot your chair up as far as you can," he said in a low voice.

"Your Honor," Parker said, still standing, "as you can see from the file, we're asking that Ms. Reid be named the Temporary Guardian pending a final trial.

"Because—"

"Because, as you'll hear from the testimony, the guardian, who had Alzheimer's, was hit by a car and died."

The judge glared in Yvette's direction. "I remember." She turned back to Parker. "Proceed."

Parker took Marian through routine questions about herself before getting to the meat of the case. She grew more relaxed, as Parker had told her she would.

"Now, Ms. Reid, would you tell her honor why you are asking to be named guardian of your son?"

Marian turned in her chair until her eyes met the judge's, as brown as dark chocolate. Every nerve-ending in her body stood on edge.

Taking a deep breath and gripping the armrests, Marian said, "I gave birth to a baby boy when I had just turned seventeen almost forty-one years ago." She was glad Bryan had been ordered out of the courtroom. "The nurses weren't supposed to, but they let me hold him. He had the most beautiful eyes . . ." She cupped her elbows across her middle. "Mama made me sign the papers to give my baby away." She swallowed to moisten her throat.

The judge stared at her.

"Years later, after I saved some money, I hired a lawyer and found out my baby hadn't been adopted. Something was wrong with him so the people didn't want him. He was placed in foster care."

The bulldog stood. "Objection to the narrative form—"

"Sustained." The judge leaned back in her chair. "Proceed by question and answer."

Parker said, "What did you do then, Ms. Reid?"

"My lawyer filed a lawsuit here in Houston, where Robert had been placed, asking that I be given my baby back—only by then he was a little boy. My lawyer found out that my rights had never been cut off."

"So did you go to court?" Parker asked.

"Yes, but CPS said that Robert would have problems if they took him away from his foster mother. They said he was retarded; he was attached to her; he wouldn't understand why he was taken away from the only mother he'd ever known."

"So what happened next?" Parker wrote on his legal pad.

Marian glanced at the judge again. "The judge ruled against me."

Judge Lawrence frowned.

"It wasn't you, Judge," Marian said. "It was an old white man with a beard."

The bulldog snickered. Parker shook his head slightly again.

"When was the next time you went to court?" Parker asked.

"Assumes facts not in evidence." The bulldog again.

"Did you take further legal action?" Parker glanced at the bulldog as if waiting for another objection. The bulldog kept his seat.

"Wait a minute. I need to tell you. Dorothy—she was the guardian—felt sorry for me so she told me I could come and visit

Robert. So I visited him quite a bit until I got married and had a baby. And then only occasionally."

"And then the next thing you did?" Parker asked.

"When Robert was about to be eighteen, I hired another lawyer so I could be his guardian." She smiled at the judge. "By then, I'd been visiting Robert for years, even if it wasn't every week, but he knew me. That's an issue for autistic people—by then they'd decided he was autistic. It takes a while for them to remember people sometimes. To recognize them. But Robert knew me."

The bulldog rose again. "Objection."

"Counsel." The judge glanced Parker's way again.

"Yes, Judge. And what happened in that hearing?"

"I lost again. Same reason. And I don't understand that, Judge, because Robert knew me and wouldn't have been afraid to live with me. I'm his mother."

"What did the judge do, Ms. Reid?"

"Well the judge—still not you, Your Honor—put in the order that I could have regular visitations with Robert. I guess in case Dorothy got angry at me or something, which she would never do because she was a wonderful woman." Marian struggled to hold back tears.

"So you've been visiting Robert ever since?" Parker asked.

"Yes, and I've studied autism. Read lots of books. Talked to a psychiatrist. We get along well, Robert and I." She shrugged. "As well as anyone can with someone with Autism Spectrum Disorder. You have to be very direct and concrete with him. I've taken him on outings." She smiled at the judge. "He likes trains. We went to the train museum the other day, before Dorothy—"

Parker cut her off. "You think you could handle Robert living with you full-time?"

"I know I can. A carpenter has built a nice room for Robert in my condominium with a window and closets. Plenty of room for all his collections."

"Are there any other reasons you want Robert to come live with you?"

"I'm his mother, Your Honor. No matter what the experts say, no one can take care of someone as lovingly as a mother. I love him." She thought about Eva. "Robert's best interest will always come first with me, no matter what."

Parker stood. "Pass the witness," he said and winked at Marian.

Marian was glad that was over. The bulldog's cross-examination was next. She'd been cross-examined before. Maybe she hadn't spoken up for herself like she should have, but she would that day. She wasn't going down without a fight.

The bulldog got halfway to his feet, and the judge said, "Proceed, Mr. Buchanan."

"Thank you, Your Honor." He fell back into his chair. It groaned under the burden. "Now, Ms. Reid, it's true you could have kept your baby if you'd really wanted him, right?"

Marian had heard that question before. She wouldn't let it rile her. "No, sir."

"You were seventeen years old at the time Robert was born, is that not true?"

"Yes, sir." She clasped her hands in her lap and held them as still as she could.

"People go to prison for felonies at seventeen in this state, isn't that true?"

"I have no idea. You're the attorney, not me." She glanced at Parker who wore an almost imperceptible frown. Okay, so she had to rein in her temper.

"Well, they do. So now you know."

Parker jumped up. "Argumentative, Your Honor."

"Sustained."

Marian swallowed her snappy response.

"For all practical purposes, Ms. Reid, seventeen is an adult, isn't it?"

"No, sir."

"So you think a seventeen-year-old is still a child?"

"Yes, sir."

"But old enough to engage in sexual intercourse."

Parker jumped up. "Objection. Is that a question, Judge?"

"Withdraw the question. In fact, you think sixteen is old enough to engage in sexual intercourse, don't you, Ms. Reid?"

"Objection, Your Honor," Parker said. "What possible relevance could anyone's sexual activities as a teenager have to the issue before the court today, namely, where is the best place for a forty-year-old autistic man to live?"

"Sustained. Mr. Buchanan, stay on point. This hearing is taking up the court's valuable time."

"Yes, ma'am." The bulldog sat down.

Marian tried to thank Parker with her eyes. He'd already done more to protect her in that one instant than her previous lawyers put together.

"Okay, Ms. Reid, tell the court how many times you've been to visit with Robert in the past year."

Marian shrugged. "I have no idea."

"Well, was it once a week? Fifty-two times?"

"No, not once a week. I live on the island, he lives in Houston, fifty—"

"Objection, non-responsive," the bulldog said.

"Sustained. Just answer his questions, ma'am," the judge said.

"Okay, ma'am, how about twenty-six times? Did you visit Robert every two weeks this past year?"

"At least that. I wasn't keeping track."

"How about twelve times? Did you see your son at least once a month over the last twelve months?"

Marian glanced from the bulldog to the judge to Parker. "I didn't write it down anywhere. I go to see him as often as I can. I have a life, a shop to run, friends—"

"If you love your son as much as you say, why would you let several months go by without seeing him?"

"That didn't happen often. In fact, I can only remember it happening once, Mr.—"

"Buchanan. Sorry I didn't introduce myself to you, Ms. Reid." He eased about halfway out of his chair and feigned a bow. "I'm Elbert Buchanan, Robert's attorney."

Robert's attorney? How did he get to be Robert's attorney? What's more, who was paying him? If he was truly Robert's attorney, why was he sitting with Yvette like he was representing APS?

"I asked you a question, Ms. Reid," Mr. Buchanan said.

Marian shook her head. "What was it?"

"Why did you let several months go by without visiting your son?"

"That was a long time ago. What does it matter now?" Marian again glanced at Parker. He watched her, his caterpillar eyebrows drawn together. She couldn't remember what she'd told him about Greta.

"Objection. Answer the question," Buchanan said.

"It was a very unusual circumstance. I did call Dorothy, though, and check on Robert."

"You called and checked on Robert."

"That's what I said."

"Did you speak to Robert?"

"Well, no. Robert isn't big on telephones."

"So you didn't speak to him. Didn't you think you should at least say hello to him? At least let him hear your voice?"

"No."

"You didn't think it was important for him to hear his mother's voice over that two-month period?"

"He doesn't know I'm his mother, first of all, Mr. Buchanan, and secondly, he doesn't like the sound of voices coming from telephones."

Marian saw Buchanan's face light up when she said Robert didn't know she was his mother. She was ready for him when the next question came.

"He doesn't know you're his mother? Why is that, Ms. Reid?"

"Because the last judge ordered me never to tell."

The judge scowled, her lips pressed firmly together. Buchanan stared at Marian for a few moments as if deciding whether to pursue that line or to go elsewhere. Parker flashed his eyebrows at Marian as though trying to lift her spirits.

"And you're good at following orders, keeping secrets, and keeping your promises, aren't you, Ms. Reid?"

What was he getting at now? "I try to do what I'm supposed to do."

"So you not only never told Robert you're his mother, you never told him he had a sister either, did you? And my guess is that you never told his sister she had a brother. Am I not correct that you promised your mother you wouldn't tell anyone about your illegitimate baby? And you never told your daughter or your ex-husband?"

Marian thought she might throw up. Who would have told either Buchanan or Yvette about Greta? It could only have been her mama. Marian whispered, "No, I never told the kids about each other."

"Beg pardon?" Buchanan said, cupping his ear. "I didn't hear you."

"I said, I never told the kids about each other, Mr. Buchanan."

"Have you told them now? I mean, if you want Robert to come live with you, wouldn't he need to know about his sister?"

Marian threw up her hands. "If he doesn't know I'm his mother, how could he ever know about his sister?"

"My point exactly, Ms. Reid. You were allowed to visit him whenever you wanted. You took him on outings. You established a relationship with him yourself. But if you really loved him so much, why did you not ever take him down to the island, introduce him all around—especially to his sister—and really make him a part of your life? Pass the witness, Your Honor."

Marian swiveled around in her chair, glancing from Parker to Buchanan to the judge. She would not let that pass. She blurted, "Because she's dead. She's been dead since she was a little girl."

"We'll take a ten minute recess," the judge said and swept off the bench.

Marian felt like she would burst. She needed to get out into the fresh air. She stumbled out of the courtroom, past Bryan, down the elevator, and onto the courthouse steps. Gripping the railing, Marian was gasping for air when Bryan and Parker found her.

Bryan put his arm around her waist. "Are you all right?"

Marian kept her head down. She had that sensation in the back of her throat that comes before vomiting. She swallowed several times and took several deep breaths.

Bryan handed her a water bottle, and she sipped. Finally, she felt better. Bryan took her hand. She sat down on the top step and looked at Parker. "What did he mean he was Robert's lawyer?"

"The judge appointed him Robert's attorney *ad litem*. It's different from being the guardian of the person and of the estate, which is what you're asking for. The attorney *ad litem* is supposed to do what he or she thinks is in the ward's best interest."

"So the judge already knew who Mr. Buchanan was when we went in there this morning?"

"Oh, absolutely," Parker said.

"And she already knew what the case was about," she said, squeezing Bryan's hand. She didn't understand one thing about the system except that she'd been screwed twice before and didn't want it to happen a third time.

"Yes, but I had to put everything on the record in case we appeal."

"Appeal? Omigod. I hope it's not going to come to that." Marian took another sip of water.

"Me, too," Parker said. "Listen, could we have a few minutes alone, Bryan? I hope you don't mind."

Bryan let go of her hand. "No, go ahead. I'll wait outside the courtroom."

"We'll be right up." Parker put his arm around Marian and helped her to her feet.

As soon as Bryan went inside, Parker said, "I'm not sure how well this is going."

"You think the judge hates me? She seemed to respond when you were asking me questions."

"I'm not going to lie to you, though, Marian. Buchanan did a job on you. That promise thing."

"It's not my fault. That judge from years ago . . . I don't know what I thought would happen if I broke my promise."

"He had no right to ask you to make a promise like that."

"You think this judge thinks I'm not telling the truth?"

"I don't know. Listen, we only have a minute." He searched her face. "I'm not sure we should put Bryan on."

"Why? If Bryan doesn't testify, I have no one."

"Maybe you could find someone who would testify in rebuttal after Yvette and her report. That won't be until Monday."

"I don't know who." She bit her lip. Everyone in the neighborhood had their own businesses to run. Veronica had to stay with Robert. "You think the judge shouldn't know I have a boyfriend? Is that a bad thing? I thought it might be good for the judge to see that Robert would have a man in his life. He hasn't had anyone since Dorothy's husband walked out."

"I'm not confident that Bryan will do you any good," Parker said, swiping his hand across his bald head, wiping away perspiration. "It's your decision, though. It's your case."

Marian trusted Parker's judgment, but without Bryan's testimony it would look like she had no friends or family who cared enough about her to come to court. And God knows whom Yvette had rounded up.

"We've got to put him on, Parker. He's all we have. I'll take the risk that the judge thinks bad of me for having a boyfriend, but without Bryan, I'll look like I don't have any friends."

"All right." He prodded her back. "Let's get in there."

Marian pulled a tissue from her pocket and wiped her forehead. The heat and humidity only took a few minutes to have an effect in the summer. Marian touched Bryan's shoulder as they walked by. They took their places just as the judge came in.

"Call your next witness, Mr. Benavides."

"Bryan Mosley," Parker announced.

The bailiff opened the small door that separated the public from the bench and bar. He followed Bryan to the witness stand and adjusted the microphone.

Parker looked at the judge. The judge nodded.

"State your name and where you live for the record, please."

"Bryan Mosley. Galveston, Texas." His eyes rested on Marian.

Parker asked Bryan a few other background questions before launching into questions relating to the case.

"What is your relationship to Ms. Reid?"

"We're friends. Old, old friends."

"Close friends?"

"About as close as two people can be."

"Then you know about Robert?"

Marian froze. She hadn't told Parker Bryan was Robert's father so what was he getting at? There was no way he knew. If he did, surely he wouldn't say anything to Bryan while Bryan was on the witness stand.

"Yes. Marian took me to Houston to meet Robert just a few days ago. He's a nice, if rather strange, young man."

"You understand what this hearing is about then?"

Marian gripped the armrests.

"Yes. Marian wants to become Robert's guardian."

"What kind of woman is Marian Reid, if you don't mind my asking, Mr. Mosley?"

"Warm, generous, and loving." His eyes met hers.

She knew Bryan would make everything all right.

"You've seen her demonstrate these traits?"

"Yes and heard about her generosity from her neighbors."

"Objection." Mr. Buchanan stood. "Hearsay."

"Mr. Mosley, you're not allowed to repeat what someone else said," the judge said.

Bryan looked over his shoulder at the judge. "Yes, ma'am."

"Now, let me ask you something more delicate," Parker said. "Exactly what is the nature of your relationship with Ms. Reid?"

Bryan looked into Marian's eyes. "I want to marry her."

Chills ran up Marian's arms, all the way to her neck.

"And you say this knowing she wants Robert to come live with her for the rest of his life?" Parker put his hand on Marian's shoulder as he spoke.

"I love her very much."

Parker stood. "Pass the witness."

"Mr. Mosley," Mr. Buchanan said, "what kind of mother is Ms. Reid?"

"I haven't been around when she's been mothering anyone, sir, so I don't know. But I'm sure she was—"

"Objection, non-responsive," Mr. Buchanan said, half-standing again.

"So you don't know what kind of mother she'd be to Robert, is that correct?"

"I'm sure she'd be—"

"My point is, you don't know, correct?"

"Correct." His eyes met Marian's.

"You've met Robert, you said."

"Yes, sir."

"You said he was strange."

"He has autism."

"I understand that, Mr. Mosley. Did you like him?"

"Well enough, I suppose."

"Did you spend any length of time with him?"

"He showed me his room. His train collection. Made the trains run around on the track he built up near the ceiling. Showed me his books, all color-coded on his bookshelves."

"How long were you two together?"

"I don't know. Ten minutes. Fifteen or twenty at the most."

"Did you observe him prior to the time you spent alone with him?"

"Yes. Watching TV. Pacing around the house. He seemed a bit agitated at the time."

"Annoying?"

"Not really, though Veronica seemed to be somewhat irked by his behavior. Said he required a lot of watching over." He looked at the judge again. "She's his foster sister. I heard her say she wished Marian would hurry up and get him. She's been stuck in the house with him since her mother died."

When Marian heard the word "stuck", a gong rang in her head. Is that what he thought? That anyone caring for Robert was stuck? She watched his reactions as he answered the next few questions.

"Mr. Mosley, based on your observations at the time you met Robert, do you think Ms. Reid is capable of taking care of Robert? Do you think it would be in Robert's best interest for the court to name Ms. Reid as his guardian?"

Bryan looked directly at Marian. Then at Parker. Then at the judge. "I wasn't expecting you to ask me that."

"Just answer the question, sir," the judge said.

"Would you repeat the question?" His eyes met Marian's again.

"Certainly. Let me rephrase it for you. Based on your observations, not as an expert," Buchanan glanced at Parker, "just as a layman, what do you think would be in Robert's best interest? To be placed with Ms. Reid? Or in a situation with people of his own kind?"

"He does seem like a lot to handle." He rubbed his chin.

"Don't look at Ms. Reid for your answer, Mr. Mosley. We all know what she wants. What do you think?"

Bryan shook his head. "Well . . . I really think he would be better off in a home for autistic people."

Marian's cheeks burned as if she'd been slapped hard. She shrieked. "Bryan!" Everything turned red and black and lights flashed before her eyes. She pulled away from Parker's hand and ran from the courtroom.

As she fled, Bryan's voice followed her. "I could help pay for it, honey! You could visit him regularly! I'd pay for you to visit him whenever you wanted!"

Chapter 31

J ANE AWOKE TO WHAT SOUNDED like thunder. She should get out of the rain. The old dime store awning would do if she could get there before the sky burst. She was warm under the covers and didn't want to move. Another rumble came from far away. Maybe the storm wouldn't come.

She opened her eyes and saw padded sofa arms. The blurry ceiling wasn't the sky, but a pattern of some sort. Wrapped around her wasn't her old blanket but a soft duvet inside a furry zebra-print cover. Remembering where she was, Jane cackled.

The hospital had been clean and comfortable, and she could have lived out her days there. Eva's apartment, though, wonderful didn't begin to describe the place. Now that she'd had a rest, she'd explore. Would Eva have brought her up there, given her a warm nightie, made up the sofa bed, shown her where the bathroom was, and left her to her own devices if she didn't trust her?

She liked the idea of someone trusting her again. In the streets, people skirted her like a mangy dog.

She stretched and folded her arms on top of the comforter for a few more minutes of pure joy; then she'd look for something to eat.

Thunder again. Rain pelted the windows. *Putt, putt. Putt, putt, putt.* A door opened and closed, footsteps thudded on the stairs. Euphoria swirled around her head.

Eva poked her head in. Her face softened when their eyes met. "The weather wake you?"

She wore jeans and a cotton sweater and pink high-top tennis shoes. She'd spiked her hair. Jane had seen her with her hair that stiff before, when Eva dressed up to go someplace.

Jane sat up and maneuvered herself so she could lean against the sofa arm. "Have I been lying around being lazy very long?"

Eva sat on the edge of the sofa bed. "Take all the time you need. Are you hungry?"

Jane wondered whether she should be straightforward with the girl. The thing is, she could always eat, but she didn't want Eva to think she was greedy. She'd already done so much by bringing her there. She stared at her for a moment and decided to tell her what she needed. Wasn't that what all the magazines said to do? She read a lot of magazines. The dumpsters always had them. "I could eat. I mean, if that's okay."

"I brought a sandwich up earlier. It's on a plate in the kitchen. And soup is sitting in the microwave, just press the button that says Easy Minute START. You can get something to drink out of the refrigerator."

Jane bit her lip. Eva didn't want to see her cry, she was sure of that.

"I'm going to freshen up for tonight."

"Okay." Jane pressed her lips together.

"Make yourself at home. Just like real roommates. You know about Artwalk, don't you?"

"Of course. When is it?"

"Not until tomorrow, but I thought I could show you things this afternoon and tonight, before it gets here."

"No problem."

"Only if you're up to it. Nothing difficult and when you're tired, you can come back upstairs."

"No time like the present to get to work. Tomorrow, I'll be on the inside of it."

"Inside of it?"

"During the Artwalk. Part of the inside of the world. I've been on the outside of the world for a long time."

"Mind if I hug you?" Eva asked and reached over, giving Jane a gentle hug.

Jane put her arms around Eva. It had been a long time since she'd had a hug from someone. A hug that didn't lead to other things, things she would continue to try to forget. "You're a good girl, Eva."

Eva didn't speak. She jumped up from the sofa bed and ran into the other room.

Jane had that Christmas morning feeling and hoped no one would wake her from the dream. She pulled a cotton robe over the nightie and crawled out from under of the covers, putting her feet into slippers Eva had left for her. A bit of a chill filled the air. Eva kept the air conditioning low. Even when Jane had been married, with a husband who brought home a paycheck, they'd kept the air on seventy-eight degrees in the summer. Sometimes she'd lower the thermostat during the day while her husband wasn't home.

While the soup warmed in the microwave, Jane opened drawers and cabinets. The dishes all matched. She'd had nice china once, but she'd sold it in a garage sale before moving to Galveston, before moving out of her house. She'd sold most of her belongings, keeping only what she needed to survive.

The microwave beeped, and Jane put the warm bowl of cheesy

broccoli soup on the table beside the sandwich. She could have put her face down and lapped it up like a dog, but instead, she found a spoon. A cloth napkin lay on the placemat. She went to the refrigerator for something to drink. A plastic jug of milk, a pitcher of iced tea, small cans of juice like the new guy next door had given her, twelve-ounce cans of soda, bottles of beer and wine, jars of pickles and artichokes and mushrooms, smaller jars of jams, real butter—

"Can't decide what to drink?" Eva stood in a thick, red terry robe. She reached into a cabinet and pulled out two glasses. "Let's have juice."

"Apologize if I've been holding the door open too long." She didn't want to do anything to make Eva angry.

"No problem." Eva extracted two cans of orange juice and closed the door. "Want to have your lunch now?"

After pouring their juice, Eva plopped down in the chair opposite Jane's. She pulled the belt tighter around her waist and hiked one bare foot up on the chair rung. "Have you ever worked a cash register?"

Jane put down the half of the chicken salad sandwich. Eva might not want her when she found out she didn't know how to do much. "Not since high school, and I bet they're different now," she said with her hand in front of her full mouth.

"No reason you can't learn."

Jane swallowed after chewing a good while. "Will you teach me?"

"We can start this afternoon. Tomorrow night I'm hoping for a crowd. I'll run the register. Sunday, we'll work on it a bit more."

"Whatever you say."

"What did you used to do? I mean, when you worked?"

"I was a housewife until my husband died."

"I always hated that term. Like you were married to the house, right?"

"In my day, that was what everyone said."

"Domestic engineer," Eva said.

"Yeah." Jane spooned the soup. She'd had this one before, when cardboard containers got thrown in the dumpster.

"There's not much training to running a shop. I'll do the ordering and bill paying. It's a matter of keeping the place clean and the shelves stocked, serving people. A bit of table service. I don't encourage that, but if they order something I don't have handy, I'll take their order to the table."

"I've seen you."

"I bet you have. I bet you could tell me stories about the people on Ledbetter Street."

"Maybe." Jane didn't mince words.

"If you were a domestic engineer, I bet you can bake."

"I used to be pretty good at baking and cooking. You want me to bake?"

"Maybe," Eva said.

"But not today." Jane finished the orange juice.

"No, today, if you're up to it, you can wait on customers and send them down to me to pay. Also, keep an eye out for shoplifters. When no one's around, I'll teach you how to use the cappuccino machine and cash register. The others aren't as hard." Eva's eyes danced.

"Why are you doing this?"

"I already told you, Jane. Is that really your name?"

"Yes." She held the second half of the sandwich in her hand. Would Eva make her throw it out? It was so good, she didn't want to throw it away.

"Do you think you'll be up to helping this afternoon? I feel kind of guilty putting you to work right away. You probably don't even have your strength back."

"You keep wondering if I'm up to it. I'm stronger today after a week's vacation in the hospital than I've been in a while. I'll tell you if I can't keep up."

"Deal," Eva said. "I'm going to get dressed. You mind clearing up?"

"Want me to put the bed away?"

Eva glanced at the sofa bed. "Nah. You could straighten the covers, that's all. That way we don't have to kill ourselves pulling it out again later. No one will be here but us."

Jane wondered about that clothing store lady who was Eva's friend.

"And you can shower when the thunder and lightning quit or wait until later," Eva said. "I have something else you can put on, too."

"Quit it, Eva." She grinned at the young woman. "I can wear what I had on earlier. Save whatever you have for the Artwalk." As soon as Eva walked into the bedroom, Jane dug around the kitchen drawers until she found plastic wrap. Once she got the half sandwich wrapped, she put it under her pillow and straightened the sofa bed.

Chapter 32

AT THE END OF FRIDAY, MARIAN felt like she'd been run over. She was lucky not to have been held in contempt of court, Parker said, when he'd found her. Bryan had left, and they were on a lunch recess.

The rest of the afternoon, Yvette occupied the witness stand. She and the bulldog focused on Marian's failings. After Denby's direct testimony, Parker took her on cross-examination, but Yvette never faltered from her stance that Robert belonged in a home.

During the night, a tropical storm moved across the island. Wind driven rain struck the bedroom windows so hard it sounded like ice breaking. Anna, shivered and hid under the duvet, wincing at each crack of thunder.

On Saturday morning, Marian peered out at the soaked streets and bedraggled trees and sympathized with the merchants hosting Artwalk that evening. Unless the skies cleared, people would stay home. The crowd would find something else to do. Troy's opening would be ruined.

None of that seemed important to her that morning. If she couldn't have Robert, nothing mattered. Bryan had shown his true feelings. She couldn't believe that after he had professed to love her, had said from the witness stand that he wanted to marry her, that he could betray her.

Carrying a carton of coffee again, Chloe arrived for work. She wore a royal blue cotton blouse with embroidered flowers and a pair of jeans.

"How'd it go yesterday?" Chloe set the coffee down and picked up a duster. After a few minutes of silence, Chloe asked again.

Marian took the mop to the front door to take care of the water that had blown in under the door. "We're picking up again on Monday, though I don't have much hope."

"I wish there was something I could do." Chloe straightened some blouses on one of the rounds. "Want me to unpack the boxes stacked up behind the divider?"

"If you want. You need to inspect each piece. Sort the clothes into stacks to be laundered, hung up, or folded and placed on shelving. Some stuff will need to be washed and ironed. We'll talk about that later."

"No problem." Chloe dragged the first box toward the counter where she had set down her coffee. "Box cutter?"

"In the drawer." Marian glanced across the street at Coffee & More. Eva moved about behind her own counter with someone, though Marian couldn't see who it was.

She perched on a stool to review the accounts from the day before. Eva approached the door of Coffee & More. Marian thought she might be coming over, but Eva stopped and stood talking with someone. Marian wanted to ask her forgiveness. Tell her about Bryan and what happened at court the day before. But when Eva spotted her and turned away, Marian knew Eva wouldn't care.

The sky had gone from gray to almost black and cleared again. After a while, Marian got up and climbed the stairs, arriving at the top just as her phone began to ring.

"You haven't forgotten the funeral, have you?" Veronica asked. "I was hoping you'd come early and sit with us in the family room."

One more cross to bear. For heaven's sake, did she hear herself? After all she'd been through over the years, was she going to give up living now? "I'll be there, honey. I met with Chloe, who's helping out in the shop, and I've just come up to get ready. I'll see you in about an hour and a half."

"Before the service you'll bring me up to date on what happened yesterday?"

"Definitely. It was a nightmare." Marian hung up and went to dress.

When she opened her garage door, the water had gone down. The streets were clear. The sun beat down from a blue sky. She started the car so she could sit in the air-conditioning and pulled out her cell phone, punching in Eva's number. After several rings, voice mail came on. She punched in the number again. The phone rang several times and went to voice mail. "I really need to talk to you. Won't you please call me? I'm leaving now for Dorothy's funeral, but I'll be back for Artwalk."

Marian pounded her fist on the steering wheel. "Damn it. How did everything get to be such a mess?" She drew a deep, shuddering breath and backed into the alley. The weekend was still young. Eva might forgive her. And someone might still turn up to testify for her. In her dreams.

Chapter 33

ROBERT SAT IN THE FRONT row with Veronica and her husband and children and stared at the casket. Marian sat on the second row among other people who, she learned, had been foster children.

"Mother," Robert said when he'd entered the main hall at the funeral parlor. He took long strides to the front of the room and stood over the coffin. "Mother. Mother." He didn't seem to understand why Dorothy didn't get up and talk to him. Marian didn't understand why they had an open coffin. Veronica insisted Dorothy would've wanted it that way.

Though there was no indication of the injuries from the accident, Dorothy had become quite thin in recent months and didn't look much like herself. The body in the box wasn't the woman Marian had known and loved. Dorothy had been a giant of a woman when they'd first met, over six feet tall and two hundred pounds. When she'd wrapped her arms around Marian, Marian knew she'd been hugged.

Veronica said since they couldn't know how Robert would take Dorothy's death, if he saw them close the lid on her, saw her being carried away, and put into the ground, maybe he'd accept that she wasn't coming back. Maybe he'd be able to transfer his attachment to Marian more easily. Social worker talk, but Marian understood Veronica's intentions were good.

Later, Robert stood over the grave, refusing to be drawn away. He stood and stood with sweat running down his body as the cemetery employees went about their work, setting the flowers to one side in a large pile, walking around him. Marian watched from the background. A long fifteen minutes later, Dorothy's coffin was sunk, inch-by-inch, into the hole. Robert kept vigil until the workers covered the grave. Marian took his hand, gave him a yellow rose—Dorothy's favorite flower—and led him to her car to take him back to Dorothy's house.

Chapter 34

TO HELL WITH THEM.

To hell with all of them. Bryan. Eva. Yvette. The bulldog. Marian belted a turquoise silk blouse over a long linen print skirt and donned blue leather sandals. She was going to have fun and not let anyone know how much she hurt inside.

Before going downstairs, she stood at her picture window and watched the people on Ledbetter Street. Clutching wine glasses and cans of beer, they clustered on the corner. Couples arm-in-arm. Laughter. Mariachis played outside Miguel's Taqueria, the trumpet blasting. At The Pit, Winnie stood at a grill on the sidewalk and handed out barbecue samples. Sitting in every available chair at Eva's tables, people sipped coffee and munched baked goods. Troy stood just inside his open door as though in a receiving line. He spotted her and beckoned to her to come down.

Marian hurried back to the bathroom and pinned up her hair, draped beads and chains around her neck, and changed her regular glasses to sunglasses to cover her bloodshot eyes. Time to get out there, find a drink, and have a good time, despite the past two days.

By the time she crossed the street, she could barely see the top of Troy's head in the center of the gallery. He broke off his conversation and pushed his way to her, taking her hand and speaking into her ear. "You look wonderful. I have wine for the customers, but tell Julio to give you a Margarita. There's a pitcher hidden in the Dr Pepper box."

Marian forced a laugh. The din made it hard to carry on a conversation.

"When you come back, I'll introduce you to the artist."

"Okay." She preferred wine to Margaritas, since Margaritas often made her very drunk, but one wouldn't hurt.

Edging her way through the crowd, she eventually arrived at the end of a long line of people at the bar. As she waited for the people in front of her to get their drinks, she looked around the room. A large group encircled a tall, long-haired woman who looked like she'd been transported from the 1960s, complete with beaded headband. Rain Fennel.

When she reached the bar, Marian asked loudly, "Julio, Troy says to give me a Margarita."

He dug around in the Dr Pepper box before handing her a mountain of frozen Margarita in a huge glass with a green stem shaped like cactus. Marian licked the sides of it like an ice cream cone so it wouldn't spill. The salt on the rim would make her look five pounds heavier the next day, but what did she care? There was no one left to impress. The bittersweet tequila and lime seemed to be a symbol of her situation.

Squeezing through the circle of people around Rain, she waited for an introduction. Rain's wheat-colored hair flowed down her wiry body to her waist. She wore hip-hugging bellbottom jeans, a skimpy knit top that showed a bit of belly, and a belly-button ring. She even had a toe ring in place of shoes. Marian wondered whether there was something between Troy and Rain and if not, why not? The woman was hot.

She thought of her short-lived reconnection with Bryan. Her memories were in a muddle. Hadn't he hugged her and been supportive just a few days earlier? Hadn't he said he loved her and wanted to marry her? If he hadn't been in favor of getting Robert, why didn't he say so? Why tell it to the judge? He couldn't have made the case any worse if he'd been deliberately trying to sabotage things.

"Hey, again," Troy said into her ear. Taking her elbow, he steered her to Rain and shouted, "This is the woman I was telling you about. She lives across the street."

What had Troy told Rain? She shook the younger woman's hand. "Looks like you're a big hit. Congratulations."

"Thanks," Rain said. "Want to have a drink after?"

Marian sipped her Margarita. "I'd like that very much." No, she wanted to say, she really didn't want a drink after. She wanted to jump off the seawall.

"See you later then."

Marian raised her voice. "Bye, Troy." She spotted Lorette, the nurse who lived on the next block, and they hooked up on the sidewalk.

"What a crowd," Lorette said. "Good for him."

"Yeah," Marian sucked at her drink again as it began to drip over the sides. "He makes a mean Margarita, too."

"You dog. All I got was wine. You must be something special."

"He's being neighborly, that's all. Want to go down to the next block?"

"Sure. God, I could hardly breathe in there."

Eva was at her cash register. Another woman—a small, older

woman—waited on people behind the case holding cookies and muffins. She sure looked like that homeless woman. Had Eva brought her home from the hospital?

Lorette had walked on but came back. "Yes, it's Jane. You didn't know?"

"When did that happen?"

"Yesterday."

"I guess I forgot." She didn't want everyone on the street to know she and Eva were estranged. Eva glanced Marian's way but either didn't see Marian or pretended she didn't.

"That's not what I hear."

Marian wanted to go inside but knew she wouldn't be welcome. "Does everybody know we had words?"

"Pretty much." They skirted a family who stood in the middle of the sidewalk. "What were y'all fighting about?"

"I don't know," Marian said.

"God, there are people here I've never seen before. There are always tourists and people from Houston, but there're really weird people. That woman across the street looks like a World War II-era German hausfrau."

Marian glanced in the direction Lorette pointed. The woman had blond braids circling her head. She wore black Doc Martins—which looked like combat boots—black knee socks, and a black jumper with a tiny pullover under it. A black leather purse that looked like a satchel hung crosswise over her shoulders. "Doesn't she know it's July?"

A man wearing a dark winter suit jacket over a black T-shirt and slacks spoke to the woman. They set off with another couple.

"Weird, definitely weird," Lorette said. "She looks like a Nazi. Speaking of clothes, I like your outfit. You ought to dress like that more often."

"Thanks," Marian said. "I decided to let it all hang out."

The aroma of burning flesh and spicy barbecue sauce filled the air at The Pit. Winnie gave out samples in little paper cups. A raggedy-dressed man with bushy black hair, a long beard, and wide-set eyes walked up. "Ma'am," he said to Winnie. "I come here from California and run out of money. Can I have something to eat?"

Winnie stepped back to the doorway and called over her shoulder into the restaurant, "Mickey. Bring me another platter."

"You gotta love her," Lorette said.

"Both of them." Marian swallowed several times.

"Hey, Winnie," Marian called as they started past.

Winnie waved them over. "Take your glasses inside and get refills."

Marian and Lorette walked back to the kitchen where Mickey chopped brisket.

"Came in out of the cold for a drink," Lorette said.

"Yeah, you wish it was cold," Mickey said. "Where are all these people coming from?"

"Beats me." Marian sucked down the remnants of her Margarita and held out her glass.

"You sure you want another that large, Marian?" Mickey looked at her sideways. "You're not used to drinking."

"Fill it up." Marian wiggled her glass. "I'm out to have a good time tonight."

"What about you, Lorette?" Mickey reached for Lorette's glass.

"Wine." She handed over her glass. "Smells good in here."

Mickey put the glasses down, wiped her hands on a towel, and went to the refrigerator, where she poured red wine for Lorette and Margarita from a large pitcher for Marian.

"Okay, thanks, we're outta here," Lorette said. They scooted through the tables to the street.

The tequila tasted stronger than in the one she'd gotten at Troy's.

Biting into a big frozen lump, Marian said. "This is good. You sure you don't want one?"

"Me and tequila don't mix. Come on, let's cross the street before some asshole runs us over." They headed toward the old five and ten.

People zoomed up and down Ledbetter Street, jamming on their brakes at the red light. Several folks rode bicycles.

Lorette pointed toward the end of a line of people. "Those people with the huge goblets of red wine are that rich lawyer and his third wife who moved into the lofts in my block." The man worked his way through the crowd like a politician up for re-election. The woman wore a purple felt, wide-brimmed hat with long black feathers and a red hatband with her khaki shorts and halter-top. Marian began to laugh.

"What's funny?" Lorette asked.

"Don't you see it? The people. The people." Marian slurped her drink.

Lorette looked at her. "I guess so."

"I hope my ex-boyfriend doesn't show up here."

"Rumor had it you had a boyfriend. He's already an ex?"

"So you heard about that, too?"

"Do you, or do you not live on Ledbetter Street? Come on, let's go."

"You know, I need to go back and talk to Eva."

"She won't talk to you. Besides, you don't want to cause a scene."

Marian put her face very close to Lorette's. "I need to talk to my friend. She's going under the knife on Monday. I need her to know how I feel."

"It's the Margarita speaking. Let's go back to Troy's gallery or get something to eat. I bet you haven't eaten tonight."

Marian headed back toward Eva's. "Come or not."

Lorette shook her head. "You're on your own."

Marian pushed through the door at Eva's, bumping several people in the process. "'Scuse me. Sorry," she muttered.

"Hey, Marian," Derek, a tiny man with a paunch as round as his head called to her.

Marian waved, but didn't falter in her determination to reach the counter. A cleaned up, non-stinky Jane was helping Eva. "Hey, Jane."

"Good evening, Ms. Reid," Jane said, her eyes sparkling. "Can I—may I help you with something?"

Moving over to where Eva stood, she said, "Eva, we've got to talk."

Eva gave her a sharp look. "I've got nothing to say to you. Get out of my shop." She turned her back and walked away.

Marian felt like a mule had kicked her. She headed back toward the front door. When she got there, she asked the man at the nearest table if she could leave Troy's Margarita glass and pick it up later.

"Sure," he said. "You okay, Marian?"

She recognized him as one of her tenants. She rarely saw them after renting her units. Most of them slid their rent under her door. "Need something to eat, I think."

"Chips and *queso* right behind you."

Marian layered chips and cheese on a clear plastic plate and slipped a napkin in her skirt pocket. She went outside and chomped it down. When she was through, she didn't feel any better, but hoped it would offset the booze. She crossed the street in the middle of the block, paying little attention to the traffic, and stepped inside a gallery.

"Hey, Violet," she called to the owner, "how's it going? Got any goodies tonight?"

"Great—check it out in the back," said a small redhead, in the midst of conversation.

When she wended her way to the rear of the gallery, a short, bearded man with a long ponytail, asked, "Wine, ma'am?"

"Sure." Taking the wine glass from him, Marian stepped over to a table and filled a plate with fruit salad. "Thanks," she called and went out the side door onto the sidewalk, coming face-to-face with Bryan.

"Marian, I—"

"Stay away from me." She was so taken aback, she walked into the street. A car blew its horn. She turned and ran the rest of the way across, not looking back, not wanting Bryan to think he should follow.

She slipped into the next store. They sold antiques but displayed art on the walls. She needed to find someone to testify for her on Monday. Spotting the table with food, she headed that way and found Lorette standing behind a portable bar.

"Marian, want some ouzo?"

"What are you doing here?" She didn't need anything else to drink but desperately wanted something after seeing Bryan. She held onto the edge of the bar.

"Harry had to pee." Lorette handed her a tiny cup filled with clear liquid. Marian tossed the ouzo down her throat and felt the burn. "Thanks, girl. Anything to eat here?"

"Some pita triangles. I think there're bits of lamb left. Make a plate."

Marian found an almost empty tray of food just past the bar. She picked at the remains.

"It's getting late," Lorette said. She came over and handed Marian a refill.

"I don't think I'd better," Marian said.

"What could it hurt? It's only a bit larger than a thimble."

Laughing, Marian took it from her. "You're right." She gulped it. "I hate the way it tastes, but it sure burns good going down."

"Want another?" Lorette asked.

"I really am declining this time." Marian stuffed a piece of pita bread into her mouth. The cold lamb tasted greasy, but she needed more than chips, cheese, and fruit in her stomach. After she swallowed, she asked, "Hey, what're you doing on Monday?"

"Working. Why? I wish Harry would come back."

"Could you get off? I need someone to testify for me."

"Let's see, I could tell the judge how much you like ouzo."

"No, I'm serious, Lorette. You've known me a couple of years."

"And I'd seriously consider coming to court for you another time, but Monday is the day after tomorrow. No time to make arrangements." She whacked Marian on the arm with the back of her hand. "What're you thinking?"

"Oh." Marian's hopes faded. "Maybe for the final hearing."

Lorette nodded. "Just give me lots of notice, and I'd be glad to, sweetie."

"Well, I have to get back to Troy's," Marian said. "I'm supposed to have a drink with that artist, Rain."

Lorette wiped the bar with a dishtowel. "Y'all have fun. I gotta go see if Harry fell in. He was pretty loaded."

Music blared from a bar half a block away when Marian crossed the street toward Troy's. The fresh air would make her feel better. Winnie had taken everything inside at The Pit. Noise came from inside, people wanting dinner.

Marian walked to the window at Coffee & More. Eva wiped the counter, but Jane wasn't around. She tried the door. Locked. Eva made eye contact and kept wiping. Why couldn't she understand? She averted her eyes and continued walking on down to Troy's. A few stragglers hung around. Troy graciously engaged them in conversation as he moved toward the front of the gallery. He winked at Marian and indicated she should go on back.

Marian found the sofa and almost fell into it, glad to be sitting. Rain walked up to her.

"Hello again," Rain said. "It's Marian, right?"

"Right," Marian said. She pulled a napkin from her pocket and wiped her mouth and then her forehead. The humidity and heat seemed to affect her all at once.

Rain handed Marian a glass of wine and sat in the chair adjacent to the sofa. "So you own the vintage clothing shop across the street? I'd love to come in and see if you've got anything that would fit me."

"It's vintage and pre-owned. You're welcome any time." Her stomach gurgled.

Troy sat down next to Marian. "That's the lot of them. Quite a bit of interest in your work, Rain."

"Super," Rain said. "What a cool crowd."

Troy turned to Marian. "You see how many people were out on the street? I heard this was one of the best Artwalks ever. What'd you think?"

Something in Marian's mouth tasted metallic. She swallowed a couple of times and started to answer, put her wine glass down, and stood. "I'm not feeling too well." She took a step toward him and threw up.

Chapter 35

LATE SUNDAY MORNING, MARIAN AWOKE to Anna's licking her face. She lay there, head throbbing, mouth tasting like the inside of a garbage can, and wondered how she'd gotten home. She wore only her bra and panties. Her other clothes lay neatly folded on a chair.

After showering and feeding the dog and herself, she called Veronica. "What's happening in your part of the world?"

"Robert's pacing between television shows. I was hoping you'd show up."

"I can't. I just can't face driving into Houston again today. I had a horrible night last night at Artwalk, and Eva's still not speaking to me. I'm so sorry."

"Honey, I understand. It'll all be over soon enough." Her voice held a motherly tone.

That's what Marian was afraid of. She had a feeling that if she lost the temporary hearing, that would be it. "I've got to ask you a huge favor. I don't know who else to turn to. Do you think you could come to court and testify for me?"

"I don't see how. The neighbor who watched Robert when Mom disappeared only did it because it was an emergency. Mom was just too busy to make many friends."

Marian's head pounded. Veronica was her last hope. "You want what's best for Robert, don't you?"

"But there isn't anyone to take care of him. The only other lady Mother ever used is on vacation."

"What about those former foster children who were at the funeral?"

"If I'd known, but they've all gone back where they live."

"I have no one else. If someone doesn't come forward and testify for me, they're going to send Robert to a home."

"I can't bring him with me. What would we do with him while I was on the witness stand?"

"I could take care of him outside while you testify. And you can at least say you've seen me with Robert and tell the court you think I'd be a good mother, a good caretaker for him." It occurred to her she didn't know if Veronica thought that. "You do think so, don't you?"

"Of course I do. I'd never do to you what Bryan did."

"Thank God. I was worried for a minute."

"You know I love you like a sister."

"Yeah, I thought Bryan loved me, too."

"Sounds to me like he doesn't want to share you with Robert."

"Enough of Bryan. He's history. So you'll come?"

"Well, A. I don't think it's a good idea to bring Robert to court. And B. You'd have to run it by your lawyer. You're supposed to stay in the courtroom during a trial. But I'll see if I can come up with someone to stay with him."

"Thanks. I'm relying on you."

After they hung up, Marian took some painkillers and went back to bed where she stayed for most of the day.

Chapter 36

EVA AWOKE IN THE RECOVERY room to Jane's sweet old face leaning over her. "How do you feel?"

Eva closed her eyes, and when she opened them again, Jane loomed over her still, or was it again? Was the surgery over?

The bandages squeezed her chest, making it hard to breathe, so the answer had to be yes. "I know I'm alive, because it's starting to hurt," she croaked.

Jane took her hand and stood staring at her.

"I'm okay, Jane. You can sit down."

"I've been thinking how fast stuff changed," Jane said. "A few days ago, you sat next to my bed."

Her dry mouth made it hard to speak. "Water?"

Jane helped her take a sip.

"I didn't mean to drag you into my problems when I first thought of giving you a job," Eva said when she lay back. "I didn't mean for you to be my babysitter." She wet her lips and swallowed, her mouth still dry.

Jane chuckled. "It's okay."

"Would you get a nurse?"

"She was here when you woke up the first time." Jane stepped out of the room.

Eva hurt inside and out. She couldn't help thinking about Marian, hated that they'd gotten crosswise. Something had gone off inside her when Marian broke her promise.

Jane returned, a nurse behind her. She waited by the door while the nurse checked Eva over.

"It hurts like hell," Eva whispered as the nurse examined her.

"We'll take care of that. You're going to be fine." She peeked under the sheet. Looked at the drip. Checked Eva's vital signs. Wrote on her chart. "Hungry? Want lunch?"

"Maybe a little something," Eva said. "And drugs, quick."

"No problem," the nurse said. "I'll be right back."

When the nurse returned, she gave Eva pain pills and a glass of water. "Let's get you to your room."

Later, Eva awoke in a different room. Another nurse came in, helped her to a sitting position, and fluffed the pillows after adjusting the bed. "That's better. Your meal will be here in a moment. Does your mother want to go down to get a bite to eat while I check your bandages and take care of a few other things?"

Eva and Jane exchanged glances. "She's my friend, not my mother," Eva said.

Jane shook her head. "I ate before I came. I'll step outside."

Eva said, "You don't have to."

"That's okay. I don't like blood and guts. I'll be in the waiting room."

Eva closed her eyes. Though the pain wasn't as bad, she hated any pain and had no intention of suffering. She cooperated with the nurse, and when she opened her eyes again, found the nurse gone and a tray on a table next to the bed. Jane sat in an easy chair.

"Have a pleasant sleep?"

"Can you push the tray table over here, please?"

Jane did and tucked the napkin into Eva's neckline. "You got any family I could call for you, Eva?"

Eva sipped the juice. "Touché." They both laughed. "Have you really eaten?"

Jane reached into the pocket of her jumper and pulled out half a sandwich. "Don't worry about me, young lady. I'm liable to eat you out of house and home."

"I wanted to tell you. You did real well Saturday night. I know I practically ignored you all day Sunday, but I had a lot on my mind."

"Sure you did. You didn't take me on to raise. I got a lot done cleaning out the storage room—my room—with Lupe and Lorette. By the way, the barbecue girls are handling the shop today."

"That's sweet." Eva sipped soup through a straw. It hurt to raise her arms. "Not bad for hospital soup. Needs salt."

"It's hard to ruin Campbell's chicken soup. I recognize it by the smell."

"Don't feel like you have to move downstairs real quick, Jane. I mean, we'll have to find you furniture and all."

"I don't. I'm going to keep my eye on you for quite a few days and run the shop. I can do it, Eva. You watch. It's just like running my own kitchen except there's customers, instead of family. I can do it."

"I know you can. We're going to make a great team."

"I'm thankful for your trust." Jane ducked her head.

The door opened, and Lorette popped her head in. "How's our girl?"

"I'm not a girl," Eva said. "I had some girls, but they're gone. And I'm sitting right here."

"Well, you were out last time I checked."

"I was told I'm going to be fine, but this is the pits. I hate the smell of hospitals, everyone's patronizing attitudes, and being restricted to bed."

"You have a good nurse," Lorette said, resting her hand on Jane's shoulder. "She was a good patient, and now she's a good nurse."

"Thanks for coming by, Lorette," Eva said. "Will you spread the word on the street that I'm going to be fine, and tell them I don't want them coming up here?"

"Aw, let people do for you if they want to," Lorette said.

"Tell them to save it for when I get home." She finished the soup and pushed the table away. "Tell them I expect them to bring lots of food. But I'm glad to see you."

"Thanks. Anything I can do for you?"

"No. Jane's got everything under control."

"Okay. I'll stop by later." She gave Jane a thumbs up.

Jane said, "Now what else can I get for you, ma'am?"

"Turn your chair around, and let's see what's on daytime television, unless you want to take me on at rummy again."

Chapter 37

"**NOBODY'S HERE," MARIAN SAID WHEN** she and Parker entered the courtroom Monday morning. "It's like an iceberg in here." She pulled her jacket lapels together and shuddered.

"We're early," Parker said. "We can go ahead and set up. Maybe we'll have time to get something warm to drink."

The bailiff came in and greeted them. The door opened behind them. Bulldog Buchanan and Yvette entered practically arm-in-arm. Marian still didn't get it. If he truly represented Robert, he should have talked to her. Had he even met Robert? Veronica didn't mention that he'd been to the house.

"Good morning." Marian gave them a terse smile.

"Good morning, Ms. Reid," they said together and not without smug looks.

Parker took her arm. "We still have time for that cup of coffee."

"I'll wait outside the door," she whispered. "I don't think I could swallow a thing right now."

"Suit yourself." He headed back down the aisle with Marian following.

Marian kept a lookout through the doors to make sure that Mr. Buchanan didn't touch Parker's stuff. She glanced at her watch. Where was Veronica? Parker said his re-cross of Yvette wouldn't take long. Would the judge wait if they couldn't guarantee they'd have what Parker called a rebuttal witness, or would the case end with Yvette? She got out her cell and punched in Dorothy's number. It rang and rang, and the answering machine picked up."

"Veronica? If you're there, pick up. Hello?" The beep cut her off.

Yvette and Mr. Buchanan had their heads together, laughing. How dare they laugh? To her, Robert was a human being. No matter what they thought, he had needs only she could fulfill.

"Still nobody?" Parker caught her by surprise. She flinched.

She shook her head and rubbed her arms. The coffee aroma brought back memories of her father, after church services, standing in the back of the sanctuary, talking with friends.

Parker finished and glanced at his watch. "It's time." He held the door for her.

The judge entered the courtroom the same time they did. Marian felt like she was marching to the gallows.

"It'll be all right," Parker whispered.

She'd been obedient to her mother, to the court, and it looked like it was going to cost her. She'd live through it. But if they sent Robert far, far away, he'd be cut off from everyone who loved him. What kind of life would that be for him?

"Good morning." The judge nodded. "Re-take the witness stand, Miss Denby."

"Yes, ma'am." Yvette, wearing a turquoise suit and spike heels, bounced to the witness stand.

What did people like Yvette know about sacrifice and love? She seemed more concerned with whether Marian's shop might fail than with Marian's love for her son.

Mr. Buchanan concluded what Parker had explained was re-direct, and it became Parker's turn at Yvette again. He held a copy of her report, which the judge had allowed into evidence.

"Good morning, Miss Denby. Just a bit of follow up, if you don't mind." Parker flipped through his legal pad as if he couldn't remember what he wanted to ask.

She looked very at home on the witness stand.

"Isn't it true that Ms. Reid has always done everything that has been asked of her?"

Yvette glanced at Mr. Buchanan. "I guess so."

"No guessing, Yvette. You've had access to all the records involving Robert and his case with Children's Protective Services and Adult Protective Services, is that not true?"

"Yes, that's true."

"You reviewed those files before this hearing began, like a good investigator should, isn't that true?"

She nodded. "Yes."

"You have never seen anything in the files that indicate that Marian Reid has not done what every governmental agency has asked of her, correct?"

"You're confusing me."

"Come now, Yvette. We all know you're a law school graduate. Just, please, answer my questions."

"Counsel," the judge interrupted, "if there is any admonishing to be done in this courtroom, I'll be the one to do it."

"Yes, ma'am." Parker stood and sat again. "Yvette, Ms. Reid has done everything that's been asked of her, right?"

"Yes." She had the good grace to squirm.

"And this go-round, she's visited her son regularly, taken him on outings, arranged for a psychiatrist for him when he comes to live with her, and even built a bedroom for him, correct? So that he could have a place for his things, and his privacy, yet still be close enough so she could keep an eye on him, true?"

"I guess—yes. That's true."

"What I've heard you say is that there are no circumstances under which you would approve Ms. Reid as Robert's caretaker. In other words, no matter what the situation, you don't think he should ever live with his mother?"

"His biological mother." She arched an eyebrow. "And you're correct."

"I'm having a little difficulty, after hearing you testify for what," he glanced at his watch, "between Friday and this morning almost five hours, what exactly is it that you object to? Seems to me that you've been all over the map." Parker straightened in his chair.

"Objection, argumentative." Buchanan didn't even attempt to stand up.

"Sustained."

"Is the reason you don't approve of Ms. Reid because she gave her baby away when she was seventeen, or because she has a life on the island and doesn't visit him every day? Is it because she never introduced him to her daughter and her friends, or because she dared to have a boyfriend? Is it because she obeyed the previous judge and her mother, or because she's never kissed the feet of Adult Protective Services?"

"Objection." Mr. Buchanan lurched from his seat. "That's a multifarious question, Judge. He can't ask her all of that at the same time."

"Sustained. Mr. Benavides, you know better than that." She scowled at Parker.

At the back of the courtroom, the door opened. In waltzed

Marian's mama. A sharp pain struck Marian's temple. She clutched Parker's arm in a death grip.

The judge said, "Ma'am if you're a witness, you'll have to wait outside."

Claire glanced at the bulldog and Yvette, shot a look that spoke of ancient history to Marian, and left the courtroom.

Parker stood and addressed the court. "Withdrawn, Your Honor. No more questions."

Chapter 38

"CALL CLAIRE VERNON TO THE stand." The bulldog looked pleased with himself.

Through blurred vision, Marian met Parker's gaze. "My mother," she mouthed.

Her mama had assumed the air of a beauty contestant crossing a stage. In a way, the courtroom became another stage for the woman who'd spent many hours of her life in pageants. Walk smooth, gliding, gliding. Steps light, no echoes from heels tapping. The only person in the world able to keep a linen suit practically creaseless. Head high. Slight smile but otherwise wearing no expression so as not to wrinkle the face. Hair as coifed as the queen mother's. Neither a glance to the left, where Marian sat, nor to the right where her allies sat, eyes strictly on the judge, her true audience.

After being sworn, Claire tapped the microphone and stated her name.

"You are the mother of the movant in this cause, are you not?" Bulldog Buchanan asked.

"Yes, sir, and the biological grandmother of the person who is the subject of this lawsuit." Claire's eyes never wavered from the bulldog.

Parker poised over his legal pad, ready to scribble notes for his cross-examination.

"Where do you live, ma'am?"

"Georgetown, north of Austin, and Galveston, in a beach development called Beachtown." She held her handbag in her lap, her hands folded on top.

Marian's vision cleared. She became aware of her breath, dry palms, and heat radiating through her body. Hate filled her for the woman who'd given birth to her, and Marian knew she'd crossed a bridge. Her mother had taught her to stuff her feelings, saying, her whole life, *It's not nice to hate people.* The awareness of her feelings overwhelmed Marian almost as much as feeling them.

Questions pierced her consciousness. Did her mama see this appearance, her testimony, as her crowning glory? Her greatest achievement? Her final victory? She knew now that her mama had never loved her. Had, in fact, hated her for a reason unknown to Marian.

"Tell the judge why you have come forward today."

"Objection," Parker said as he jumped to his feet. "Object to this open-ended question. He hasn't established this witness even knows what this hearing is about."

"Sustained." The judge peered over her glasses at the bulldog. "At least attempt to lay some kind of foundation, Mr. Buchanan."

"Yes, Your Honor. Okay, Claire, are you aware that we're here today to decide where your grandson, Robert, will live for the rest of his life? Where his guardianship will lie?"

The judge cleared her throat. "Not we, *me.* Mrs. Vernon, it's my decision and mine alone."

The bulldog stood. "I didn't mean to imply—"

"Just move on, Mr. Buchanan."

"You do understand why we're here, Claire?"

"Most definitively. Robert's long-time guardian passed away, and Robert has to move somewhere."

"Yes, ma'am, precisely. You're aware of Robert's disability?"

"According to Yvette, he's autistic."

"You're aware of the nature of that disability?"

"I am," Claire said, still not glancing Marian's way. "I have researched it at the library. Those people must have strict supervision and can never fully function on their own."

Those people? Marian scooted back her chair, but Parker pressed her arm, pushing her down, whispering, "Stay calm. I'll handle this."

She hoped he would. He needed to be as aggressive as Buchanan. Was he up to it?

"All right," Buchanan said. "You're Marian Reid's mother. You probably know her better than anyone in the world."

Claire looked at Marian. "Through and through. Better than she knows herself."

Marian shivered. What a claim to make. The arrogance.

"In your opinion, is Ms. Reid capable of taking care of a man with such disabilities?"

Her mama made eye contact with the judge. "No, Your Honor. She is not."

White knuckled, Marian could hardly restrain herself.

"Explain your reasons for that opinion, Claire."

Again Parker stood, "Objection. I ask that Mr. Buchanan be required to proceed by question and answer."

Buchanan held up his palm. "No problem, Judge. Claire, I take it you have solid reasons for your opinion. Please, give one reason why you think she, that being your daughter, Marian Reid, should not be put in charge of your grandson, Robert."

Claire gripped the microphone and leaned toward the judge. She cleared her throat rather loudly. "She let her daughter Greta get hit by a car." Like a handball, her voice bounced off the courtroom walls, reverberating, seeming to go on forever.

Marian clutched her stomach. How could she? How could *any* mother, say such things, do such things to her only child? She kept repeating to herself, "Be calm, be calm, be calm," like a mantra.

"And so, naturally, you have a fear that something may happen to Robert under her care?"

"Naturally. The welfare of my grandson is my number one interest." Her huge sigh gave the impression of utmost concern.

Parker's furious writing left deep grooves in the legal pad. He'd shoot Claire a look and write, and look and write with an intensity Marian wished her earlier attorneys had shown.

Buchanan's smugness betrayed him. "Claire, tell the judge if you have another reason why your daughter should not have care and custody of Robert."

"Yes, I do." She seemed pleased with herself. "I fear the strain of having to take care of a severely handicapped person would be too much for Marian and could cause her to suffer another nervous breakdown."

Marian ran her fingers through her hair. At least she'd told Parker everything. At least he'd had a chance to think about how he would defend her if her mama did exactly what she was doing. The pressure with which he made notes tore the paper. He flipped the sheet over and continued. What happened to lawyers maintaining a dispassionate distance from clients? If she hadn't been the brunt of the testimony, Marian would have smiled at Parker's feelings at the events taking place.

"Tell us about that, Mrs. Vernon—Claire."

"Yes, well, let me see." Claire's eyes cast up to the ceiling as if trying to jog her memory. "I believe she was twelve the first time she had a nervous breakdown. Yes, twelve and in the sixth or seventh grade."

Marian could only grip the armrests when what she wanted to do was go up to the witness stand and thrash the bejesus out of her mother.

"By nervous breakdown, ma'am, do you mean—"

"Objection, leading." Parker stood and crossed his arms about his chest. Dropping back into his chair, he resumed writing.

"What do you mean by nervous breakdown?" Buchanan asked. He sat, pen in hand but never made a note.

"We had to hospitalize her, poor dear."

"And how long did they keep her in the hospital?"

"Six weeks and then six weeks recuperating at home." She turned to the judge. "I had a tutor come in so she could pass to the next grade."

"How had she behaved to indicate she'd suffered a nervous breakdown, as you call it?"

"It's not what I called it. That's what they said at the mental hospital. Anyway, out of control. Screaming. Crying jags. Tantrums. Extreme lethargy after one of her fits."

Buchanan nodded and stroked his chin as if he were an old sage.

The judge peered over her glasses at Marian. Marian met the judge's eyes. Should she give up now? Or let her mama bury her deeper? She thought of Robert in a home where he didn't know anyone, where no one knew him, where no one loved him. That kept her going. She'd never give up. She'd see this thing to the end.

"Thank you, Claire. I realize this must be very difficult for you."

Buchanan glanced at Marian. "Very difficult to say these things about your daughter in open court."

Like hell, Marian thought.

Claire put her hand to her mouth. "Do you want me to continue?"

"Oh, yes, ma'am," Buchanan said when Parker stood to object again.

"Marian was a wild child. She seemed to be normal in every way after that nervous breakdown until she got to high school when she began to . . . sexually act out, I believe they call it."

Marian almost laughed. Her mama had certainly boned up on current terminology.

"By that, you mean she engaged in sexual intercourse?"

"Yes, that's what I mean. Whether or not she had multiple partners, I don't know. However, she became pregnant at sixteen."

"That would have been with Robert? I mean, she didn't have multiple pregnancies, did she?"

"Your Honor!" Parker's chair banged against the short, wooden wall behind them.

It didn't take a genius to understand what her mama and Buchanan were calling her. Marian felt limp with exhaustion.

"Counsel—approach the bench."

Parker scowled as he strode to the front of the courtroom. Buchanan trotted close behind. Marian kept her eyes on her hands. She couldn't hear what the judge said, just the chastising tone of her voice.

When Parker returned, he shook his head at Marian. She had no idea what that meant, but it couldn't be good.

"Proceed," the judge said.

"Yes, that was with Robert," Claire said to the judge. "She got pregnant with Robert at sixteen, and I sent her to Ft. Worth to stay with her grandmother and deliver the baby at the home for wayward girls."

Buchanan nodded. "And then what happened?"

"She gave birth to Robert and put him up for adoption and returned home where she finished high school, graduated, and went off to college."

"And so life went along smoothly for awhile?"

"I thought so, but in college she got involved with the wrong people."

"Really?" As though surprised at this turn of events.

"Her young man was a drug user. A ne'er-do-well. She wouldn't give him up. I assume she used drugs as well."

"By drugs you mean illegal, mind-altering substances?"

Claire nodded. "I was forced to pull her out of college and bring her home. I enrolled her in a local university. She had to learn skills. I couldn't go on supporting her forever."

"So everything rolled along smoothly after that?"

"She met a fine young man from a well-to-do family. They married. I put on a beautiful wedding. Marian got pregnant not long after the marriage."

"That was Greta?"

Claire folded her hands as if in prayer. "She was a beautiful baby. I mean, in spite of that red hair. Bright and rosy-cheeked. She walked early and talked up a storm."

"And then what happened?"

"And then, and then—" Claire bowed her head and sniffed. The court reporter pushed a box of tissues at her. Grabbing a handful, she patted her face.

"Take your time," Buchanan said.

After a minute or so, Claire said, "And then one day apparently Marian took the baby to the zoo. She had a balloon, and when they headed to the parking lot, the balloon came untied from Greta's wrist and began floating away. Greta ran after it and a car hit her." Claire covered her face with tissues.

"And you blame Marian for her death?"

"I can't help it. A good mother would have had her in a stroller or in hand. It never should have happened."

Buchanan stood. "Pass the witness."

"Oh, wait. Wait. Wait," Claire said. "Judge, I want to point out—"

"Objection." Parker rose to his feet again. "No question—"

"It's all right," the judge said. "I want to hear this."

Claire raised an eyebrow at Parker and turned in her chair toward the judge. "I just want to say, Your Honor, that I just want what's best for the boy—the man—my grandson. I even told Yvette there that I would be more than glad to pay for his support at the institution she suggests sending him to. I could set up a trust so that when I die he'd be taken care of."

A shiver erupted down Marian's neck and across her shoulders. Marian knew at that moment she was looking at the all-time, undefeated, world champion of control freaks. If the judge had the slightest concern about what the lifetime cost of providing for Robert was to the state, Claire had just addressed that issue head-on. Marian could only hope no one would be taken in by Claire's offer. As little as Marian knew about the law, she didn't see how the judge could make an order that could be enforced if Claire had a change of heart.

"Now I pass the witness," Buchanan said.

Chapter 39

"YOUR HONOR, MAY I HAVE about thirty seconds with my client?" Parker asked.

The judge nodded, a look of interest crossing her face.

Parker turned to Marian. "Listen, we only have a moment. I don't want you to react in any way to my cross-exam of your mother. I did research into your parents' divorce, looked at their file, delved into your family history a little more—" He looked rueful.

Marian didn't know what he was getting at. "Why are you telling me this?

"You trust me?"

"Yes, but you're frightening me."

He clasped her hand for a moment. "Just don't react when you hear my cross. I'm going to have to take her apart."

Marian searched his face. "Do what you have to do to get me my son."

"Good deal." He winked at her and stood again. "May I proceed, Judge?"

"Please do." The judge leaned back and crossed her arms.

Parker scooted his chair out a little into the aisle and leaned forward, elbows on knees. "Mrs. Vernon, I'm Parker Benavides, and I represent your daughter in this matter."

"I'm quite aware of who you are."

"Now, it's true, isn't it, Mrs. Vernon, that Marian was an unwanted pregnancy?"

"I don't know what you mean, young man." Claire stiffened.

The pain in Marian's gut was like a sucker-punch. Was that how he intended defending her? Discrediting her mother? Make it all her mother's fault? Okay.

"All right. Let's go back. I understand you were a beauty queen. A high school beauty queen?"

"If you want to call it that." Her head tilted to one side as she smiled the smile Marian had seen in so many photographs.

"Not if I want to call it that," Parker said, "you were. County Fair and Rodeo Queen, am I not correct?"

Claire nodded, still smiling. "Yes."

"And Homecoming Queen at your high school?"

"Both Football and Basketball homecoming queen."

"Sweet," Parker said, nodding. "And you won many pageants, including runner-up for Miss Texas."

"*First* runner-up." She stirred in the chair. "I should've won that."

"Eventually you married a fine young man from a well-to-do family?"

"Yes."

"A banker's son?"

"Evan. We were going to go to California. He thought I would do well out there. Maybe the movies."

"Movie queen," Parker said. "Quite an ambition for a small-town girl, but then you got pregnant."

A sharp glance at Parker and then, "We wanted children."

"But not then—not at that time."

"It was unexpected." She glanced at the judge.

"You wanted your chance in California, your big chance."

"I would have been a big success."

"A baby would weigh you down. You wanted to get rid of the baby, but your mother made you have her, am I not correct?"

Claire's mean look reared its ugly head. "My mother. Humph. My mother could have lent me the funds to have the baby taken care of, but she wouldn't. My mother could have taken the child to raise, but she refused to do that, too. If it wasn't for my mother—"

"Thank you." Parker wheeled his chair back behind counsel table and flashed a look at Marian.

"My mother—"

"Objection, non responsive," Parker said. "Now, let's talk about Marian's childhood for a minute. Marian was the apple of her father's eye, as they say, right?"

"A daddy's girl." Claire had resumed her grandmotherly persona, a demure smile gracing her face.

"She loved her daddy like nobody's business, correct?"

Parker squeezed Marian's arm again. He touched her so much that she wondered whether he thought it would settle her down, like petting a dog. She was much calmer during his cross-examination than when Buchanan questioned her mother.

Claire folded her arms in front of her. "She followed him around like she was his shadow. Before she grew old enough for school, he'd take her to the bank, and let her color in her coloring books in an empty office, take her to the cafeteria for lunch, and let her get whatever she wanted. He made her fat. A little chunk of a girl."

"And you didn't like that."

"Didn't seem normal for a man to favor his daughter that way."

"Well, at any rate, it's true that Marian doted on her father, and he, on her."

"Yes, it's true."

"And when he left you, he wanted to take her with him to raise, and you wouldn't let him, true?"

"That was abnormal in those times. Whoever heard of a man raising a daughter—unless her mother was dead, and then the child should be raised by her grandparents or an aunt, certainly not by a man."

"Well, to summarize, you fixed it so that Marian could never see her father again, isn't that right? Through implications about their relationship? And when she found out she'd lost her father," Parker rose from his chair, "the one person in all the world who loved her, she was furious. And, yes, she threw a fit. She wanted her daddy. And you had her locked up in a mental institution and called it a nervous breakdown. Isn't that correct, Mrs. Vernon?"

"No, that's not what happened. I told my lawyer. I told the judge of his abnormal obsession with our little girl. It was the judge who said he couldn't see her anymore."

"I see," Parker said, resuming his seat. "I think we all see."

"Objection to sidebar, Judge." Buchanan said.

"Sustained." The judge pointed at Parker. "Mr. Benavides, I'm warning you."

"Sorry, Judge." He made a few notes. "Now, let's talk about Marian's second breakdown, shall we?"

"Second breakdown. All right." She patted her eyes with the tissues.

"The second time Marian was locked up in a mental institution, she'd lost her daughter. Her baby daughter, Greta."

"Exactly. Her husband left her, and what was I to do? She wouldn't get out of bed. I had to do something, so I called her psychiatrist, and they came and took her away."

"And kept her in a mental institution at your behest. And gave her shock treatments."

"Not exactly my behest, young man. The doctor thought it was best."

"Right. The doctor you hired. The doctor you paid. And it wasn't until her nana, her grandmother, intervened with an attorney for Marian that she was able to get out of that place. Isn't that correct?"

"Well, if you want to put it that way."

"It's not me who is putting it that way, is it, Mrs. Vernon? That's the way it was, right?"

"If you say so."

"Do I need to bring the probate court records from Galveston to prove it, Mrs. Vernon?"

Claire wriggled in the witness chair. "Her grandmother did hire an attorney. Her attorney did get her released from the hospital. But I'm not sure—"

"Thanks very much, Mrs. Vernon. And as to Robert, you didn't want her to have that baby, did you?"

"Pardon? I didn't want her to get pregnant if that's what you mean. I had no idea her behavior had deteriorated—"

"No. I mean, when you found out she was pregnant, you wanted her to have an abortion, didn't you?"

"Objection!" Buchanan climbed out of his chair.

"Just what is the nature of your objection, Mr. Buchanan?" the judge asked.

"Uh, assuming facts not in evidence." He scowled.

"Judge, this is cross-examination," Parker said.

"Overruled. Sit down, Mr. Buchanan."

"Isn't that true, Mrs. Vernon? You wanted her to have an abortion, but she flatly refused."

"I didn't want her to end up like—I didn't want her to make the same mistake—well, she was just too young to have a baby, that's all."

"And you and she battled it out, right?"

"Yes."

"You let her have the baby as long as she would give it up for adoption."

"We came to that agreement. She went to Fort Worth and stayed with her grandmother until the baby was born."

"You made her agree, further, that she would never tell anyone she was pregnant, right?"

"She'd brought enough shame on us with her institutionalization, after all."

"And that included the biological father of the child, isn't that correct? You made her promise she'd never tell the father?"

"We agreed she wouldn't tell anyone. No one would know but my mother and myself. We thought it would be better that way. She could return after the summertime and make a fresh start at school."

"You mean, you thought it would be better that way."

"He's badgering her, Judge," Buchanan said.

"Sustained. Move along, Mr. Benavides."

"You didn't want her life ruined like yours, by having the baby, I mean. And you didn't want her bringing any more shame upon the family than she already had, is that your testimony?"

Buchanan rose again. "Compound question, Your Honor. Object."

"Withdrawn," Parker said. Turning to Marian, he whispered, "Anything else you want me to cover?"

Shivering, Marian's mind flew in all directions but she couldn't think of anything. No one had ever spoken up for her like that since before her father left. Not even her husband. "I don't know what else you could ask."

The courtroom door behind them squeaked open. Veronica stood holding Robert's hand. Marian pulled on Parker's sleeve. "The cavalry's arrived," she whispered, hoping Veronica would save the day.

"I'm counting on it," he whispered back. "One last question," he said, addressing Claire. "Ma'am, have you ever met your grandson Robert?"

Clearly startled, Claire looked at Buchanan, Yvette, and finally, the judge. "To be perfectly honest, no."

"In fact, you wouldn't know him if you saw him, would you?"

Buchanan lumbered out of his chair again. "That's two questions, Judge, and argumentative to boot."

"Sustained."

Parker stood. "Pass the witness."

Veronica and Robert sat on the bench behind Parker and Marian, Robert on the inside.

Marian mouthed the words "Thank you."

The judge said, "Are y'all witnesses in this case?"

"I am, Your Honor," Veronica said. With her jeans and western shirt, she could've just ridden in from the ranch, but Marian was just glad they'd come. Well, at least, Veronica. Robert looked like he'd just woken up.

"If you would stand and raise your right hand," the judge said.

Veronica stood and raised her right hand. Robert looked to his right and left, got up, and raised his hand also.

"If you aren't going to testify, young man, you needn't be sworn," the judge said.

Robert continued to stand and hold his hand up. He faced forward but did not look at the judge.

Marian rose. "Your Honor, this is Robert."

"I thought as much." She nodded. "Okay." She administered the oath. "Now I must tell you that as witnesses, you have to wait outside in the hall to be called."

Veronica took Robert's hand, and they headed back the way they'd come, Robert's gait as stiff as a wooden soldier's.

"Now, where were we?" the judge asked.

"I just passed the witness," Parker said.

Buchanan said, "Attorney ad litem rests."

"Mrs. Vernon, you may step down," the judge said. "Rebuttal witnesses, Mr. Benavides?"

"Yes, Your Honor. We'll call Veronica Reasoner."

They'd just reached the back of the courtroom. She whispered to Robert, pointed to Marian, pushed the door open, and prodded him outside.

Marian rose. He couldn't be out there alone. He'd be scared and not know what to do with himself.

"Where is your client going, Mr. Benavides?" the judge asked.

"Veronica," Robert called from the back of the courtroom. Arms dangling by his sides, he ambled up the aisle.

"I'm sorry, Your Honor," Veronica said as she reached the witness stand. "I guess he couldn't wait for Marian to get out there. He wants to see where I am." She called out, "See, I'm right here. I'm okay. Now go with Marian." To the judge, Veronica said, "He's been agitated since Mother passed away. I don't think he understands where she went, and that she won't be coming back."

Marian waved at Robert. "I'm coming Robert. Wait up."

Robert turned back toward the door. Before he reached it, he did an about-face again. "Veronica," he called.

Marian said, "Robert, go back." She scooted between Parker's chair and the bar separating spectators from the attorneys, meeting Robert before he pushed through. The bailiff closed in behind her. "He'll be okay," she whispered to the bailiff. She took Robert's arm.

"Robert, you're not allowed to come up here. Veronica's all right." She pointed at Veronica. "See? Veronica's okay. Now, how about sitting down on this row behind me?" She opened the small door and stepped into the gallery. "Sit over here, Robert. Behind me. That's where I sit." She pointed to her chair. "You can sit right here behind me." She led him to a spot on the bench directly behind her chair. Glancing at the judge to find her watching the whole scene, she asked, "Okay, Judge? He's not testifying." The judge nodded.

Claire, who'd been standing in the aisle near the rear door, slung her purse over her shoulder and sailed outside.

"Behind Marian," Robert said. "Sit behind Marian."

"Yes. You can see Veronica, and if you need something, you can ask me."

"Sit behind Marian." He sat down and twisted his hands in his lap.

"I'll be right in front of you." Marian pointed and circled back around to her chair. "Sorry, Judge. He'll be okay."

The creases in the judge's forehead grew, but she didn't say anything. Veronica sat in the witness chair and fidgeted. Buchanan and Denby huddled together.

Parker whispered, "Okay, now? I want to get this testimony in."

She wondered if Robert had just cost them the case. She would've preferred the judge not see Robert. Not see him being difficult.

"Mrs. Reasoner, I'm Parker Benavides, Ms. Reid's attorney. Can you tell the judge who just came into the courtroom with you?"

"My foster brother, Robert. He's okay, but you have to watch him. Or at least make sure he doesn't get out of the house without supervision or unless he has strict instructions about what he's supposed to be doing. He can do tasks if he's told exactly what to do." She leaned back in the witness chair. "He's very literal."

"Do you know the person beside me?"

"Marian Reid. A very nice woman."

Marian glanced at Robert to see how he was faring, but his face was as deadpan as ever.

"Okay, ma'am, do you know why we're here today?"

"Marian wants Robert to come live with her. She wants to be his guardian."

"Do you think that Marian can take care of Robert?"

"Yes, definitely. She's very capable. She could take care of Robert very well."

Parker asked, "Ma'am have you been present when my client, Marian Reid, has been around Robert?"

"Many times, sir. Most recently over the past few weeks."

"So you've seen them interact together. How do they get along?"

"Very well. Just like what you saw today. Often Marian can handle Robert better than I can. He seems to listen to her better. I don't know what it is. Maybe because she's been a mother longer than I have, she's firmer. Not to be argued with."

"You love Robert?"

"He's like a brother to me."

"Why is it that you're not asking for him to live with you?"

"I'm married. I live on a ranch-farm. I work part-time and have two young children."

"In other words, your plate is full."

"Overflowing, sir." She smiled at the judge.

"Would you have any qualms about Ms. Reid having full guardianship of Robert for the rest of his life?"

Veronica shook her head. "None at all."

Marian's insides warmed. Perhaps all was not lost.

When it was Mr. Buchanan's turn at Veronica, he asked, "Ma'am, do you remember I was at your mother's home last night?"

"Yes, sir."

"Good," Buchanan said, with a glance at the judge as if to say, *See, I did my job.* "Do you remember what you told me last night?"

"Which thing?"

"Well, you remember that we had a conversation about Ms. Reid visiting Robert."

"Yes, sir."

"And you said that you had never seen the two of them alone together."

"Sir, if I'd seen them alone together, they wouldn't have been alone." Veronica looked exasperated. "What I said was that I'd never been around them when my mother was not around. Until she died, that is."

"In other words, you've never observed Ms. Reid mother Robert. Your mother, who Robert saw as his mother, had always been in the vicinity?"

"That's what I said, sir."

"So it's fair to say, isn't it, that you don't know what kind of mother Ms. Reid would be, do you?"

"I've seen her take care of him. He responds to her. She's good with him."

"Objection, non responsive," Buchanan said, again half-rising from his chair.

"Sustained," the judge said.

"Your own mother had always been present when you'd made your observations, correct?"

"Correct. But Marian's taken Robert on outings without my mother."

"But you have never been in the position to observe Marian with Robert and without your mother, that's true, isn't it?"

Parker stood. "Asked and answered."

"Sustained," the judge said.

"Pass the witness," Buchanan said.

"No further questions," Parker said.

Veronica said, "I just don't know why Yvette hates Marian so much that she would do this to her."

"Objection! Objection!" Buchanan pounded the table. "There's no question out there."

The judge glowered at Veronica. "We'll take a ten minute recess," the judge said as she stepped down from the bench.

Marian turned to Parker. "No matter what our witnesses say, he makes them out to be worthless."

"I'm sorry, Marian." Veronica joined them. "I did the best I could." She held Robert by the hand and led him out to the hallway.

Robert said, "I'm sorry, Marian. I'm sorry."

Marian hugged Veronica and lightly hugged Robert even though hugging him was mostly only going through the motions. He didn't hug back. "It's not your fault. I'm so grateful you showed up. I nearly fell out of my chair when I saw you."

Veronica laughed. "I did try to find someone to stay with him. I finally decided that we'd better just come. Sorry I couldn't control him."

"That might not have been a bad thing," Parker said.

"Cafeteria," Robert said.

"In a minute, Robert," Veronica said. "The judge just took a break, and when she comes back, we'll see about the cafeteria."

"It's okay, Veronica." Marian draped an arm around her shoulder. "I love you so much for coming, but y'all had better head out now."

"We have to make a stop first. I made a promise about a chicken leg. Will you call us when it's over?"

"You'll be the first to know what the judge decides. After us, of course. Now run along." Marian put her cheek against Robert's arm. "Bye, Robert."

"Cafeteria."

"Robert. It's *I want to go to the cafeteria.* Say it," Marian said.

"Robert wants to go to the cafeteria, Marian."

"Right." Marian waved them on. Turning to Parker, she said, "Just give me a minute in the restroom."

After pulling herself together, Marian exited the restroom adjacent to the courtroom. Figuring Parker must have gone back inside without her, she opened the door to see him poised at their table. "Your Honor, we have other witnesses we'd like to bring if you could give us a continuance. Of necessity, the hearing was quick so some of our witnesses couldn't come."

Shaking her head, the judge said, "Not now. Maybe you can bring them to the trial, if there is one."

"Barring that, Judge, we rest." He beckoned at Marian.

"No re-rebuttal," Buchanan said. Both he and Parker sat down.

Marian scooted behind Parker, sat down, and clasped her hands under the table.

"Well, here's the thing," the judge said, with a look at the APS table. "I've heard from the state in the form of Yvette Denby who has no real good reasons to send Robert to a group home, especially when he's apparently functioned just fine in a single parent home for many years. And I heard from a very selfish man who professed to love this woman but obviously wants her all to himself. And the testimony of Ms. Reid's mother was off the charts. I haven't seen such a self-absorbed person in all my years."

Marian reached for Parker's arm. She felt like she'd burst.

"It's about time someone gave this poor lady a chance to mother her son. Ms. Reid, you may have temporary guardianship with all the rights, powers, privileges, duties, and responsibilities of a guardian effective immediately. And I'm appointing Sylvester Garza as Guardian Ad Litem to do an independent home study on your home. He should show up there in the next week or so. Unless something drastic happens, I expect the guardianship will be made permanent."

Tears crowded Marian's eyelids, but she wasn't about to cry over the court's order. She was just too happy. She rose from her chair. "Oh, thank you, Your Honor. You're doing the right thing." The judge nodded and gave Marian a thumbs up.

Marian hugged Parker so hard he protested. As she waited for Parker to pack his briefcase, her opponents walked grimly to the door. She still didn't understand how Mr. Buchanan could have been so against her without ever having met her. But he was forgiven. Yvette was forgiven. Everyone was forgiven. Even Bryan, though their relationship was over and done with. She could never be with a man who put himself first, especially when there was someone with greater need to consider.

As they walked to the back of the courtroom, Parker said, "Interesting Guardian Ad Litem the judge appointed."

"In what way?"

"Sylvester Garza is my cousin—on my father's side." He laughed.

Marian gasped. "You think the judge knows that?"

"Oh, she knows. She knows it very well."

Marian laughed, too, as she walked past the door he held for her. And she thought, *Third time's the charm, Dorothy. You were right.*

In the hallway, Marian spotted Claire talking to Yvette and Buchanan. She signaled Marian to stop and hurried over to her. "You've got what you wanted, dear," Claire said, taking Marian's arm. "I've been thinking. I could help you with Robert's expenses since I'm sure you'll want to take him to the best doctors, and of course, outfit him with proper clothing. And if you need to hire someone to look after him—"

Her mama would never quit. "You don't get it, do you Claire? And you never will." With two fingers, Marian picked up her mama's hand and removed it from her arm. "I don't want your money." She slipped her purse over her shoulder. "I forgive you, but don't expect to ever, ever be invited into our lives. Our relationship is over. Finished. Ended. Terminated." Marian took Parker's arm and strolled to the bank of elevators to be taken away.

Chapter 40

EVERYTHING LOOKED THE SAME WHEN Marian arrived home. Somehow it should be different. She cuddled Anna in her arms and walked to the front window. A few people sat at the small metal tables in front of Coffee & More. Inside, Jane pressed her nose to the glass door and looked up at Marian. Neither of them made a move to acknowledge the other.

After she fed Anna, she peeled off her clothes on the way to the bedroom and threw herself on the bed. The glow of the stars and planets she'd stuck on the ceiling years earlier looked like the night sky overhead. The following day, she'd become a full-time mother again with—what had the judge said—all the rights, powers, privileges, duties, and responsibilities. Even if she'd had the energy to celebrate, who would share her joy? Not Bryan. Not Eva. She could only hope her other friends on the street would welcome Robert and would understand when she had less time, when she couldn't mother *them* anymore.

Marian dozed. When she awoke, she pulled on her bathrobe

and walked into Robert's bedroom. It looked a bit like an oversized cupboard with two walk-in closets. Still, what did Robert need except a bed, a chest of drawers, a place for his collections, and a chair? And a shelf that ran all the way around the inside of the room for his trains.

The carpenter had built a raised platform bed fixed to the wall. Robert wouldn't be able to move the bed, but he could shift the rest of the furniture around if he wanted. When she picked him up, they could bring the bedding, chest, and chair upstairs.

After dining on leftovers, Marian changed into shorts and a shell and headed across the street. She had to know how Eva had fared. Inside, Jane dusted shelves. She wore one of the outfits Eva had picked out for her at Marian's shop.

"Hello Jane."

"Good evening, Miss Marian."

The woman behaved differently from the bag lady Marian remembered. It wasn't just the clothing, though the green blouse with rolled-up sleeves, flowered skirt, and clean apron tied around her waist were a vast improvement over the rags she used to wear. Her skin looked pinker. Her cheeks bloomed. Her eyes sparkled. Someone had cut her hair, and it fell in wisps around her little wrinkled face. Marian could see, now, Jane couldn't be anywhere near as old as her mama.

"I—I came over to find out how Eva is doing. You seem to be well, I must say." Marian glanced around the place. It was neater and cleaner than she'd ever seen it. Somehow, though, it didn't feel the same. Coffee & More had always been welcoming, like a second home, but that was because Eva had always been there. Now it was only Jane. Could she be trusted? Was Eva taking a risk leaving the place entirely in Jane's hands?

"Eva's still in the hospital, of course. I only came back tonight because the barbecue girls couldn't cover for us. They have their own business to run." She stepped behind the counter and put the rag away. Marian followed her when she walked to the bathroom and washed her hands. "As for me, I'm doing great. Still tire easily, but getting stronger every day."

"Uh, Jane—I want to apologize for what happened in the alley."

Jane stepped close to Marian. "No need, Miss Marian. A happy accident. You was—were—watching out for your friend's place. I was in the wrong and got my just desserts when I fell. But you didn't cause it. My fault." She held out her hand. "Want to be friends?"

Marian stared at the little pixie-faced woman. When they shook hands, Jane had a warm, firm grip and smooth, leathery skin.

"Thank you," Jane said. "You're a forgiving woman." She picked up a broom. Marian didn't know what the dynamics were between Jane and Eva. "Will Eva be in the hospital very long?"

"Oh, Miss Eva's going to bounce back quickly. She'll be home soon." She moved a chair to sweep under it. "But don't you worry, I'm going to take real good care of her."

"Oh. Do you think—"

"I'm not one to get into another's business, Miss Marian. I don't get paid to think. What's between you and Miss Eva stays between you and Miss Eva."

"It would be okay if I visited her though, wouldn't it?" She wanted nothing more than to see Eva, to apologize again. She missed her friend.

"I wouldn't go there just now, Miss Marian, if you want my advice. The late hour and that being major surgery and all."

"You're right. Maybe I could go in the morning. The thing is, I've got to go back to Houston to pick up my son."

Jane's face softened. "So you have a son . . ."

"Eva didn't tell you about my son? What did Eva say about me?"

"I mind my own business. I know nothing." Jane pulled open the front door and swept a little pile of dirt over the threshold, chasing it onto the sidewalk and into the street.

Marian followed her. "Jane, could you stop for one minute and talk to me?"

Jane leaned on the broom. "She's going to be just fine."

"I'm so glad. Do you think she'll forgive me?"

Jane met her eyes. "I really can't tell you, Marian. She made me promise that if you came over here after you got home, I wouldn't say anything. You come back after she gets settled, and I'm sure she'll be up to seeing you."

"But she's okay?" She wondered whether Jane could be withholding information.

"She's all right. Come back in a couple of days."

"In the afternoon? In the evening? What time?" What if Eva was worse than Jane said? What if Eva was all right but never wanted to see her again?

"Mid-afternoon would be good."

"Jane, when I come home I'll have uh, extra responsibilities. I won't be able to run across the street if I want to. I'll have my son to take care of."

Jane started sweeping the sidewalk. "Bring him with you. Like to meet him."

"Okay." She glanced down the street to make sure no cars were coming. "But tell her when you see her in the morning that I came by, would you? Please?"

"I certainly will. See you again soon."

Marian walked back home and climbed the stairs. She lay on the bed and wept. Tears of exhaustion and relief and love for her son and of hope for the future. She fell asleep fully clothed, waking in the middle of the night to kick off her shoes and crawl under the covers.

Chapter 41

AT DOROTHY'S THE NEXT DAY, Marian packed most of Robert's things into the car's back seat and trunk. Veronica promised to bring the rest before she went home to her family. She looked worried but admitted she knew everything would be okay.

Veronica tried to hug Robert, always awkward at best. Hugging meant encircling him with one's arms, barely touching. Most of the time touching Robert, besides holding his hand, was out of the question. It startled him and could be painful, not just emotionally, but physically. Not always. It was hard to know. She did manage a kiss on the cheek—his—not hers.

As Marian and Robert drove back down the Gulf Freeway toward Galveston, he sat in the passenger seat and called out the color of cars. "Red car. Little red car. Big red car. Twenty-three red cars."

When they reached the wetland area of the Galveston county

mainland, Robert said, "Railroad tracks, Marian. Railroad tracks on the water."

"I know. When the train is on them, it looks like the train is traveling on the water. Sometime I'll bring you out here when the train is on the tracks so you can see how weird that looks. Would you like that, Robert?" She wondered what she sounded like to him. And what went on inside his head.

"I would like to see that train, Marian." Robert stared out the window.

"We're going across a big bridge in a few minutes, the train bridge goes right next to the Causeway Bridge. You'll be able to see it."

"That's good. I want to see the railroad bridge."

"And we have a railroad museum here, too. Remember I told you that when we went to the museum in Houston."

"I want to see the museum."

"Okay. We'll go someday. But not today. Today we get you settled in your new home."

"Okay, Marian. But soon. We will go to the museum soon."

She reined in a sigh. They crossed the bridge with Robert intensely focused on the railroad bridge and didn't talk the rest of the way.

When they parked in the garage at the condo, they lugged Robert's things up the back stairs. Anna greeted him with a growl and a bark, but not aggressive barks like she had at Claire. Robert stared at Anna, expressionless. He'd never had a pet.

"Put out your hand." Marian leaned down and held out her hand to Anna who licked it and jumped up and down at Marian's feet while keeping a respectable distance from Robert. Marian scratched Anna's head and under her chin and around her ears. Anna clearly wanted to be picked up, but Marian wanted Robert and Anna to get to know each other.

"Her name is Anna. Give her your hand so she can learn your scent."

Robert didn't appear alarmed at Anna's growl. He leaned over from the waist like a wooden stick figure and hung his hand down low enough for Anna to smell. Anna sniffed and nudged him with her nose. But when Anna growled a second time, Robert growled, too.

Marian covered her mouth. They still stood on the landing. She was afraid to breathe, afraid to disturb the moment.

Anna let out a lesser growl, and Robert imitated her again. She stepped forward and licked the back of his fingers. One little lick. Robert didn't pull his hand away, but he glanced at Marian, deadpan. Always deadpan...

"I think she likes you."

As she said that, Anna licked his fingers more. He turned his hand, and Anna licked his palm. He slowly walked his fingers to the top of Anna's head and scratched her in the center between her ears. Anna jumped up on her hind legs in a jig, her tail flying high. Robert stood up as though startled but petted her, cupping his hand at the back of her head and stroking the dog. "Anna the dog."

"Yes, Robert. Anna the dog." Marian wanted to cry, to see her son taking to Anna so easily, and Anna returning the feeling. Things were going to be all right. Robert might have some hard days ahead, be confused as he should be, but everything would end up being fine. Could the judge have sensed that? She was grateful the judge was giving her a chance after everyone had been against her.

Robert stretched out his arms, and Anna hopped into them. He glanced at Marian as if asking permission. Elated, Marian nodded. Afraid to do anything that might alter the situation, she stood as stiffly as Robert had been a moment before and watched him cradle Anna in his arms. After a few moments, Anna licked Robert's face. He put his nose to her neck and sniffed. Unbelievable.

"Let's get you situated," Marian said, walking toward the bedroom. "Bring Anna, bring one of your bags. I've got one." She led the way toward his room, and he followed.

Robert sat on the edge of his new bed and stroked Anna who seemed very content in his arms. Marian put his clothing away in one of the empty walk-in closets. She talked to him the whole time, even though he didn't reply, and explained that he'd be living with her now. She told him one walk-in closet was for his collections, his trains, his books, and things he'd saved from his childhood. "If you need better lighting in there, we can add big florescent lights. You can arrange things anyway you want. This is your room. Those are your closets."

He stroked Anna. "Robert's room. Robert's closets." Monotone as usual.

"Come on," she said when she was through unpacking and had gotten his help to stack his bags on the highest closet shelf.

She led him to the bathroom and hoped the potpourri wasn't too strong for him. She'd forgotten he was sensitive to certain smells. "This is our bathroom. We'll share. You'll knock if the door is closed. I know you understand, but if you can't remember, you can ask me." She turned his face to hers to be sure she had his attention, but he pulled back and looked sideways.

"I just want to make sure you're paying attention, Robert. I'll also knock if the door is closed. Okay, look, we each have a sink. You get the one on the right." She patted his sink. "I get the one on the left. See, Robert, I'm putting your shaving things next to the sink on the right."

"Yes, Marian. This is my sink," he said, patting his sink. "That is your sink."

"Robert, we have a bathtub and a shower. You can take a bath if you want, but you have to clean the bathtub." Rubbing her lower back, she said, "My back just won't take it."

She slid open the shower door. "See, this is our shower. This is how you work the knob. The large knob controls the flow of water and whether it is hot, or cold, or warm. Turn it to the right for cold, left for hot, and leave the little arrow pointing upward for warm." She demonstrated for him. "Pull it up hard for a lot of water and down for a slight shower, which is good when you're cleaning." She glanced at him to see if he understood. He seemed to grasp it.

Pulling on his sleeve, she led him to a small closet in the bathroom and slid open the bi-fold doors. "This is our washer and dryer. Put your dirty clothes in the hamper here, and I'll wash our clothes when we have a full load." Again she scanned his face to see if he'd respond. He stared, but at what she didn't know.

"Mother gone." He stroked Anna.

"Yes, Robert." Marian took a quivering breath, pulled again on his shirtsleeve, and moved on. She led him to another small closet in the opposite corner. "Robert, this is the toilet. The door will automatically swing closed behind you. It's an antique door from the five-and-dime store that used to occupy this building. Do you know what an antique is?"

"Yes, Marian. An antique door. It's old. An antique door."

"Do you need to use the toilet now? It was a long drive from Houston."

"No, Marian."

Marian led him downstairs to the shop. "This is where we work. This is my shop. I'll have jobs for you to do. Right now, we'll have something to eat, and then you can open those large boxes over there."

She led him back upstairs where Anna finally jumped down.

She encouraged him to wash his hands. "If you're not careful, she'll let you carry her around all day."

"I like Anna. She's a good dog. I like her." He went to the kitchen sink and washed his hands.

"I'm glad. I like her, too. Sit anywhere," she said, pointing at the table. She was pleased about Anna. She'd read that autistic people and animals communicate very well, but she wouldn't have believed it if she hadn't seen it.

She opened the foil-wrapped packages Veronica sent with them. Leftovers from the meal at Dorothy's house after the funeral.

She filled two plates and heated them in the microwave. When she set one in front of Robert, Anna scurried to his feet.

"We don't feed Anna from the table," Marian said. "Don't even think about it. Here, Anna. Let's get you your dinner." She poured Anna's food from a bag in the pantry. Robert watched them. "She's on a schedule. She gets fed twice a day, morning and evening. She's little, so not much if you feed her. We don't want her to turn into a fat old lady dog."

"Okay, Marian. I won't over-feed Anna. We don't want a fat old dog." He watched Anna eat.

"Robert, people eat three times a day, right?"

"Right, Marian. We eat three times a day. And snacks."

"Yes, snacks. Just like at Dorothy's. I made a schedule for you. It's here pasted on the inside of the pantry door." She opened the pantry door again and showed him the poster boards pasted to the inside. The psychiatrist she'd consulted had advised her to make him a visual schedule. She'd cut out pictures from magazines and made charts with pictures. "When you have a minute, you can study your schedule, okay?"

"Okay, Marian. Can we eat now?" He held a fork in his hand.

"Sure. I'm hungry, too."

After dinner, they went downstairs to the shop. Chloe had already closed up and gone home so just the two of them were there. Afraid to give him a knife, Marian handed him a plastic letter opener that had sharp edges. Part of his job at the grocery store had been opening boxes, so he'd used a box cutter, but she wasn't comfortable with that; he could slice into garments. Robert walked over to the boxes and set about opening them. Marian kept an eye on him while she unpacked and thought of Dorothy and years of caring for Robert from the time he was a tot.

That night, Marian lay in her bed and listened to Robert pace in his small bedroom. She could hear soft footfalls. Like a caged animal, he walked from one end to the other and back again. She'd peeked in on him when he stopped; he sat in the chair and rocked, cupping his elbows and staring into space.

Marian had fallen into bed exhausted. She knew she'd get used to caring for Robert, get used to their routine, but after just the first day, she was worn out.

The next day, after breakfast, she took Robert downstairs and introduced him to Chloe when she came in. "Chloe is the young lady who works for us, Robert."

Chloe smiled and put out her hand. Robert looked at it.

"You shake hands when someone holds out their hand," Marian reminded him. She wasn't sure if he usually shook hands when he met people when she wasn't around.

Chloe reached for Robert's hand and lifted it up and shook it. "Like that. That's a hand shake, Robert."

Robert eyeballed her and their hands and then shook her hand once up and down and dropped it. "Chloe, hand shake."

Chloe glanced from Robert to Marian and back. "I hope we'll be friends."

"We'll be friends," Robert said.

In the middle of the day, after having had an almost sleepless night, Marian turned the shop over to Chloe and took Robert upstairs, telling him they both needed a nap. She lay there, listening to his footsteps. She was already lonely for adult conversation, but glad she at least had Chloe. She missed Bryan. And Eva. And her friends on the street. She wondered what had been going on with Winnie and Mickey and Lorette and Lupe and Miguel and Luther and Troy.

She had convinced herself that Bryan was ancient history, but now she wanted him. She missed the companionship. And the sex, if she had to be honest. The sex had been wonderful after a long, dry spell.

Marian rolled over onto her stomach and pressed her face into her pillow. She was like an addict—a co-dependent? She had dreamed of reuniting with Bryan for so many years, true, but it hadn't worked. Wasn't meant to be. She didn't really want Bryan. He was selfish. He was wishy-washy, unstable. If he didn't love her enough to even try, things never would've worked out in the long run. She needed to get used to that idea and get over him.

But she loved him. No, she fantasized about him. She'd dreamed all those years about who she thought he was, not who he really was. He was not that dream person. What she was crying for was the loss of a fantasy.

But what if he'd given it some thought and realized how wrong he'd been? Maybe he was too proud to call her and apologize. She hadn't seen him since Artwalk. He'd probably had a chance to think it over. But what about Robert? She knew how Robert might react if Bryan came into their lives and changed his mind and left again. It was bad enough for normal children when a parent left. No, no matter what, she wouldn't sacrifice Robert's health and stability for Bryan, whether Bryan ever wanted to come back or not.

LEDBETTER STREET

Robert's movements stopped. Did he finally lie down or pick up a book? Was he sitting and holding Anna? She wondered what he saw inside his head. None of the experts seemed to know for sure. They couldn't measure him like they measured regular people.

Tomorrow, she would renew her efforts to help Robert find where he fit into her life. She would call around the University of Texas Medical Branch to see if there were any support groups for each of them. It would be mother and son making a life. Right now, what she needed was rest. And someone to talk to.

Marian woke up after forty-five minutes. Startled at herself for forgetting Robert, she jumped off the bed and looked in his room. Empty. She found him in the living room. He stood at the window and stared into the street, like Marian often did.

"You all right?" she asked as she came up behind him.

"Yes, Marian. Want to go outside." He looked at her out of the corner of his eye, expressionless.

"Want to run across the street to Coffee & More? I want to see my friend, Eva. You haven't met her yet."

Robert nodded. "Yes, Marian."

"Okay, let me get some shoes." She hurried back toward her bedroom, calling over her shoulder, "Are you hungry? We can get something at Eva's, okay?"

"Okay, Marian. Okay."

When Marian came back with her shoes and wallet, Robert sat on the top step. A tall, gilded mirror hung over the stairs. Robert stared at his reflection.

"You look fine. A very handsome man, if I do say so."

Robert's face remained impassive.

"Stay, Anna," Robert said. "Nice girl." He patted the dog and scratched her ears.

"Yes, very handsome," Marian said and realized she repeated

288

herself again. "Let's go." He bounded down the stairs, and she scrambled after him, determined to get past Jane no matter what.

When they reached the street, Robert ran across, and Marian realized what she'd said. She had to be careful. Robert was literal. She'd said run, and he'd run.

She crossed the street after him. They found Jane behind the counter. "Hey, Jane."

"Good evening, Ms. Reid."

"What's this Ms. Reid stuff?"

Jane shrugged. "What would you like?"

"Jane, this is Robert." She turned to Robert. "Robert, this is Jane."

"Hello," Robert said. "Jane."

"Nice to meet you, Mister Robert," Jane said. "What would you like?"

Marian said, "A large hot tea, and he can pick out something in the cabinet if he's hungry."

"Coffee," Robert said.

"I thought you liked tea." Maybe it was Dorothy who liked tea and Robert never had a say in it. Who knew?

"Coffee and that," Robert said, pointing to a large scone with orange bits on it. "Okay, Jane, the coffee lady."

"Whatever he wants. I'll pay when I come back down. I'm going up to see Eva, and don't try to stop me."

"I would never do such a thing," Jane said with a sniff and an arch of her neck. She turned her attention to Robert. "Now, young man, do you have a particular scone in mind, or will any of them do?"

"Robert, stay here with Jane. I'll be back." Marian took a deep breath to calm the flutter in her chest and headed upstairs. Eva was not in the living area. Panic gripped her. Did she have to remain bedridden? She opened the bedroom door. Eva lay sleeping.

Marian walked around the far side of the bed and sat on the edge. "Eva, wake up. It's me, Marian." She shook her arm.

Eva opened her eyes. She didn't say anything for a few moments, just looked at Marian. "So you finally deigned to cross the street and come see me?"

"Eva, I—"

Eva's face broke into a grin. "I'm just kidding. How are you, girl? Give me a hug but don't squeeze me."

"Is it bad? I should've known it would be this bad. Don't go making light of it. I know you haven't been downstairs." Marian put her cheek to Eva's and patted her shoulder. "I'm so sorry," she whispered. "I should've been there. I tried to see you before I brought Robert home, but Jane said you were still in the hospital."

"Jane." Eva snorted. "She's a trip. Really protective and such a warm person, Marian, you'll see."

"I'm glad. I'd hate to think a bad person was your caregiver."

"I'm sorry about how I treated you, sorry about Dorothy. Don't know if I ever told you that." She sat up and tucked the covers around herself. "I should have figured out a way to go with you to her service."

Marian was touched. "Thank you for that, but I want to know about you. Tell me all about your surgery. Can I get you anything?"

"Pour me a glass of water from that pitcher, will you?" She pointed at a plastic pitcher and cup.

Marian brought her the water and sat on the edge of the bed again. "Eva, please. It's killing me. Please tell me it wasn't so bad."

Eva handed the cup back after taking several swallows. "It was terrible, but they got all the cancer. Think it's gone now. Hadn't spread to my lymph nodes."

Marian couldn't find the words to say anything; she simply

stared at her friend. She tried to hold the tears back, knowing Eva thought women who cried were just being sappy.

"No crying, Marian. Look at it this way, I'm flat-chested now, no boobs to worry with." She brushed her fingers through her hair as though to look nonchalant. "I bet I look a mess."

Marian wiped her eyes with her fingers. "You bet you look a mess? They took both breasts, and you bet you look a mess? Are you serious?"

Eva clenched her jaw. "Yes, I'm taking it very seriously, but you know me, kid. Got to make the best of it."

"God. You know I love you. I'm so sorry I wasn't there. Maybe I should've tried to get the case reset. At least by a couple of days. You should've slapped me silly and told me to get my head out of my rear. Are you okay now? Do you have to have chemo and all that?"

Eva stroked Marian's arm. "First of all, you were all wrapped up in the Bryan and Robert thing. I was a bitch. I've never had kids, but I think I know how much Robert means to you.

"Second, it's all worked out fine. I was hurt, but the thing with Jane is fine. Really. She's a great lady and is going to be a big help to me in the shop from now on. All my problems are solved."

"Sure they are."

"I'm apologizing, girlfriend. Let's put it behind us."

Marian perched on the side of the bed. "When you threw me out, I wanted to step in front of a car. I could see you through the window later, but you wouldn't even look my way. I didn't know I could hurt someone so badly." Eva lay there quietly.

"I was too angry. I wanted you to know how much it meant to me, but I didn't want to accept how important Robert was to you. I've been thinking a lot about it since I've had nothing else to do. I guess sometimes I don't communicate very well."

"Maybe I should have seen that. I'm sorry. I couldn't think about anything except Robert and Bryan and losing Dorothy. Bryan and I are over, on top of everything else."

"Oh, God, I'm sorry. I was just thinking about myself."

"I guess we both were. So how long do you have to stay in bed? I can't believe you look as good as you do." She took Eva's hand. She wished she could do something to relieve her pain.

"Is that a compliment, girlfriend?"

Marian laughed. "I thought the recovery time was really long. How come you're not still in the hospital?"

"Well, I didn't have reconstruction. I just couldn't see the use in that. It's not like I'll ever have a husband or a boyfriend who'll care if I have breasts." Tears spilled from her eyes. "When they told me what you had to go through for reconstruction, I said no way. So I'll get these little jelly thingys to put in special bras. If I miss my girls too much, I can stick 'em in and look like I have boobs."

"Oh my God." Marian found a box of tissues, dried Eva's tears and blotted her own. She crawled up on the bed and gently put her arms around her friend. She stroked Eva's hair. For once, it wasn't gelled into spikes. It was soft, like a baby's. "I've missed you so much."

"Me, too," Eva said.

"So I guess Jane's taken my place."

"It's like my mother's taking care of me. But I don't want you to think that's why I took her in. It's not. I just couldn't leave her out on the street." She sobbed into a corner of the sheet. "Poor lady."

"I know. You think you have everybody fooled, but we all know what a soft heart you really have."

"She could never take your place, though."

"You're heart's big enough for both of us. "

Marian and Eva lay on the bed for a long time. Eva described the details and showed her what was left of her chest. Marian told Eva about Bryan's testimony, her mama trashing her and wanting to pay to put Robert away, what the judge said, and Robert coming home.

A bit later, Jane stuck her head in the door. "If you're up to meeting someone, I have Robert here."

"Bring him in," Eva said.

Marian stood and brushed at the wrinkles in her clothes. "Come in, Robert." He took hesitant steps inside the bedroom, his arms swinging by his sides.

"Eva, this is Robert. Robert, say hello to my friend, Eva."

They both said hello at the same time.

"Eva sick?" Robert asked.

"Yes," Eva said. "But I'm getting better. Did Jane give you something to eat downstairs?"

"Coffee. Cake."

"An orange scone," Jane said. "I think you have a new fan."

"I'm glad," Eva said. "You're welcome to come anytime, Robert. We're like family here."

"Family," Robert said. "Like family, Eva the sick lady."

Eva glanced at Marian as if to ask why he said what he'd said. Marian shrugged. She'd have to explain later how associating each person with something helped Robert remember them. "Well, I think family has had a long enough visit. We have things to do. Jane, if you need any help at all in the shop, I'll be glad to come when I can, so just let me know. Chloe's working for me, and Robert's working now, too."

"Jane told me about Chloe," Eva said. "That should work out well for her and the baby."

"I hope so. She's really a nice girl, but God, so under that man's influence. Well, I'm glad I got to see you."

"Me, too. Let's not be strangers again," Eva said and took Robert by the wrist. "You either, Robert."

"No strangers again," Robert said.

"Take it easy," Marian said. "I'll be back tomorrow." She leaned down and kissed Eva's cheek. "I love you. Let's never get crosswise again."

"Take it easy," Robert said.

Marian led Robert down the stairs and out onto Ledbetter Street. After she got him settled in front of the TV, she locked the bathroom door, turned on the radio and the shower. She got in and stood under the water, blubbering until she could no longer stand.

Chapter 42

"**ROBERT, LET'S GO FOR A** walk," Marian said a few days later, turning off the TV. "Put your tennis shoes on, and we'll go out and breathe fresh air."

"My favorite show."

"You know what I told you. They're all on the DVR." She pointed to the box on a shelf.

Robert turned toward Marian, got up, and walked to his room, forever like a wooden solder. He returned with his shoes on and started down the stairs.

Marian followed. Just as they started to go out, Troy opened the door to his shop and stepped onto the sidewalk. Embarrassment flooded her. He was probably the one who had put her to bed after Artwalk, which meant he'd seen her get violently ill. A bit of memory came back, more than she wanted. She stopped Robert before he opened the door, giving Troy time to lock his own door and walk away. A younger man followed him. It was Luther, the artist who used to live in the next block, the one who'd had hepatitis.

He looked healthy. They laughed as they set off down the street. How long had it been since his collapse? More than several weeks, a month, or longer?

Luther was gay. The thought had crossed her mind that Troy might be interested in her. Obviously, she was mistaken. Troy was new on the street and was being a friend to her, that's all. Not that she wanted a man in her life after Bryan, but she'd been flattered. Didn't he tell her he'd been married, and his wife died? She'd heard of men who'd been married and turned out to be gay.

Troy and Luther went into Miguel's. Marian opened her shop door and steered Robert the opposite way. Locking it behind her, she hurried to catch up with her son's long. loping strides. They walked toward Fisherman's Wharf Restaurant.

"Slow down," she said, pulling on his sleeve. "Take a breather."

"A breather?" Robert slowed to a snail's pace and started breathing fast and deep.

"Okay, that's an expression. Haven't you heard that before?"

"An expression? Slow down. Take a breather?"

"Yes. Though it's one you might take literally, especially when we're out walking. Remember, my legs are shorter than yours."

"Short legs can't walk fast."

"As fast, anyway." She hooked her arm through his.

The closer they got to the docks, the stronger the scent of salt air. They passed the restaurant and its grilled-fish aroma and strolled around the corner. The tall ship Elissa sat tied to the dock, wood gleaming in the late afternoon sun. "Want to go on the ship?"

"Yes, go on the ship." Robert jogged to the roped-off area.

"Hang on, and let me pay." After she paid, they climbed aboard. Marian had quit worrying about small things like Robert's losing his footing. He was very able physically and needed to stay active. She had so much to learn about him.

"Robert, this is the Tall Ship Elissa. It's very old, built in 1877. Some people found it in Europe. You know what Europe is. I'm sure you've seen it on your globe."

Robert glanced at Marian. She followed him around the deck as he looked and touched and stared up at the masts and sails, all wrapped and tied. The oil from the woodwork left a slight residue on her fingers.

"Europe is made up of those countries across the Atlantic Ocean, a large body of water off the East coast of our country." He probably already knew all that.

"Somebody found this old ship in a salvage yard in Greece. She'd been used to haul cargo, and for fishing and stuff, and was run down. People got together and raised money to bring her to Galveston. When she arrived, they raised more money to fix her up, millions of dollars. It took a long time. A lot of people volunteered. They sail her, and let people like us look at her."

Robert headed for below-decks. He stood next to the ladder. "Marian, I want to go down."

"All right, go ahead." She'd never toured the ship. She was a stranger to one of the biggest attractions in Galveston.

Robert seemed to know what he was looking at. He scrutinized everything. Again, she realized she shouldn't underestimate him.

An hour later, they trudged over to Willie G's restaurant where they sat at the bar and breathed in the smell of cooking seafood. She ordered iced tea for Robert and a glass of white wine for herself.

The bartender set a bowl of peanuts and pretzels before them. Robert stared at everything as though he would have to describe it in detail later.

"You can eat that, Robert," she said.

She glanced around to see if anyone she knew happened to be there. K. D. Lang's music played in the background. Marian wanted to stroke Robert's back, but wasn't sure whether he'd be too sensitive to that kind of touch.

Robert picked peanuts out of the bowl and lined them up on a napkin. After he made two rows, he picked pretzels out and lined them up on another napkin. When there were two rows of pretzels, he pushed the bowl at Marian. She set it at arm's length. Robert picked up the peanuts one at a time and ate them.

"Well, what have we here?" Bryan's voice came from behind. When she turned, he stood at her elbow, close enough for her to catch his scent. He looked dapper as always, a crease as sharp as a straight razor in his slacks, starched sports shirt, shined loafers. About a week's growth of white fuzz covered his thin face. He also wore new glasses, designer frames.

The wine in her stomach soured. "Hello, Bryan."

They looked at each other a few moments until Bryan peered around her and said, "Are you going to say hello to me, Robert?"

Marian gripped Robert's elbow. She still didn't know what Bryan knew or what Robert understood. Robert didn't respond. He just kept eating the peanuts. He probably didn't recognize Bryan. He'd only met him once.

Bryan shrugged. "So how are things going? Since Robert's with you, I take it you're now his guardian."

Marian said to Robert, "Drink up. We're going home." She swallowed the last of her wine.

"You don't have to leave on my account," Bryan said.

Marian placed money on the bar and slid out of the high-backed barstool. "Come on, Robert. Let's go." She tugged on Robert's sleeve. He scooped up a handful of pretzels. When they got to the door, she held it open and Robert went out.

Bryan followed them. "Do you want to talk sometime?"

"I have nothing to say to you." Her eyes met his, but she held strong and followed Robert out the door.

Chapter 43

JANE HADN'T NOTICED THE HOSPITAL smell in Eva's bedroom until Friday night when she and Marian went to help Eva downstairs. She'd have to figure out what made it so strong.

"She's not to lift her arms much, Miss Marian," she said, "so I slipped this blouse over her bandages and buttoned it up for her. It looks okay, doesn't it?"

"Very nice." Marian smiled at Jane.

Eva said, "Quit talking about me like I'm not here. I look fine. I don't know why you two have to make such a big deal out of my going downstairs."

"When we go down, hold onto the rail with your right hand to steady yourself and hold my hand with your left so you can balance," Marian said.

"I lost my boobs," Eva said, "not my mind. I think I can manage a flight of stairs."

"I'll bring a lap rug," Jane said, "in case you want to cover up."

"Cover up, hell. It's summer outside."

"You'll be inside," Jane said. Eva was funny when she fussed, but tried not to hide her smile.

"Whatever," Eva said.

"I think she's feeling better." Marian led the way, putting out her hand for Eva to take.

Jane followed them. She'd never wanted to interfere with their relationship. In the few short weeks they'd known each other, Jane had grown to love Eva, too. Like the daughter she'd never had. Marian and Eva mended their friendship, but it didn't affect Jane. Every day she lived on Ledbetter Street, they were more and more like family.

"Surprise!" A chorus of voices rang out.

One of the women sang, "For she's a jolly good lady."

Robert sat at the counter on the far wall with his hands over his ears.

Eva stopped. "What the hell are y'all doing here?"

"We just came by to tell you how glad we are that you're back on your feet," Mickey said.

"Well, my feet maybe, but not the rest of me," Eva said. "But I'm getting there." The look on her face told Jane how much she appreciated the attention.

"Missed having someone bitch at me when I get coffee in the morning," Troy said. He crossed the room and tousled her downy hair. "We don't know each other well, Eva, but I'm glad you're up and about. I hope we get to be better friends."

"Well, ain't that sweet. Is that Luther over there? Jane tells me you're all better, Luther, and living with Troy next door. Doing any painting?"

Luther blushed. "A little. Seems like everyone in the neighborhood had something go wrong at the same time. Good to see you."

"Not a little painting," Troy said. "A lot, and he's really good."

"That's what Jane told me," Eva said.

Jane couldn't have been prouder if she'd been his mother. "Hey, Luther," she said, bobbing her head. Luther flashed her a grin.

"We just came by to wish you well, Eva," Winnie said. She crossed the room and leaned down, squeezing Eva's shoulders gently. "We gotta get back to The Pit."

"You're not staying for cake?" Jane asked.

"Cake—hey, it's not my birthday. I just walked downstairs for God's sake."

"It's sort of a *welcome home* cake, even though you've been home for almost a week now," Marian said. "We wanted to share our happiness with our Ledbetter Street family."

Lorette edged closer to Eva. "Want me to help you to a chair?"

"That's all right, Lorette. I'm not a cripple." She walked over to one of the tables and sat down. "Okay. Thank you all for coming."

Chloe stood in a corner. She wiggled her fingers at Eva.

"It's a carrot cake. Healthy. Come back later and get a piece," Jane said.

"See you," Miguel said. "Lupe can stay, but the man, he has to go back to work."

"Aw, get out of here, Miguel," Eva said.

Miguel kissed the back of her hand. "Glad you're okay, Amiga."

Troy said, "We're going back to the gallery. Okay if Robert goes with us, Marian?"

Jane walked to where Robert sat hunched over. "Robert, want to go with Troy and Luther?"

Marian nodded her approval.

Robert slid off his stool. "Okay. Go with Troy the man and Luther the artist." He followed them out the door.

Several other people left to get back to their businesses, but most of the women stayed. Jane stepped behind the counter. "Want me to get anyone anything? Of course, you'll be paying."

Lorette pulled up a chair next to Eva. "I'm sure glad you're doing better. We've missed you around here."

"Thanks, Lorette," Eva said. "I'll take a latte," she said loudly.

"Should you be having caffeine?" Lorette asked.

"One latte is not going to kill me. Besides, I don't remember the doctor limiting my caffeine."

Jane showed Eva the cake and set it on the counter beside plates, forks, and a knife. "If you want cake, come and get it, except for you, Eva. I'll bring you a slice." Never in her entire life had she been around so many nice women. Again, she thought of how living on Ledbetter Street was like living with a large family. She'd always wanted sisters and brothers. She had wanted more than one child, though Howard wouldn't hear of it.

Lupe came around to help her. "You've learned a lot, Jane. It's like you've worked here for ages."

"Like being in my own house, except all these fancy new machines." She pulled out two cups. "And a lot louder and smellier. But good smells."

"Is Troy gay?" Marian asked when she pulled up a chair. "I was thinking he and Rain might have something going, but now Luther's living with him."

"He's gay?" Lorette said. "Too bad. Kind of cute."

"Luther's gay," Eva said. "Right Jane?"

"Yep, a gay blade, as they used to say." She set a latte before Eva and a chai tea in front of Marian. Steam rose from the cups.

"Thank you, Jane," Marian said. "I didn't even say I wanted anything."

"You're welcome, Marian," Jane said and winked. She wanted Marian to like her. "Hey, Chloe girl, you want anything?"

Chloe looked at her hands. As far as Jane knew, Chloe was acquainted with everyone but hadn't been included inside this circle until now.

"Don't be shy. You're going to pay for it," Jane said.

"A Coke?"

Chloe's expression made Jane think of a whipped puppy. She'd felt the way Chloe looked when she was living in similar circumstances.

"Diet, or regular?"

"Diet," Chloe said. She sat in a chair on the other side of Marian.

"Like you need to be on a diet," Lorette said.

"Darryl doesn't want me to get fat." She bit a cuticle.

"Chloe, I hate to say anything, but isn't Darryl in jail?" Lorette asked.

Chloe looked at Lorette. "Yes, ma'am. But he'll be getting out soon. He told me he cut a deal with the district attorney so he won't have to stay in jail as long as we thought."

"He told you?" Marian asked. She took cups from Jane and passed them to the others. "I thought Children's Protective Services told you not to see Darryl."

Chloe glanced at the other women's faces. "I don't want to discuss it. Couldn't we just talk about Eva or what's happening on Ledbetter Street?"

"Chloe," Marian said, placing a hand on her arm. "No one's accusing you of anything. We just want to help."

"Darryl called and told me to come see him at the jail," she said, crossing her arms and staring at the table.

"You didn't have to go," Lorette said.

"You don't understand," Chloe said. "I have to do what Darryl says, or he'll get mad. I can't let him get mad."

"Oh, Jesus," Eva said.

"He needs me, Eva. I can't turn my back on him when he needs me so badly."

"Chloe, I saw what he does to you," Jane said, handing her a diet Coke and a straw. "This is your chance to get away from him."

"I can't help it. I can't leave him."

"Yes, you can, damn it," Lorette said. "Just don't go see him, or talk to him, or let him come around when he gets out."

"You don't understand. None of you understands." Chloe picked up the diet Coke can and pushed back her chair.

Jane put her hands on Chloe's shoulders, prodding her to sit back down. "No use getting mad at us, little girl. We're your friends."

"What about the baby?" Marian asked. "What's going to happen to Leo?"

Chloe stared down into her lap. "I'm having a trial next week."

"What?" Lorette asked. "For what?"

Chloe's eyes grew round. Jane knew what the girl would say before she even spoke.

"They want to take my baby away from me for good." Chloe gripped her drink, the soft aluminum indenting from the pressure of her fingers.

"Oh, no. No, Chloe," Lupe said, shaking her head. "Why would they do that? Are you not doing what they put in that paper for you to do?"

"They wanted me to promise I'd divorce Darryl and never see him again." She ran her fingers through her hair and rested her elbows on the table, staring at each woman in turn. "I can't do that."

"Can they ask someone to do that?" Eva asked.

"They can do whatever they want," Marian said. "Believe me, I know. They won't let you keep him if you agree to keep Darryl away from him?"

Chloe shook her head. "They don't think I can protect Leo from Darryl."

Jane and Marian exchanged glances. Jane thought that might be true.

"There are other things they could do, though, aren't there?" Lorette asked.

"Like what?" Chloe asked.

"Couldn't they put him in foster care and let you visit?" Eva asked.

Chloe bit her lip as tears welled up in her eyes. She shook her head.

"Well, couldn't they?" Eva again.

Chloe choked and wailed, "They want to put him up for adoption!"

"Oh, God."

"So I guess they're going to the judge to get your rights cut off? Why didn't you tell me?" Marian asked.

Chloe pulled napkins out of the holder on the table. "My lawyer said I stood a better chance with a jury."

"You're having a jury trial on Monday?" Eva asked. "You want us to come to court with you?"

"You're not going to court with anyone, Miss Best," Jane said. "You're not even staying down here very much longer." She crossed her arms and stared Eva down.

Eva rolled her eyes. "Well, someone can go to court with her."

"That's okay; you don't have to." Chloe wiped her eyes. "I'll have my lawyer."

Several of the women shook their heads. Jane recognized the dazed expression on Chloe's face. Her mother used to get that look, like she'd been hypnotized and couldn't understand the events around her.

Eva raised her voice. "Will at least one of you go to court with this poor girl?"

"I'll stop in, Chloe," Lorette said. "Sometime during the week."

"Me, too," Lupe said.

"Now I know why you needed time off," Marian said. "You could have told me."

"You had your own problems." Chloe hung her head, her hair falling forward to cover her face. "I didn't want to bother anyone."

"Well, we'll all be there to give you moral support, except for Miss Best here," Marian said, inclining her head at Eva. "At least, to let you know we're here for you if you need us."

"Okay," Eva said, "that's settled, now let's dig into this cake before my nurse puts me to bed."

Jane laughed. That's what she'd been. Eva's nurse, her employee, her friend. When Eva got better, she'd show her what she'd been doing downstairs in the room that Eva had given her. But for now, she'd keep doing what she'd been doing and wait and see what happened.

Chloe slurped the last of her soda. "Thank you, gals," she said. "I know you want the best for me."

"We need youthful blood on this street," Lorette said.

"I'd say it balances out," Jane said. "An old hag like me and a sweet young thing like Chloe." She was going to like being a permanent fixture on Ledbetter Street. She'd work really hard to make sure that's what she'd be, so hard that Eva wouldn't know how she ever got by without her.

Chapter 44

THE FOLLOWING WEEK, MARIAN PEEKED through the doors of every courtroom until she found Chloe, in a simple white blouse and flowered skirt, sitting at a table. To her surprise, Parker Benavides stood talking with another attorney and the judge at the bench. Marian slipped onto a wooden pew. A jury filled the jury box. A young woman sat at the table next to Chloe's. The court announced a recess a few minutes later.

"Marian, what are you doing here?" Parker asked.

"I came to support Chloe. She didn't tell me you represented her."

Parker looked as comfortable in the Galveston courtroom as he had in Houston. If he could win Robert back for her, he could do anything.

He glanced over his shoulder at Chloe. "I should've realized you two knew each other."

"She works in my shop, Reid's Ritzy Rags."

"The court appointed him for me," Chloe said.

He ushered them into one of the conference rooms. "We'll stay in here while on break. I don't want the jurors to hear anything we're saying."

"I guess my timing's off. I managed to stash Robert with Jane and thought I'd run over. How's it going?"

"The jury doesn't like me." Chloe crossed her arms.

"We're not giving up hope," Parker said. "These damn CPS workers think they can tell people how to live their lives. They have no right to try to force Chloe to get a divorce."

"I was afraid of that," Marian said. "You have to quit seeing Darryl."

Chloe shook her head. "I can't promise that. I know he hurt Leo, but I don't know how to explain it. I just can't get loose from him." She hugged herself.

Parker patted Chloe's back. "He's getting out sometime this week. He pled to a state jail felony and relinquished his rights to the baby. With good-time credit on his sentence—he didn't have to do much time."

"He'll be coming for me," Chloe said. "I told him not to come to court, but I bet he does."

Parker clenched his jaw. "You have to tell him not to, Chloe. They'll terminate your rights in a New York minute if he shows up in the courtroom."

Chloe stood and rocked back and forth on her heels, her arms clutching her stomach. "I don't want to lose my baby. I love Leo. I don't want them to take him."

"Darryl's still here in Galveston, in the county jail? He didn't go to prison?"

Chloe said, "By the time he went to court, he was in jail long enough they said it was no use sending him away. He could finish his time out here."

Parker and Marian's eyes met.

"I could go to the jail with you while you tell him not to come to the courthouse," Marian said.

"You don't have to do that." Chloe shook her head. "I don't tell him anything. I'll *ask* him when he's getting out, if he knows for sure, and *ask* him not to come here."

Parker glanced at his watch. "Let's go. Break's almost over."

Marian hugged Chloe. She smelled like bath soap. "Good luck."

"Thank you for coming. I'll be all right."

Parker touched Marian's shoulder and whispered, "You're a gem, Marian. I'll be over sometime this week to see you and Robert. See how you're doing. And I'll bring my cousin."

Marian caught her breath. She had yet to meet the court-appointed guardian *ad litem*. But Parker assured her everything would be fine and not to worry. Hugging Parker, she said, "Good luck. I'll try to make it back on another day, if I can."

Poor Chloe. Pathetic life with a man who'd probably kill her some day. Although Marian wanted to help, she knew Chloe would have to figure everything out for herself. No one could do it for her.

When she reached her car, she switched on the air-conditioning full blast and rested her head on the steering wheel. Parker had won her case, but Chloe's was another matter. Her friend survived her surgery and made up with her. Robert already was an asset in the business and a joy to have around, even if she was worn out sometimes. He was adjusting well. And she had more friends than she could say grace over. If only Chloe could be so lucky.

When she fetched Robert from Eva's, he was playing a handheld video game, his focus totally on the little machine. The psychiatrist said to let him try new and different things and see how he responded. Dorothy had done a lot with Robert, but electronics and science had come so far, more could be done to stimulate him.

"Where'd he get this thing?" she asked Jane.

"It's a Gameboy micro something or other. Troy brought it to him. He said he was getting stuff ready to donate and came across it." Jane wrinkled up her forehead. "He's a damn liar."

"Yeah," Marian said. "He's a nice man. I feel like Robert's been adopted by the street."

"Well, he has, Ms.—Marian." Jane cackled. "What's not to love about Robert?"

"Come on, Son," Marian said. "Time to go to work. You can bring your new toy."

"Time to go to work, Marian," Robert answered. He got up from the table and raised his hand to Jane. "Goodbye. Time to go to work. Goodbye."

"At least he recognizes you, Jane," Marian said. "That means a lot. It takes him a long time to recognize people, but I guess seeing you just about every day has helped."

"I'm waiting until he says my name when he first sees me. Then I'll know for sure he knows who I am," Jane said. She wiped the counter. "See you folks later."

When Marian and Robert entered Ritzy Rags, Marian flipped on the lights. Robert dragged his stool up to the front counter and continued playing with the Gameboy. He faced the door, looking at the game, at the door, out the window, and back at the game again.

Marian left her purse in the back of the store on the stairs where customers couldn't get to it without going past the two of them. "Robert, you want a cold drink?"

"No, Marian," Robert said, in a loud voice. "No cold drink. Person coming."

"Okay. You'll be fine. Just keep an eye on them. I'm going to run upstairs and change my clothes. Buzz me if you need me."

"Yes, Marian. Buzz me if you need me," Robert said in a louder tone than usual.

Marian smiled. Robert could do a lot more than he'd been given credit for. In two weeks, especially with the suggestions of the doctor, he'd been remarkably responsive. She'd found she could leave him alone in the shop, and he'd complete any tasks she gave him. If a customer came in and needed help, Robert would come and get her or buzz her. And as for Anna, Robert had taken over feeding, walking, and cleaning up after her. He and the dog were inseparable.

She hurried up the stairs. Robert would be all right for a little while, but he didn't like being alone for long. Throwing her dress on the bed, she changed into white capris, a bright red cotton blouse, and thick-soled moccasins. She grabbed a clean glass out of the dishwasher, climbed back down the spiral staircase, and got a diet drink out of the refrigerator, pausing to turn on the CD player. When she got closer to the front, she heard a male voice on the other side of the wall.

Luther had dragged the other barstool up and was sitting next to Robert. "How's it going, Marian?" He held a Gameboy as well. They'd been playing side-by-side like two young boys.

"It's going, Luther. What's up?" She set the drink down. Though thin and slight, Luther looked like he'd fully recovered. His skin was tanned. The summer sun had bleached out his hair.

Luther tapped his lips. "I wanted to ask if I could put one of these in your window." He held up a handful of flyers.

Marian took one and read it. "Congratulations. Your own show at the next Artwalk." She hurried around the counter and hugged him. "Of course we'll put one in the window. We'll put two, one on each side of the double doors. What a score for you. Hand me that tape, Robert."

"Thanks," he said. "I've never had my own show before. I think Troy's taking a risk, but I can't talk him out of it."

She taped the flyers on the windows where anyone who came into the store would see them. "From what Jane says, you're a talented artist. What a *coup* for the street, to have our very own artist having his very own show."

"Jane, again. She's something, isn't she?"

"What do you mean?" She squeezed behind the barstools and put the tape back under the counter. She took a key out of her pocket and turned on the cash register.

"She's the one who told Troy about me," Luther said. "Didn't you know?"

"What do you mean she told Troy?"

"Troy told me she asked him to look out for me when I was in the hospital. So Troy came to the hospital, and that's how we met."

Marian pulled out a dust rag. Jane seemed to have a hand in everything on Ledbetter Street. "Of course," she said. "Troy was new to town and didn't really know anyone. Some of us were surprised you two hooked up so quickly."

Luther cocked his head. "Wait, wait, wait, wait, wait. What do you mean 'hooked up'?"

Robert said, "Hooked up. Hooked up."

Marian stopped dusting and glanced past Robert at Luther. "Well, aren't you two . . . um . . . a couple?"

"Troy?" He burst out laughing. "Ha. Don't I wish."

She threw the rag on the counter, walked to where they sat, and looked Luther in the eye. "Troy and you aren't together?"

"Troy is about as straight as they come."

"Straight as they come. Straight as they come." Robert parroted Luther.

She cleared her throat. "I didn't know that."

Luther pointed at her. "I know what you're thinking."

Robert made an unusual sound, like a snort, and both of them looked at him. Was Robert laughing?

"That's funny," he said. "Funny man."

Marian and Luther looked at each other and grinned. Did Robert even know what they were talking about? Marian shrugged. So Troy wasn't gay. Very interesting.

"I need to get going," Luther said. "I wanted to ask you something, though, Marian. Can Robert come over sometime and paint with me?"

In his way, Robert looked from the Gameboy to Luther.

"Troy said that we ought to see if Robert likes to paint," Luther said.

Robert said, "Yes. Robert paint."

"You want to paint with Luther, Robert?"

"Yes," Robert said again, actually looking at Marian. "I want to paint with Luther."

"Well, I guess it's yes," Marian said. "But, Luther, uh well, not during busy days. I need his help. Mondays would be good, though. Would that work for you?"

"Mondays. Sure. I'll come over and get him. And Marian, you don't have to worry. I'll take care of him."

Marian's face flushed. Her eyes met Luther's. "Do I come across as that protective?"

"You don't have to apologize. You're his mom. I won't let anything happen to him."

She nodded. "Okay. I trust you."

"That's cool," Luther said. "It'll be early in the mornings. I like the light then. Okay, Robert." He put his hand over the Gameboy and stuck his face in front of Robert's. "I'll come get you next Monday, and we'll paint."

"Okay," Robert said. He held the Gameboy in both hands and stared at it until Luther removed his hand.

When Luther left, a woman passed him in the doorway. Marian greeted her and said to Robert, "You have to move your stool back and put that game away for now."

Robert dragged his barstool back to the far right corner of the shop and got back up on it. He unbuttoned his sport shirt and stuck the Gameboy inside and buttoned it back up. Marian shook her head and asked the woman if she could help her find anything in particular.

Robert sat on his hands and rocked. The woman went from circle to rack, jerking clothing to the right, and then dragging the items one by one back to the left as she rejected them. She lifted some off the rack and examined them before hanging them back. Each time the hanger made a low screeching sound on the metal circle, Robert's face screwed up, and he emitted a tiny gust of air. Since Robert had come into her life, Marian had become very aware of the noises that customers made. The first day they had opened together, Robert held his ears and moaned each time a hanger made that high-pitched screech.

Marian watched him now. His face screwed up, and his shoulders hunched to his ears as he rocked back and forth. Marian had talked to him, explained that he shouldn't moan so loudly. She had given him waxed paper to rub on the top of the racks so the garments would slide more easily. They kept a box under the counter.

When the woman went to the back to try something on, Robert jumped off the stool and got the waxed paper. He tore off a sheet and rubbed the top of the rounder. He straightened each item the woman had touched. Only Robert could discern the appropriate spacing between each garment. He hung them perfectly, straightening the item if it needed it, the hanger facing the correct way, and moving the piece some fraction from the next, set by the calculator in his brain.

Robert could hardly wait until customers left the store before he'd straighten the clothing. It had taken numerous explanations over several days to convince him to wait until the door closed behind the person, and the store, empty. Fixing things while a customer tried on clothes was okay, Marian told him, so long as he didn't interfere with their shopping. Robert became antsy if there were many customers, or someone stayed a long time, so Marian taught him to sit on his hands if she couldn't find other things for him to do.

Marian was elated as she watched her son busy with the clothing. Everything had to be just so. Lined up. Stacked neatly. Jewelry hung in alignment. Accounted for. Nothing got past Robert. Not a speck of dust. Nothing.

Chapter 45

THURSDAY AFTERNOON, WHEN JANE RETURNED downstairs after lunch, Eva threw back the covers and climbed out of bed, tiptoeing to the closet. For several days, she'd been screwing up her courage, growing more energized. She was sick of lying around in bed. Time for her to quit letting herself be coddled and get back to work. Time also to reconcile herself to the fact that her girls were gone. She hadn't yet looked at herself full-length with nothing but scars where her breasts had been.

Lifting her arms about halfway to her head didn't hurt nearly as much as she'd feared. She dropped the pajama top on the floor and stepped in front of the full-length mirror. She revealed the bare truth to herself little by little. She'd seen her chest when the bandages were being changed, but this was a different perspective. It was downright about as ugly a thing as she'd ever seen, but just being able to see it meant she was alive.

She ran her fingers over the healing scars. She knew she didn't need boobs. Still, the red, the flatness, the scarring . . . . She forced a smile. The doctors said they'd gotten everything. Several breast cancer survivors had telephoned her and asked her to lunch, told her there was a survivors group they'd like her to join. They'd assured her that the worst was over, but her life was not.

The following Friday, she'd go back to the medical branch so the doctor could check her over, make sure she was healing, and release her until her long-term checkup. But she wasn't staying in bed until Friday. She was going to dress and go downstairs and show the world that it hadn't licked her.

No more crying or wallowing in self-pity. She had Jane, Marian, and now even Robert.

Eva buttoned a cotton sweater over her chest. She'd shop for the bras and stick the gel thingys in there later. When she finished dressing, she sneaked downstairs and caught Jane outside, washing windows.

"Get in here," she called.

Jane hustled inside, a wad of newspaper in one hand and a bottle of vinegar in the other. "What are you doing down here?"

"I'm sick of being treated like a baby."

"Well, it's about time," Jane said. "I take it you feel frisky enough to watch the counter while I finish the windows?"

"Get back outside to work."

Jane chuckled and went back outside. Eva knew she'd found a jewel. She began checking the contents of each cabinet and drawer to see if they needed supplies. She stuck her head inside the downstairs restroom. It had never been cleaner, the white porcelain shining like new.

Jane had transformed the storage closet. The walls were painted taupe. Several unfinished paintings hung on them. A small chest of drawers and a single bed stood on one side. An antique tiger oak wardrobe sat at the end of the room. Two small chairs sandwiched a café table. Crowded, but livable.

Jane could move in any time. Eva wasn't sure she wanted that. She liked having Jane upstairs. From her bed, Eva could see Jane straighten up the sofa bed each morning. Not only had Jane kept Coffee & More going, but she'd cleaned the apartment, caught rides to the store for groceries, and nursed Eva.

Lorette said Jane put leftovers on the back stoop for the street people. And Jane asked Mickey and Winnie to leave their leftovers out, too, instead of pitching them.

Eva checked the display cases. Pastel paper rosebuds and doilies framed the inside of the glass, vastly improving the presentation. Paper napkins folded into little cones, a glass vase, and fresh flowers sat in the center of each table.

Outside, Jane talked with someone who lived in the next block. She kept tabs on everyone on the street, and everyday she had filled Eva in.

There were also gift sets of cups and saucers for sale. They were identical to Harry's. And packaged teas in colorful containers were stacked up on one end of the counter. Had Jane bought duplicate items so they could compete with Harry better?

After waiting on a customer, Eva dug around until she found the ledger. Jane had made an entry for each day's receipts. The amounts she'd paid to the vendors were in one column and the daily receipts in another. The cash register readings, two from each day, were stapled to the pages. Jane was amazing. She hadn't kept one penny. Even grocery receipts were inside an envelope clipped to the binder's cover. There were a couple of entries Eva didn't understand, including a large one to Harry. Could Jane have persuaded Harry not to sell coffee?

Eva wandered through the aisles. No dust. Everything neatly

lined up. Fried pies in place. She picked up a newspaper and took it to a table near the door. She was happy to be home, in her shop. It was as if she had just awakened from a long sleep that began the day she discovered the lump.

Across the street, Robert was focused intently on something. She'd seen him from her upstairs window. Sometimes he sat on the barstool with his back to the street. Sometimes he swiveled around and stared outside.

A youngish bald-headed man drove up, parked in front of her place, and jogged across the street. He was in shirtsleeves and dress pants, no jacket.

The wind blew from the North. Eva walked outside. "Have you checked the weather?" She asked Jane. "Is a cold front coming?"

"Bigger than the first one," Jane said. "Smells good, don't—doesn't it?" She walked a pile of wet newsprint to the trash barrel. "Might get down to a livable temperature."

"It's a little early, but even a bit lower would be good."

"Yep. I'll take even five degrees," Jane said as she wiped down a table.

"I've been looking at the ledger. What's that bookkeeping entry about Harry's?"

Jane snorted. "Me and Harry made a deal after Artwalk. I promised we won't sell art if he would give up the coffee business."

"He went for that? We've never had art."

"I told him we would. We'd hang art before the next Artwalk. The competition's tough enough without us, I told him."

Jane was amazing. "And he believed you."

"I would've, too. There are plenty of artists who wouldn't mind hanging paintings in your shop. If we want some, Harry'll provide them and get the commission."

Jane was pretty smart for an old broad. Eva glanced across

Ledbetter Street at Marian's, resisting the urge to cross over and see what was going on. She went back inside when another customer walked up. After she filled his order, she focused on the newspaper again until Jane came inside, a grim look on her flushed face. Jane got a bottle of water from the refrigerator and made a note on something and sat down with her.

"You aren't wearing yourself out?" Jane asked.

"Me? You look like you're fixing to melt into the ground yourself. Is everything okay?"

Jane pressed her lips together, her eyebrows knitting. "Aw, I'm okay. Just wondering about things."

"Is it money? We can afford to pay you for your work."

"We? Who's that? You got a silent partner?"

"We. You and me. We need to get you paid. You were nice enough not to take any salary while I was laid up, though that wasn't necessary."

"Me and you?" She grinned.

"How've you been managing with no money?"

"Oh, I didn't need anything. Marian gave me clothes. I had everything else I needed, food and drink."

"Did you buy that beautiful tiger oak wardrobe I saw in the back?"

"From Tiny. I owe her for it."

"Tiny?"

"The one who used to live next door before those two ladies got together."

"Lorette, you mean." Jane was so honest she'd rather owe someone money than bother Eva with salary issues while she was recovering.

"Yeah, Lorette. I call her Tiny, cause she's so tall."

"We can go over the books tomorrow, if you like. By the way, what you did to that room is way cool. But I'll miss you if you move downstairs." She laid her hand on top of Jane's. "You've been such a good mother to me since my surgery."

Jane turned up her hand and squeezed Eva's. "Would you teach an old woman how to drive? That way we don't need no one—anyone else. It'll be just the two of us."

"I could teach you more than that, Jane, but by the way you've been running things around here, maybe I can't teach you as much as I thought."

"We could learn from each other," Jane said. "I never had a daughter, but if I did, I would've wanted her to be just like you."

Their eyes met and held for a few moments. "Hell, let's not go getting mushy." Eva pulled her hand away.

"Oh, Lordy," Jane said. "Looks like Marian's upset enough to bust a gusset."

The bald guy hurried out to his car and sped away. Was it bad news about Marian's own case or about Chloe's? His face had been as dour as Marian's when she stood at the door.

Eva got up to go see what was the matter. Jane grabbed her hand and pulled her back down.

"Let go, Jane. I need to get over there."

"Sit down. Wait a few minutes and see if anything else happens." She let go of Eva's hand. "Hey, look to the left."

As they watched, Troy crossed the street, his long legs making short work of the distance. He paused at the door, yanked on the handle, and waltzed inside like he belonged there. Eva bit her lip. She thought down the line, he just might.

Chapter 46

"MAN COMING, MA—RIAN," ROBERT SAID, in his monotone.

Marian glanced at Robert, wondering at the new way he said her name.

Before starting on the decorations for his party, her goal was to finish tagging and clipping slacks for the size ten-to-sixteen section of the round. She gave them to Robert to hang, since he was so exact, and piled the decorations on the counter. Robert seemed as excited as he was able to be, examining each roll of colored crepe paper, the balloons, and the banner that said HAPPY BIRTHDAY ROBERT.

Troy came to the door and smiled when he saw Luther's notice. He pushed through and was greeted by Anna's barking and bouncing around until he stroked her back.

"Hey, y'all need help decorating?" His hair was windblown; his face, brown as a nut from the summer sun.

"Troy," Robert said.

"I see that," Marian said. "Wait, Robert, you said, Troy." Robert had his back to her, straightening the slacks, making sure each pair was exactly the same distance from the next. He didn't respond.

"Troy, that means he recognizes you. He knows you." The work everyone on the street was doing with Robert was paying off.

"Pretty wonderful feeling when he calls you by name, when he recognizes you," Troy said. He picked up a roll of blue crepe paper. "Where do you want to start with this?"

"That means Robert's been seeing you enough to remember who you are, or else he's made great progress in the last few weeks."

"Or both." He stood with the roll of paper in his hand.

"What are you doing here, anyway?" It was early for the party and even for decorating. "Jane said she'd help later."

"I saw Parker run in and out. I wondered if Chloe's case was over."

"You know, Troy, for someone who's new on Ledbetter Street, you sure have gotten involved in everybody's lives."

"It's all in the family, isn't it?"

"I guess so." She liked his sense of humor. "You knew Parker was appointed to represent Chloe?"

Troy rubbed his chin. "Yes, I did. You told Eva. Eva told Jane. Jane told Luther. Luther told me."

"Par for the course. Boy, was I shocked when I went to the courthouse on Tuesday and saw them together." She clipped a pair of slacks and put them on the round. "Anyway, I ran over there this morning to hear the final arguments. Parker said they got a verdict just after lunch. The jury terminated Chloe's parental rights."

"That was quick," Troy said. "Poor kid."

Marian perched on a stool. "Sorry, I have no other place for you to sit unless you want to sit on the spouse's sofa by the door."

"It's okay. I don't mind standing. In fact," he said, holding out the crepe paper, "I don't mind helping decorate."

She beckoned to him. "Why don't you bring the ladder up

front?" She walked him to the back and pointed to the ladder. "Parker said after the judge released the jury, he saw Darryl waiting for Chloe outside. Parker tried one last time to talk to Chloe, to convince her she didn't have to go with Darryl. I don't understand. What's holding her to him when they no longer have a child?"

Troy carried the ladder to the front and set it against a wall. "I never could see a man hitting a woman or a kid. Got tape or thumbtacks?"

"All Chloe could say was she couldn't help herself, she just couldn't break loose from him. I talked to Chloe before, and that's what she told me, too. And that night at Eva's party, Chloe told us all the same thing." She handed him a roll of double-sided tape. "Chloe and Parker were walking out of the courtroom when Darryl grabbed her by the arm. She left with him."

"What's going to happen to Leo?"

"He'll be put up for adoption. Did you ever see him? His blue eyes were so dark, they looked ebony." She could still feel the little bundle she'd held in her arms when Chloe had come to the shop the first time. She glanced at Robert, picturing his face the only time she'd held him in her arms as a baby. She knew the kind of pain Chloe must be feeling, knowing she'd never see Leo again.

"I don't think I ever saw her baby except when he was covered up when she walked down the street." He mounted the ladder and stuck blue crepe paper to the wall.

"His eyes weren't like Luther's or Robert's. More like the night sky. Poor little boy. Chloe said she really loved him, but she's sick. Sick as Darryl. Addicted to love, but in a bad way." How alike she and Chloe were in many ways. She didn't mean to judge Chloe. She didn't want to be like those girls in her high school who'd gossiped about her.

"She let him control her," Troy said. "I'm not sure that's the same thing. You want me to stick green up here, too?"

Marian realized she'd been daydreaming and shook her head. Would she ever get past the memories of Bryan? Looking up into Troy's attractive face, for a moment, she wanted to touch his cheek. "I don't know why we sometimes let ourselves get into bad relationships, have stupid lapses in judgment, and don't have the courage to make the break. Or even why we let them abuse us one way or the other."

"Are you talking about Chloe, women in general, or yourself?"

Did he know about her? The way Ledbetter Street was, he probably knew all the details. Who was this man, and what did he want?

She chastised herself. What had he done? He'd brought her home drunk after she vomited on him. He'd cleaned her up and put her to bed and never mentioned it. She hadn't seen him much since Artwalk unless he was drinking coffee at Eva's, or talking to Robert, or walking down the street with Luther. "Sure, stick green up there, too."

Marian and Troy met halfway up the stepladder where she handed him the green paper. He smelled earthy. "I never thanked you for taking care of me the night of Artwalk. I know it was you."

"I didn't ask to be thanked." He climbed back up.

"Well, thank you, anyway."

"You're welcome." He stuck the green paper over the blue and began twisting them together.

Looked like he had decorated for parties before. "And thank you for being so nice to my son."

"I like him very much. He has a curious mind."

Warmth spread through her like a hot drink. "You've been very kind, and I appreciate it."

"I hear you thought I was gay." The lines at the edges of his eyes crinkled.

Marian covered her face with her hand. "Luther has a big mouth."

"He thought it was funny."

"I'm not the only one who thinks—thought so." Her voice came out in a croak.

"Well, I can assure you, I'm not gay." He rested a hand on her shoulder.

"Okay, fine. I believe you."

"Woman coming, Ma—rian," Robert said, his voice unusually loud.

"All right, Robert." Her eyes met Troy's. "I can handle the decorating if you need to go."

"I'll stick around a few minutes and get this done. Then I have to get back to the gallery. Luther can only watch it a few minutes."

"Woman. Woman. Woman coming." Robert jumped down from his stool and hurried to the window, alarm in his voice. "Chloe."

Marian and Troy ran to the window. Chloe hobbled down the sidewalk toward them, drawstring bag clutched to her chest, hair disheveled, clothing awry. Blood ran down her chin. One of her eyes didn't look right. Marian flung open the door and pulled her inside.

"My arm," Chloe cried.

Marian let go. "Here, sit on the sofa. Let me get ice." She hurried to the back of the store.

When she returned with two bags, Chloe's things rested next to the couch. Troy sat beside her, an arm around her shoulders. Robert stood before her. "Chloe hurt, Ma-rian," he said.

"Yes, Robert. Chloe, put this on your lip." Marian knelt down. "Your poor face. Put this other one on your eye and cheek." She brushed Chloe's damp hair back. "Do you think your cheekbone is broken? Should I call 911?"

"Call 911," Robert said.

"No." Chloe held the ice bag against her mouth a few moments. Although her words were slurred, she said, "I don't think so. Just very bruised, as usual."

"Okay for us to know what happened?" Marian pressed her lips together, trying not to say something nasty about Darryl.

"Thought he was going to kill me," Chloe said, glancing at Robert. She pinched the fabric of Robert's jeans and shook it. "I'm okay, really."

The three of them stared at her.

Troy finally said, "Can we get you anything else? Should Marian check your legs to see if you have cuts that need doctoring? Those scrapes on your arms need cleaning. Marian can take you in the back."

"I've left him." Chloe smiled, showing them her bloody gums. "Will you call Parker? Ask if he'll call my caseworker, and see if it's not too late? Maybe I can still get Leo back."

Marian held her breath, afraid to speak.

Chloe put the ice bag back on her mouth and pulled it away again. "I don't know what happened. We were walking to the bus after we bought our tickets. Darryl said something like to forget Leonard, that I could always have another baby."

Troy gently steered the ice bag back to her lip. "Shh. It doesn't matter. It's okay."

Chloe looked at Troy. "He called me stupid. I don't know what it was, but I realized that I didn't want to keep giving up my babies for the rest of my life because of Darryl."

Marian sat cross-legged on the floor and let Chloe talk. Troy's eyes shifted to Marian's. Even Robert took a step back from Chloe, as though giving her room to tell her story.

"When I said I wasn't going with him, he said he was going

to kill me." She searched their faces. "Can you believe I said for him to go ahead? I didn't cower. I didn't beg. I just stood there. I think he must've realized I wasn't backing down this time." Chloe shifted around on the sofa and grimaced. "I just made up my mind that taking care of my baby was worth more than anything. I won't ever let anyone hurt a child of mine again. Could I have a drink of water?"

"Hold on," Marian said. "I'll be right back."

Chloe put the ice bag to her mouth, and Marian hurried to the refrigerator. When she returned, she opened the bottle of water and handed it to Chloe.

"Oh—that's so good—nice and cold."

"You don't have to finish telling us, if you don't want to," Troy said.

Marian wanted to know how Chloe had the strength to defy Darryl, but she wasn't going to drag it out of her.

"I want to," Chloe said. "He usually only hit me in places where people couldn't tell. This time he started on my face, like he wanted to make me look so bad no one would want me. I just kept getting up and standing there. You got another Kleenex?"

Marian got the box of tissues and put them in Chloe's lap. When she finished blowing her nose and wiping the blood away, Chloe said, "People on the bus started yelling at Darryl to stop. The driver came and helped me off the ground. Did I want him to call the police? I said would he get Darryl on the bus and drive him away from me."

"And he did?" Troy asked.

"He did. He yelled at Darryl, and another man came, and another, and they dragged him onto the bus and drove away. And here I am. I just want to get Leo back." She ended out of breath.

Eva burst through the door with Jane close behind. Troy gave them a rundown on what Chloe said while Marian took Chloe upstairs and helped her clean up.

When Marian and Chloe came back, they found the decorating complete, the clothing racks pushed to the walls and into the back of the store, and Winnie and Mickey talking to Troy. Soon, the rest of the crew came by.

Lupe hugged Chloe. "You want to come back to work? Maybe Marian and I can fix your hours so you can work for both of us, at least 'till you get Leo back."

Chloe stared at everyone, and nodded and otherwise didn't speak much, just held the ice bag back on her lip.

"If you can't afford to stay above Ron's, you can stay in the room behind my shop," Eva said, looking at Jane for confirmation. "At least until you get on your feet."

Marian called Parker. Later, he raced in and hugged Chloe. "Don't worry, Chloe-girl, I'll file a motion for a new trial. We'll get Leo back."

Chloe, with the ice bag to her mouth, nodded and wiped her eyes.

That evening, everyone locked their shops early. Jane produced a gigantic cake decorated with a red train engine. Everyone drank and ate too much, except Marian who stuck to iced tea. Robert sat as far away as he could in a corner, earplugs in his ears, Anna beside him. He managed a vague smile at people who wished him happy birthday. Luther showed up with a man he introduced as an artist who lived on The Strand a few blocks away.

Several times during the evening, Marian found Troy's eyes on her. Before the night was over, he lifted her hand to his lips and kissed her palm. "I know you've had a lot of changes in your life, but if you need me, I'm here."

Marian put her hand to her cheek, nodding. She could take care of herself and her son. But if she did enter into another relationship, even one with Troy, it would have to be on equal terms.

And Robert would always be part of it.

Chapter 47

MARIAN SHUT THE DOOR ON their final birthday guests. For the past half hour, Robert had been walking around with a trashcan, throwing out paper cups, plates, and napkins, including some that people were still using. Their friends got the hint and headed for the exit, laughing at Robert's method of ending his own party.

Troy was the last to go. He took her elbow and said, "By the way, did I tell you that Parker Benavides is Rain's first cousin?"

"No, you didn't. But I think I knew that."

"He's a very good attorney," Troy said.

"The best. Goodnight." She closed the door. "They're all gone," she said to Robert. "Whew. Did you like your party?" She wiped up spills on the counter.

"Too loud. Too loud," his voice boomed.

Marian approached Robert, pulled the earplugs out of his ears, and tucked them into his breast pocket.

"Let's get the rest of this picked up and leave the decorations on the wall until tomorrow."

"Man coming, Ma-rian."

Bryan was striding toward the shop from across the street.

"Please don't say anything while this man is in the store."

Robert nodded, pulled his Gameboy out of his shirt pocket, and climbed on his stool. Anna sat at his feet.

Marian rushed to the door and jerked it open just as Bryan pushed on it, blocking his entrance. "What do you want?" Her heart raced.

"You going to let me in?" He frowned down at her, his eyes intense.

She crossed her arms. "We're closed for the evening." She wished he'd gotten the message. What was it going to take?

"I need to talk to you. Just for a few minutes."

"It's late. You'd better make it quick." She stood aside, her hands on her hips.

Bryan brushed past her and glanced at Robert, hunched over his Gameboy as though he didn't know anyone else was in the room. Anna yipped.

"Hello, Robert," Bryan said. "How are you?"

Robert didn't respond. Marian thought he probably didn't remember Bryan. It took consistent contact with a person for many autistics to recognize them.

Anna growled low in her throat. Robert dropped a hand down and fingered the top of her head.

"What?" Marian let the door close behind him. "If you want to talk, let's go in the back." She walked away, hoping he'd follow. "Watch the front, Robert." Then remembering how literal he was, "I mean. Don't let anyone else inside."

She weaved her way to the rear of the shop. She didn't want Robert to overhear their conversation.

Bryan followed. She perched on the edge of the staircase, one foot on the bottom rung and one on the floor. "Okay, what is it?"

"You're not making this easy, Mar."

"You have something to say, say it. I have stuff to do." Was this it? Would he admit he knew he was Robert's father?

"If I had a hat, it'd be in my hand, Marian. I came to apologize. I was wrong."

"Yes, you were." She crossed her arms again.

"So you accept my apology?"

"Bryan, it doesn't matter." She struggled for words to tell him it was okay, that she had her son and that was all that mattered. He'd forced her to choose, and she'd chosen her child. "We're not together anymore so it doesn't matter one way or the other whether I accept your apology. If that's what you came for, okay, I accept." She grabbed the railing to pull herself up.

He stopped her. "I want us to uh—get back together," he said. "Try again."

His warm fingers stroked the back of her hand causing it to tingle, but she didn't give up her hold on the stair rail. She'd never risk Bryan coming into their lives, changing his mind, and leaving again. It would be terrible for Robert and not so good for her, either. She searched the face she'd dreamed about for almost forty years. She'd longed to hear him say those words. But she couldn't do it, couldn't risk her son. Bryan seemed sincere. And he probably was— at that moment.

She pried his hand off hers, one finger at a time. It wasn't that she didn't love him. She loved the idea of him. But it wouldn't work. The knot in her stomach loosened. This was the right thing to do.

"Bryan, it's not going to happen. I appreciate how you feel, but we're not getting back together."

"Marian, I really care about you."

Marian winced. "I care about you, too, Bryan. That doesn't mean we were meant to be together. It only means I had to get you out of my system." She shivered. How could she explain without insulting him? He wasn't reliable. He'd failed her more than once. She couldn't risk it again. Couldn't risk what it could do to Robert even if she could take the risk herself.

He moved closer to her and put a hand on her cheek. "I love you. I need you."

"I understand how you feel, Bryan. But you need to understand me. Your feelings aren't returned. I thought I felt the same, but I've come to see that I don't."

"You can't change your mind so quickly."

Marian shook off his hand and stood. "Bryan, I had a dream, an ideal of who I thought you were. I thank you for that. But that's not love, not a lifelong, sustaining love. Can't you accept that?"

He stared at her, his eyes roaming over her face, forehead to chin, eye-to-eye. She met his gaze.

"Is there someone else?"

She wanted to groan but chuckled instead. "Why do men think there must be someone else? Can't you just accept that you and I were trying on our relationship like a set of clothes? The clothes didn't fit. Nothing personal."

"So I'm nothing but an old pair of—"

"No theatrics, Bryan." She took his arm. "Now come on, you go home. We have to get this place cleaned up and get to bed." She put her hand on his back and gave him a gentle shove. "I need to check on Robert."

Bryan preceded her to the front of the store. He looked Robert over, his eyes lingering.

She walked to the counter and picked up the spray cleaner and paper towels. "You take care now, you hear, Bryan?"

Bryan gave her the once-over, glanced around the store, and looked again at Robert. "Is today your birthday, Robert?"

Robert looked at Bryan, meeting his eyes in a direct way that surprised Marian.

"How old are you?"

Her breath caught.

"Forty-one," Robert said, bending over his Gameboy again.

Bryan's eyes, that older version of Robert's, met Marian's. She stood riveted in place. The next few seconds passed like centuries. What he did then confirmed that she'd made the right decision.

He opened the front door. "Goodbye, Marian." He stepped through and didn't look back as he crossed the street.

Marian ran to the door and pushed it closed, resting her forehead on the cold aluminum frame, proud of the way she'd handled herself. When she heard Bryan's car drive away, her eyes met Robert's. In a few quick strides, she reached him, throwing her arms around him. "It's just us from now on, Son." She wondered whether he understood what just happened.

Robert clapped a hand on her back and patted her several times. "It's okay, Ma—ma. Everything's going to be okay."

Marian looked into her son's face. He'd called her Mama. He knew who she was. He stared back at her, deadpan as usual. There was no sense saying anything. It was what it was. She ran her fingers through his short reddish-brown curls, clamped a hand on his shoulder, and said, "Let's get this done, Son, and go to bed."

About the Author

Susan P. Baker, a retired Texas judge, is the author of seven novels and two nonfiction books, all related to the law. As a judge, she dealt with murder, kidnapping, incest, stalking, child support, child custody, and divorce. Prior thereto, she practiced law for nine years and, while in law school, worked as a probation officer. Her experience in the justice system is apparent in her writings. Currently, she has two mysteries and two suspense novels in progress.

Susan is a member of Texas Authors, Authors Guild, Sisters in Crime, Writers League of Texas, and Galveston Novel and Short Story Writers.

She has two children and eight grandchildren. She loves dark chocolate, raspberries, and traveling. An anglophile, she likes to visit cousins in England and Australia (her mother was a British war bride). On her bucket list are a trip to New Zealand, a long trip back to Australia, living in England for several months at a time, visiting all the presidential libraries and authors' homes in the U.S., and driving Route 66.

Read more about Susan and sign up for her mailing list at

http://www.susanpbaker.com
Like her at http://www.facebook.com/legalwriter
Follow her on Twitter @Susanpbaker.

Made in the USA
Coppell, TX
13 May 2023

16790258R00193